From Woodstock To Eternity

A Free Spirit Finds True Freedom

50th *Anniversary Edition*
1969 ～2019

John D. Cooper

DEDICATION

To my ever faithful wife, Lisa,
who still runs with me,
chasing my rainbows.

"Incredible, very entertaining, gets your attention immediately and doesn't let up. Wow!!!!! From another person who attended Woodstock. Awesome!!!! I highly recommend this book."

Smilin' Jimmy   5 stars   ☆☆☆☆☆

"Amazing Real Book!!! Thank you for writing it and then sharing it with us!!! Oh how I remember the days of my youth!!! My Parents were so right about my music and lots of other things!!! THANK YOU AGAIN!! Loving the readings in this BOOK!!!"

Kenneth   5 stars   ☆☆☆☆☆

"*From Woodstock to Eternity* is not only captivating, but it clearly shows God's redemptive plan for mankind through the author's own transformation."

Paul and Jenny Speed: Founders "Whatever It Takes" Ministries http://witministries.com/

"... whether you lived through these turbulent times or whether you are learning about them from an inside view... This read will give you hope, no matter what you may have gone through or are going through."

JR Polhemus Lead Pastor, The Rock, Castle Rock, Colorado

Cover design: Josh Clark

Cover images:

Woodstock poster: © INTERFOTO/Alamy/BA1G5A
Florida Coast at Night: *www.photos4u2c.com*

Back Cover image:
Sunset: © iStock.com/pailoolom

Introduction

August 15, 16, and 17, 1969. Hundreds of thousands of hippies converged on a farm in upstate New York. The Woodstock Festival became the symbolic portrayal of a peace and love movement that came and went in just a few short years. Though its time was short, the effects and influences of this era were profound, and are still with us today. This book will take you on an odyssey from the development of the Woodstock ideology into the world of international pot smuggling, and through the spiritual victory of one who made it to the other side.

How did Dustin Morgan get here? What dreams, experiences, and ideals could bring him to the point where he would risk his life and his future for the chance to make it rich? He loved the adventure, the prestige and the pleasures of the drug dealing lifestyle. Little did he know that the things he grew to cherish would bind him like a slave. Even when he heard the Spirit call, he simply could not give up his old life.

But this is not the end of the story. The ups, the downs, the bondages, and the freedoms are not unique to this one man, or to this generation in history. They are common to all. The deliverance and victory are also available to all who seek it. This is the story of one such wanderer who found the key to eternity.

JDC

Based on a true story

Table of Contents

PART TWO

From the Author

Throughout history, many time periods stand out as exceptional in charting the course of the world. They are usually marked by new discoveries that open up new frontiers, or they involve desperate struggles that determine the fate of mankind. Such was the case in the days of Columbus, and in the great Westward expansion of the United States. In recent times, two World Wars have settled the issue of freedom or tyranny for much of civilization and defined the political boundaries of nations.

The people who experienced these events certainly knew they were living in historic times. Those who were born after World War II entered into a period of discovery and adventure as well, only theirs was in a different realm. Their frontier was that of the mind, uncovered and unleashed by the advent of psychedelic drugs. A number of unique factors bonded with this new phenomenon to create a period of unprecedented harmony, creativity and social upheaval. It all came together on a farm in upstate New York in an event known as Woodstock. The sub-culture of those who lived out that ideology came to be known as the Woodstock Nation.

For those who were drawn to it, the allure of this culture was romantic and seductive. Many saw the idealistic dreams of peace and harmony as the solution to all of mankind's problems. However, the emphasis on pleasure and drug use wreaked havoc on the moral fabric of a generation and left many ruined lives in its wake.

This book is based on a true story, as told through the eyes of a young man who wanted to get everything he could out of that era. The history is real, and the history is fun, but sometimes it can be a hard, painful teacher. It has been my desire to create an adventure story that will deliver the opportunity to experience a colorful period of history and see the hope that is available from heaven.

John D. Cooper

Like our page and share your stories, ideas, and dreams at

www.fromwoodstocktoeternity.com

 FromWoodstockToEternity

 @eternalpioneer

For Inquiries or info contact:

eternalpioneers@gmail.com

Available in paperback and Kindle

www.amazon.com
Search: *From Woodstock to Eternity*

www.amazon.com/dp/0692368523

Also available at www.barnesandnoble.com

From Woodstock To Eternity

A Free Spirit Finds True Freedom

The Smell of a Culture

There was nothing quite like it. Flying through the night, inside a musty old cockpit filled with the rumble of turbocharged engines. Morgan breathed in deeply. Ahhh, the smell... pungent and intoxicating, but not physically. It intoxicated his inner being... the part that brought forth visions and spurred him into action. He gripped the throttles, relishing every jolt of adrenaline, living out the pinnacle of a lifestyle he had grown to love and that now had him in complete control. All of this had been ignited by an aroma, and in this case, that aroma was the hallmark of a sweeping ideology. It was the smell of the counter-culture. The unmistakable and unforgettable fragrance of a plane full of weed.

Inside, the only illumination came from the panel lights... the altimeter, airspeed indicator, and radio stack. The captain, Dustin Morgan, and his crewmate, Grady, gazed up at the vast array of stars, so clear against the black expanse, the moon shining with a soft whiteness, gently casting its rays over the ocean. Up here they were merely a speck in the dark, a part of the night canvas. The earth was down there, with all of its people and their cares, far below.

1

Many landmarks defined the long, monotonous trip from "down South"... land masses with people groups from vastly different cultures slowly passed underneath. Tiny flickers of light identified dwellings on the small out islands of the Bahamas. They served as visual waypoints along the route, like signposts on an aerial highway pointing them to their destination. There was Great Inagua. After a while, off to the far right, Cat Island and Eleuthera. Still to come was Nassau, with its dazzling spectacle of casinos and nightlife, followed by Chub Cay.

Cruising over a sparsely lit island, Morgan turned to Grady,

"What do you suppose it's like for those people down there?"

"Huh? What'd you say? I was day-dreamin'"

"Here we are, flying from one civilization to another, hundreds of miles over vast expanses of water, heading for the mainland of modern America... and there they are, their whole world wrapped up on a small island in a one room hut. Have you ever thought about that?"

"What in the world are you talkin' about? Have I ever thought about what?"

"Maybe they're the ones who are happy, who really know what life's all about. They probably have the keys to all wisdom, and we're the ones who are really lulu."

"Speak for yourself, Captain. I know this... we both have to be lulu to do what we're doin'. Do me a favor. Just keep it together 'til we get there."

"No, really. Look down there... that one little speck means one little hut. And they're content to live off the land and the sea in the same spot for the rest of their lives. They've probably never given any thought to what life would be like beyond basic survival."

"Yeh, yeh. Don't start thinkin' too much, or you'll hurt yourself. What am I supposed to tell the Boss when I get back? 'Well, we were doin' OK 'til Captain Morgan wigged out on one of his mind trips, and we crashed in the ocean. We crawled up on the beach and got rescued by one of the natives. I had to leave him behind though, 'cause he thought they had the keys to all wisdom, and he wanted to live with 'em in their little hut and eat clams the rest of his life.'"

They cracked up, laughing and snorting. They needed to laugh, just to break the weight of their mission. Up ahead, they could see the lights of Grand Bahama Island ascending out of the horizon. Once they put Freeport behind them, a glorious string of big city lights would come into view, outlining the nightscape of the Florida Coast. The last act of the drama was about to unfold, and Morgan drew it all in.

"Yes, here we are, as planned, everything is going nicely."

Now the curtain would rise on a show in which this renegade air cargo crew would be the major players... A Moonlight Run over Palm Beach.

The trip began at a loading point in a desolate patch of bushes and dirt known as the Guajira Peninsula. Once on the ground, a Colombian ground crew swarmed the plane, pulling up with gasoline drums and bales of marijuana. While some workers topped off the gas tanks, three more stacked bales into the cabin. The entire turn around took about ten minutes.

Cruising north over an endless expanse, there was nothing but open sea and hours without a glimmer of light. Then, a dark form came into view, and a cluster appeared on the right, signifying civilization. Isolated lights in the hills, a few more outlining a little village or town, then the massive and brilliant display of tenements, highways and skyscrapers that defined a large metropolis.

The first land mass they encountered was Haiti, with Port au Prince passing on the right as they headed toward the Bahama chain. Morgan brooded over the poverty on the island, "Those poor people, I can't imagine living in their conditions."

A few years back, he had flown a charter with a group of businessmen to the city of Cap Haitian, on the north coast of Haiti. The taxi ride to the hotel took them right through the middle of town. As they entered the village, the dirt street was lined with mud and stucco shacks along both sides. Most of them had roofs pieced together with scraps of corrugated tin. They were painted in bright, pastel colors of turquoise, lime green, and coral.

At first glance, it had the picturesque feel of a happy Caribbean port scene. But as the crowd of villagers parted around the slow moving taxi, the truth became painfully clear. This was no thriving paradise of natives with baskets full of tropical fruit.

The closer he looked, he was astounded to see that many of them were stark naked! Especially the kids, not a stitch on them. They came upon a ditch running through the middle of the street and a putrid odor suddenly enveloped them. Could it be? He asked the taxi driver about the smell.

"Dat's de sewer, mon. Eet goes right down de middle of de street."

Oh, Lord! They piss in the ditch, and live along side of it, and walk in it. Yuck!

The squalor caught him completely off guard. He had been to Mexico and the Bahamas and seen people living in "poverty," but nothing like this. This was beyond poverty, this was tragedy. The worst part of all, there was no hope of ever coming out of it.

He pondered their only alternative. "No wonder they float in rickety boats and risk drowning at sea to get to the United States. I would too."

The main difference between this island and the other Caribbean islands… no one was smiling.

Morgan shook his head and came back into the cockpit. Grady looked at him with a smirk.

"What's the matter with you? Stay awake, now. We got a long way to go."

Grady was the chunker, the guy who threw the bales out the rear passenger door while flying 100 feet above the ground at 110 mph. Right now he was feeling light hearted as they flew through the calm night sky. You could never tell by looking at him what kind of convoluted business he was up to. He was the picture of joviality. Relaxed, looking out the window, cracking jokes like he didn't have a care in the world.

Back at the airstrip in Colombia, one of the loaders asked him,

"Do you ever worry about flying a plane load of pot over the ocean into the United States at night?"

To which he replied in his thick New Jersey accent,

"Whaddya want me to say? I'm scared!"

Then he pulled his sunglasses halfway down his nose, looked at Morgan with a half grin, and winked. Morgan chuckled inside,

"They're looking at me too, wondering if I have the sense to be scared. After all, I'm the pilot. But it's a job, and somebody's got to do it. Besides, there's no backing out now. On the contrary, I need to refocus and put it in high gear. It's going to take everything I've got to bring it home, so worrying about it won't do any good."

His mind brought up a scene from *Gone With the Wind* with Scarlett O'Hara staring off into the sky. *"I won't think about it now, I'll think about it tomorrow. After all, tomorrow is another day."* I hope I get another day to think about it. He pushed those thoughts away.

"Tell me, Grady, why do you do this?"

"Huh? Whaddya mean why do I do this? I just do it, you know."

"Well, I was wonderin'. Were you ever a hippie?"

"What do you think? Do I look like a hippie? I oughta bust you in the chops." He shuffled in his seat like he was ready to make a confession. "Well, to be honest, I grew my hair out, took some acid. It's been a while."

Morgan chuckled, "Yeh, I thought so. Even you tough guys had your fling with Lucy in the Sky. Problem is, you didn't do enough of it. Ever since I started dealin', it's been for a cause. I always thought that, if smokin' pot expands the mind, makes people mellow, and brings people together, then it must be a good thing. So, that means I am doing my part to contribute to the hippie culture by being a supplier of dope. And, the more dope I supply, the more I help promote the Revolution."

"The Revolution? You been readin' too many comic books."

"You know what I'm talkin' about. The Beatles' *White Album*. It had Revolution and Revolution number 9."

"Yeh, the Beatles were OK. I liked their earlier stuff. Some of that weird stuff I just couldn't understand."

"Well, Revolution number 1 was about the wild-eyed, Molotov cocktail throwing loud mouths who thought they were speaking for everybody else. In reality, they were only speaking for themselves, and everybody else thought they were a bunch of nut jobs.

"Revolution number 9 didn't have any words. It didn't need words. It was a psychedelia infused sound blast that painted the revolution of the mind. If you were straight, it sounded like a bunch of noise, but if you were tripping, it was like a roller coaster ride in a locomotive going upside down through the loop.

"The main message was that revolution starts with a metamorphosis of the psyche, and out of that, you have a different view of the world. I personally think they wrote it on acid, for people on acid, and that it only makes sense on acid. That's why, if I deal large quantities of LSD and weed, I'm helping to advance the cause of Revolution 9. Instead of just participating, I am a promoter. Kind of a missionary zeal, you might say."

"I might say you're a complete basket case, but I know what you mean. Back in those days, there was a lot more good feelin' going around."

"Don't you ever have any of those ideas? Do you ever think about doing this for the psychedelic impact you're having on people by bringing in tons of pot?"

"Yeh, when I started out, I did. But that's all gone, kiddo. Peace and Love is over. Now, I just do it for the money. All we are is a Red, White and Blue All American Capitalist Enterprise cleverly disguised as a morally depraved, hippie counter-culture supply run."

Grady looked away as if he was tired of the exchange. He stared out the side window at the lights going by underneath, gradually drifting off as Port au Prince receded behind them. Morgan shifted around, trying to relieve pressure points and keep the circulation going.

The next phase was the strait between Cuba and Haiti. Off his left wing were the lights of the U.S. military base in Guantanamo. He was sure they saw him on their radar, and he visualized jet fighters pulling up alongside with men in flight helmets, pointing down as if he had a flat tire.

Once they were well north of Haiti, Grady helped Morgan perform the fuel switch from the main airplane tanks to the auxiliary drum tanks. To access these tanks, a splice had been made in the fuel line under the floor near the fuel selector switch. The spliced line had a valve that enabled fuel to flow from the fifty-five gallon drums to the left inboard tank of the airplane.

Morgan hoped the mechanic who rigged this set up knew what he was doing. If they were going to have a problem, it would most likely be a fuel leak and a spark. That would be bad, he thought. He couldn't escape the visual image,

"I can think of better ways to go than in a mushrooming ball of flame over the Caribbean, trying to do an honest day's work."

With the cross-feed set for "left to right," the fuel flowed from the drum tanks, into the left inboard tank, and through the cross-feed to the left and right engines. If everything went OK, they kept on cruising like nothing happened.

"Well, I think I got it." Grady finished the connection and raised himself up. The engines barely skipped a beat as they picked up the fuel from their new, unconventional source.

Morgan sighed. "Good, that makes me feel a whole lot better. All we need now is smooth sailing into Florida."

After another long stretch, the lights of Nassau ascended out of the horizon to meet them.

Grady spoke up, "So, how we doin' Commander, we gonna make it?"

Morgan sat back in his captain's seat and pondered the question. The Piper Navajo's engines purred with a low growl, operating perfectly. With plenty of fuel and landmarks showing the way, a wave of assurance flowed through his gut, and he sensed for the first time that everything was going to be all right.

"Yeh, we're gonna make it... or die tryin'."

They gradually closed in on Florida's sea of lights, and Morgan cycled through a few frequencies, listening to the chatter on approach control to get a feel for the traffic flow. Their entry point would be north of Palm Beach, somewhere between Jupiter and Ft. Pierce. His mind raced,

"I've gotta find of an "off" frequency that won't be assigned to anybody. I think I'll add five hundredths to the approach frequency of 124.6, just to be safe."

Morgan carefully adjusted the radio to 124.65 as they edged closer and closer to the lights on the coast. As long as he remained outside of controlled airspace, he was not required to make contact with anybody. And if he got low enough, he could evade radar detection altogether.

Morgan was faced with a difficult decision. "I've got to make up my mind how to avoid their radar. Should I try to look normal and come in high, or get down on the deck?" Worry descended on him like a blanket, and for a moment, the dread of capture invaded his thoughts. "What if they intercept me? Should I comply? Should I run?"

But it didn't matter. They already had him pegged.

The Game of Pursuit

Officers Jansen and Craig were in a briefing room of the U.S. Customs entry office at Palm Beach International Airport. The trackers had been monitoring an echo on their screen for some time as it slowly moved up from the south. Even without a transponder code, the plane was visible as a blip, just without any altitude information. Watch Commander Grey drummed his fingertips on his desk, knowing exactly what it was.

"Jansen, Craig, come take a look at this. See that echo right there? We've been watching him come up from the south for some time. This guy has no flight plan, no customs clearance, and up to this point, has made no official contact with any controller on the ground."

Grey looked around with a sly smirk,

"Looks like we got us another doper. That makes three this week... business is booming. Jansen and Craig, suit up and get your crews ready for intercept."

Jansen briefed Craig,

"I'm going high, you go low. Keep me in your sights. When we find him, we'll put the pinch on him. Come up from below and behind... I'll come in from high and behind. He'll never see us 'till we're on him."

"Yes, sir. Roger that."

"We'll talk on 124.65"

"Roger, 124.65"

The two flight crews jogged across the tarmac to board their jets, firing up two Cessna Citations with an ear piercing whine. With their clearance to taxi from ground control, they began their roll to the active runway.

"Palm Beach tower, Cessna two zero Juliet is ready for takeoff, runway one zero left."

"Cessna two zero Juliet, cleared for takeoff runway one zero left"

"Roger, cleared for takeoff, one zero left. Two zero Juliet."

Flying twenty miles to the east, Morgan had a bird's eye view of Palm Beach at night. It was a dazzling sea of lights forming a band along the coastline, then fading into the sheer blackness of the countryside. A glowing ribbon along the coast clearly defined Highway 1.

He craned his neck to scan left and right, up and down. A rotating beacon marked the location of Palm Beach International. Out of the massive display emerged a blinking speck of light. On this night, the traffic was taking off toward the east, toward them. Most of these flights turned one way or the other, so at first it was not particularly noteworthy.

Eventually, the blinking speck separated itself from the crowd. Morgan kept his eye on this one as it progressed from down low on the left side of the plane. Each time the speck flashed, it marked a path moving upward from left to right, steadily inscribing a sharp angle on the dark sky. It was still coming at them.

The speck kept climbing straight on, getting closer and closer, until it was off their 10:00 position. Now it was above them, and it presented an ominous sight, somehow projecting a message that it was not a friend. Morgan got a bad taste in his mouth as he considered who it might be. It hung in the air at the 1:00 position, right in front by only a couple of miles. Then he saw another one following along, coming from the coast, going east. The second dot had disappeared down below, and another shiver rippled through his body. He knew it was still out there.

"Did you see that?"

Grady leaned forward and peered outside. "Yeh, what do you think it is?"

His heart pumped loud and fast. It can't be... I've never had this happen before. What if it's a Customs jet?

Radio crackle, "Hey Craig, do you see him?"

"Yep. Got 'im in my sights. What do you make of him?"

"That's our boy. I got him at 12 o'clock"

The radio Morgan had set on 124.65 suddenly came alive with this conversation! He couldn't believe his ears. This was supposed to be a dead channel! The logic unfolded in his mind, and an awful coincidence dawned on him.

"Customs is using the 'off' channel that I purposely set to be 'dead' as their own discrete channel! We are now listening in to those blinking specks' conversation, and we are the ones they're talking about! Unbelievable!"

"You ready to make him into a sandwich?" the voice said in a stern, military kind of voice.

"Roger that."

Morgan frantically called out to Grady,

"Look outside. Quick! Tell me if you see those dots."

Grady strained to scan up and down. "Nah, can't see 'em. What's goin' on?"

"I think they're Customs planes and they want to make a sandwich out of us."

Morgan's palms began to sweat. His mouth was bone dry. In an instant, two flashing specks had drawn a line between his dreams of glory and an ominous future. He mouthed the words to Grady,

"They're heading for us right now."

"I got that. What are you gonna do?"

"The only thing we can do is go dark and make a run for it."

"Let's go."

Lights off. Throttles back to the stops. Hold the nose up until airspeed bleeds off, then over and down. Down, down, down. Airspeed climbed to the red line. Grady clutched his arm rests as the G forces compressed his torso against the leather seat. Morgan gripped the yoke and dove. Nine thousand feet. Seven thousand. The altimeter spun backwards. Three thousand. Strangely, the cocky, macho man chatter on 124.65 from Whoever It Was stopped the minute they became invisible.

Pressure hit the ear drums and the old Navajo whistled through the air. Every seam strained under the force of the wind. Maxed out on weight, they fell like a cannonball. Morgan's mind whirled,

"I don't know why I think I can out run a jet with my whale of a plane, but I've got a mission to accomplish. I gotta deliver my load."

Two thousand feet. One thousand feet. No lights, over the water, the coast of Ft. Pierce Florida dead ahead. He pointed out a dark, unlighted area along the coast to Grady,

"OK, I'm bringing it in right over there."

"Sounds good, Commander. Just tell me when I need to get things ready."

Billy Mitchell and the other deputies on graveyard shift relaxed in the breakroom, drinking coffee. On a table by the wall, a newspaper covered every square inch of surface area. Someone in the corner was filling out a crossword puzzle. Next to the coffee pot sat a box of donuts with the lid wide open.

The St. Lucie county sheriff's substation was just like any other emergency service base. Sheriff department, police department, EMS station. The cars were equipped, the ambulances were stocked, and the guns were loaded. They were all dressed up with nowhere to go. Meanwhile, a TV blared in the background, someone was sleeping in a bunk that smelled like dirty feet, and all of this could change in the blink of an eye.

Deputy Mitchell was pulling night shift with his partner, Deputy Evans. Sandy the dispatcher was leaning back in her chair, reading a magazine. The night dragged on, quiet and uneventful. Evans tried to break the monotony,

"Maybe we'll get some action downtown. You know that area with the yellow street lights is bad news. If they don't have a murder a week down there, they're hurtin'."

"You ain't lyin'." Mitchell took a sip of his coffee. "Somebody's gotta act up somewhere. People say bein' on call is hours of boredom punctuated by moments of sheer terror. I guess tonight it's gonna be hours of boredom punctuated by hours of boredom."

He lifted a donut out of the box and tapped it with his finger, making a dull clicking sound. "Y'know, if someone could make these things stay soft and chewy for more than an hour, they'd be a millionare."

Deputy Mitchell leaned back in his chair with his mouth wide open, the stale donut dangling overhead between his thumb and middle finger.

ZZZZRRRRROOOOOMMMMM!!! The twin-engine plane roared overhead at one hundred fifty feet, obliterating the silence.

Mitchell fell backward on the floor, coffee and donuts flying everywhere.

"Holy crap, what was that?!" He rolled over and pushed himself up, kicking his leg around, trying to escape the burning wet spot.

Evans headed for the door. "Damn! That was a doper..." He ran outside and peered into the night. All he could hear was the fading sound of engines in the distance. "He went right over our station!"

Sandy grabbed the microphone. "Attention. Be advised. We got a bandit over the office heading west. All units west and north be on alert. I repeat, low flying aircraft proceeding west over I-95."

Inside a sprawling brick ranch house, two men sat in soft leather recliners, sipping lemonade. The ranch was outfitted with rustic elegance. Shiny, lacquered logs dominated the decor in every aspect... support beams, fireplace mantel, furniture. The couch and loveseat were upholstered in rich calfskin, and the hearth was made of natural river rock. All the light fixtures were hanging wagon wheels with miniature lights mounted around the wheel rims.

The Boss and his driver, Casey, kicked back in their recliners as they followed the action over an altered police scanner. This scanner could listen to law enforcement frequencies, while the walkie-talkie radio picked up the chatter from the ground crew at the drop sight. From this vantage point, the Boss would know if anything went wrong with the drop, if the cops showed up, or if they were going to show up. In that case, he could give the ground crew advance warning, and they could tell the pilot to go to plan B.

Everything was monitored from this well-appointed command center. The Boss's wife kept their glasses full of lemonade and nervously whiled away the minutes, dusting everything in the living room, trying to occupy her time.

The Boss looked at Casey and shook his head.

"Does that fool pilot know he just buzzed the Sheriff's office?" He lifted both of his palms up in dismay. Casey shrugged,

"I don't know, Boss. You never know about Morgan. I'm pretty sure he didn't do it on purpose."

"I don't know about that. Morgan gets a wild hair sometimes, but he hasn't failed us yet... this should be interesting." The Boss shifted around in his chair and took another sip of lemonade.

"I've always wondered about that boy."

Air Drop

Palms whizzed by, houses whizzed by... the pace sizzled as the darkened airplane cruised over the tree tops at 150 miles per hour. Off in the distance, red radio tower lights blinked above the wingtips. Morgan was on high alert. His senses were firing on all cylinders as he executed every procedure. This was where the rubber met the road. No time for fear. All he had ever learned and experienced came into play right now. His kept his eyes set on the gauges, constantly scanning the panel, then checking outside. Altitude, airspeed, manifold pressure, turn coordinator, gyro, keeping the plane out of the trees as he penetrated the Florida countryside.

"I have to keep it right on one hundred and fifty feet." He prodded himself relentlessly, struggling with the altitude. Small corrections. A quick look outside for obstructions, then back to the panel. He looked for landmarks that led to the drop zone, flying visually.

Morgan picked up the walkie-talkie.

"Big Boy, this is Wagon Master, over." He looked at his radio, "I sure hope this thing works." The radio crackled.

"Wagon Master 10-4, this is Big Boy, come in."

In the command center, the Boss listened to the exchange. He turned to Casey, "Where does he get these names? Big Boy? Wagon Master?"

Morgan, "We've got thirty one Indians sittin' on a fence."

Ground, "10-4, thirty one Indians."

Boss to Casey, "Sittin' on a fence?"

A few gut wrenching seconds later.

"Big Boy, we're comin' in. Gimme the lights."

"Roger that."

"Well, Casey I guess it's time to go to the airport. If the cops don't get 'em they should be ready to pick up in about 30 minutes."

"Boss," Casey said, "do you think that pilot's all right? He sounds a little unbalanced."

"Don't worry, son. It's obvious you haven't met too many pilots."

The ground crew was pumped and ready for action. They set up two flood lights at the beginning of the stretch. One on the left and one on the right. They repeated the procedure at the end of the stretch. One on the left and one on the right. When the call came to turn on the lights, the plane was just a few miles away, lined up for the most dangerous part of the trip... the drop.

This maneuver required mastery over the airplane in a very unique application. The pilot had to configure the plane for "slow flight" with the flaps extended, using the throttles to maintain one hundred miles per hour and an altitude of one hundred feet above ground level. Grady would be in the back, with the door open, throwing fifty pound bales out as fast as he could. Any lower and he might hit the trees, any higher and the bales might break apart or be scattered beyond recovery.

If Grady didn't dump everything in one pass, Morgan would have to circle around and set up again. Meanwhile, he was hoping nobody in the area would look up and see a twin-engine plane with no lights flying around at tree top level and call 911.

"OK Grady, it's that magic moment. When I turn the inside lights on and off real quick, that's your signal to start throwin'. When I turn 'em on and off again, stop throwin'."

"Yeh, and if you hear a loud scream, that's me goin' out the hatch."

Grady unbuckled his seat belt and pulled himself over the top of the bales to the back of the plane. Morgan took a deep breath and steadied himself, tightening up his acuity and staying relaxed at the same time. He throttled back. The heavy airplane slowed. He gradually lowered the flaps. The plane wanted to rise, but he held it down. The airspeed bled off, and just before the plane began to sink, he re-applied power. The airspeed indicator settled to a speed of one hundred ten miles per hour. The altimeter read one hundred fifty feet.

Grady let down the staircase door and a tremendous force of wind rushed in. He set himself in the back of the plane, trying to calm his thumping heart. He spread his feet apart, balanced his weight on each leg, took a deep breath, and waited for the light. Grady hadn't paid much attention to religion, but because of his Italian roots, he knew he was Catholic. From somewhere deep inside, he uttered, "Mother of God, give me strength." Morgan saw two lights ahead, just beyond a farm road, one on the left and one on the right.

"Just a second. Here we go."

Light on – light off. The plane lurched as Grady grabbed the first bale and rolled it out the door. Number two. Number three. Number four. Every ounce of Morgan's focus was burned into the flight instruments and operating controls. Sink down, add power. Too slow, lower the nose. Not below one hundred feet. Not below one hundred miles per hour. The plane bounced and heaved. Thirty seconds seemed like an eternity. Two more lights appeared... one on the left and one on the right. The end of the run. Light on – light off. Grady stopped. He pulled the door up and latched it then fell back against the rear bulkhead, heaving and gasping for air.

Morgan pushed the throttles forward to climb out. He nursed the flaps up, a little at a time, and the airspeed picked up. As he gained altitude, he craned his neck to the right to see Grady behind him, laid out in the back of the plane.

"How many you got left?"

Grady wheezed, "I... got... them... all."

Morgan was astounded. "Are you kidding? Nobody's ever done it on one pass before!"

"Just take me home... I can't do this every day... It's too much like work."

Morgan keyed the walkie talkie, "Big Boy, that's it. We're movin' on."

"10-4. Roger that."

Relief washed over him like a waterfall, instantly tossing aside the tension and stress and replacing it with euphoria.

"We're gonna make it! All this time, it was anybody's game, but now it's over! All I've gotta do is fly to Melbourne and land the plane."

He was relieved, naturally, and a great sense of joy welled up in his chest. However, there was something inside that would not let him fully relish the success of the mission. Something was telling him that what he was doing was wrong, and that he was walking down a bad road.

Setting his course for Melbourne airport, his mind wandered to a bar scene not too long ago.

The bar top was formed out of mahogany wood, with a middle section filled with clear resin. Embedded in the resin were tiles depicting images from a Monopoly board. There was Boardwalk and Park Place, Get Out of Jail Free, and the restaurant namesake, Marvin Gardens. The decor was solidly tropical Florida. Fishing nets were strung up in the corners with shells and starfish hanging in them. Mounts of deep-sea fish adorned the walls, and huge ropes lazily sagged around the outside decks. The presence of driftwood abounded in the beams, the tables, and the posts.

Scattered around the walls were plaques with amusing sayings...

"Teach a man to fish and you'll never see him again"

"Work is that annoying time between fishing trips"

"When Momma ain't happy, ain't nobody happy"

Morgan got a kick out of the yellow, diamond shaped caution sign that said,

"Mother-in-law in trunk!"

He didn't have a mother-in-law, but figured if he ever got one, that would be a good place for her.

He straddled the barstool, hunched over, working on his sixth rum and Coke. In the background, Jimmy Buffett crooned "Son of a Son of a Sailor," and he let himself drift off with the tropical rock. What was that he said? Something about loading tons? Yeh, you got that right.

The music was light-hearted and happy as it bounced along, the marimbas tinkling in the background. Jimmy sang about the unique privileges of having the sea in your blood. You could almost hear the Caribbean breeze blowing through the palm trees, feel the sun caress your face, and smell the salt air coming off the sea.

"Blow me down! Avast and away! Blimey mateys, if it ain't Captain Morgan himself!"

Chuck roared through the door, unrestrained and boisterous as usual. As the lead lineman, he worked at the airport where Morgan taught as a flight instructor. He pulled up a stool and ordered a St. Pauli Girl.

"Hey, Cap'n, what's your poison?"

"Rum and Coke."

"Bartender, rum and Coke here." Chuck pointed to Morgan.

"Comin' right up."

He leaned back on his stool and studied the logo on Morgan's t-shirt, squinting to read the writing on the faded garment. It had an image of an olive tree in the middle, and the tree was encircled with a border of words. Across the top of the circle it said, "Tree of Life Coffee House." Underneath, the footer said, "Jesus is Lord."

Morgan's seventh rum appeared before him and he swished half of it down. A slight spin went through his head, and he muttered, "That's more like it. Now we're gettin' somewhere."

"Hey, what'd you do, go Jesus freak on us?" Chuck laughed.

"Always been a Jesus freak," Morgan slurred, "Nothin' strange about that. You believe in Julius Caesar?"

"Whaaa? Do I believe in Julius Caesar? You some kind of emperor worshipper or somethin'? Man, you got more problems than I thought."

"No, c'mon. You believe Julius Caesar was real, right? That he really lived on earth?"

"Yeh, of course he did. Everybody knows about Julius Caesar." Chuck took a big pull on his Pauli Girl and waved his hand off in the air. "E tu, Brute?"

"That's just it. How do you know he existed? It's because history books are accounts that have been handed down from generation to generation. Somewhere there was an eye-witness account of Julius Caesar that somebody wrote down. The same thing goes for Jesus. Isn't the Bible a collection of eye-witness accounts of what happened when He was alive? Jesus lived around the same time Caesar did. There's probably more proof of Jesus than there is of Julius. So, if you believe Julius Caesar lived, you gotta believe Jesus lived."

"Ok, Ok. Whatever you say. That's enough for me."

He got this revelation on a trip to the East Texas town of Paris, Texas, where everyone went to church and said, "Yes ma'am" and "Yes sir." It was during this time he came to believe that Jesus really lived on planet earth, that He was God's Son, and that God had raised Him from the dead. Ever since that visit, the Holy Spirit would not let him off the hook. Even when he was stone drunk in a bar, Morgan could not deny Christ. About the only conclusion you could draw from this was that he was very, very confused.

If he was confused then, he was really confused now. Here he was, landing a plane after successfully delivering a load of marijuana, and the Holy Spirit chose *this* time to talk to him. How could he have the Holy Spirit and run pot at the same time?

"Now that's a good question," Morgan said to himself. All he knew was a fight was raging inside as he eased the throttle back and flared to land.

"Well, Commander, does this mean we get to live?" Grady had been gripping the armrests, stiff as a board.

Morgan held his breath, maneuvering the last critical seconds to caress runway nine right with the main wheels. He gradually lowered the nose wheel and blew all the air out.

"Yep. We live to fight another day." He rolled to a stop, pulled off the runway, and picked up the mic.

"Melbourne ground, Navajo one niner x-ray, taxi to the ramp."

"Roger, one niner x-ray. Taxi to the ramp."

Grady seemed to melt in his seat as he stretched out his fingers. He turned to Morgan and said,

"You saved my life, and I owe ya one. You ever need anything, or need me to take care of somebody for ya, just let me know."

Morgan returned a smile, "Just doin' my job, but I appreciate it. We both did good work."

He taxied the plane to a remote area of maintenance hangars along the airport boundary. Rolling up to a chain link fence, he throttled back to idle. Both mixture controls came back to the stops, and the propellers wound down. He felt the overhead switches and shut off the right magnetos, then the left magnetos. Finally, he clicked the battery switch "off."

Grady jumped out of his seat, glad to be on solid ground, and headed back to open the stairway door. While he was back there, a tremendous wave of guilt washed over Morgan. He grasped the yoke with both hands, laid his head down between them and uttered a helpless prayer,

"Father, forgive me, for I know not what I do."

Suddenly, a bright light shone in the left window. Morgan raised his hand to shield his eyes from the glare diffusing through the plexiglass. Unfortunately, it wasn't Jesus or an angel. It was a spotlight from a Cessna Citation. A bullhorn blared out,

"United States Customs. Come out of the plane with your hands up."

Morgan slumped. "I shoulda known they were still out there." He had kept his fear at a distance, but a great, sinister unknown had always been hanging overhead.

Out on the ramp, two jets were lined up with uniformed men emerging and spreading out. They formed a perimeter around the Navajo and its crew. Two of them separated and took up positions on either side of Morgan and Grady. They stood ramrod straight, feet apart, poised and ready with their machine guns.

One of the officers made his way to the door of the plane, the other one headed straight for Morgan.

"I am Customs Officer Jansen. May I see your pilot's license please? Also, I need your registration and airworthiness certificate."

Morgan handed his license to Jansen with quivering fingers.

"Nervous? You should be." Jansen carefully examined his paperwork and wrote something on a pad. He asked him to confirm his personal information.

"Are you Dustin Morgan?"

Meanwhile, Officer Craig leaned inside the door of the plane and looked around the empty fuselage. If he found one seed, they were busted.

"Well, it's got that smell," he said.

Jansen glared at Morgan with the hard look of authority.

"Where did you come from?"

What could he say? He had to make up something.

"You see, sir, we were just ferrying this plane from Ocala."

"Ocala?" Jansen raised an eyebrow, amused.

"Yes, Ocala."

"Ocala is northwest of here. We've been following you since you were off the coast of Palm Beach."

"Well, that must have been somebody else, because we just ferried this plane from Ocala."

"Do you have anyone in Ocala who can verify you were there?"

It was now a game of cat and mouse. The exchange had turned into a theatrical routine, where everybody knew what was going on, but no one could say it. In a twisted, bemused sort of way, Morgan got a twinkle in his eye and said,

"I doubt it."

With no twinkle in his eye, Jansen said, "So do I."

He kept his stern gaze on Morgan and handed his license back to him, along with the papers for the airplane.

"Have a good night." He motioned to his crew.

The two agents, along with the officers, walked stiffly back to their planes and climbed aboard. The jet engines screamed as they fired up for their trip back to Palm Beach. Morgan couldn't believe his eyes. He watched them slowly roll away and taxi toward the runway. He had dodged a bullet and he knew it. A sigh of relief sent shivers through his body.

"I really thought I was a goner."

As soon as the jets were out of sight, two car headlights came on behind one of the hangars. The Jaguar slid out of the darkness and pulled up outside the chain link gate.

"Get in," said the Boss. Grady and Morgan quickly settled into the exquisite leather seats, glad to make their escape. "What did they say?"

"They said, 'It's got that smell.'"

How the West Was Won

*"The call of the horizon finds quick response
in the heart of every wanderer."*

Louis L'Amour, *The Walking Drum*

The air was filled with the sounds of a busy wharf... the shouts from the crew, the creaks and moans of a ship against the moorings. The Mayflower gently floated up and down as the Pilgrims prepared to board. Driven underground for their strict adherence to a life of holiness, the group had resorted to desperate measures. They would sail to a New World, one that was completely unknown, making the endeavor so much more than a move from one house to another. They would be forsaking families and friends, cities and countries... a civilization that had developed over eons for an unexplored wilderness.

Then the day and the hour came when they drove their animals on board, carrying all they could up the ramp. The great sails went up, and the waves slapped against the hull of the magnificent vessel as they lined up along the rails. With mixed emotions and memories of a previous life, the families strained to absorb every last detail of the skyline... their one last gaze at the vanishing European land mass. It receded into emptiness behind them, and they turned to the scene ahead. An endless expanse of sea to the horizon, the bow of the mighty ship rising and falling with the swells. From now on, all they had were their dreams and a determination to conquer the unknown.

Two hundred years later, one of the most ambitious mass undertakings in history was underway. In 1817, construction began on the Erie Canal which would take cargo and people west from Albany to Buffalo, New York. When it opened in 1825, scores of adventurers dreaming of a new life lined up on the banks of the newly built canal.

The air was bursting with excitement, alive with the chatter of a great multitude, full of expectations. The cool morning air was sharp and crisp with the aroma of campfires, percolating coffee and biscuits beginning to brown. A constant hum hovered while the throng went about their duties. Keeping camp, grooming their animals, watching the kids. Dogs and cats ran around freely, chasing each other in their timeless game.

A descendant of one of those Pilgrims was a farmer named Zebulon, and he was not the only one with that fire in his heart to break out of the world he thought he was trapped in forever. As the dawn broke, he stretched his back, taking a swig of hot coffee. His ears relished the sound of history on the move. People talking, shouting, laughing, pots clanging, wagons creaking, little ripples of the Erie Canal bouncing against the barges at the dock.

"Ah, look at all those people... my, my. All smitten with the same bug. I guess I'm not so crazy after all."

All throughout the crowd, people from every background were talking about the possibilities of the future "out there." It was time to load up, and the dock masters bellowed out their orders as the canal barges began to take on passengers.

"No," he said to himself, "I don't have to spend the rest of my life tilling the same field, working the same shop... no end in sight to the monotonous drudge – no escape. No, this is the escape! If I don't take this chance, my children will be doomed to the same meager existence I've had. When you put it that way, I'm doing this for them, so they can rise up and meet all the challenges waiting for them. The only dreams they have now are based on what they already know. Possibilities are out there to become something they haven't even discovered yet!"

Zeb shouted, "Ezra! Hanna! Get over here. C'mon, let's all stay together."

He took another pull on his coffee and it satisfied him like the taste of hard work and adventure. Hot, black and right off the coals. His nose was delighted with the mixture of pine trees and camp smoke. The unforgettable smell of livestock permeated his nostrils as the drivers harnessed their mules and horses. He could feel the sharp morning breeze on his face, the coffee cup in his hand, and the leather boots on his feet.

But wait, Zeb had another sense of "feel" as he soaked up the unforgettable scene. There was a tingle in his spine and a surge of adrenaline in his heart. Feelings of power and euphoria lifted his soul, and he felt like he was going to float up off his feet. A smile broke out on his whiskered face.

"By golly," he said with a tear welling up in his eye, "we're going West!"

This was the heart of a true pioneer. It wasn't enough for him just to have a dream and work hard to fulfill it. He was ready to gamble on a promise afar off that was powerful enough to spur him into action. He was willing to leave behind all known quantities of his present reality because he saw them as limitations. And, those limitations were like chains to him. He might as well have been in leg irons in a dungeon with one little window where he could look outside and watch the world grow and change while being forced to tolerate an eternal hell of sameness.

When he saw an opportunity to break free of those limitations and latch onto an enterprise with untold possibilities, he had to take it. He was compelled to open that door. If he did not discover what was on the other side, he would not be able to live with himself. It didn't matter that some would die, others would suffer shipwreck, still more would become discouraged and turn back. He never believed it would happen to him. If he dwelt on the hazards, he would never know if he could have made it. With a heart full of wonder and a stiff resolve, he refused to let caution triumph over glory.

Morgan saw the movie *How the West Was Won* when he was twelve. The scene at the Erie Canal of the Prescott family, ready to get on the barge with no idea what was ahead, ignited a spark. He became infatuated with the adventure and freedom of the "Promised Land." Years later, he could still see the image of the raft going down the Ohio River with the oars paddling away and the music singing that wistful, uplifting melody,

"Away you rolling river. Oh Shenandoah, I long to hear you, Away, I'm bound away, 'cross the wide Missouri."

Morgan often imagined to himself, "Oh, if I had only lived back then, I know I could have done that!" Everything about the movie affected him... the indescribable journey of going into the unknown, the wagon trains, the riverboats, the dance halls... ah, the breath of adventure! He got a bad case of the bug.

If he had kept his focus in the right direction, his dreams would have produced noble achievements. However, good visions, which would produce noble actions, which would result in grandiose achievements, could be switched to another track simply by a change in perspective.

It all depended on the "lens" he saw life through, and that lens was molded and developed by the influences in his life. For Morgan, his lens became tainted, and his pioneer spirit deformed until it took on a much different mold. In this recipe for a twisted adventurer, add story after story about the new counter-culture. Mix in some peer pressure. Spice it up with the message from the music.

"Born to be Wild" by Steppenwolf. "Are You Experienced?" by Jimi Hendrix. Pulsating, reverberating guitar sounds. Notes screaming and spinning with a driving beat as the music carried you off somewhere unique to each person's wandering thoughts. The message was clear. Expand your mind, explore the unknown realms... in your head and on the open road.

The Rock and Roll of Elvis turned into the progressive rock of Cream. The cute, long haired "I Wanna Hold Your Hand" Beatles morphed into the psychedelic *Sergeant Pepper's* Beatles, along with the acid rock of Jefferson Airplane, The Grateful Dead, and the

Doors. The invention of birth control spawned the ideology of free love. Anti-war sentiment was epidemic as the coffins came pouring in from Vietnam.

The social and cultural upheavals of the 1960's infiltrated the fabric of what was normal and made it hallucinate with vibrating patterns, covering it with paisley. Tradition was out the window, the status quo was now the *Establishment*, and everything had to change just because it had to. The mood of the era was intoxicating and alluring. It was history in the making. Early on, Morgan sensed there was a tectonic cultural shift taking place, and he wanted to be part of it.

In July 1967, Time magazine came out with a cover story, "The Hippies: Philosophy of a Subculture." The issue explained the reasonings and ideologies behind the amazing spread of the cause. What many people passed off as a temporary fad took root in every corner of society. From small rural school houses to the most prestigious college campuses. From the city to the country, from Switzerland to New Zealand. Life magazine had dedicated issues to hippie communes, the anti-war movement, psychedelic drugs, and even marijuana dealing.

Morgan plopped down on a couch in his parent's house and opened a magazine to a picture of two arms, stretched out, holding a kilo brick of pot. It was an expose on big time marijuana dealers in Haight Ashbury. The mood of the article painted them as entrepreneurs pursuing a noble calling requiring great skill and intelligence. They lauded the creativity of these underground capitalists with proclamations like, "If these dealers were employed in corporate America, they would be highly successful businessmen."

Morgan set the magazine down and allowed himself to wander.

"Can you imagine what it would be like to have that kind of status?"

The taste was sweet in his mouth, and now he saw what he had to do to get it. The article mentioned the risks, but they didn't faze him. All he saw was the glory of becoming a legend.

The fantasies massaged his thoughts until something very odd began to happen. The wheels and pulleys of his life manipulated the "lens" of his soul, which took his pioneer spirit and put beads and flowers on it. There weren't any wagon trains anymore, but the West was still out there, and it still beckoned with promises of wild exploits and untold opportunities.

Scare Tactics

A cool fall breeze blew down the quiet street in Georgetown. The 1961 Rambler sat idling at the curb with the AM radio playing "Black is Black" by Los Bravos. Roy stretched out his hand and motioned to Morgan.

"C'mon, give me your money. You want Colt .45 right?"

"Yeh, I guess. How are you gonna buy beer when you're only seventeen?"

"You'll see. Just sit tight, I'll be back in a minute. Be ready to go when I get here."

Roy stepped out of the car and onto the curb. He began a casual walk back and forth along the sidewalk in front of the small, dark storefront with a neon sign beckoning "Liquor." Soon, a scruffy, middle-aged man came out of the darkness at the end of the street. Roy moved up alongside and started talking.

"What's he up to?" Morgan fidgeted nervously, looking around.

The man nodded his head and walked into the liquor store. Roy lagged behind, then followed him in a few seconds later. Morgan got out of the car and slid into the shadows where he could still see what was going on. The Georgetown night was eerily quiet.

"Hey buddy, whatcha doin'?" A male voice called out from the dark behind him.

The hair on Morgan's neck stood up.

"I'm waiting for my friend to come out of the store."

"Why don't you take a little walk with me real quick?" he said.

What's he doin'? Morgan was focused on the beer buying scheme, not ready to deal with anything peculiar.

"I'm not going anywhere. My friend is coming out of the store any minute now."

The stranger moved in. He was stocky and well groomed, in his mid-twenties, with a deliberate look in his eyes. He came closer, now touching the back of Morgan's shoulder. Suddenly, the car seemed farther away than before, and the need to get there much greater. C'mon, Roy, get your butt out here!

He grabbed his arm, "I said, 'Let's go take a walk.'"

Finally, Roy emerged from the liquor store, swinging a paper bag and looking around for his friend.

"There he is!" Morgan yanked his arm out of the stalker's grasp. "Hey, Roy I'm over here, let's go, NOW!"

Roy looked his way, and the stranger casually slipped out of sight.

"OK, OK. Don't get so excited. What are you doing over there? I told you to stay in the car. What's wrong with you, anyway?"

Morgan tossed him his keys and said, "Just drive." Roy pushed the start button on the Rambler and merged onto MacArthur Boulevard. Just as they pulled away from the curb, a whistle pierced the air from back on the sidewalk. It was the debased, would-be assailant, gazing at him with a wicked smile.

"Did you hear that? That guy was trying to get me to take a walk with him."

Roy shook his head. "Man, I can't leave you alone for two seconds. There's no tellin' what he had up his sleeve."

He glanced over at Morgan and smirked,

"There must've been *somethin'* about you he liked."

The color drained out of Morgan's face as they drove over Chain Bridge into McLean, Virginia.

"Oh God, give me a beer, quick."

He ripped open the six pack of Colt .45, popped the tab, and started guzzling. He lit a cigarette, puffed it down and lit another. By the time they hit the Virginia side, he had finished the first beer of his life. What a rude introduction to the real world for a sixteen year old! Oh well, he wanted adventure...

Bum bum bum bum bum – boom!
Bum bum bum bum bum – boom!

The driving beat and organ licks filled the inside of Dad's Rambler. Heads bobbed up and down in unison as the guys bounced to the song, "Gimme Some Lovin'" by the Spencer Davis Group.

Bum bum bum bum bum – boom!
Bum bum bum bum bum – HEY!

Outside, a crisp fall breeze blew by the window as they hung out on a back road in northern Virginia. Morgan leaned back in his seat and gazed at the stars. The air was filled with the smell of beer and cigarette smoke as the AM radio pounded out the music of 1960's youth.

Roy nudged him, "Well, Morg, whaddya think? How are you feelin now?"

"Actually, I don't feel a thing. What's all the fuss about? I'm supposed to be foaming at the mouth or something, like I'm out of my mind. I guess you can't believe everything they tell you about drinking. Gimme another one. I do have to go to the bathroom, though."

For centuries, parents have relied on "scare tactics" to keep their children from harm. They were usually based on hard facts... if you do this, that will happen. A mother would tell her child that a red hot stove would burn his hand if he touched it, to prevent him from experiencing the pain. If he touched it anyway, he got burned. This was not a scare tactic. This was a viable warning. 100 of the time, if you touched a hot stove, you would get burned. Simple, right? Cut and dried.

The "scare tactics" society used to turn people from drugs followed the same logic, but it was not cut and dried. The debilitating effects of drugs and alcohol were ethereal, emotional, and even spiritual in ways that could not be boiled down into absolute claims. You couldn't put a finger on it.

So, good people, who knew the better way, invented dramatic proclamations of disaster to steer kids away from driving off the cliff. But, when the kids tried the stuff anyway, and the disasters didn't happen as advertised, they began to think they knew more than the *Establishment*. Instead of turning them away from the cliff, all they succeeded in doing was creating a situation where they put rockets on their cars and thumbed their noses on the way down.

But social engineers insisted they had it all figured out about how to train humans. On the one hand, *they* wanted to outlaw spanking as too violent or harmful to a child's ego. On the other, *they* didn't mind hurting his ego by expelling him from school for having a water pistol. "Oh, *we* don't want our kids to get used to guns at an early age, so *we* need to ban cowboys and Indians and cops and robbers, and then the world would be a better place because *we* said so."

The dogs and cats running around the banks of the Erie Canal portrayed this phenomenon perfectly. To the dogs, this had always been the most exhilarating form of play, to intimidate these smaller, faster, cuter little creatures because it was fun. The dogs were the little boys in the playground, teasing the pretty little girls just to annoy them. If they could aggravate them enough, maybe they would fight back, and then oh, what fun that would be, and they could keep on doing it over and over.

The cats were the meek and tender girls, trying to protect their honor, not enjoying this escapade one little bit, and they couldn't understand why they had to scratch these slobbering, senseless, unseemly oafs to get them to quit. Why couldn't they be civil and dignified? The world would be such a better place if they weren't so boisterous and rough and crude (nose stuck up in the air, holding the teacup with the little pinky raised), don't you think?

Soon, governing agencies began imposing unimaginable situations on people. The news was full of absurd and bizarre circumstances.

"Six year old expelled for kissing girl on the hand."

"Elementary school bans dodge ball in playground"

"League gives trophies to winners and losers"

"Store prohibits employees from saying, 'Merry Christmas'"

"Mother arrested for spanking son in store"

Morgan was standing in line with a cart full of groceries. In front of him, a kid was squirming and gyrating in the shopping cart, red faced with his nose running and tears streaming down his cheeks. Totally out of control, he was screaming at the top of his lungs, throwing himself back and forth like a pencil balloon at a used car lot. Momma leaned down and whispered lovingly into his ear, "now, now Billy, just be still, you stop that now." *Whap!!* He slapped her in the face.

"Oh no, Billy, don't do that, that's not very nice."

Morgan turned to the lady behind him,

"Doesn't that make you want to take him out of the basket and tan his hide?"

"Oh, I don't think so. Why would you want to do that?"

"Come on, don't you think that kid needs a whoopin'? He's throwin' a fit!"

"Oh no, that would be child abuse. Spanking is not for today."

"Lady, the real child abuse is letting these kids grow up to be spoiled brats. They ought to arrest parents for *not* spanking their kids!"

"Oh heavens, how can you say such a thing?"

"Because they are unleashing a whole generation of undisciplined, self-centered rascals on the world who will grow up to create a depraved society! I guess it's a good thing I'm not his Dad."

"I should say so," the lady raised her nose and turned away.

"You mark my words. This next generation is going to be called, 'The Spoiled Rotten Generation.'"

The solution to all this would be to take all those *we's* and *they's* and put them in nice white suits and cart them off to a serene little spot in eastern Wyoming. There they could make their own utopia where everybody would be nice to each other all the time. And if you weren't... into the concentration camp you go!

Everybody else could then build a big glass dome over the whole thing so they could go on and live their lives. Most people would agree, but the baffling thing was, this misguided group, in the white suits, under the big glass dome in eastern Wyoming, somehow got to make the laws the rest of us thought were asinine. One of the mysteries of life.

After much dreaded anticipation, Roy and Morgan had decided to smoke some pot. For this occasion, Morgan put on the Jefferson Airplane album *Surrealistic Pillow* and turned out the lights. The acid rock wasn't loud and irritating, but rather gentle and subtle. It was soft, like a pillow, but mysterious and tantalizing, like a snake charmer playing for a cobra. The purpose was two-fold... get out the message with the words, and take you on a journey with the music.

Music had always been the anthem of a culture. Gypsy music brought visions of Gypsies dancing in the moonlight with bells and trinkets and jangling tambourines. Russian music had a room full of soldiers kicking out their legs while everybody clapped out the beat. Italian music was Lady and the Tramp eating spaghetti with two chefs romantically crooning, *"This is the night, it's a beautiful night..."*

Classical music, country music, church music... It all expressed the essence of the culture it represented, and the hippie counter-culture was no exception. In fact, the music of this generation may have been the most powerful force at work to define the heart of the movement. When people went to a love-in or a rock festival, it wasn't just a performance... It was a gathering of the tribes, fueled by psychedelic drugs, with electric vibes in the air and love in the heart.

The two psychedelic explorers laid on their backs on the floor, swirling lit cigarettes around to make trails of red in a vain attempt to have some kind of experience. Wow, man that's so neat... and so on. In fact, Morgan was disappointed, because the horror stories of Reefer Madness just didn't pan out. It will make you crazy. It will lead to harder drugs. To Morgan, this was a wacky concept.

"How does this make me want to do heroin? Putting a needle in my arm is the last thing I want to do. Why do these people say such things?"

While Morgan thought he was now all wise and had seen through the deceptions of straight society, he didn't realize he was being drawn into the very subtle work of evil.

"How do they come up with these ideas? They said I'd be stumbling around if I drank a beer, and I'm just fine. I'm supposed to get hooked on pot, but I'm not addicted. If they're wrong about drinking and smoking pot, what else are they wrong about? I'm beginning to wonder if any of their so called 'morals' or 'standards' are right at all."

Now, the tide began to turn, and instead of trusting in the way it had always been, the door creaked open to experiment. In a bizarre twist on right and wrong, the behavior that led to ruin took on the air of being innocent and good, while the healthy restraints that led to happiness and success were condemned.

It was the summer of 1968, Morgan had graduated from high school, and was getting ready for his first year away from home as a freshman in college. The change in perspective was complete. Now, it was glorious and righteous to repudiate straight society. Grow out the hair, listen to the music, talk the talk, do the drugs, flash the peace sign, and be a beautiful person. The "other side" seemed like mannequins from an outdated era. Old ladies with their horn rimmed glasses, men with crew cuts, and rednecks with their rough, leathery faces.

Morgan was all softened up for the plunge into hippiedom. As an initiation rite to the "brotherhood," he knew he had to follow through with the next phase by taking his first hit of acid. LSD (lysergic acid diethylamide) came in tablets (tabs), really small tablets (microdots), gelatin squares (windowpane), or blots on paper (blotter). The tabs could be any variety of colors, from pale green to orange California Sunshine. The blotters could be on plain paper, sugar cubes, or stamped in unique designs.

The media ground out the exaggerated claims,

"MAN ON LSD TRIP THINKS HE IS SUPERMAN – JUMPS OFF TEN STORY BUILDING!"

"You know, I heard a news story that somebody walked out into the middle of a freeway and got run over, because he thought nobody could see him."

Morgan didn't know if these stories were true or not. The message was that LSD worked on the thought processes in the brain. This made it scary, because people who normally knew they couldn't fly or walk out in traffic suddenly became convinced they could. Morgan pondered how this applied to him.

"If that happened to them, what would it do to me? What strange, extreme conflagrations would I come up with?"

The magazines described trippers seeing intense hallucinations of walls melting, trees moving, and trails following moving objects. This was marketed as something bad, that you should never do, and if you did... you'd be sorry! Deep down inside, it sounded like fun and he wanted it to be like the magazines described it. After all, it wasn't called "tripping" for nothing.

Nick, Sherry and Diane hooted with glee as they glided through the suburbs of Northern Virginia in a 1967 Mustang convertible. Morgan leaned his head back to gaze at the summer sky full of sparkling stars. This night was not like other nights. The air was unusually crisp, the sky was bigger and the stars were brighter. He had a swelling feeling in his chest and he felt light all over. His eyes were sparkling, and he was grinning so much his face hurt. Only one thing was missing. He couldn't see any psychedelic hallucinations. The telephone poles were straight, the houses weren't moving, so he was certain the little pink pill he took was having no effect.

"I AM NOT TRIPPING ON ACID!!!" He yelled into the night as he stood up in the back of the convertible, waving his hands in the air.

Nick said, "Oh, no, you're not tripping at all. Not one little bit. Now sit down and shut up! Somebody's gonna see you." Sherry and Diane were beaming with wide, dilated pupils. Diane challenged him, "C'mon, Dusty, tell the truth."

"Is this what it's supposed to be like? Where are all the melting buildings? Where's the light show? I wanna see streaks of red and yellow and blue. How come I'm not out of my mind?"

"Well, that's debatable," Sherry smirked.

Morgan leaned back and stared up at the stars. "Magical Mystery Tour" by the Beatles drifted out of the speakers. A satisfied look crept over his face as his mouth formed into a permanent smile.

"Shoot, there's nothing to this. This is a walk in the park!"

Culture Wars

Rednecks vs. Hippies

In 1968, a gathering of newly minted hippies was a peculiar sight in the college town of Blacksburg, Virginia. Long hair, pot smoking, and psychedelic music were foreign to this isolated corner of the world. But when these college kids started their freshman school year, the ones who had a taste for the new "movement" gradually began to find each other.

As the months went by, the hair got longer and curlier. Strange looking beads and necklaces appeared. The clothes became more "creative," with colors and patterns and flowers. It looked like they were going through a metamorphosis, a mutation that distinctly stood out from the rest of the population.

The normal students were frat-boy engineers, farm boys studying agriculture, rednecks studying construction and football jocks. They had flat top crew cuts and listened to soul music. The locals were called "townies" and were generally poor country kids who grew up girl watchin', cussin', and drinkin'. When they got old enough to drive, they rode around with their buddies, cruising the strip and lookin' for a fight.

The car load of townies slowed down to take a look at the unusual looking group strolling by. They had been drinking so much beer their eyes were glazed over and their cheeks were flushed with a rosy red. The one by the window wrapped a short piece of chain around his fingers and leaned out into the night air, shouting at the strange looking guys with hair half way over their ears.

"Hey, you there. What are you? You a boy or a girl?"

"Hey, shut up and go on home to momma."

"What'd you say? Look here, girlie, you shut up or I'm gonna kick your ass!" He lifted up his chain wrapped fist and shook it at the hippie. "You see this? I'm gonna make you eat this chain!"

The car rolled on down the street, moving along with the flow of traffic going downtown. It was only a matter of time before they came back. Morgan sensed a twinge of fear.

He was no stranger to backyard combat. He had grown up with playground fights and parking lot brawls. He knew that booze fired you up with adrenaline and dulled the senses, but this time, the whole troupe was stoned on pot, making everything more acute and rendering the mere thought of violent fisticuffs all the more undesirable.

On this crisp fall night in the mountains of Virginia, the ensemble consisted of the members of their hard rock band, Andromeda. Walking beside Morgan was the drummer, Gregg. He picked up the pace and turned to Morgan,

"We better move a little faster. If we can get to Hardee's it might be safer. I don't think they'll start a fight inside a hamburger joint in front of a room full of people."

"Yeh, you're right. Wish I wasn't so stoned."

They reached the hamburger restaurant and got in line. As they waited to give their order, they slowly gazed around at the strange assortment of people sitting in the booths. They soon realized they were the ones who were strange. Everybody was looking at them. Morgan reflected,

"Maybe I'm imagining things. Am I just paranoid?"

He felt like he was in a capsule looking out at a room of distorted people glaring at him with their eyes bugged out. The joint they just smoked was working on his brain, and the blood vessels in his eyes stung with sharp prickles.

He stepped up to the counter and beheld a teenager with a folded hat on his head. The kid's red cheekbones got redder and the pimple on the end of his nose developed a red, glowing sheen until he morphed into a Looney Tunes character. Morgan stifled a laugh and wanted to slap himself so he could come back to where he was now, standing at the counter, trying to order a hamburger.

The pimple faced kid leaned over and asked,

"Can I help you?"

"Uh yeh, sure. Double cheeseburger and a medium fries... and a large coke."

Man, I gotta get outta here. All these people are freaking me out. These lights are too bright, and everbody's staring at me. This sure is taking a long time... I bet I've been here half an hour just trying to get some french fries. How long can it take?

He looked at his watch. It had been three minutes.

"Here you go, sir. You want ketchup with that?"

"Yeh, yeh. Thanks."

The guys gathered together in the back, filling up the booths, next to an exit door. They pulled the wrapped up food out of the bags, and a wonderful whiff wafted through the air.

"Man, these hamburgers smell better than ever!" Morgan reveled in the aroma. "I am soooo hungry. Wow, these french fries are great!"

They devoured their meals, stuffing fries into their mouths one after the other in a crazed, unrestrained attack on the greasy fast food. The onions, pickles and ketchup blended together with the hot, juicy hamburger into a dream of flavors exploding in their mouths. Some of them closed their eyes and leaned back in the booth, savoring every chew, every burst of heavenly essence. They got lost in the ecstasy of the moment, forgetting all that was around them, where they had been, where they were going...

"WHAM!" The exit door exploded open with a horde of wild-eyed, drunken rednecks. They swarmed in, more and more until they filled up the area behind the booths. The feeding frenzy was shattered as the rednecks pounded their chain wrapped fists into their hands, huffing and snorting.

"You hippie punks! Told ya we were gonna kick your ass! You bunch of long-haired pussies! C'mon, let's go, who wants to fight?"

The red faced kid was right in the middle of them, pacing back and forth, looking for some flaw, some weakness.

"You see this?" He waved his bloody fist in the air. His knuckles were raw where the chain had peeled off his skin.

"We been fightin' all night! Now it's your turn."

Gregg was sitting next to the exit door, and the mob of bloodthirsty rednecks jostled around behind him. Suddenly, one of them grabbed Gregg's hair and pulled it, shaking his head violently with his balled up fist. Gregg looked like a rag doll as the attacker jerked him back and forth. Reaching back, Gregg grabbed the redneck's arm with his hands, trying to release his hold, when suddenly, the kid let go and ran out the door. Gregg lurched forward, gasping for air.

Somebody shouted, "Call the police!"

The dining room erupted into an arena of chaos... chairs falling over, silverware clanging on the floor, women screaming... the frantic look of terror in their eyes as they ushered their little ones out to safety.

Morgan scanned left and right. The rednecks were like a pen of bulls waiting to go out the chute at a rodeo... jerking, writhing, chattering, growling. Surprisingly, they didn't come any farther than the back row. They milled around, going through their motions, trying to look as fearsome as possible, spewing out wave upon wave of menacing epithets. He leaned over to the organist, Slate, and whispered,

"I guess they think fighting is the greatest thing since buttered grits. They really expect us to let them wail on us until we're covered with blood."

Slate sat there stone cold as he picked out one of the ringleaders and burned a hole in him with his eyes.

"I want that guy to know if he messes with me, I'm gonna take him down," Slate whispered to Morgan.

"He knows I've got his number, because he won't look me in the eye. He's purposely looking the other way."

Morgan felt powerless because he was stoned, and it had taken away all of his bravado. Slate was ready to go, but Morgan's strength was drained out into the floor. He had to come up with a plan.

Every mob has a leader. So, the best way to reason with this pack of belligerent rednecks was to identify the biggest one and face him down. He scrutinized the crowd until he locked in on one that was head and shoulders above the rest. He didn't have a chain, and he was not screaming and yelling, which made Morgan believe he could be someone with some authority.

"That's my man."

Before he could talk himself out of it, he stood up and walked toward the tall redneck. He motioned to him with his hand.

"Hey you, come over here a minute." The crowd got a little quieter and parted in two as they made their way toward each other. Morgan looked up into his eyes.

"Have we done anything to hurt any of you guys?" Morgan asked.

"Uh, no, I don't think so."

"Then why is everybody so worked up? Why do your guys want to fight us if we haven't done anything?"

"I don't know."

"It doesn't make much sense, does it?"

"No, I guess not."

"Well then, do you think you can talk to your friends and tell them we don't have anything against them, so they don't need to have anything against us?"

"Yeh, sure. I can do that."

The dining area was void of any customers. In their wake, they left upturned tables and chairs all over the room. The two negotiators were now surrounded by the whole gang of rioters, mixed in with the long haired hippies. The tall high school kid looked around and waved his hands over the assembly. The loud, cantankerous buzzing calmed down to a quiet hum.

"That's enough, you guys. These people ain't causin' us no trouble. Just leave 'em alone."

That was it! The fire, the adrenaline, the danger and the intensity drained out of the atmosphere. The wild-eyed chain slingers turned around and walked away, went out the exit door and got into their cars. They squealed their tires and peeled out onto the main street.

In the history of Hardee's Restaurants, there had never been a scene like this. The ratification of a peace treaty between rednecks and hippies. Corporate didn't even know it happened, although there should have been some kind of plaque on the wall.

Now that it was all over, the police showed up, lights flashing and sirens howling. Two officers strolled into the restaurant with their hands on their hips. They looked down their noses at the only ones left... a rag tag bunch of hippie strangers.

"What's goin' on here? What are you people trying to stir up?"

The cop examined them, convinced they were the trouble makers. He was used to the short haired, street fighting high school kids. Shoot, he knew most of them and their families. Sure, they got into a little trouble now and then, but they were basically good kids. However, he didn't know what to make of this group of college students with their hair and their clothes and that far off look in their eyes. They were different, so they had to be at fault.

Slate came forward as the spokesperson.

"Nothin', sir. They were the ones who were trying to jump us."

"Oh right, right. And you had nothin' to do with it. Why do you think a bunch of normal kids riding around for the fun of it would all of a sudden decide to beat up a group of hippies?"

"I don't know. You'd have to ask them, but I think it all boils down to a clash of cultures."

"A clash of cultures, that's cute. I guess because you're in college you think you're real smart, with your big ideas. You just go on and get out of here and don't cause any more trouble. We don't need your kind around here, anyway."

War and Peace

"Hey Buz, I started taking karate. Why don't you do it with me?"

Mark was Morgan's old friend from the high school gymnastics team. "Buz" was his nickname for "bosom buddy," so go figure.

"No, I don't think so. I don't have the time." As a boy, Morgan had taken judo lessons at the YMCA, but for some reason, karate seemed too difficult, too hard, too painful.

"Aw, c'mon man, you need to know how to fight in this world. You only get three options... run, get whooped, or fight back and win. I don't like runnin', and I intend to win. That's why I'm taking karate."

"Yeh, you got a point. I guess when you put it that way, winning is better than losing."

"Winning is always better than losing! Are you kidding? We were born to win! When babies fight for their first breath, what are they fighting for? To win the contest of breathing over not breathing.

"I hate to say it, but some people just accept losing as a part of life. They started out winners, but then they got discouraged. Maybe they were poor, or beaten by their parents. They might have been put down at school. Somebody told them they would never amount to anything, but no one ever told them they could WIN.

"Sure, you're gonna lose some battles, but you don't have to like it. You gotta pick yourself up, look in the mirror and tell that face looking back that you are gonna find out what went wrong, make a plan to fix it, and win the next time."

Mark was energized. He pounded his fist on the table, driving his point home.

"To the victor go the spoils! Win, and you get to the top of the pecking order. Win, and you keep the bullies from taking your football or messin' with your family."

Morgan folded his hands and bowed.

"You are right, Sensei. But you know there are times when fighting isn't the answer. When it comes to family or marriage, peace and love is the only way to go. I'm not married yet, but I've heard there are three words that form the foundation of a successful marriage, usually uttered by the husband. These words are, repeat after me, "I...was...wrong."

Mark laughed, "I was wrong."

"Good, you're getting the hang of it. You're gonna need that someday, and I only charge fifty dollars. Now, we all know the wife has access to these same three words, but they reserve them for very rare occasions, like dire emergencies. The husband, on the other hand, should have these words on the tip of his tongue, ready to proclaim on a moment's notice. Failure to use them within thirty minutes of the infraction will render them stale and useless, and you will suffer the consequences."

"How do you know all this?" Mark asked, "You've never been married."

"It's not hard to figure out. Seriously, though, the same could be said for any situation where people interact. Most of the time, humility is the only way out. Now, there are some people who don't think fighting should be used at any time, for any reason. I was raised by pacifist parents, so I am well acquainted with the precepts of pacifist ideology. They were peaceniks before peaceniks were cool.

"Pacifist parents consider it their duty to raise up a generation that will get along with everybody, that will end all war. They are against violence for any reason. To them, fighting is ignorant, distasteful, and socially unacceptable. So when little Johnny comes home from school with a black eye, they scold him. They don't care what happened, they just don't want their perfect little boy to engage in something so crude and ugly as a fight.

"When I was in elementary school, I endured daily beatings at recess from two bullies who would wait around to gang up on me. One would grab me from behind and hold my arms while the other would punch me in the stomach. This happened right out in the open, in front of teachers and coaches. Nobody said a word or did a thing about it."

"Why didn't you tell your parents?" Mark wondered.

"Because I thought I would get in trouble. I didn't think they would come to help, because, if they had to use any kind of force to overcome my enemies, it would ruin their argument. Since they were pacifists, they were bound by their philosophy to blame me rather than admit there was any justification for fighting back.

"A fighter parent, on the other hand, would consider it his duty to train his son how to protect himself. He would encourage him to tell the whole story and teach him how to fight so he would come out better the next time. If I ever have kids, believe me, the bullies better find somebody else."

"I was beginning to worry about you, Dusty," Mark smiled, "I thought your long hair might be clouding your brain. There might be hope for you after all."

This was the crux of the argument. Pacifists believed peace and diplomacy would win out over belligerent foes, and good would prevail. "Turn the other cheek," "Love your enemies," "Thou shalt not kill." All these were mantras for the peace and love movement. How could there ever be a situation where these ideals would not apply?

People who were not ready to give everything they owned over to violent thugs thought this approach naïve. They, too, had Christian values of goodness and love, but they recognized evil in the world, and believed that good should resist and conquer evil. Therefore, the only way to overcome attacks of force was to reply with force. They used it as a last resort, but they knew it was an unpleasant necessity.

On an international scale, they would go so far as to attack a rogue nation that was trying to subjugate the weak. Delivering the downtrodden with force was also an act of love, and in the end, it restored peace. The outcome of World War II proved to be the most convincing example of the need for force to liberate countries oppressed by the wicked and stop the spread of evil. Ronald Reagan made these comments concerning the D-Day veterans in his 40th anniversary speech on June 6, 1984,

"The men of Normandy had faith that what they were doing was right, faith that they fought for all humanity, faith that a just God would grant them mercy on this beachhead, or on the next. It was the deep knowledge -- and pray God we have not lost it -- that there is a profound moral difference between the use of force for liberation

and the use of force for conquest. You were here to liberate, not to conquer, and so you and those others did not doubt your cause. And you were right not to doubt."

These beliefs played a big part in America's role in the Vietnam War. America had been trying to stop the spread of Communism since the end of World War II. This determination led to the strategic doctrines of "containment" and "domino theory." The policy of containment stated that it was necessary to contain Communism within its post-World War II borders. When communist North Vietnam began to take over parts of South Vietnam, the United States felt it was their duty to stop the spread of Communism and save the South Vietnamese.

According to the "domino theory," America calculated that if they let the communists conquer one innocent country, they would conquer another, and another, until they spread Communism around the world. In World War II, Americans were united in their abhorrence of the atrocities of the Axis nations, and they believed that if they were not stopped they would take over the world, including the United States. They were determined not to be forced to speak German or Japanese! They threw everything they had into the fight, even to the point of self-sacrifice and rationing at home to make certain they won that war.

With the conflict in Vietnam, many Americans were not so sure about all this. The prevailing sentiment of the anti-war crowd was, "Yes, Communism is bad, but Vietnam is way over there, and it's just a backward little country full of Asian peasants, and who cares, anyway?" The average person was uninformed about foreign affairs. They didn't buy in to the doctrines of containment and domino theory. Most of them didn't know what those doctrines were or that they even existed.

Unlike World War II, nobody thought there was any threat of the North Vietnamese coming over here and making us all Communist. "So, why are we there?" And, "whatever the plight of the South Vietnamese people is, it isn't worth sending our boys over there to die for it."

Morgan sat back and watched the images on his nineteen inch black and white TV... footage of soldiers walking through a jungle, Asian peasants milling around a cluster of huts, battle shots and pictures of dead bodies. Within a year or two of graduating from high school, word began to get around that some of the guys he knew personally had been killed in Vietnam.

"Has anybody heard from Bobby since we got out of high school?" Morgan was home for the weekend, trying to catch up with his friends.

"Somebody told me he got killed in 'Nam."

Oh no! A void dropped into his gut. Bobby was one of his closest friends. They learned to skateboard together. Morgan flashed back to a group milling around the drugstore parking lot, where Bobby took a deep breath, worked his lips into an irregular circle and blew out a wad about twenty feet.

"I still remember him teaching me how to spit."

This feeling of loss became all too common as he heard the same news about others. He had to file this away as an unpleasant fact of life and go on about his business.

The following summer, Morgan was sitting in his parent's house in Arlington, Virginia, looking out the front window. A car drove up and parked along the curb. Someone vaguely familiar got out and walked up the sidewalk. "It can't be! It's Bobby!" Morgan rushed out the door and jumped on him, hugging him as tight as he could.

"What are you doin' here? You're supposed to be dead! They told me you were killed in Vietnam!"

"Well, I wasn't."

"Hey, you want a Coke or something? Stick around a while. You can help me with my van. I'm trying to panel it inside."

"Yeh, sure man. I'll give you a hand."

Morgan and Bobby worked together holding the paneling up while the other screwed it to the framework. The job brought them together after two long years, and they began to bond again.

"Man, I can't believe this! What happened? Tell me about it."

"You know all those news stories about the drugs over there?"

"Yeh, I heard about it. I saw a story about troops shooting up in their foxholes. It's hard to believe."

"Well, believe it. It's just like they said. I got into it while I was there, and it's really bad. Heroin is everywhere. The blood and gore we see is so bad the guys smoke pot and shoot up just to get away from it. It's somethin'."

They spent the rest of the afternoon finishing the paneling job, but he couldn't tell if Bobby was trying to reach out to him or what. He seemed aloof and out of touch. He didn't act like he was wildly overjoyed to have survived the war and be back home.

"What are you going to do now?" Morgan asked.

"Dunno. Guess I'll stay with my mom. She's living in Georgetown. Maybe I can get a job."

He sounded so depressed! Here was Morgan, the cosmic hippie with the great attitude, going to college, lots of friends, not a care in the world. What's wrong with Bobby?

A few months later, Morgan heard the saddest story of all from the Vietnam War. Bobby had overdosed on heroin and was dead. This time for good. Here was a guy who had experienced all the horrors of war, survived combat, escaped drug addiction, and came back to free soil. He could have made something of himself, but the demons he encountered in the jungles of Vietnam followed him home. He survived the war, but the war killed him anyway in some dank, lonely apartment in the inner city of Washington D.C.

"What's this letter from the Selective Service? A draft card?" Morgan ripped open the envelope. "Class II- S, Student Deferment. Yes! That's what I want to see! I guess this is a good reason to stay in college."

The anti-war fervor was growing wildly. The sentiment formed a major theme in the music, the slogans, and in huge demonstrations. "Make Love, Not War" was the motto. Black light posters asked, "What if they gave a war and nobody came?" The "V" for victory sign from World War II was co-opted into the peace sign, which was now the mandatory greeting for all hippies. Like everything else, Morgan just rolled with the flow. The War is bad? OK, it's bad. The government's corrupt? OK, it's corrupt. The whole military concept of killing the enemy is wrong? OK, it's wrong. He really didn't run into anyone who thought otherwise until he went home for break.

Morgan wandered into a drug store to cruise for friends. The place was pretty empty... not much traffic on a weekday afternoon. In the back was a long soda fountain counter with a few couples huddled together here and there. Off to the side was a bigger open area where some people were sitting in booths, smoking and chatting. You could hear Neil Diamond singing, "Sweet Caroline" out of the speakers.

Then he saw Mark sitting by himself, sipping a Coke. He had stayed straight while Morgan had broken through to the other side. He still looked like a crew cut jock, with side burns, a collared shirt and Weejuns penny loafers. Morgan slid into the booth across from him. Mark was his link to the straight world, his "contact," so to speak. They went through some catch up... jobs, school, small talk. Mark went first,

"Hey Buz, you look a bit shaggy. The Army will take care of that. You been drafted yet?"

"No, I got II-S. Didn't you? Aren't you in school now?"

"No, not now. Maybe later."

"You're gonna be I-A, you know. What are you gonna do then, try to get out of it?"

"Hell, no I'm not gonna try to get out of it. I enlisted!"

"You did what?! You enlisted? Are you crazy? People are gettin' killed over there, Mark. I bet you're glad you took karate."

"Yep, and I'm still taking it. I'm a black belt now. I can't wait to get there... just lemme at 'em. I'm gonna pick up those little Viet Cong chinks with my bare hands and break 'em in two." Mark held his hands up in front of him and snapped them down, like he was breaking a stick. Then he leaned back and laughed hysterically.

"Man, I thought I was crazy" Morgan said to himself, "I spent all this time and effort warping my mind with drugs just to attain this level of weirdness, and I got a guy sitting in front of me who is crazy for real!"

The draft was an evil monster that hovered like a dark cloud. Many wanted to avoid it at all costs, so they devised all manner of schemes to avoid getting called up. Get a deferment, leave the country, do whatever you had do to keep from going into the military. They concocted every ethereal philosophy possible.

"We have deep seated religious ideals and righteous indignation against killing people."

"We are beautiful people, and the very thought of violence makes us recoil in disgust."

The cold, hard truth was, they didn't want to leave their paradise of sex, drugs, and rock and roll for the demanding rigors of boot camp. They didn't want to be ostracized from their peers because of a military uniform. Or, deep down inside, they were just, plain scared.

It became a mark of honor to get a IV-F classification that permanently exempted them from military service. Someone would get their I-A draft notice, then go off to a draft board in a faraway city. When they came back, they were either free or suddenly constrained to put their affairs in order and prepare to go "over there."

Crazy Jim had been in the Virginia Tech ROTC but dropped out to be a full time acid dealer. He drove his old 1963 jalopy non-stop to California to score five hundred hits of Orange Sunshine. When he got back to Blacksburg with his happy pills, his draft notice was waiting for him in the mail. Since he was no longer in college, it was I-A. "Available for military service." Included in the notice was an appointment for a physical exam.

The Army doctor walked into the room, dressed in a white smock, carrying a clipboard. He looked over his glasses at the subject sitting on the examination table. This one had the same look that all too many of these college kids had these days. His stringy hair hung down to his shoulders, his moustache and beard were grown together, about two inches long, and he had that goofy look in his eyes. Here was another one trying to get out of the draft. "Who wants them anyway? Why do we have to go through this charade? Just send them back to wherever they came from and let the real men fight the war."

"Good Afternoon. I am Doctor Clark, the Army psychologist. They sent you to my office because of some inconsistencies in your information. It will be my job to determine your competence for induction into military service."

"Oh, I can assure you I am totally incompetent, doc." Crazy Jim said.

"Yes, I see. That is why you are here with me now. A lot of people think they are unqualified for military service, when in fact they are perfectly normal and quite capable."

"Well, like I said, I am nowhere near qualified or normal or capable."

"I understand. Are you familiar with the Rorschach ink blot tests?"

"Yeh, I've heard of 'em. We might have done some in high school."

"Very good, Jim. May I call you Jim?"

"Most people call me Crazy Jim."

"Why do you think you are crazy? You probably have ordinary feelings like everybody else. We all feel a little crazy sometimes, so that is quite normal. So... we are going to perform a couple of simple tests that are specifically designed to find that out. Now, I am going to show you some images on these cards, and when I do, you tell me the first thought that comes into your mind. Are you ready?"

"Uh, yeh, sure. Go ahead."

"OK, Jim. Here is the first one." The doctor held a card out in front of him with a random ink blot image.

"What does that look like to you?"

"AAAAAAGGGGHHH!!" Crazy Jim let out a blood curdling scream. "Blood! Blood! Get it away from me! I can't stand it! No! No! AAAAGGGHHH!" He clutched his face with his hands and shook his head from side to side, long hair flying around.

"Hmm," the doctor muttered, "very interesting. A psycho neurotic, hemo phobic reflex." He jotted some notes down on his evaluation sheet.

"Thank you, Jim. That will be enough of that. I apologize for the uneasiness this has caused you. We will move on to some other questions."

"Oh, thank God. That was terrible. All I could see was blood, and bodies, and death. I think I'll be all right in a minute."

"Yes, I am sure you will be. Take your time and breath deep. Would you like a drink?"

"Yeh, that'd be great." Crazy Jim went to the water fountain, took a long drink, and wiped his whiskers with the back of his hand.

"OK, now Jim. I need to ask you some questions about your personal life. Will that be fine with you?"

"Yeh, no problem."

"What do you think about girls?"

"Girls? They're nice, I guess."

"Do you have any girlfriends?"

"Sometimes. I don't have one right now."

"What do you think about boys?"

"What about boys?"

"Are you attracted to them?"

"Well, you know, flesh is flesh."

The psychologist scribbled on his clipboard. He glanced at Jim and raised one eyebrow, "Are you sure that's the answer you want to give?"

"Oh yeh. Like I said... at this point, what difference does it make?"

"Well, that puts the nail in the coffin." The doctor said to himself, "He's outta here." He tucked the clipboard under his arm and looked at Jim,

"I will submit my report to the board. Thank you for your cooperation."

Jim pleaded, "Wait, wait! What's the answer? Did I pass? Did I fail?"

"You are IV-F. Psychosis and sexual preference."

Crazy Jim was ecstatic and laughing wildly as he relayed the episode to a room full of friends. Morgan sat off to the side taking this all in, thinking to himself,

"I wonder if I could put on that kind of a show. I don't even know if I want to. It might not be the smartest thing in the world to have it on your record that you were rejected from the military for being mentally unstable and bisexual when you're not."

A light bulb went on. "That's it! I've got it! I'll apply for conscientious objector... the crown jewel of draft dodging. Not only would it exempt me from combat, but it would officially validate me as a peace loving person. And the girls... are you kidding? They just love guys who are peace loving and willing to suffer for it. They'll think I'm sensitive and caring..." he took a deep sigh, "sympathetic, soft and cuddly."

He crossed his arms and rocked them slowly, like he was hugging himself. Then he saw a girl across the room staring at him, squinting her eyes. Dustin snapped himself out of it and gave her a goofy smile.

"Yep. They'll never know I have no honorable intentions whatsoever... Just a dog in cat's clothing."

Morgan leaned against the side of the phone booth and gathered his thoughts.

"What am I going to say? I hope they take this OK." He pulled a dime out of his pocket and slid it into the slot. Nervously, he dialed the number for Mom and Dad.

"Hey Dad? It's me. I want to talk to you about this war thing. I mean, about the draft. Well, I've been thinking about getting a conscientious objector classification."

"Oh, is that so? What brought you to that conclusion?"

"I remember you telling me how you struggled with what you would do if you had to kill people in the War, and I kind of feel the same way. I don't want to kill anybody."

"That is true, and I appreciate that, but my convictions were based on my religious beliefs. Do you now have religious beliefs, or is it something else?"

Dustin stumbled, grasping for words. Dad was no dummy. He knew he was trying to piggy back on the spiritual principles that good Christian men died for. Still, Dad was against war and killing in general, so he told him something he never expected.

"You know, your Godfather is a Quaker minister."

"What? I didn't even know I had a Godfather."

"That's right. When you were born, we were going to a branch of the Quaker church, and he agreed to be your Godfather. He might be able to help you, since you need to have some affiliation with an organization that is recognized as having conscientious objector status."

Morgan couldn't believe his luck, "I'm a Quaker and I didn't even know it. Or, at least I have a Quaker Godfather. That oughta do it. I'll write to him right now."

His Quaker Godfather did indeed answer the letter, and said he would be happy to back him up in a quest for CO. Morgan filled out the paperwork for the application process, using his Godfather's name to certify him as a genuine conscientious objector, and waited.

A number of weeks went by until a letter showed up with the official Selective Service return address. He anxiously ripped open the envelope. If they granted the CO, he would be free from the draft for good. No more worries, no more fear of the unknown. If they didn't give him the CO, then well...

"Your application for conscientious objector classification has been denied."

"Oh no, I can't believe it!" The reality of getting called up suddenly became real again. "I proved everything to them, and I had documented evidence that I am a Quaker!"

The strings he had to pull were getting fewer and fewer, until one day, like everybody else, he achieved the ominous draft classification of I-A. Fortunately for him, the lottery system kicked in before he got called up. Morgan's number was 354.

In years to come, a lot of young men who got these deferments or left the country lived to regret the stigma that followed them. Whenever they filled out a job application, or were asked about their draft status, they would have to put down CO or IV-F. When the anti-war fervor subsided, and people started respecting the troops again, all these deferments didn't seem so "honorable" anymore. From that time on, Morgan carried the reminder of his foolish ideas with him. He regretted not going into the service when so many of his friends paid the ultimate price.

He couldn't fix the past, but he tried to pay some of it back. Whenever the veterans were asked to stand at a public event, he knew he could not stand up with them. All he could do was look at them with admiration and clap.

What Do You All Want?

Morgan flipped through the stack of posters in his hand... twelve, thirteen, fourteen, "OK, I think I've got enough." He had just picked up a fresh batch of concert posters for his band from the print shop. Their friend Chad created a drawing of a large, transparent planet with little goblins dancing all around it. In the poster, the band members were laughing, with Slate's hands wrapped around the globe, as if he was holding the planet in his lap. Across the top in bold letters it read,

ANDROMEDA
SOCK HOP – ARMORY
8:30 PM to 12:00 PM
Saturday, April 10, 1970

His plan was to start in this ROTC dorm and work his way around. Grabbing his Levi jacket, he lit up a joint and inhaled a few long, drawn out tokes. He stubbed it out and walked up to the intricately carved wooden entry door.

"This oughta be fun," he mused, "you never know who you're gonna run into in these dorms."

Morgan opened the door a crack, and a sudden blast of light hit his bloodshot eyes. He instinctively shielded them with his hand as he scanned the area for a place to hang his poster. The hallway was immaculate, with sunbeams reflecting off the waxed floor. The walls were perfectly flat, with the exception of two water fountains protruding two feet into the open space. Dormitory rooms lined both sides.

The open area was empty, void of any human traffic or movement. An active quietness hovered in the air... somebody was here, but it was eerily silent. A twinge of uneasiness told him he was not supposed to be here. The wind banged the entry door shut behind him, making him jump.

"Where did everybody go?" He took two steps. The sound of his heels hitting the hard linoleum echoed around the chamber.

BLAM!! The door right in front of him slammed open and spit out a skin headed kid in a gray ROTC uniform. His back ram rod straight... his arms fixed at his sides, slightly bent at the elbow. His neck locked in place in line with his back, his eyes straight ahead. He took two steps straight out of his room. Morgan jumped back and fixed his eyes on the freshman officer in training.

The cadet stopped at attention for half a second, then brought his right foot behind his left foot and performed a flawless right face. He marched down the hallway with perfect precision, not flinching, not wavering, exactly two inches from the wall. He marched right up to the water fountain. A sharp left face for two steps. A sharp right face for two steps. Another sharp right face, then a sharp left face to continue marching down the hall... exactly two inches from the wall.

Morgan stood transfixed with his mouth open. He had never seen anything like it. He was blown away by the cadet's precision and discipline. He had never given any consideration to the idea that a human being could be trained to such exacting requirements. But requirements they were, and that was the concept that struck him the hardest.

"What must it be like to be under such control?" Morgan asked himself. "That is so strange! He's like a robot, but he's a man. Robots are programmed... they can't think, they can't make up their own minds. Humans aren't supposed to be robots. They have sucked all the life out of this guy and turned him into an automated, brain dead, machine!"

That's what it was, it was subjugation. That cadet, and everyone like him might as well have had their minds wrapped a thousand times with bands and chains until they had no will of their own.

Then their heads were opened up, and they poured in the instructions, the rules, the involuntary servitude.

The image stuck with Morgan for a long time, and convinced him more than ever that he was on the right path. He was free, by golly, and no one was going to take that away from him. He was so glad he wasn't in that poor cadet's shoes. He would never be there, and nobody could ever make him be there. He would die first.

Later in life, with years of trouble under his belt, he looked back on this case through the eyes of maturity. He could now see the value of discipline and training for success. It took discipline to wake up and get to work on time. It took training to do a job right. If that job was highly intricate, or carried a lot of responsibility, the degree of discipline and training could make the difference between success and failure, maybe between life and death. One day he was reading in Psalm 2,

Why do the nations rage, and the people plot a vain thing? The kings of the earth set themselves, and the rulers take counsel together, against the LORD and against His Anointed, saying,

"Let us break Their bonds in pieces and cast away Their cords from us."

He pondered this perspective on freedom and bondage and tried to explain it to his wife,

"You know, back there in that dormitory, I thought I was the free spirit, the man without a goal. I thought the cadet was the one in bondage, and his spirit was bound with cords and chains. But according to this verse, the cords and chains are placed on us by the Lord, and the people who want to break the bonds are the ones who are against the Lord. Their "freedom" is Psalm 2 freedom. They want to throw off the restrictions God has put on us for our own good.

"Back then, I wanted to break loose of the Lord's limitations, but freedom from God's constraints isn't freedom at all, it's bondage. I was the one in bondage, and he was the one who was free! I was in bondage to my freedom, but his bonds gave him strength to win and freedom to succeed! If both of us were in a battle, which one would have the character to come out alive? Probably not me."

"Just what is it you all want, anyway?" Dad asked one summer while Morgan was home on break.

"What do you mean, 'what do we want?'"

"Normally, when people intentionally make themselves stand out, they want something. I want to know what your people are trying to accomplish with your love beads, the flowers in the hair, the music, the whole thing."

Dad was trying to see how all this fit with what he had been through. He was from that classic mold of the World War II generation... the one they called "The Greatest Generation." His parents were poor, he remembered the Great Depression as a time of great suffering and sacrifice. He experienced the bread lines and the soup kitchens. He knew what it was like to not know where the next meal was coming from. Because of this, he had vowed to do all he could to make sure this would never happen to his family.

He went to college, got a degree in engineering and got a job. Then the War came, he went into the Army and was stationed in Guam. He witnessed the rise of Hitler and Hirohito. He read the newspaper accounts and watched the newsreels of the battles, the bombings, and the concentration camps. He learned about the Japanese atrocities against the Chinese and the German slaughter of the Jews. He saw real injustice and brutality on a scale never before experienced by mankind.

After the War, Dad settled into a government job and began to pursue his life's work, which would fulfill his dream. That is, he got married, built a house, had kids, and built a financially sound livelihood that would guarantee his family would never go hungry.

This was what all the vets returning from the War wanted. They fought and sacrificed for the freedom to make their own way, have a family, and provide for them so they could make their own way when they grew up. So, in a manner of speaking, Dad saved the world and handed it over to his son so he would not have to experience the sufferings and depravation that he did. Then he gave him all the resources he needed to have a successful life.

Now, standing before him, was his college student boy, with his uncombed hair hanging over his shoulders, his shirt tail hanging out, unbuttoned at the top, and a peace symbol scrawled on his notebook. Dad had nerves of steel, the patience of Job and the love of Jesus all rolled into one. When Morgan finally snapped out of his youthful idiocy, he could not fathom how Dad did it. With all of God's grace from heaven, he knew he could not do that.

The fact that colleges and universities were breeding grounds for the counter-culture gave it credibility, proving it was not just ignorant, disgruntled low-lifes who were populating this movement. With this backdrop, a picture emerged of an entire generation of privileged, well-groomed, well-fed, well-educated young people, raised by survivors of a World War, turning into a mob of sandal wearing, tie-dyed, pot smoking, peace sign flashing rabble. This begged the question,

"Why would anyone in their right mind do this?"

Morgan was already an attractive, normal looking young man. What would possess him to grow his hair out and intentionally make himself look unattractive? He was already in the middle class. What advantage could he gain by intentionally making himself look like a low class bum? He already had a home, so why would he want to make himself look homeless? He already had shoes. Why would he want to run around barefoot?

In 1970, Joe South wrote a song entitled, "Walk a Mile in My Shoes," which articulated the message that people should see, feel, and experience what someone was going through before passing judgment on them. This was the reason thousands of young people who already had it made tried to look, feel and act like they didn't have a thing in the world. They wanted to walk a mile in their shoes. They wanted to experience poverty when they weren't poor. They grew their hair out so they could incur abuse for their shabby outward appearance, just like people who couldn't help it did. They wanted to experience the injustice. They wouldn't admit it, or put it that way, but that's what it boiled down to.

How could Morgan answer his Dad when he asked, "What will make you satisfied that you have accomplished your goal?"

He replied, "What do we want? Let me think about that a minute. By changing the way we look, we identify with people who are rejected by straight society because of their appearance. That would lead to the conclusion that our goal is for straight society to not judge us for our appearance, but for what's inside. I guess you could say, if the day ever comes when people don't stare at us and pass judgment on us for the way we look, don't despise us in their hearts before they get to know us, then we have accomplished our goal."

Thirty years later, Morgan was pushing a shopping cart in a grocery store, looking around at all the people. He saw long hairs, short hairs, skin heads, nose piercings, dreadlocks, and every kind of outward costume imaginable. He scanned the crowd to see how everyone reacted to everyone else. Guess what? Nobody cared... no one noticed a thing! People from completely different cultures strolled around, oblivious to everybody else. Instead of craning their necks or sending out menacing glares, they acted like everything was normal. They were there to shop, and they were looking at the food... not each other.

A gray haired old hippie with a braided pony tail stood next to a little old lady with her hair in a bun. She was picking out tomatoes while people from all walks of life milled around them. The little old lady spoke to him as if she had known him all her life.

"These are a little green, hon, don't you think? Oh, there's a nice one."

"Yes, ma'am, they sure are. Here, let me get that for you."

Morgan watched the big biker reach up and grab the tomato for the little old lady and smiled inside.

"Well, it looks like we won the culture war. The sad thing is, that old hippie doesn't even know it. Or maybe he just doesn't care."

Hitchhiking To California

The summer of 1967 changed the world. From June 16 to June 18, the Monterey Pop Festival unveiled a lineup of performers with a message for humanity... Peace, love and unchained melodies, with Janis Joplin, the Mamas and the Papas, Jefferson Airplane, and many more. The Who played, and Pete Townshend smashed his guitar. Jimi Hendrix played, and lit his guitar on fire. Then, engulfed with the roar of feedback, bass and drums, he knelt down and drew the flames toward him with his hands, trying to absorb the power and passion. Now that was creativity.

After Monterey Pop, this power and passion spilled over to San Francisco and spawned the Summer of Love. In the district surrounding the intersection of Haight and Ashbury streets, a new kind of chemistry began to form among the inhabitants. It exuded a magical sense of freedom, brotherhood, and wildness into the air. Hippies called these invisible, intuitive expressions "vibrations," and in the Summer of Love, the good vibes were everywhere.

The love was contagious and drew people from all over the country, like a magnet. The throngs were hungry to be part of something noble and glorious. They wanted to see what it was all about, feel the vibrations and expand their minds. Some were drawn by free love. Some were drawn by wanderlust... and some of them just wanted to get away.

Whatever it was, the urge to go West became a frenzy that seized many a young person from 1967 to 1970. The obsession to take the pilgrimage was lionized in songs like "California Dreamin'" by The

Mamas and the Papas, and "If you're going to San Francisco" by Scott McKenzie. In the summer of 1967 alone, one hundred thousand vagabonds descended on Haight Ashbury. Why did they go there? They went there just to be. They went to be-ins, to love-ins, to concerts, to happenings. Everywhere, on every street corner, they sat, talked, grooved, tripped, hallucinated, and just plain hung-out. They simply wanted to relish the good vibes.

People who were determined to be a part of this used whatever means they could to get out West. Some drove, others took busses or even jumped trains, like hobos in days gone by. Those who didn't have a car, or enough money for bus fare, improvised another way to make their journey. So many people embraced this new form of travel that it became a huge phenomenon. Overnight, the sight of an occasional wanderer standing on the side of the road grew into a giant wave of hitchhikers.

Hitchhiking used to be a last resort for people down on their luck, accompanied by a stigma that had always been one of suspicion and danger. The driver didn't trust the hitchhiker, and the hitchhiker didn't trust the driver. Both of them were sure the other was going to rob or rape them at gunpoint, then leave them dead on the side of the road.

But now, it was a social happening. The change in attitude was spawned by people with an altruistic attitude towards their fellow man. It was the righteous and expected thing to help out the poor soul on the side of the road. They had no problem stopping for them, because giving a ride was all part of being in the brotherhood. Before long, so many nomads shook off their fears and picked up their backpacks they became a common sight along America's roadways.

Canned Heat's "On the Road Again" drifted out of Morgan's AM radio. The soft, rhythmic shuffle filled his head with dreams of sticking his thumb out on a remote, lonesome road with the wind blowing through his hair. This was another rite of passage he had to accomplish. The harmonica wailed, the bass carried the rhythm, and the soft, skipping drums made the beat slither and slide. The mood was toxic and enticing. It seemed to say, "Come with me, out to the highways, off to places unknown, off to experiences unknown, connect with the flow of what's happening."

Ever since he heard about the outbreak of flower power in San Francisco, Morgan knew he had to go. When the Summer of Love hit in 1967, he was in high school and still too young. The next summer, he was on track to go to college, and couldn't just up and leave, although a lot of people followed the advice of Harvard professor Timothy Leary, who preached, "Tune in, turn on, drop out." This fever hadn't completely jelled in Morgan's heart in the summer of 1968, but by 1969, it was unstoppable.

"I gotta get outta here. I gotta get on the road."

Morgan was home for summer break, and he was apoplectic that he may have missed out on the mass migration to California. Standing in his bedroom, he took a look around, scanning the artifacts of his life. His eyes settled on his bed, all nice and made up by Mom, his AM radio alarm on the headboard. He remembered how he wouldn't let himself go to sleep until they played a Beatles song. There was the Magic 8 Ball, sitting on the dresser, waiting for him to ask a question.

He scanned the big cork board Dad had made for him. Plastered all over were certificates of achievement, vacation souvenirs, banners and pictures. Talk about a walk down memory lane! A bittersweet sentimentality swept over him as he recounted the fond episodes, the friends, the old places in his past. At the same time, he knew he wasn't that person anymore. The combination of maturity, hormones, peer influence, and new ideas had separated him from the idyllic years of his youth.

Now, home from college, full of energy and wanderlust, he had to move. He felt like a big cat in a cage, stalking around in circles, surrounded by barren walls. The quietness and tranquility of the empty house was unbearable! Suddenly, from somewhere deep inside, a vision sprang up, and the gears in his mind began to turn.

"I know what I'll do. I've been putting this off for too long, but it's about time. If I get started right now, I can make some headway by nightfall. But I need to hurry up and get on the highway." He looked at the Magic 8 Ball, beckoning him from his dresser.

"Should I hitchhike to California?" He shook it up and turned it over for the answer.

"Outlook not so good."

Oh, really? What do you know? You're just a piece of plastic. I better get movin'. The more I dawdle, the better the chance I'll back out.

Morgan pumped himself up, "Guess what, hippie boy, you're going West!" He hastily penned a note to Mom and Dad, telling them what he was going to do. Then, with one last look around, he took a deep sigh, locked the door behind him, and walked down the suburban street to the main highway. The sun was shining bright overhead as the traffic whizzed by. He stood there, a block from his house and stuck out his thumb for the first time.

On the Road Again

That night, Morgan rode through the mountains of western Virginia. The roads were dark and mysterious, cloaked in a blanket of fog, winding back and forth around hairpin turns. The ride he picked up outside of his parent's house turned out to be a good start, the driver going all the way to Winchester. Morgan had been on this road many times before, but not like this. This time, the road was full of intrigue, launching him into the odyssey of his dreams. He leaned back in his seat and watched the blur of the trees. Little cabins whizzed by on the side of the road indicating a change of geography. The city behind, the mountains and valleys ahead, and beyond that? The same thing the pioneers saw... wide open spaces and wide open possibilities.

"I wonder if they felt like this when they headed down the river for the first time," Morgan wondered, "Riding on a raft with all your earthly belongings, the current moving you along, watching the trees on the bank glide by." The freedom rose in his heart. It felt like someone was pumping him with a giant air pump. Pull up, push down. Pull up, push down. Wave upon wave of exhilaration washed over him. The essence of what he was doing went through his head over and over, and each time he pondered it, he got that pumping feeling.

"What a rush," he said, with his face plastered against the car window, "What a rush."

Later that night, they reached Winchester, Virginia, and his first ride dropped him off on the side of the road. Morgan's gaze followed the tail lights as the car disappeared into the darkness. He picked his backpack up by the shoulder straps and moved it off to the shoulder. The moon was almost full and gave off a gorgeous glow as he took in the spectacle of stars. The night was still, and the air clean and fresh. He drew in a deep, cool breath, then exhaled slowly.

Stretching his back from side to side, he watched the road for any signs of life. This was a far cry from the mad, sixty mile an hour, four lane stampede on Lee Highway. Out here, it was a car here, a car there, and long moments in between with nothing but night sounds.

"If I don't get a ride soon, I'll be here all night. Hope I don't get stranded in the middle of nowhere with a bunch of hillbillies." All of a sudden, he flashed back to the gang of red-faced, chain swinging rednecks from the Hardee's in Blacksburg, and got a cold chill up his back.

"That's just what I need... a car load of wild, drunk country kids pulling up and asking me if I'm a boy or a girl." Morgan got a new sense of urgency to flag down a ride. He peered down the road, into the blackness.

"I wonder if there's anybody out there..."

Soon, two white lights appeared in the distance.

"Oh, good." He stood up straight and stuck his thumb out. An old pickup zoomed by, blowing his hair in his face and scattering gravel.

"Well, shoot, it's gonna be a long night."

Behind him, the red lights went on, and the truck slowed to a stop, as if the driver had second thoughts. Morgan grabbed his backpack, ran down the road, and looked in the window at a gray haired old farmer.

"Whatcha doin', kid? You need a ride? Get in." Relieved, Morgan jumped in and slammed the door. He took in the musty smells of the old cloth seat and the dirt.

"Hey, thanks for stoppin'"

"How far ya goin'?"

"I'm going to California."

"Well, I'm just goin' to the next town, but maybe that'll help you get on down the road."

The rest of that night, Morgan caught one short ride after another. As the sun peeked over the eastern horizon, its shimmering rays cast a glow of light on the first day of the rest of his life. A cloverleaf intersection loomed ahead, and he finally reached the artery that would take him West. Interstate 70.

"Here ya go, bub. This is as far as I can take you. Be careful and watch yourself."

The driver let him off at the cloverleaf. Morgan was coming up from the south, so it circled down to the right, 270 degrees to merge into the main highway. He surveyed the scene before him. It was obvious he wasn't the first one here. The sight was surreal, right out of the magazines. Starting at the top, they were scattered around the ramp, more huddled under the overpass, still others strung out all the way onto the freeway itself.

Morgan marveled, "Look at all those people trying to get a ride! How do you figure out who they're stopping for? And besides, who's going to stop on the main highway?"

Just then, a car slowed down and pulled over to the shoulder. A guy and two girls picked up their packs and got in. The car pulled out and disappeared down the road.

"Dang! I guess it does happen, after all. That was pretty neat!"

Sure enough, after thirty or forty minutes, he caught his first ride on the road that would take him over the horizon... A rowdy group of college kids going to Columbus, Ohio.

"Hey kid, you got permission to be out here?" A crew cut jock yelled at him out of the window. "We're gonna take you home to Momma."

Morgan jumped back, "You ain't takin' me anywhere." He knew he had a baby face. He still had peach fuzz, and he hated to admit it, but he probably did look like a girl with his long hair. His only consolation was his college friend, Cutter, who reassured him, "I don't think you look like a girl at all. I'm glad you're not a girl, 'cause you know what? You would make one ugly girl!"

He refocused his attention on the driver, not sure what to do.

"OK, kid. Hop in. We're just kidding. We'll take you as far as we can go. Where you headed?"

"I'm headed for California."

"Well, I hope you make it. You sure don't look old enough to be doin' this."

The day wore on, and Morgan's progress was erratic. He got long rides, he got short rides. He had long waits, he had short waits. Daylight began to wane and it was getting dark. The street lights came on as he cruised into the outskirts of Indianapolis. The fatigue weighed him down after being up all night. He hadn't slept since the day before when he woke up in his parent's house back in Arlington. He left on an impulse, so he hadn't thought out anything except to pack his clothes and a few cans of sardines from the cupboard.

Now that night was falling, it was time to come up with a plan for a place to sleep. He didn't have the money for a motel, so that only left one alternative... the side of the road. He imagined being curled up in a drainage ditch, trying to sleep with cars and trucks zooming by. That won't work.

A sea of lights illuminated the highway as the car penetrated the suburbs of Indianapolis. The exits were coming more frequently now, the stone retaining walls and chain link fences flashing by. Morgan stared out the window at the growing density of the city and knew he had to do something. He saw something up ahead. Is that a bunch of trees on that rise? I need to get up there, into that grove. He nudged the driver,

"Hey buddy, can you let me out here?"

"Right here, on the side of the road?"

"Yeh, pull up to that fence coming up. That'll be great. I really appreciate the ride."

"OK. You say so. Hope you make it."

Morgan walked up to the fence and heaved his pack over the top. Grabbing hold of the chain link, he climbed it like a monkey, lifted his legs up and over, then jumped down on the other side. He grabbed his pack and disappeared into the tree line.

A short distance inside the trees, the ground rose sharply with a steep embankment. Morgan struggled with his heavy pack, slipping on loose stones as he climbed. Once on top, the wooded area appeared to be an isolated piece of forest, even though the Interstate was roaring by only a short distance down the hill. He shuffled around in the leaves and found a good place for his sleeping bag. Unstrapping it from the frame, he rolled it out on the ground and snuggled up inside. In the distance, a small house was nestled in the trees with a single porch light. A dog barked once. Then twice. Morgan dropped off to sleep and dreamed of a man standing over him with a shotgun.

After a fitful night, he woke up suddenly and rolled out of his sleeping bag. Moving fast, he strapped his pack together and slid down the embankment. He threw the pack over the fence, climbed it again, and trudged out to the freeway. Still exhausted, he found a flat spot on the shoulder, arranged his backpack like a pillow and stretched out on the asphalt. Resting his right elbow on the road, he stuck his thumb in the air.

HONK! HONK! HOOOOOOONK! "What the....?" Morgan woke up with a jolt and realized he'd been sleeping on the side of the road. The sun hit him in the eyes, and he shook the sleep out of his head. Dazed, he rolled over and pushed himself up. About thirty yards behind him, he saw a huge, charcoal gray luxury car idling with the brake lights on. It was a beautiful sedan with a sloped back and a black vinyl roof.

"What is that?" he wondered. "Oooh, that car is a beauty." He walked up to the sleek, shining marvel, taking in every color, every stylish line. "Can it be? My God, it's a Buick Riviera!"

The car was brand new, a 1969 model, rumbling as it idled on the shoulder, waiting for Morgan to get in. He couldn't believe his luck. He wanted one of these ever since Dad went looking for cars a couple of years ago. He sat in that showroom model, sinking down in the plush leather seats, clutching the automatic stick shift, knowing it was way too much car for them to afford. He could only dream. Now, he got to ride in one for a little while, but then he stopped himself. Wait a minute, the kind of people I know don't own Buick Riviera's. And, the kind of person who does wouldn't stop for a hippie sleeping on the side of the road. This ought to be interesting.

"C'mon, c'mon, hurry up and get in. I ain't got all day." Morgan opened the back door and slid his backpack onto the back seat. "Hey, be careful, there. Watch whatcha doin'. Don't mangle the merchandise."

Above the back seat, pinched in between the sides of the headliner, was an expandable coat rack, lined with suits.

The people I know don't wear pin striped suits, either. Who is this guy? Morgan settled into the soft leather front seat and shut the door. The tires let out a short squeal as the car lurched onto the highway. Soon, they were cruising west through Illinois, heading for St. Louis, Missouri.

"What's your name, buddy?"

"My name's Morgan, what's yours?"

"People call me Jimbo. Saw you layin' on the side of the road and decided I needed some company. I gotta have somebody keep me awake. Been driving for two days."

Jimbo was a rough looking character with a thick New England accent. Morgan couldn't tell if it was New Jersey, New York or Boston, but it was thick. He was probably in his mid-thirties, with a pock marked face, mussed up black hair, big hands, thick fingers and long black hair on his arms. He was strong and tough, about six feet tall, with an air of cocky unholiness. He hung his hand over the steering wheel, casually dangling a cigarette, with two big rings on his fingers. Everything inside smelled and looked like new leather, except for the ashtray, which was overflowing with cigarette butts. He was treating this car like it was a twenty year old piece of junk.

They rode for a while, neither one saying anything. There really wasn't anything to say. They had absolutely nothing in common, and Jimbo was more than a little intimidating. There was an aura of evil around him. He wasn't straight, and he wasn't a hippie. He didn't look or act like your average insurance salesman, but he was wearing a collared shirt, expensive oxford shoes, and had a closet full of suits in the back.

"Hey buddy, you gotta talk to me. I picked you up so you could keep me awake. Now talk."

"Huh? OK, OK. This is a pretty nice car... you must be doin' pretty good for yourself." Morgan didn't expect to get his life story, but Jimbo rambled on.

"Yeh, it's OK. I just got outta the pen, so I bought it and hit the road. I need some fresh air."

"You were in the pen? What for?"

"Murder."

"Murder?"

"Yeh, it was second degree. This guy started razzin' me in a club and we got into a fight. I smashed his face down on the foot rail of the bar and stomped on the back of his head. The guy croaked, what can I say? Couldn't help it... he started it."

Oh boy, here we go. Most people have never had a casual, private chat with a convicted murderer, but now Jimbo's spilling his guts as if they were having an afternoon tea party. Morgan tried to act nonchalant.

"Yeh, you get what you ask for, all right. He had it comin'. So how many years did you get?"

"They gave me twenty, but I did seven. Got out last month, as a matter of fact. Me and some guys hit a pharmacy warehouse in New Hampshire. We got about a half mil in drugs. We sold it all and split the money. I bought this car and got outta town. Bought all those suits, too. Those are hundred dollar suits back there."

"Yeh, nice." Morgan could care less. "So where are you going?"

"I'm goin' to San Diego. Lookin' for some grass."

If that don't beat all. He's not even a hippie, and he's dealing drugs, but that's not the way you're supposed to do it. You're supposed to smuggle the pot from a third world country in a romantic, clandestine manner, then sell it to your friends and have this sensation of camaraderie and brotherhood... not raid a warehouse and steal the drugs with armed robbery.

Facing this reality gave Morgan a brief glimpse into a darker side of his warm and fuzzy culture. His hippie element, and Jimbo's Mob-like element were joined together by two things: Drugs and money. So, as much as he hated to admit it, the cold hard truth was... it was *criminal.*

I know one thing, I don't wanna get on his bad side. Probably not a big fan of peace and love. Just about then, Jimbo looked at Morgan with a sly grin, "You wanna come with me?"

Morgan's could feel the malevolence in the air. "Not on your life."

Jimbo let out a chuckle. "You're all right, kid. I'm glad I gave you a ride. We're gonna make a great team."

From that moment on, Morgan's mind raced with schemes to get away. Knowing Jimbo had been in jail for the last seven years only intensified the gloom.

"This is really creepy. I mean c'mon... a murdering, ex–con, drug warehouse robbing, New England thug? Who knows what kind of stuff goes on in the mind of somebody like that? I don't wanna find out, either."

He felt the knife in his pocket, but knew it wouldn't do any good. The next sign said, "Columbia 18." Suddenly, Jimbo let out a groan.

"Oh no, my temperature gauge is going up. I must be overheating." He turned off the air conditioner and slowed down. "This can't be happenin'. I just bought this piece o' junk!"

He nursed the car as far as it could go, and barely made the exit for Columbia, Missouri. He pulled over to the shoulder, got out and raised the hood. A cloud of steam billowed out of the radiator as he stood there, hands on his hips, shaking his head.

Morgan quickly opened the glove box and rifled through Jimbo's papers. He found a pill bottle full of black beauties and dumped out a handful. He stuffed them in his pocket, putting the rest back in place. Then he slipped his pack out of the back seat.

"Hey, where do ya think you're goin'?" Jimbo lunged, but Morgan was already past him. His walk turned into a trot, then a jog. Jimbo stayed with the car, hands on hips, staring at Morgan as he hurried up the exit ramp. Behind the Riviera, a car pulled over to help.

Cursing, Jimbo turned back to the steaming engine. Morgan reached the top, breathing hard, and looked around. Nothing. Glancing back at Jimbo, he knew this was his only chance. He walked across the road and down the ramp feeding back onto the Interstate.

A delivery truck pulled up. "I'm not supposed to pick up hitchhikers, and I'm not going very far, but if you want a ride, get in."

"You don't know how bad I need one right now."

Morgan settled back, took in a long sigh of relief and gazed at the Missouri countryside sweeping by. The driver turned to Dustin,

"So what's it like, hitchhiking across the country?"

"Well I've only been at it two days, but I've got some doozies."

Morgan went into an animated account of the Jimbo story. It was behind him now, so he was free to laugh, to mock, to embellish every minute detail. He went to great lengths to describe the murder, the prison time, the drug robbery and the beautiful Riviera. They were both in stitches, laughing so hard they had tears in their eyes. It felt so good to recount the whole episode as past history. It wasn't an hour ago he was living it for real.

The driver looked at him, "Sounds like a pretty bad dude. You're lucky nothing worse happened."

"Yeh, well, I'm just glad I got away from old Al Capone... I don't know what he had up his sleeve. So, how far ya goin'?"

"Well, like I said, I'm not going very far. I've got a local delivery route, and my next turn off is two exits up the road. It's probably a little less than forty miles."

A short drive later, the truck pulled over on a desolate country road, and Morgan got out. He looked one way, and it went on forever. He looked the other way, and it went on forever. From his observation point on the overpass, he could see for miles in all directions. The landscape was sparse, with miles of open fields, a house here and there, some silos off in the distance. A hawk sailed overhead in a lazy circle.

It dawned on him that he could be in the worst of all predicaments for a hitchhiker... no traffic. It could be hours before a car came down the road, and if he didn't pick him up, it could be more hours.

Morgan's imagination ran wild. "The sun will go down, the stars will come out, the night will be full of crickets and coyotes. And there I'll be, staring into the night, waiting for a car to come by. Then the sun will come up, burn me to a crisp, and go down again. Next thing I know, I'll be a bleached out skeleton with long hair and hippie beads, standing on the side of the road with my arm sticking out and a bony thumb up in the air.

People will drive by and say, 'Erma, would you look at that? I bet that feller's been out here for two months, and nobody stopped to give him a ride. The birds have picked 'im clean!' 'Yes, Homer, that sure is a cryin' shame. That's not a very good spot to hitchhike, anyway. Not many people come down this road.'"

He shook the picture out of his head. You think too much. You better get down on that Interstate and get a ride. That's your only hope.

A few minutes later, Uh oh, what's this? A state trooper turned on his lights and pulled over. He got out of his car and walked up to Morgan with his hands on his belt.

"Missouri highway patrol. Do you have any identification?" Morgan handed him his driver's license.

"You know, son, it's against the law to hitchhike on the Interstate. You're going to have to stay off the main road."

"Really? You know there's nobody coming down that ramp."

"That's not my problem. I can't let you stay out here, so pick up your stuff and get off this highway."

The trooper hung around until Morgan walked back up the ramp, then pulled out and faded from view. Twenty minutes went by, then thirty, then forty. From the east, he saw a car coming down I-70, going very fast. It roared under the overpass and Morgan got a good look. It was a charcoal gray Buick Riviera.

Good thing that cop got me off the Interstate when he did. Funny how that works. As soon as the Riviera disappeared in the distance, he ran onto the interstate hoping to heaven someone would stop before the cop came back. Or Jimbo.

An hour later, it was flashing lights, an aggravated trooper, and a nervous hippie.

"I thought I told you to stay on the ramp."

"Yes sir, you did, but you don't understand. If I stay up there, I may never get out of here."

"That all may be true, but I can't let you hitchhike on the Interstate. It's against the law. Now I'm telling you, if I come by here again and catch you on this road, I'm gonna have to take you in."

The trooper got in his car and pulled away again. Now, it was time to get radical. A car appeared out of the emptiness. Morgan jumped up and down, waving his arms like a windmill. Please stop. Please, please, c'mon do it for me. He pumped his thumb up and down.

WHOOSH! The car blew on by. Another car showed up. Same thing, both hands waving, jumping up and down... even stepping out into the driving lane. The car swerved, horn blaring. He was frantic, knowing it was only a matter of minutes before arrest and imprisonment descended on him.

A box like van appeared over the hill, moving slower than the others. Morgan put on his show and lo, and behold, it stopped! There must be a God! He stumbled over himself trying to pick up his pack and run to the waiting step van. It had psychedelic markings painted all over the outside, with swirls and shapes and rainbows. Gasping for breath, he stopped at the front door and looked inside. There was a guy with long hair, about his age, with no shirt. He had a girlfriend, or a wife, with long, straight blonde hair and a toddler on her lap.

"At last, someone I can identify with." This was the first hippie ride he'd had the whole trip.

"Hey brother, what's the problem? You were giving off some wild vibes back there."

Morgan told them about the trooper and being stuck out on the country road with no cars.

"Well, I'm Dan and this is Mary. We're going to Denver. That's about six hundred miles from here. At the rate we're going, I figure it'll take us about ten hours. I'm gonna drive all night, so we'll get there sometime tomorrow morning. You can use the bed in the back of the van whenever you're sleepy."

"Hey, I just might take you up on that if you don't mind. Want some black beauties?"

Morgan stayed up for a little while to talk and watch the sun go down. They were in Kansas now, and the land was dead flat as far as the eye could see. The horizon was bigger than he had ever imagined, and it made the perfect backdrop for a stunning sunset. There was a thin cloud cover in the West, accented with puffy cumulus clouds. As the sun dropped behind them, a bright orange hue began to paint itself across the sky. The light dimmed, and the orange became darker and bolder, with the sky forming a band of rich blue overhead. Suddenly, the sun peeked out from behind and shot out huge shafts of orange light in beams that emanated from the magnificent glowing circle. They shone down from the heavens to the earth, from one side of the horizon to the other, as if the sunbeams were the curtain and the Kansas plain was the stage.

Morgan was in awe. He halfway expected to hear a heavenly chorus of angels. The incredible painting of the sky with its royal blue, brilliant orange, and giant rays of sunlight brought up an image. It looked like 'JESUS IS LORD' should be emblazoned in big block letters across the sky. He didn't know what else to say or think. There was nothing else to say or think.

After a glorious show of colors, the sunset faded, and night fell over the wheat fields and corn fields of Kansas. Morgan thanked the couple again and crashed in the bed. It was his first good night's sleep since he had left home.

The End of the Road

Dan and Mary dropped Morgan off in a park in downtown Denver. He strolled around as a small gust of wind rustled through the pine trees, giving him a taste of cool, crisp air. Across the lawn, he saw a small group of hippies huddled in a circle, sitting cross legged in a yoga position. Probably smoking a joint. Morgan decided to test the water.

"Mind if I join you?"

"Hey, not at all, brother. Have a seat." The joint came around, "where ya from?"

"Just got here from Virginia. Trying to get to California."

"Well, I'm Harry. We're from Pueblo. We're just up here for the day and we're going back tonight. You need a place to crash?"

Morgan breathed sigh of relief.

"Hey thanks, man, I don't even know where Pueblo is, but I sure can't stay here."

Harry turned to one of the other guys in the group and asked,

"Doesn't Ed have an extra room at his place?"

"Yeh, I think so."

Turning to Morgan, Harry said, "even if he doesn't, I'm sure we can find something. You can crash with one of us for a little while if you wanna come to Pueblo."

Three days later, Morgan and Harry were up late in Ed's apartment. Ed and Harry had taken some acid, but Morgan's stomach was a little upset, so he decided not to. Ed asked Morgan,

"You wanna go to the coffee shop? It's the only spot in town."

"I really don't feel too good. You guys go ahead."

They rolled up the streets in Pueblo pretty early, so by eleven o'clock, Ed and Harry came back to the apartment. Morgan's stomach pains were much worse, leaving him moaning on the couch. Harry cocked his head and pointed his joint at him,"

"You don't look so good. You sure there's nothin' we can do?"

"Nah, it's gotta be food poisoning or something. It'll go away sometime."

The two trippers spun records and talked the night away while watching the new stranger writhe in agony. When morning broke, they went out for breakfast to get some fresh air.

"Are you gonna be OK while we go into town?" Harry asked.

"Yeh, go ahead. I'll be all right."

Morgan got up from the couch that had been his infirmary for the last twelve hours. He assumed a position that had become all too familiar, dry heaving in a toilet. In an instant, a searing pain tore through his side and his guts felt like they had been ripped out of him. He let out a blood curdling scream, but there was nobody around to hear him.

"Now that's not normal," he gasped, breathing hard. "We got a problem here for sure."

Morgan held onto the handrail and hobbled down a long flight of stairs, one step at a time. He lurched and stumbled for the house next door, then banged on the door, over and over, louder and louder. He could only imagine what he looked like. Long scraggly hair, pale white face, mouth hanging open, doubled over with his shirt undone.

"I'll probably scare the hell out of whoever opens this door."

A young lady cracked the door and peered outside. Taking one look at Morgan, she put her hand over her mouth, horrified, and cried out,

"Oh my God!"

"I gotta go to the hospital. I'm sick and I don't have a way to get there. Please, can you take me to the hospital?"

"Oh, I don't know. Oh my God." She slammed the door.

"Sheesh! I'm guessing that's a 'no.' Now I've gotta climb back up those stairs."

Morgan haltingly made his way across the lawn toward the apartment. Just then, Ed and Harry pulled around the corner and jumped out.

"Hey, what're ya doin', man? Why are you out here?"

"I gotta go to the hospital. Somethin's wrong."

They pulled up to the emergency room entrance, and Ed slowly craned his neck, looking for a space. Oblivious to Morgan's condition, the guys moved at a snail's pace, driving up and down the rows. Finally, they parked in a lot a football field away from the hospital, across a wide open stretch of lawn. By the time they walked into the hospital, Morgan collapsed on the floor in front of the registration desk.

He woke up in a small cubicle surrounded by curtains. Another excruciating cramp hit him as a doctor walked in. Morgan tried to sound upbeat,

"Hey, Doc... Got any morphine?"

The doctor cracked a friendly smile, "We'll get to that in a minute. You were right, you definitely have a problem. It's appendicitis. Not only that, your appendix has ruptured, probably when you had that jolt of pain this morning. When that happens, the poisons in the appendix spread all over, and they can kill you. It's a good thing you got in here when you did. You may have had only a few hours to live. You are a lucky man."

"A few hours to live? Wow! So what can you do about it?"

"We will have to operate and remove your appendix."

The word stung his heart, but not because of the pain. The glorious image of California faded away, replaced by a heavy stone of frustration.

"I should have known when I asked the 8 ball. I wanted it to be real, but there was always a little voice saying, 'You can't do it. You'll never make it.' And guess what? I'm not gonna make it."

With a pained resignation, he asked the doctor, "How soon can you get started?"

"Since you are under twenty one, we have to get your parent's permission to operate."

"What? Are you kidding? My parent's permission? What if you can't get a hold of them? What if they say 'no'?"

"Well then, we can't operate."

The doctor walked out and pulled the curtain behind him, leaving Morgan to his thoughts. He was flabbergasted.

"Here I've gone to all these pains to be independent, and now they hold the keys to whether I live or die? This is crazy. What if they did say 'no'? Would they say 'no' because I left? Would they say 'no' for all the nights I came home with cigarettes and beer on my breath? Surely not. Surely they'll forgive me for all the bad things I've done to them."

Mom and Dad sat down for dinner and said grace.

"God is great, God is good, now we thank Thee for our food."

They were used to eating alone since their son went to college, but this time it was different. He should have been home for summer break, and his absence was ominous. Since the day they found a note on the refrigerator, they had been unsettled, not knowing what was happening to him on the open road. Of course, his physical well-being was not the only thing they were worried about. They couldn't understand what was going on in his mind. Why had he given himself over to this new hippie movement? What kind of damage would it do to him in the long run?

The phone rang. Dad pushed his chair back and walked over to the black, rotary dial telephone. He picked it up, and Mom strained to listen to the muffled voice in the receiver.

"Hello..... Yes, that's me.... Yes, we are his parents... Uh huh.... Oh, I see... Is that right? OK... Yes, I give my consent...... OK, thank you very much for calling. Goodbye."

Dad hung up the phone and slowly turned to look at Mom. His face showed deep lines of concern and compassion.

"What is it, dear? Is something wrong with Dustin?"

"Honey, pack your bags. We have to go to Colorado. We have to get our son."

Woodstock

The summer heat in Arlington, Virginia was miserable at 105°. It was August, and Morgan was back at the home he left only a month before. But what a month... a little worse for the wear, recuperating from an appendectomy, his head was still reeling from all that happened on his foray into the wide open spaces.

Mom and Dad came out and released him from the hospital. They also had to pay the bill, which just reinforced the point that he still needed their care. Then they took a classic American family vacation in the mountains and caught trout. It was his first glimpse of the towering granite faces of the Rocky Mountains, and they stunned him with their beauty and majesty. He knew right then he would have to see more of Colorado.

"Ring, Ring, Ring!" Morgan carefully got up, walked into the kitchen and picked up the receiver on the old black telephone. He was beginning to feel a little perkier.

"Morgan's mortuary. You kill 'em, we chill 'em. You stab 'em, we slab 'em."

"You'd feel pretty silly if this was your Dad's boss." It was one of his college friends, Rick. "Listen, we have a carload going up to that rock festival in New York. Woodstock, I think they're callin' it. You wanna come along?"

"Is that what I've been seeing on those red posters in the head shops?"

"That's it. You heard about Atlantic City, right? The one they had last week?"

"Yeh, I heard some good things. Didn't they have a lot of big bands?"

"Oh, you bet. Janis Joplin, Iron Butterfly, Credence Clearwater, you name it. Can you imagine seeing all those groups at one time? Well, this Woodstock thing is gonna be even bigger. It's three days long, and everybody's gonna be there. There's one spot left in the car, so if you wanna go, you better tell me now."

"OK, great. Count me in."

"The festival starts Friday the 15th, so we have to leave early Friday morning. It's about a five or six hour drive, so if we get a good start, we should be able to see the bands Friday night."

"Wow, sounds like fun. See ya Friday."

The car pulled up on schedule Friday morning, August 15, 1969. Rick rolled down his window,

"Ya ready to rock and roll?" Throw your stuff in the back."

Morgan squeezed his backpack in the trunk and they headed north. Once they were clear of D.C. traffic, Rick pulled out a bag of gelatin capsules filled with brown powder.

"Anybody want some mescaline?" Holding the bag open, he offered it to each one. Hands dove in, fiddling around, trying to get hold of the slippery brown caps. This simple, generous act instantly energized the atmosphere in the car.

The mescaline generated a mellow, excitedly happy feeling. Pretty soon, they were a bunch of talking, laughing, singing hippies. The mescaline waxed and waned, producing intervals of high laughter and low quietness. Finally, driving through the countryside of upstate New York, they approached the streams of traffic flowing into the historical event that would become known as Woodstock.

Gary, the driver, peered outside, "Hey man, look at those cars up ahead. They go on for miles!" Craning his neck over the steering wheel, he put together a plan.

The scene was surreal. Nothing but cars and people. Frustrated drivers pulled onto the shoulders, bumping over curbs, frantically maneuvering anywhere to find a place to park. In some cases, they just abandoned their vehicles, donned their backpacks, grabbed their coolers, and started walking. The hillsides were crawling with swarms of two-legged creatures, all going the same direction. They were headed for Max Yasgur's farm where the phenomenon of Woodstock was building and expanding into something bigger than anyone had expected.

"We're not getting' anywhere. I gotta do somethin'." Gary hastily turned the wheel and gunned it, spinning his tires to pull off the road into a small opening on the grass.

"Well, fellas, we're here. This is our parking spot for the next three days. Grab your stuff and start walkin'."

Woodstock

Written by Joni Mitchell
Recorded by Crosby, Stills, Nash and Young

Well I came across a child of God, he was walking along the road
And I asked him tell where are you going, this he told me:
Well, I'm going down to Yasgur's farm,
Going to join in a rock and roll band.
Got to get back to the land, set my soul free.

We are stardust, we are golden, we are billion year old carbon,
And we got to get ourselves back to the garden.

Well, then can I walk beside you? I have come to lose the smog.
And I feel like I'm a cog in something turning.
And maybe it's the time of year, yes, and maybe it's the time of man.
And I don't know who I am but life is for learning.

We are stardust, we are golden, we are billion year old carbon,
And we got to get ourselves back to the garden.

By the time we got to Woodstock, we were half a million strong,
And everywhere there was song and celebration.
And I dreamed I saw the bomber jet planes riding shotgun in the sky,
Turning into butterflies above our nation.

We are stardust, we are golden, we are caught in the devil's bargain,
And we got to get ourselves back to the garden.

Gary brought a tent, so a couple of guys wrestled with it and took off, disappearing into the masses. Falling in with the flow, Morgan passed what was supposed to be the main gate. It was pushed off to the side, twisted and leaning against a chain link fence. The crowd flowed through the opening like water through a chute. As the numbers swelled, the spectacle took on a life of its own. Voices from the crowd all echoed the sentiment.

"Wow, can you believe how many of us are here? This is just far out... I mean, it's really far out there."

"Yeh man, the vibes are building, you can feel it. There's so much peace and unity. This many of us here, all together. Wow!"

Morgan soon realized he had lost his friends and wondered if he would ever see them again. It really didn't matter... he knew he'd get by. What mattered was the enchanting mood of so many of his kind coming together in one place. Yes, he was a "cog in something turning." What that something was, was hard to capture, but it was happening all around him.

"One thing's for sure, this is for us, for all of us who are leaving society, who believe in making love, not war, who thrive on total freedom... this is the movement. The flat tops and the old straight folks aren't here. This is a gathering of the tribes."

Everything he had been reading about for years, and the whole conglomeration of hip people he had come to know, was all here. California was here. The hordes of hitchhiking wanderers were here. College hippies, city hippies, country hippies, ex-military hippies... they were all here, and they were all part of something turning.

Soon, the flow of humanity poured into the concert area. There was a huge open bowl, like an oversized amphitheater, with scattered figures of people rapidly filling it up. It was a patchwork quilt of blankets, sleeping bags, and more people.

Morgan stood on the rim of the bowl, looking down at the massive stage. On both sides were enormous stacks of yellow metal scaffolding that made up the sound towers. He reflected on his own band in college and sighed, wishing they were good enough to have that kind of equipment.

Large tents sprang up on either side of the trail going into the grounds, some for first aid, some for food or water. Morgan passed these by, thinking he would be able to come back and get a hamburger and fries later. He strolled along, one member in a throng of happy, laughing, vibrant hippies, moving in unison. He was shirtless, his long hair hanging over his bare shoulders, his heart humming with the privilege of being able to participate in such a happening. Marching with the crowd, he mused to himself,

"This is it, baby, this is it."

He passed groups of people huddled together off the side of the trail. Some were passing joints, and some just stretched out on the ground. He decided to infiltrate a circle of people passing a pipe. He stepped off the trail and sat down in the grass. The pipe came around to him.

"Hey man, you want a hit of hash?"

"Sure." The young hippie held his lighter over the pipe as Morgan took a deep draw. He held it in, fighting back the inevitable cough.

"Where you from?"

"D... C..." He let it out, "How 'bout you?"

"We're from Canada."

"Canada? Man, that's a long way."

"Oh, not too bad. Hey, this is really somethin', ay? People from everywhere. I met a bunch from Arizona, I even ran into a guy from England."

One of the Canadians was older than most of them. He was stocky, with streaks of gray in his short beard and a small ponytail tied up behind his head. He was calmer and more reserved than the others, as if his age had worked in him a quality of wisdom. He had a knowing little smile behind his whiskers, and he looked at Morgan with a sparkle in his eyes.

"You know somethin'? There's angels here, too."

"Angels? Really? I never thought of that."

"Oh sure, with all this peace and love and good vibes, I mean, there's gotta be angels around here. They're walking among us. I've seen 'em."

"Uh yeh, sure. Probably so."

Just then, Morgan saw two of his friends from the car walk by on the path above him. He yelled out,

"Hey, you. Don't I know you? We rode here in the car together."

"Oh yeh, its Morgan, right? How about that? Can't believe we found you. We set the tent up in a place called the Hog Farm. You go up to the T in the road, then turn left. Well, just follow us, c'mon."

Morgan stood up and grabbed his pack. He waved to the Canadians, "Hey, thanks for the hash. I'll be looking out for those angels."

"All right, peace, ay?"

Morgan followed his friends down a gradual slope that led to a concentration of tents and people that was the Hog Farm... a communal group of "Back to the Land" types who, among other things, were setting up a free kitchen to feed as many as they could during the event. They looked like pioneer farmers with long hair and beards. The women wore denim and flower patterns, with straight hair to their waist and no makeup. They could have passed for a group of sod busters from the 1800's, except for the whiff of marijuana in the air.

He thought to himself, "These people are the salt of the earth who have really dedicated themselves to the movement. They are all the way in."

There was still time to burn before the music started, so Morgan decided to take a stroll through the campsites to savor all he could. One theme that kept popping up was how peaceful the gathering was, and how extraordinary it was that so many people could congregate together and get along. After all, the posters billed the event as "3 Days of Peace & Music."

Could it really happen? As many as 500,000 people could be here before it's all over. That's the population of a large city! And we're living together for three days without one fight. As if the collective "we" could take credit for accomplishing this amazing feat of love and show the world how it should be done. If they would just listen to us, we could end all strife and fighting, and there would never be any more war! Amen to that!

Morgan was abruptly snapped out of his trance by a commotion coming out of a tent.

"I just want to come inside. What's wrong with that?"

"I told you, I don't want you in here. Now, all you have to do is walk away, and everything will be fine."

A girl was standing outside the tent with her hand over her mouth, watching. Morgan asked,

"Hey there, what's going on?"

"I'm not sure what the whole story is, but Jimmy is tripping, and Sam doesn't want him inside the tent. I don't know why Sam doesn't want him there, but the idea that Sam told him to get out makes Jimmy want to get in more. I don't think Jimmy even knows why he wants to get in the tent anymore, just that Sam doesn't want him to, so they keep going back and forth."

Sam came out of the tent, pushing Jimmy backwards and out into the clearing.

"Now get out of here and stay out. I'm not going to tell you again. DO NOT COME INSIDE THIS TENT!"

Sam turned around and went back inside. Jimmy was bent over, grabbing his head with both hands, hallucinating and agonizing over some kind of inner thought struggle. He cocked his head back, running his fingers over his face, then through his hair, turning around and around in circles. Ultimately, the same influence that compelled him before turned him around and forced him back to the tent. He opened the flap.

"But I want to be in here. Can't you understand?"

Out the door again came Jimmy with Sam behind him, pushing him along. This time Jimmy lurched for the tent, beside himself with a maniacal urge to reach his destination of acceptance. Sam grabbed him by the collar before he could make it two steps. He landed a roundhouse punch on the side of his head, knocking him down, then rained blow after blow across Jimmy's face. The smacking sounds of flesh hitting flesh mixed with the piercing sounds of Jimmy's screams. Sam continued to wear him out until Jimmy collapsed into a sobbing heap on the grass. His face was a grotesque mess of blood oozing from his nose and mouth.

"I told you to stay out, but you wouldn't listen." Sam turned away, calmly wiping his hands on his pants, and slipped back into the tent.

The girl standing nearby leaned over Jimmy, gently patting him and rubbing his back. Jimmy heaved and sobbed as she wiped the blood off his face.

"I'm so sorry, Jimmy," she said, trying to comfort him.

A tall, skinny hippie with no shirt and a beaded necklace came up the trail and asked the girl what happened.

"Oh, they had a terrible fight," she said.

"Bad vibes, sister. So sorry about the bad vibes." And he walked on by.

Morgan had simply stumbled onto this impromptu bout. He stood there, watching the girl and Jimmy, analyzing the drama. "Well, life's tough, but he asked for it. Must be one of the hazards of tripping. You get bound up by your own uncontrollable thought blurbs. Maybe that's what causes people to jump off skyscrapers. Time magazine should have tried a scare tactic like this:

'MAN ON ACID GETS ASS KICKED FOR BEING STUPID.'

Maybe that would have kept me from doing it."

He ambled back to his tent, grabbed a blanket, and headed for the big bowl. When he got there, the scene had changed dramatically. Instead of a smattering of individuals here or there, the hillside was covered with people from the front of the stage to the top of the rim. It was pretty obvious he'd better find a spot now or never.

The sights and sounds formed a mishmash of a carnival, a stage show, and an Indian rain dance. There was the constant, high level chatter of thousands of people crammed into one area. Standing up in the group on the right was a wild looking shirtless longhair, swaying with his eyes closed, his head bobbing back and forth as he beat on a set of native drums. A girl with long, straight blonde hair was next to him, playing a flute. The air was filled with the vibes of an enormous, festive rendezvous of a band of gypsies.

The traffic jam of people was constantly moving like a slow flowing stream. A young kid emerged out of the mob, quickly weaving in and out, yelling into the air, "Orange Sunshine, four dollars!" A couple stopped him a few feet down the path, and the transaction began.

The tower of speakers came alive with a thump, thump on the microphone and a short squeal of feedback.

"Testing, testing. One, two."

Morgan took a deep breath and started zigzagging down to the front. It was like an outdoor summer theater multiplied and condensed exponentially. There were no gaps between the outstretched sleeping bags and blankets. Nobody had lawn chairs spread out two feet apart. On the contrary, any openings that existed were rapidly being filled in. People tip toed through, balancing on one foot, then the other, trying not to step on someone's head or fall face first into somebody's lap.

"Excuse me. Pardon me. Coming through..." Morgan joined in the routine, inching closer and closer to the front, looking intently for a break in the human mass where he could carve out his own spot. He got as far as sixty or seventy yards from the stage and realized there was no going forward from here. He looked around in a circle and saw a small bare spot.

"Hey, is anybody sitting there?" He called out to a couple on a blanket.

"Nope. It's got your name on it."

Morgan hurriedly dropped his blanket on the ground and spread it out as far as he could.

"This is great!" He said to himself. "Two hundred feet from the stage right in the middle on the first night. Unbelievable."

He laid down on his blanket and kicked back, reflecting on his day so far. "Just think, I started out this morning in Arlington, Virginia, and here I am in the middle of Woodstock." He meditated a while on the wonder of it all, staring up at the sky. Overhead were some helicopters, all part of whatever they needed to put this thing together.

After a few minutes of small talk with his new neighbors, he got up to take a look around. The trail coming into the festival was still packed with a moving stream of newcomers. The amphitheater steadily took in more and more, and the sense grew that the pilgrimage they made was turning into an unprecedented event. It was a monumental happening, not just in the present, but in the whole course of history, in "the time of man." Starting from the left, he scanned the crowd, enjoying the wild cacophony of sounds, the motley diversity of the people.

His gaze came around to the right and settled on someone only fifty feet behind him. It was Slate, the organist in his band!

"Hey, Morgan, what are you doin' here? Come on up here." Slate waved at him with a big grin plastered on his face.

Morgan knew that wild-eyed smile, "Oh gosh, he's tripping." He looked down at the couple beside him. "Can you watch my spot for a second? I see somebody I know. I'll be right back."

"Yeh, sure. Go ahead."

Morgan carefully picked his way back to Slate, and sensed a strange attitude about him. He looked around, back and forth, up and down. Then he stared at Morgan with slanted eyes.

"Man, this is crazy. I can't believe I saw you. All these people here, and we're only a few feet apart."

"Yeh, what do ya think? This is really wild, huh?"

"It's even wilder trippin'. It's freaking me out. This is too big. I think they're up to somethin'."

Morgan reacted instantly, "Oh no, here he goes again, getting paranoid about the government. I've had enough of people weirding out on acid today."

"You see those helicopters up there?"

"Yeh, so what?"

"I've been watching the strobe lights. They planned this whole thing. It would be real easy for them to get this whole crowd of hippies in one spot and open fire. They could wipe us all out at once.

Good night, how does he come up with these ideas? "Are you serious? They're just up there lookin' at us. It's probably the news or TV or somethin'."

"No, no. Something this big couldn't just happen on its own. They're making me nervous. I gotta get outta here."

"But Slate, you just got here. You have one of the best seats in the house, and the bands haven't even started yet. Why does there always have to be some secret, overshadowing power? You gotta stop thinking Uncle Sam is out to get you."

"Oh, that's just it. They would like nothing better than for us to think everything is normal. Then we'll let our guard down, and they can do away with us once and for all. They have to get rid of us, 'cause we're getting in the way of their plan."

"Their plan? What plan?"

"There's gonna be a war, Morg! Can't you understand that? All this nuclear stuff with the Russians and us is going to end up in one big, all out world war. They want it that way."

"Who?"

"There's a power structure behind everything that we don't know about. It controls all the governments in the world, and they want this war so they can rule everything. The CIA is in on it. The KGB is in on it, and who knows who else. They're all in it together, but we're in their way, so they gotta get rid of us! It's gonna happen!"

Slate was flaming with adrenaline as he worked himself into a frenzy. Morgan rattled his head and shook out all the junk he just put in there. For a second, he mulled it over to see if there could be any truth to it. None of it registered.

"Man, if you want to miss the event of a lifetime because of your conspiracy theories, then have at it. I'm gonna enjoy myself. See ya back at school."

Morgan headed back to his blanket, tip-toeing through the hippies. He turned around, and Slate was still standing there with his mouth open, head tilted back, looking up at the helicopters. Later that evening, he looked back to where he last saw his freaked out friend. He was gone.

Richie Havens took the stage. He passionately strummed his guitar, rocking back and forth with tears rolling down his face, while a drummer pounded out a beat on two tall African bongos. Richie whipped up the crowd, singing the word, "Freedom," over and over again with a bouncing native beat. The crowd was enraptured, clapping and swaying, shouting "Freedom" along with him. After all, freedom was what this was all about. Freedom from prejudice, freedom from stereotypes, freedom to do what you want, freedom just to be free.

Between bands, the announcer walked up to the microphone with a piece of paper in his hand and read off some news updates. Only these updates were a little bit different from your average evening broadcast.

"Ladies and gentleman, I have a few announcements. The green acid is good... the brown acid that is circulating around us is not specifically too good... of course it's your own trip, so be my guest... stay away from the pink acid. The brown mescaline is bad. The Orange Sunshine is good, I repeat, the Orange Sunshine is good." There were random cheers from around the audience. Morgan was amused.

"What kind of gathering gives quality control reports about the LSD?"

The concert moved on with bands he had never heard of, so Morgan decided it was time for one of those hamburgers he thought he saw on the way in. He gauged how far it was to the tents on the rim of the bowl, and how much trouble it was going to be to get out and get back in.

Thirty minutes later, he stepped out from the last row of people and onto the road leading into the site. He inspected the various tents in the area, and soon discovered no one was in them. No hamburgers and no french fries. Not only that, there was no food at all, and there wasn't going to be any food.

It was getting late, and there were only a couple of acts left, so he decided not to battle the crowds any more. He walked back to the tent, cold and weary.

"Hey, buddy, get on in here. They say it's supposed to rain."

Just then, a drop landed on the tent, followed by a rapid pattering on the canvas. Morgan rolled out his bag and snuggled in as the drops turned into a shower.

The Hog Farm

The next morning, people were walking through mud up to their ankles.

"Oh no, what a mess," Gary said as he peeked his head out the screen. Not to be deterred, Morgan took off his shoes and walked barefoot to the concert area. He surveyed the drenched, mud splattered crowd milling around the big bowl. It didn't take long to conclude it was not worth it. The guys had already said they were staying behind on the Hog Farm, so he turned around to go back, resigned to the fact that he wasn't going to see any bands today.

"Hey, you're back. C'mon in this tent... it's too miserable out there." Two of the guys were inside, smoking a joint.

"Rick rustled this up somewhere. Here, take a hit." Morgan drew in deeply, then laid back on his elbows. It's nice to be dry, but dang this is frustrating. After a little while, the rain stopped and a sharp hunger pang hit his stomach. He hadn't had a real meal since the breakfast he had before he left home.

"Have you guys found any food around here?" he asked.

"Somebody said the Hog Farm was serving something down at their soup kitchen. I don't know if you want it, but it's supposed to be free."

"Beggars can't be choosers. I'm getting to the point where I'll try anything."

"Well, we've gotta do something about eating, too. If you're going down there, let us know what you find out."

Morgan took his place in the long line, and finally got his plate of "soup." He couldn't tell exactly what it was, but the main ingredients appeared to be rice, beans and lentils. He found a log to sit on, and began to savor his free lunch. Not too bad, all things considered. The fact that he hadn't eaten in two days made it taste even better.

He looked around and contemplated the moment of history unfolding all around him... hippies taking care of hippies at

Woodstock. He welled up with pride that these people, who were now his people, could show so much compassion and generosity. He looked down at his plate of brown rice. Of course, it needed salt.

A commune hippie walked up, holding his plate of rice and beans. A friendly smile peered out from behind his long, wavy hair.

"Mind if I join you? I'm havin' a hard time finding a place to sit."

"Sure, man. Have a seat." Morgan scooted over to make room. "Didn't want to eat alone anyway. What's your name?"

"Cosmo. I'm with the Hog Farm."

"Hey, great, Cosmo. I'm Morgan." Morgan reached out, and they exchanged the hippie handshake. "This is pretty far out, huh? It's really great for you guys to provide all this food."

"Yeh, man, peace and love, ya know. We gotta take care of each other or we're doomed."

"You got that right. Y'know, this food is a life saver, but I almost feel guilty, like I shouldn't be taking a handout."

"Ah, no, man. Don't feel guilty about it. This is what it's all about."

"Yeh, a lot of us got caught off guard. But up to now, I always took care of myself. I was just thinkin'... since I left home and went out on my own, then I should accept the fact that I've got to provide for myself. After all, if I shook off my parent's authority, why should I expect them to keep taking care of me?"

"Huh?"

"Look at it the other way. If I take care of myself, I earn the right to be my own boss, right?"

"Yeh..." Cosmo looked uncertain, wondering where this was going.

"That means I don't depend on anyone to provide for me or protect me anymore. And if I goof up, I got nobody to blame but myself... my parents are no longer responsible for my mistakes. Does that make any sense?"

"Yeh, I guess so, man. You are getting' way out there, though. What's all this got to do with a plate of rice?"

"I'm getting to that. OK, here I am, out on my own, in the middle of Woodstock." Dustin waved his hand over the crowd. "Now, today,

I discover that I am unable to take care of myself, and that rattles up a nerve somewhere that I failed. I failed to see far enough ahead, or whatever. So, do I expect the *Establishment* to air drop supplies to me because I didn't plan ahead? No! That would mean I am still obligated to them, because I need them. Can you see that?"

"I don't know, man. I just live on the commune and they feed me."

"What if you left the commune? Would you still expect them to feed you?"

"I guess not. I never really thought about it."

"OK, let's get back to the rice. According to this line of reasoning, if I accept what the Hog Farm gives me, I come 'under their wing,' so to speak. I am subject to their limitations. But, if I was in a position to say, 'No, thanks' to the rice, I would be free to make my own choices."

"But this food is free, man, you don't have to do anything. No strings attached."

"I know that, but there are some strings you may not have thought about."

"Like what?"

"Well, for one, we have to eat it *when* they serve it. We can't just walk up any old time, day or night, and get a snack. Number two, we have to eat *what* they serve. Burlap bags of beans, lentils, and rice translate into lots of bean, lentil and rice stew."

"Yeh, they're hopin' to keep it going for the whole festival." Cosmo smiled, nodding his head. "Lots of people, though."

"Well, even if they are able to keep it up, it's going to be the same old thing. No more, no less."

"Well, beggars can't be choosers."

"That's the whole point. Do you ever wish you could have a steak instead?"

"Aw man, I ain't got that kind of money... that stuff's for rich folks."

"Well, if being rich means you don't have to eat beans and rice the rest of your life, they might have something there. All I know is, if you want it bad enough, you'll go out and get it. As long as you have to rely on a handout, you're stuck with what they give you. If you want salt on your rice, or if you want to upgrade to a hamburger, you're gonna have to do it yourself."

Morgan didn't know he was playing with political fire. This was just common sense. Going through that line, sitting on that log, and contemplating that plate of tasteless rice made it clear that if he wanted more than a menial existence based on welfare, he was going to have to go out and do something for it. All he wanted was freedom, like Richie Havens said, but if he resigned himself to take what others would give him, he would be in bondage to them, and to that level of existence.

What really amazed him was that so many would eventually surrender to the enslavement of government provision. After a period of time without working, they would become adverse to work, and by necessity, succumb to the standard of living that government subsistence enveloped them in. They were content to get by on bare minimums, so long as they didn't have to work.

"Not for me," he vowed, "not by a long shot."

When he got back to the tent, his friends were packing their bags.

"How's the soup?" Greg asked with a smirk on his face.

"Oh, it hit the spot. Don't think I want to make a habit of it, though. Where you guys goin'?"

"Well, with the rain and all, and no food, we decided to get out of here while the gettin's good. We'll leave the tent for you, if you want. I'd appreciate it if you could get it back to me. Rick's staying, and he'll help you with it. Otherwise, we'll take it with us now."

"No, if Rick's still here, we'll get it back somehow."

Morgan spent the rest of Saturday exploring his sector of the Hog Farm. He sat around camp fires, smoked joints, shared bottles of wine, and listened to the stories of people from all over the country. Occasionally, someone would pick up a guitar and strum a song like "If I Had a Hammer" or "Like a Rolling Stone." Every part of the picture came together to form a panorama of the movement, and Morgan was enjoying it immensely.

He didn't have to feel on guard, or worry about saying something stupid. If he did, everybody knew that we all have our quirks, and that's OK. He found what he had been craving all along, since growing up in the neighborhood, the playground, in school. Everyone was accepted for who they were, no questions asked, and they were free to be whatever they wanted to be.

He knew there was an honor code... be honest, never rip anybody off. At least, that was his honor code for those known as "good people," and everyone at Woodstock seemed to be "good people." He felt so naturally adapted to this culture.

Woodstock represented all these ideals, and the music articulated every thought, concept and philosophy. Joe Cocker said it all when he screamed out his version of the Beatles song, "With a Little Help from My Friends." He belonged, and he was going to pour himself into it, lock stock and barrel.

After a good night's sleep Saturday night, Morgan began to feel anxious about spending so much time away from the music. It did seem silly to be here, in the middle of the biggest rock festival in history, and not see any groups. He went through the food line one more time for a breakfast of Hog Farm granola. Once again, he was thankful for the food, and he took a moment to contemplate their communal, alternative lifestyle.

"I wonder if that's for me. It might be fun, living off the land, bein' out in the country. Talk about leaving society. Seems like you could get awfully isolated, though."

Throwing that idea out the window, it was time to find some good acid and see some bands. It was already mid-afternoon when he saw a young kid selling brown tabs.

"These any good?"

"Oh yeh, don't listen to the reports. This is pure LSD, and it takes a little longer to come on you, but you'll like it, I guarantee it. Just don't take any more thinkin' you're not getting off. That's why people are going to the OD tent. They end up takin' two or three, then they hit 'em all at once. Be patient. You'll get off, for sure."

"OK, how much?"

"Three bucks."

"Here ya go. Hope you're right."

"Oh, I'm right. Happy trails."

Hendrix at Dawn

The weather on Sunday wasn't any better. There were pockets of clear sky, but the rain kept coming in downpours, turning the festival into a quagmire. The bands continued to play in between the showers, while the crowd endured the deluge. It had been an hour since Morgan dropped the brown acid, and he didn't feel a thing.

"Man, I can't get off for nothin'!"

The sun began to set, and the August evening approached with a moist, cool breeze followed a blast of rain. About this time, he felt a cold chill go up his legs, through his back and out the top of his head. His teeth gave a few short clacks and the shiver left as quickly as it came.

"Now, what was that? The chill in the air, or am I getting off?" He had his answer in a few seconds as the next wave worked its way through his body, followed by another. His mouth got a strong taste of a rushing metallic twang. Now he knew he was in for a ride.

"Whoa, Nellie." A grin spread across his face, and he was sure he looked like a goofball. "It's about time. This is gonna be a good night."

Suddenly the crowd around him looked different. The faces of people who were just people a few minutes ago morphed into cartoon characters, and he had to force himself to keep from staring. He walked to the edge of the amphitheater and studied the crowd that had been there for the last three days. He knew what he had to do.

There was a lull in the storm, and Morgan set himself, determined once again to navigate his way toward the front. Again, he performed the awkward dance of inching and balancing through the crowd. The yellow towers got closer. He was barefoot in the mud, picking his way through the thick forest of people standing near the stage. Somewhere behind him, he heard comments floating around the crowd.

"Those government bastards are seeding the clouds! That's what those helicopters are doing."

Oh, come on! Here we are, trying to prove to the world that we are a legitimate force to be reckoned with, and they have to make us look like a bunch of idiots. The next thing you know, they'll be parading around the stage, holding up signs and chanting, "The End Is Near."

Morgan wasn't far off. Earlier in the morning, a radical activist named Abbie Hoffman jumped out in front of the Who and started blabbering about some supposed injustice. The lead guitarist, Pete Townshend, bonged him on the head with his guitar to get him off the stage. The funny thing was, nobody seemed to think there was anything wrong with Townshend clobbering Hoffman in front of the whole world. Everybody knew that listening to the Who was better than listening to some weirdo rant and rave, so he had to be removed.

As it turned out, Hoffman was loaded on acid, just like the others Morgan had witnessed who succumbed to incoherent thought blurbs. And once again, they had been taken out by an act of force. He had a surprising lack of difficulty in processing the irony. It was unusually funny in a way... the only conclusion had to be,

"Some people just can't hold their acid."

Morgan wasn't having any trouble holding his acid, however. He was having a ball, the little brown pill doing its job with great aplomb. The bands played through the night, and he was fueled up and ready to go. By the time he found a place to call his own, Ten Years After was midway through their set. Alvin Lee led his group through a high-speed romp of "I'm Goin' Home," and Morgan went to a level of rock and roll heaven he had never experienced. Nobody had ever played a guitar that fast! The hard driving, relentless beat stoked his psychedelic energy like coal in a locomotive. The Band was next, singing the opening strains of the hippie anthem, "The Weight." *"I pulled into Nazareth, I was feelin' 'bout half past dead..."*A magical mood settled on the throng.

The combination of high powered vitality and deep, brotherly love was a tonic to Morgan's heart. The acid intensified it, and while he was peaking, he felt so warm inside, he wondered if he was going to burn up. He watched most of Johnny Winter, but the peak passed, and he came crashing down... all his enthusiasm drained out like his plug was pulled. He had a sudden urge to get somewhere familiar, so he wormed his way out of the crowd and back to the campground. Once inside the tent, he crawled into his sleeping bag and shivered, twitching his legs. Strangely enough, he fell right into a deep sleep.

A few hours later, it was now Monday morning, August 18. The rain had stopped, and the sun was shining through the screen flap. Suddenly, a stampede of footsteps pounded past the tent. He poked his sleep-fogged head out the screen, rubbed his eyes and saw a guy pulling his shirt on while stumbling up a hill.

He shouted out like Paul Revere, "Hendrix is playing!! Hendrix is playing!! I've been here all weekend, and I'm not going to miss Jimi."

"Well, he's right," Morgan said to himself, "If I don't see anybody else, I better see Jimi Hendrix."

His legs were rubbery as he crawled out of the bag, the memories of just a few hours ago coming back to him like they were a dream. He wound his way closer to the stage, and heard the howling, high pitched sounds of Jimi's guitar.

"Oh no, I hope I haven't missed too much."

He crested the hill overlooking the stage and the bowl of people. If he had any concerns that he might not be able to get through the throng, they were quickly erased. Amazingly, only a small part of the crowd was left, and they were mainly concentrated into a dense pack in front of the stage. You could draw a line in an arc midway through the bowl with everyone that was left standing in front, and bare ground covered with splotches of clothes, blankets and waste in the back.

Morgan was incredulous. "This is unbelievable. The master of rock is here to show us how it's done, the greatest electric guitar player of all time, and half the people have already gone home?" He strolled down the slope, picking his way around the trash, stepping on sleeping bags half submerged in dried up mud. When he got to the back row of onlookers, he was almost as close to the stage as he was the first night, about seventy yards out, right between the two yellow speaker towers. The band was so close he could see the wrinkles on their faces and the knobs on Jimi's guitar.

Hendrix launched into the opening riffs of "Voodoo Child," plunging into a screaming guitar sound that only he could make. He fired out lick after lick at lightning speed, the shrill notes warbling and vibrating and shrieking. He man-handled the "joy stick," making his guitar roar and moan like the winds of a monster tornado. The reverberations erupted in wails and controlled feedback that pulled the sound around like a rubber band. Pull---ing this way, and stre---tching that way, bending, groaning, peaking in squeals and explosions.

Many emotions flooded Morgan's mind. The brown acid had worn off, so he had to rely on something else to stimulate his senses. He had to make do with the combined vibes of Woodstock. And they did just fine.

He closed his eyes and let the rhythmical power of the acid rock take him away. The images of the last three days rolled through his mind. The overwhelming onslaught of people from everywhere. The gathering of the tribes. The Canadians, the angels, the swells of peace and brotherhood. The generosity of the Hog Farm, the open market of psychedelic drugs. The acid reports. The smiles on everybody's faces, the "hello, brother," "hello, sister," "peace, man."

Jimi said it all in his brief chatter between songs,

"You proved to the world what can happen. A little bit of love, and understanding, and *sound*."

Hendrix went straight from "Voodoo Child" into the opening notes of "The Star Spangled Banner." He raised his arm high in a salute to the crowd, his fingers formed into the peace sign. The adoring audience flashed the sign back in unison. The twisted, exploding version of the National Anthem painted the picture of everything the revolution stood for, and Morgan knew he was a part of it. Woodstock had sealed the deal... he sold his soul. A great swelling of emotion rose up in his heart, and he could not contain it. He raised both hands into the air, with his fingers forming the "V," and cried like a baby.

Did they prove to the world what could happen? For a three-day interval of time, the results were remarkable. There were three deaths, two births and one fist fight. But data alone did not address what constituted the feat of Woodstock. Love had beaten the odds. They showed the world that a multitude of people could live at peace with one another.

The sheer power in the numbers demanded the counter-culture be taken seriously. This one-time occurrence became the symbol of the generation Abbie Hoffman later called "Woodstock Nation." Before Woodstock, hippies were seen as annoying misfits. They were a nuisance that mainstream America hoped would die out like any other fad. After Woodstock, their status was elevated as an ideology that became both a social force and a political force.

There was no question the Woodstock generation affected American culture in many ways. Fifty years later, hippie slang had become mainstream. People still flashed the peace sign, in its wide range of displays. One of the most popular formats for radio was still Classic Rock, simply because all the creativity was used up by the mid 1980's. Disco came on the scene, and the musical world went downhill from there. It never recovered.

The underlying political doctrines also made an impact. The country could no longer overlook the national mood of pacifism, as it applied to the Vietnam War. Declining moral standards would soon have the support of the legal system. Anti-capitalism became popular, because hippies abhorred commercialism in any form.

The term "commercial" became a smear, an insult of the highest order. Anything that was mass produced, average quality, or designed to appeal to the multitudes was "commercial." Pop bands were commercial, if they conformed to the mold of the record producers. Even marijuana could be commercial if it was only average or "regular."

"How would you like it if somebody called your pot 'commercial'?"

"Well, by dog, I don't reckon I'd stand for it."

This loathing of commercialism was tied to a rejection of materialism. If you became wealthy, you must have stolen it, inherited it, or abused others to get it. The idea that somebody could earn money the old-fashioned way, through honesty and hard work, was out of the question.

So, was it OK to make money, or not? On his way home from Woodstock, Morgan stayed in New Jersey with some friends he met hitchhiking out of the festival. For three days they smoked red Lebanese hashish, got the munchies, went to Dairy Queen, and pigged out on hot fudge sundaes.

After two days of this, Morgan started running out of money, to the point where he had to make a choice. One more delicious bowl of soft serve or save what he had left for more important things... like real food? He confided in one of the girls about his dilemma, and she said in a sweet, flowery voice,

"Don't worry about it, Dustin, money just doesn't matter."

He knew right then and there he'd have to solve this one on his own.

If there was any hand-wringing going on about the worthiness of money, one thing was for sure. Drug dealers didn't have that problem. There was one capitalistic enterprise at Woodstock that was exempt from all conspiracy theories or contempt. On the contrary, the dealers were heroes, because they supplied psychedelic fuel to the masses, and it didn't matter they did it for cold, hard cash. Morgan was quick to pick up on this reality, and he tucked it away. He wouldn't mind being a hero someday.

Drug dealing was based on the time honored economic force of supply and demand. There was low demand for the brown acid, and the kid had a lot of it, so his was three dollars. Down at the bowl, the Orange Sunshine dealer had a product with a good review that people wanted, so his was four dollars. Of course, herein lay the hypocrisy. It was OK for acid dealers to make money, because they were essential. Everything else was expected to be free. But, you could break the hippie "code" as long as you were providing something that made everyone feel good.

Not everyone fell for the Woodstock fever or "drank the Kool-Aid," as they say. Most of the older generation saw the images of long haired, bandana wearing kids waving their peace signs, and were not impressed. To them, the whole thing was a colossal laughingstock and a funny farm. All their ideals of world peace and love seemed unrealistic and naive.

"What do they mean, they want to turn the whole world into Woodstock? Do they really expect everybody else to become like them? If they think I'm going to grow my hair out and wallow in the mud, they got another thing comin'!"

Their fears were very real as the counter-culture philosophies continued to grow and mutate. But just as these free spirits were certain the Great Establishment wanted to enslave them and force their ways down their throats, they adopted the same role of tyranny, forcing their ideas of how things should be down everybody else's throats.

Now, the loonies in the glass dome in Eastern Wyoming really did want to make the whole world like Woodstock. They wanted everybody to agree with their ideas, and if you didn't agree, then too bad... they would force their view of what is right and proper on you. Kind of like the French Revolution, Socialism, Communism. If everyone became equal, who was going to clean the toilets? They would all be like the commodes at Woodstock.

Later that fall, Morgan was back on campus at Virginia Tech for his sophomore year. The band got together again to practice, and he was dying to find out what happened to Slate at Woodstock.

"Man, I was just tripping too hard. I got hold of some bad mescaline, and it really messed me up. I told the guys with me I was leaving, and they better follow me out if they wanted a ride home. It was pretty funny. Everybody else was desperate to get in, and I was driving against the traffic, crazy out of my mind trying to get out. I did a lot of thinking while I was coming down. By the time we made it back, I knew what I had to do. I went straight."

"You went what? What do you mean, 'you went straight'?"

"Just what I said. No more acid, no more mescaline, no more drugs, period."

"You're not even going to smoke any dope?"

"Nope. Nothin'. I've been straight ever since I got back from Woodstock, and I don't see myself going back. I can already tell I'm sharper and more creative. Some of the big rock guys are going straight, too. You should try it."

"I don't think so... that would be abandoning the Cause. I'm tellin' ya... you stop smoking dope and the next thing you know, you'll be wearing a suit and a tie."

"No, I'm right. I know I am. One of these days, you'll see that I'm right, too. You'll see that straight is the only way to go."

Ironically, the Achilles' heel of Peace and Love would be the incessant quest for self-gratification. The craving to explore new realms of feeling good was insatiable, and in just a few short years, the social phenomenon of beautiful people would take on shapes that were not very pretty.

But for a little while, for a sweet moment in history, we were stardust, and we were golden.

Haight Ashbury

San Francisco

Written by John Phillips
Recorded by Scott McKenzie

If you're going to San Francisco
Be sure to wear some flowers in your hair
If you're going to San Francisco
You're gonna meet some gentle people there

For those who come to San Francisco
Summertime will be a love-in there
In the streets of San Francisco
Gentle people with flowers in their hair

All across the nation, such a strange vibration
People in motion
There's a whole generation with a new explanation
People in motion, people in motion

For those who come to San Francisco
Be sure to wear some flowers in your hair
If you come to San Francisco
Summertime will be a love-in there

A stream of people flowed along the sidewalks, surging like a fluid mass going up one way, down another, parting around a fire hydrant, veering off to cross the road. It flowed like a sea of moving heads, rhythmically drifting in many directions. Zooming in, it became clear this was not your average group of city folks. If this were Wall Street, you would expect the throng to be neatly groomed, sporting suits and ties and business attire.

But not this crowd. Since the Summer of Love, the neighborhood had been growing and blossoming with thousands of hippie pilgrims from all across the country. Everyone was clad in jeans, tie dyed shirts, and various applications of leather. They adorned themselves with all manner of beads, rings, bracelets and fringe.

The San Francisco architecture added to the charm. Magnificent buildings sat side by side, with an occasional break for a narrow walkway or alley. On the ground floor, the sidewalk was lined with picturesque shops of every kind. Quaint little coffee shops, restaurants, markets, record stores and head shops. Above these were second floor houses and apartments in an eloquent, Victorian style. The bay window designs were three-sided or rounded like towers on a castle. The exterior trim was elegant, with wide, rounded borders along the housetops, and intricately carved rails outlining the windows. Many of the doorways were accented with archways and columns, highlighting the entrance to the home.

The resplendent design and workmanship pointed to a time when this district enjoyed the prestige of being one of the wealthier quarters in San Francisco. In the early 1900's, the famous cable car lines came through here, sparking a boom in upscale construction. But after the Great Depression, the values went down, many houses became vacant, and this became a low rent district, ripe for the influx of hippies.

The heart of this district centered on the intersection of Haight Street and Ashbury Street, which became known far and wide as "Haight Ashbury," or simply the Haight. Four blocks to the west, Haight Street ran into Golden Gate Park where hippies gathered for love-ins, be-ins, rock concerts, or just a place to groove.

In the summer of 1967, the euphoria was electric, and the numbers continued to swell. Although the phenomenon would continue for another couple of years, some thought the pure idealism had peaked and was already wearing off. After the Summer of Love, on October 6, 1967, the locals staged a mock funeral, "The Death of the Hippie," to signify the end of a scene they considered played out. They wanted to send a message something like this:

"..this is the end of it, don't come out. Stay where you are! Bring the revolution to where you live. Don't come here because it's over and done with."

Strolling along the sidewalk, weaving in and out among the colorful throng, a young adventurer who had been trying to get here for the last three years was hoping it was not over and done with yet. This was the summer of 1970, and Morgan was relieved to find the spirit still alive. It almost seemed as if Woodstock moved here. Maybe it wasn't what it used to be, but he didn't know any different, and he wanted to absorb as much as he could.

For this reason, Morgan had taken a hit of Orange Sunshine to thoroughly relish his moment of glory. He moved through the crowd, constantly looking around him, soaking up the vibes. On his left, in an alley, three people huddled in a circle, sharing a joint. Further along, he noticed a couple leaning against a car. The guy had a head full of black, curly hair, wearing round, purple sunglasses and strumming a guitar. The girl next to him was grooving and slithering, with her arms bent at the elbow, nodding her head in time with the beat. Morgan continued walking, while gazing at the dancing girl, and bumped into somebody coming the other way. He spun around and fell back in with the flow.

He glanced down and found himself looking straight into the eyes of a Siberian Husky. The dog was pure white with deep, dark blue eyes. He had a studded leather collar and looked wild, like he just came out of a remote Alaskan wilderness. Morgan worked his gaze up the leash to the owner, who was a young man, about his age, with chiseled cheekbones and straight blond hair down to his shoulders.

He looked from the dog to the owner and back to the dog... they both looked alike! He had the same wild look in his eyes the dog did.

"Nice dog," Morgan said, and kept on truckin' up Haight Street.

The acid kicked in, with a tingle in his fingers and a throbbing in his chest.

"Oh boy, here we go," he said to himself. "Like Country Joe says, 'eat flowers and kiss babies, L-S-D.' Don't think I want to kiss any babies, though... Now look at that up there."

Morgan fixed his eyes on a girl hitchhiking further ahead, her hair braided into long blonde pig tails, adorned with a white daisy. She was wearing a buckskin jacket studded with beads and trimmed with fringe. If you could put the classic, down to earth, psychedelic, beautiful hippie chick into a painting, she would be it. She didn't even look real, so he had to find out.

"Hey, where ya goin'?"

"Oh, I gotta get home. Just trying to catch a ride."

"This whole scene is great, isn't it? I mean, I just got here."

"Oh yeah? Where ya from?"

"Virginia."

"Oh, wow. Yeh... really far out. It's the people. The vibes are great."

Morgan got lost in the conversation, enthralled in the wonder of being here, talking to this hippie girl. He wasn't trying to make any advances, he felt too awkward for that. Even if he wanted to, he was tripping so hard he would have messed it up anyway. A VW van pulled over.

"Hey sister, you need a ride?"

"Sure, thank you." She climbed into the front seat. Morgan didn't know what else to do, so he climbed in, too. The driver was a guy named Jerry, and he started talking on and on to the girl about something, while Morgan listened from behind the front passenger's seat. He had now infiltrated the life blood of the Haight, riding around with two natives, cruising down Haight Street, then off on a side street. The rows of quaint houses and apartments rolled by as he got higher and higher.

"I need to get out right there, up ahead," she said, pointing.

Jerry pulled over to the curb, the girl said, "Thanks" and "Peace," and jumped out. Morgan followed her with his eyes as she walked down the street, his mind trailing off into a daze.

"Where you goin'?" asked Jerry. Morgan snapped back to the moment. With the girl gone, he was lost, he didn't know what to say.

"Uh, I don't know." Jerry examined him for a few seconds. He had seen that look before.

"Well, let's go see what's goin' on at the Fillmore."

Morgan couldn't believe his luck. Now he was going to the Fillmore auditorium where every California rock band got its start! The Grateful Dead, Jefferson Airplane, Country Joe and the Fish, you name it.

To Morgan, Jerry was the perfect prototype of the Haight Ashbury hippie. If he could get inside Jerry's head, and get a small picture of his life, he could get a picture of the Haight.

"Where did he come from? How did he make it after he got here? What does he think about? Do the same things go through his mind that go through mine?"

"Nobody here came from here," Jerry said. "I came out two years ago from West Virginia."

"What'd ya do then? How did you make it?"

"Oh, I struggled. Built up a clientele sellin' acid and whatever else I could find. The problem is, so many of them are from out of town, like you. I base my business on repeat customers, but most of them never come back."

"Well, if you can score for me, I'll come back. I would love to have a good acid contact in San Francisco."

"Yeh, that's what they all say. There's the Fillmore up ahead."

When they got there, it was closed.

"Ok, what now? You wanna come over to my place? Do you have a place to crash?"

"Yeh, I'm crashing with some college kids in Berkeley, but I don't have any place to go right now."

"Well, you can come with me and ride out your trip. I'll take you to a good place to catch a ride back when you're ready."

Like many of the other Victorian houses in Haight Ashbury, Jerry's had a long, wide staircase that led up from the sidewalk to the front patio. He opened the beautifully engraved door and they climbed more stairs to the second story. He guided Morgan through a kitchen back to his room.

"My old lady's gonna be here in a little while, but make yourself at home." He shook a greenish gelatin capsule out of a film tin and put it in the palm of Morgan's hand.

"Here, hold on to this."

As he turned to stash the little can, Morgan gazed down at the capsule and popped it in his mouth. Jerry closed the drawer of his dresser and gave Morgan a puzzled look.

"What did you do with that cap I just gave you?"

"I ate it. What was it?"

"Psilocybin," he chuckled, "you're gonna be one high dude. I'm goin' out to get us some weed. You stay here and chill out. Don't go anywhere. I'll be back in a little bit."

Just as Jerry was walking out, his girlfriend Lorie walked in. Jerry pulled her aside,

"Hey babe, take care of my new friend 'til I get back, OK?"

"Sure, baby, sure. No worries... I'll take good care of him."

Lorie stretched out on Jerry's bed while Morgan remained sitting in the only other chair in the room. Long moments went by, and she seemed to be making suggestive gestures at him. Reclining on her side, she pulled one shapely leg over the other, rolling closer to him. With a slithering motion, she stroked her right thigh with her hand, looking at Morgan through deep auburn hair. His thoughts ran wild.

"What is she doing? Am I seeing things? She's Jerry's girlfriend, but she acts like she's trying to seduce me, or wants me to seduce her. What if she's not? What if she is? What should I do? Where's Jerry anyway, it's sure been a long time. I hope he's not gonna rip me off. But then, why would he leave his old lady with me, if he was going to rip me off?

"What's the protocol? Maybe this is all part of free love or something. Am I supposed to make a move? Will she be insulted if I don't? I better just keep my hands to myself. I don't want to get slapped or shot. Especially while I'm tripping."

"Hey buddy, are you all right?" Lorie pulled her hair out of her face and wrinkled her eyebrows with an uncertain stare.

Morgan realized he'd been staring off in a daze, looking like someone who couldn't hold his acid. He shook his head and laughed. "Yeh, sure, I'm Ok. I just popped some psilocybin on top of some Sunshine."

"Oh, baby. You're gonna have a wild ride."

"I'll be all right. Where's Jerry?"

The VW van pulled up to an intersection, and Morgan got out. He checked his pockets to make sure he had everything.

"This street will take you down to the freeway that goes across the bridge to Berkeley. You should be able to get a ride here, no problem. Hope everything works out for ya."

"Yeh, Jerry, thanks a lot. I'll be back next year. Take care."

"Peace, man."

Morgan watched as the van turned and headed back the way they came. The flowery, bustling hippie district where all the peace and love was, was called the Upper Haight. The area he was in now was the Lower Haight, and they were definitely not the same. The elegant, brightly colored Victorian style houses had given way to drab, industrial looking block apartments. The flat, brick fronts of the buildings formed walls along the sidewalks of every street.

It was dark and it felt even darker. In contrast to the lively street life of Haight Ashbury, there wasn't a person in sight. He surveyed his surroundings from an intersection at the top of a hill. The street he was supposed to take was three lanes wide, one way, with parallel parking spots marked on both sides. It went straight downhill, and in Morgan's condition, it looked like a wide, black asphalt ski jump descending into sheer blackness. He saw three men coming his way.

"Hey, can you tell me if this is the way back to Berkeley?"

"Buddy, what are you doin' out here? It's not safe. This is gang turf. If they see you out here, they'll rob you for sure."

Two of them were young, in their early twenties, and they were alert, seemingly friendly. The other one was much older, with deep wrinkles in his face, long gray hair, hunched over with a bottle in his hand. He was stinking drunk.

"Hey, kid, you got any change on you?" He stumbled toward Morgan and sneered at him with crooked brown teeth and bloodshot eyes.

"No, I don't"

"You see this cut in my coat?" He turned and showed a slash in the back of his second hand blazer. "I got that last night. You know what I did? I cut him right back. Only I didn't miss." He moved up next to Morgan and grabbed his pocket, rubbing it in his hand to see if there was any change in it.

"Hey old man, get your grubby hands off me." Morgan pushed the drunk away. In his mind, he knew this was the time to act... to make the first strike. But what would the other guys do? He didn't know what the "rules" were. Would they take up for the old man, or was it every man for himself? That second of vacillation made it too late. The drunk wobbled back with a sinister chuckle and a short knife in his hand. Morgan pondered,

"I wonder if this nasty old soul is a glimpse into the future. Is this what all of us are going to look like in our old age? Inebriated, scraggily haired, poverty stricken, begging for handouts, living in the slums? Not a pretty picture."

The drunk moved in closer.

"Think you're pretty tough, don'tcha? I'm gonna get that change in your pocket, if I have to cut ya for it."

One of the young guys saw what was going on and intervened.

"John, get out of here, leave him alone. I don't know why you get like this."

He stumbled into a hallway, collapsed on the stairwell and passed out. The stench in the enclosed area was horrible. There was a pile of dirty clothes and a sleeping bag bunched up in a corner, and the air smelled like urine.

"Don't pay any attention to him, he's harmless. Where you from, man?"

"D.C. Just got here this week. I came out looking for peace and love."

"Well, there ain't no peace and love out here, I can tell you. But, hey, cool. I used to be from D.C. Don't worry, we'll take care of you. Now, what are you tryin' to do?"

"I need to get back to Berkeley."

"Ok, we'll stay with ya until you catch a ride." Just then a door slammed somewhere down the block. The two young guys flattened their backs against the building, pulled out their knives, and nervously looked in all directions. Nothing there.

A black car turned onto the street, and he watched it cruise down the hill. It veered off toward the far left lane and slowed down, finally stopping, way down there, in one of the parking spots along the curb.

"Do you think they're stopping for me?"

"Go on down and see, the worst they can do is say no."

Morgan ran down the incline, "in this neighborhood, they can do a lot more than say 'no'." He reached the car, out of breath, the adrenaline of fear and acid putting a wild, frantic look on his face. He stared at the rear door of the car as it opened. A huge black man rose up out of the back seat. Two big, round, bloodshot eyes rolled up to meet his.

"Can I help you, brother?"

The blackness of the street, the car, the night, all formed a cloak of dark danger. Morgan jumped back in terror as his hallucinating mind flashed visions of a massacre. He envisioned them emerging out of the car, bright, gleaming metal knife blades in their hands... his body covered in blood, lying in the gutter. His jaw dropped, and his eyes opened up wide, aghast... he turned and ran back up the hill as fast as his rubbery legs would take him.

Huffing and blowing, gasping for air, he told the guys waiting at the top of the hill, "They were going to mug me." They pushed him into the reeking hallway where John was, still passed out on the stairs. Pulling their knives again, they flattened out against the wall, staying in the shadows, stealthily peeking around a stairwell to see down the hill. After a few minutes, they came casually strolling back into the hallway.

"Really? They were going to mug you?"

"I thought I saw knives, and I had this image of them stabbing me and leaving me bleeding in the street."

"All they did was get out of their car and walk into their house. They're probably laughing their asses off about some lily livered white boy."

"Well, you can never be too careful."

"OK. You wanna try again? We'll stay a little bit longer, but we gotta go."

"Yeh, I gotta get out of this place." Morgan walked back out on the street, looking all around, and waved his thumb at every car passing by. Eventually, one pulled over in a normal way, clearly intending to give him a ride. With a sigh of relief, he approached the vehicle that was his ticket to safety. He waved back at the two mysterious, unknown protectors. They raised their fists in victory, giving him the thumbs up, and he opened the car door.

"Man, you look frazzled!" The driver's name was Dean, and he had a much more familiar look... long black hair, hippie attire, friendly, good natured. Morgan melted into the seat and confided in him that he was tripping, and that the psilocybin should be kicking in any time now. With Dean as his captive audience, he entertained him with all that happened. It made for a great story, and they laughed heartily, becoming instant friends. They merged onto the Bayshore Freeway that would take them over the San Francisco – Oakland Bay Bridge, and Dean said he knew exactly what Morgan just went through.

"Yeh, that's a pretty bad neighborhood back there. A lot's changed in the last few years. It's not the same as it was, that's for sure."

He asked Dean, "So, what do you do?"

"I'm a dealer."

"Another dealer. The chain of supply to exercise the mind. The economic engine that drives the hippie industry. Pretty far out."

Mendocino

Jimmy the cook sat on a log, stirring a large pot of stew over a campfire. Five miles into the back country of Big Sur, Morgan had found a small hippie outpost in an isolated campground. At suppertime, everyone contributed to the evening concoction. If they were lucky, somebody had a little bit of meat.

Jimmy was a thin, young black man who spent the summer in this campground with his dog, sleeping in a two man pup tent.

"So Jimmy, where are you from?" Morgan asked.

"Oakland. How 'bout you?"

"Virginia. I came out to see the Haight last year... it was pretty nice, but some things weren't so nice. I came back this year, hopin' to get one more shot at the Summer of Love before it fizzled completely."

"Well, it be fizzled, I can tell you that."

"Really? That's a shame. So, since you're from Oakland, you would know all about that."

"Yeh, I guess. I never went down there much. I'm from the inner city... downtown."

"Is that why you're out here, in the middle of a Redwood forest?"

"Oh yeh," Jimmy nodded his head, stirring the pot. "It's a whole lot better than Oakland... if you want the good vibes, you better be in the woods. You might catch some up north, if you want to head up that way."

After three nights of communal stew, Morgan decided to fend for himself. He noticed some trout in a stream running through the campground... they weren't very big, but trout was trout. He scouted the limbs overhanging the little brook until he found a tangle of fishing line wrapped up in a wad. After an hour of unthreading the line, he borrowed a handful of flour, mixed it with a few drops of stream water, and made a paste of dough. He pinched a little ball on the hook and gently lowered the offering into the water, behind a trout facing upstream. As he carefully pulled the dough ball upstream, alongside the little fish, it abruptly turned and nailed the bait. Two fish later, Morgan had a nice little feast of campfire roasted brook trout.

"Like I said, if you want something better than what the masses are willing to accept, you have to do something different."

From Big Sur, he followed Jimmy's advice and headed north to Mendocino, in Northern California.

"Let me see that Uncle Henry over there."

The middle-aged woman with long, silver streaked hair reached into the case and pulled out a beautiful bone-handled knife.

"There ya go, hon."

The general store was a combination of clothes, camping equipment, cooking utensils, and fishing gear. This was coastal mountain country, so he stocked up on pans, matches, rice, and salt. Everything he might need for a primitive existence.

"This knife comes with its own sheath. Genuine leather, too. You can have it for fifteen dollars."

"Man, that's a lot, but it's a beauty. I'll take it. I'll take that camp hatchet, too."

Whiskey Ed had spent the better part of the winter putting together his driftwood palace on this strip of sand blanketed with round rocks. At the point where the rocky beach met the land stood a sheer cliff ninety feet high. Using the cliff face as a wall, he arranged pieces of driftwood to lean against it for support. He hung rugs on the walls for artistic design, and added pillows and blankets to make it soft and cozy. He burned candles at night, and kept the incense going at all times.

On this day, Whiskey Ed lounged with a couple friends from town, drinking whiskey and smoking dope. Many "tourist" hippies had come and gone, so he was not surprised at the sight of this new intruder coming down the path. What was amusing was his outfit. This kid looked like a Barbie Doll, or rather a Ken doll. Actually, he looked like a five year old with a new Davy Crockett costume. New knife, new hatchet, clean clothes, no whiskers.

The newcomer stepped off a rock and paused to take a look at Ed and his elaborate, driftwood bungalow.

"Well, who do we have here...? Daniel Boone?" Whiskey Ed snorted. His friends roared in mocking laughter. Morgan ignored the ridicule,

"Any of these available?" he asked, pointing to some driftwood shelters.

Ed stumbled toward him, showing a row of crooked, yellowed teeth, his breath reeking with a horrible stench. He took a swig from his bottle and waved his arm in a wide arc over the panorama. "Sure, take your pick."

Morgan walked over the slippery rocks to a pile of driftwood someone had formed into a cocoon with just enough space for one sleeping bag. He started a fire, cooked his rice and crawled into his one man shelter. Looking back at Whiskey Ed's hut, a lantern cast shadows against the rocks with the sounds of riotous hooting and hollering in the distance. It wasn't long before they all passed out, allowing Dustin to breathe a sigh of relief.

The next morning, he quickly decided this was not for him, so he hiked back up the trail to a scenic overlook on Highway 1. An old International Harvester truck swung in to give him a ride. The truck's bed had been modified with wooden fence slats on the sides to create a wider, deeper hauling capacity. The back was filled with long haired, bearded country hippies. One of them yelled out,

"Hey, you wanna come with us? We have a commune about five miles from here. You got a place to stay?"

"No, I don't. Yeh, why not? Are you sure it's OK?"

"Yeh, hop in."

That evening, Morgan found himself in a lodge that served as the Great House for everyone at the commune. They made the main evening meal here, and all the women worked together in the kitchen as the workers gradually filed in from the fields. After dinner, they settled into a humming, cozy atmosphere with a fire in the hearth. It was like a page out of a Life magazine cover story. Marijuana smoke drifted through the air as the kitchen crew passed around a joint.

A short while after sunset, a couple named Red and Carlita invited him to spend the night in their cabin. They walked across the compound to a small, rustic house made out of redwood timbers. Once inside, Red pointed to a corner and said,

"Set your backpack over there. You can crash on that mattress."

The house looked like a psychedelic fur trapper's cabin. An antique lumberjack saw hung at an angle on the wall, and a wood burning stove sat in the middle of the living room. There was a Grateful Dead poster above the doorway, and the furnishings had a paisley, viney type of design in deep earth tones. Carlita's dress was one piece of flowered fabric that draped to the floor. The air was filled with the scent of incense.

Red leaned back into an overstuffed pillow and lit a joint. He exhaled,

"A few years ago, a little old lady wanted to use her money to help us hippies, so she donated the land, with the condition that we would farm it and give her a share of the profits. In exchange, she lets us do whatever we want, including putting up homes and the main lodge. It's a great setup. We have a good thing goin'."

Dustin settled in his chair and relished the moment. He wanted to stay up and get to know these people, but Red said,

"We have to hit the sack. Daylight comes pretty early."

At 5:00 the next morning, Red shook him out of a deep sleep.

"Up and at 'em, man. We get up with the chickens around here. Lots of work to do."

Morgan's body was in shock. He hadn't gotten up this early since his paper route in high school.

"Man, this is painful. Do you always get up this early?"

"When you work on a farm, you gotta keep farmer's hours. Breakfast starts at six. After that, you can stay here and work with us, or you can hang out at the Great House. Someone will take you back out to the main road."

The Great House was a beehive of activity. The breakfast of oatmeal and biscuits was over, and the women settled into their system for cleaning up. The dining area came alive with hustle and bustle... people scooting benches around, scraping off the dishes. The air was filled with the sounds of clanging pans and chatter. Outside, trucks were pulling in and out, the workers busy loading up tools and supplies. The big truck that brought him here was once again filling up with hippies, jostling about feverishly, making room for each other.

"Where's everybody going?" Morgan asked Red.

"Out to the fields. We work this farm from dawn to dusk."

There's that word again. WORK? Dustin felt like Maynard G. Krebs on Dobie Gillis. "These people are really hard at it. I got nothin' against doin' what you gotta do to get by, but this is too much like reality."

At 7:00 AM, he was on the highway, hitchhiking south to San Francisco. It was so early, his head was still in a daze, but he definitely had a good jump on the day. By late afternoon, Morgan was back in Haight Ashbury. He walked along Oak Street, trying to find Jerry's house. In just one year, the place had changed dramatically. No more bustling exuberance, no more shoulder to shoulder masses of happy hippies, no more flowers in the hair, and no more music. Jimmy was right... it be fizzled.

He stared down each side street until he recognized the neighborhood. It appeared the pall of the Lower Haight had extended its shadow to infect the Upper Haight. The houses with the grandiose staircases were barricaded with black iron bars on all the first floor windows and doors. Instead of a quaint, colorful, Bohemian village, it felt more like an urban prison.

"This is sad. How could this be?" Morgan sensed a wave of heartache as if he had lost a good friend. He climbed the stairs to Jerry's old house. He contemplated the bars across the door as he rang the doorbell. He rang it a few more times until he heard footsteps. From behind the door, someone grumbled,

"Who's there?"

"It's me, Morgan. I was here last year."

The door opened, and it was one of Jerry's roommates... a thin, dark-skinned man with a frizzy head of hair who looked as if he had aged more than his years. He poked his head out and looked both ways.

"Yeh, whaddya want?" There was not a drop of joy or kindness in his voice.

"I'm lookin' for Jerry. I told him I would be back."

"Jerry doesn't live here anymore."

"What's the deal with the bars on all the windows?"

"Gangs, man. They took over the Haight. It's dangerous to go out. You better get out too, while the getting's good." He brusquely shut the door.

Morgan couldn't help mourning the perverse deviation of Haight Ashbury from its former glory. The "Death of the Hippie" ceremony in 1967 proved to be prophetic, but nobody wanted to believe it. After Monterey Pop, the Summer of Love, and Woodstock, could this explosion of good vibes and brotherly love really have vanished that quickly? Was mankind so depraved that he couldn't abide peace and love for more than a couple of years? Something made this movement unsustainable. Morgan wondered if the answer could be found in some deep, philosophical understanding of the universe, but he reasoned to himself,

"Nope, it's probably nothing more than good, old-fashioned greed and ego. The basic nature of man. When the warm fuzzies are gone, it all boils down to taking care of Number One."

Whatever happened in the Haight was a forerunner of what would eventually happen to hippiedom in general. When *"Hey sister, you need a ride?"* gave way to *"Who's there?"* it became the death knell of a free and trusting ideology.

The Great Unraveling

Georgetown

*"Knock, knock, knock.... tap, tap tap. "*Morgan's friend, Alex, was at the window, and Georgetown was calling. For their maiden voyage, Alex had clandestinely secured his parent's car. The year was 1967.

"OK, OK," Morgan whispered, putting his finger over his lips. He silently formed the words, "I'm coming."

He slithered out the window of the basement and belly crawled through his mother's flower bed. Brushing himself off, they stealthily slipped through the bushes and made their way to Alex's car. Alex put it in neutral, and Morgan pushed from the rear to get the car rolling. It gradually built up speed as he ran alongside and jumped in the door. At the end of the block, Alex started the engine, and they were on their way to D.C. They didn't have anything in particular to do... they just wanted the thrill of sneaking out and being up in the wee hours of the morning in the alluring, forbidden realm of Georgetown.

The hip movement was new and fresh. Like any other wave of creative thinking, it started out full of energy and vitality. There was a new understanding of things, a new prism to see life through, and those who latched onto this revelation were bustling and vibrant. The two young escapees could feel this as they cruised the sidewalks. There weren't that many shops open at this hour, but they got a couple of hamburgers at White Castle and hung out for an hour or so at an all-night coffee shop on Wisconsin Avenue.

They sat and talked and smoked forbidden cigarettes, making comments about the people milling around them. If anyone appeared to be unusually strange in any way, well, that was all the better. The air had a sense of electricity, and they felt privileged to be a part of it. After 4:00 AM, it was time to go home and sneak back inside. The sleep they lost was worth the sacrifice... after all, how many high school kids, in 1967, got to hang out in Georgetown at three o'clock in the morning?

In late August 1969, a couple weeks after Woodstock, Morgan was again wandering the streets of Georgetown. The air was alive with good vibes, and the streets were hopping with activity. The love and peace fervor from the last few years had grown into a thriving gathering of like-minded souls. Around every lamppost stood a group of three or four, shooting the breeze, enjoying the fellowship. The stairways were full of young people sitting and reclining, watching the scene go by. Morgan and his friends were gathered in front of People's drug store, talking to a tall young man fresh from Woodstock.

"I just got back. Took me a while. Made a lot of detours. All I've got is the pack on my back. I picked up this sleeping bag at the festival."

Morgan was amazed. "You got that sleeping bag at Woodstock? How'd you do that? Weren't they all buried in the mud?"

"Yeh, everybody just walked off and left their stuff. There were hundreds of them lying around. I picked out the best one I could find and took it with me. I stopped at a laundromat and washed it, and "Poof," here it is. Good as new."

The hip movement was now in its hay-day. The "British Invasion" was in full swing with the rise of The Who, Led Zepplin, The Rolling Stones, and many more. Woodstock just happened, and the culture was growing by leaps and bounds.

What started out as little groups in hubs all around the country had expanded into a wave of counter-culture ideals that were beginning to influence all aspects of society. When you walked down the street, there was energy. People were smiling, bobbing to the music, and the buzz of lively conversation filled the night. In Georgetown, on this night, as in hip centers everywhere, there was joy in the air.

By the early 1970's, a disturbing trend in drug use began to surface. Fatalities began to show up in newspapers, Time and Life ran articles about it, and news of it drifted home from the battlefields of Vietnam. It was ugly and foreboding, scary and distasteful, eating away the life of the happy hippie from the inside like a cancer... it was a deadly scourge called Heroin.

Morgan had personal contact with this scourge through his friend Bobby, who had just returned from Vietnam. Heroin seemed as foreign to him as the rice paddies of Southeast Asia. It didn't belong in the arena of other counter-culture drugs. It came from an era of greasers and ghettos and dark, inner city tenements. It was dirty, and creepy and dangerous. Worst of all, it involved needles.

Hippie drugs like pot and LSD were nothing like heroin... they stimulated the mind and made people happy and giddy. They did them for fun, for entertainment, for recreation. They could take them or not take them at will, but heroin physically infected the body with an uncontrollable craving. Most people had heard about going "cold turkey" where they tried to stop taking heroin suddenly and completely, only to be ravaged with indescribable anguish that most addicts could not endure.

In 1971, a movie called The French Connection hit the theaters exposing the havoc heroin could wreak. From Morgan's point of view, it was just an entertaining show about another culture that didn't exist anywhere near him. None of the people in that movie looked like anybody at Woodstock. They were mobsters and gangsters from the city. When word leaked out that this poison was filtering into the hippie communities, he couldn't believe it. Why would anyone take that ominous, foreboding step into certain bondage?

The usual culprits were at play. Peer pressure, lack of contentment with what they had, and curiosity to try something new. This was

Morgan's first glimpse into the idea that recreational drug use could become addictive. At first, he had rejected all notions of the "gateway" theory as a scare tactic. He didn't believe smoking pot would lead to heroin, but now he saw it happening in some of his friends.

They didn't go directly to it, but whatever switch they had to flip in their soul the first time they tried marijuana opened the door to experimenting with other activities that were off limits. That "switch" had broken down their moral boundaries and loosened their bonds, but not necessarily for a good thing. They had proudly proclaimed freedom for themselves, to do whatever they wanted, but their new found freedom had only run them headlong into slavery. This time, he believed the scare tactics. The common understanding was, if you did heroin, you became an addict.

In the summer of 1970, a night in Georgetown sadly confirmed all he had been hearing. The streets were much less crowded. People still lounged on the steps of the townhouses, but instead of having eyes wide open with smiles on their faces, their eyes were half shut, and they looked deflated. Shoulders hunched over, heads hanging down. Instead of lively chatter and dancing to the beat, they were "nodding" with a heroin induced downer.

Morgan strolled along, taking this all in, and saw a friend he had known since the sixth grade. Stevie now had perfectly straight black hair over his shoulders and halfway down his back.

"Hey Stevie, remember me?"

Stevie looked up slowly and puts his hand on Morgan's arm to steady himself.

"Yeh, Dusty, how ya doin'?"

"I'm doin' great man. Whatcha been up to?"

"Can't talk much now, man, I'm down, really down."

"Down on what, on junk? You a junkie? How'd that happen?"

"I dunno. Just went from one thing to another. Started smokin' pot, then acid, now this."

"Man, you don't have to, you need to quit."

"Too late, man. It's got me now. Good to see ya, man."

Morgan stared helplessly as Stevie turned away to sit down and rest his head against a wall. Two or three of his high school friends had already died from heroin overdoses, and he felt like he was watching Stevie for the last time.

The devastation didn't stop there. Soon, there was an outbreak of death announcements for beloved rock stars. On September 18, 1970, Morgan was driving through the rolling countryside around his college campus with Led Zeppelin's "Dazed and Confused" on the FM radio. The DJ broke in, "Sorry ladies and gentlemen, we have an emergency announcement. Please stand by." The voice of a newscaster came on.

"We have received reports that rock star Jimi Hendrix has died. The cause of death has not been determined, but is under investigation. Again, Jimi Hendrix is dead at the age of 27. We will now return to our regular programming."

It didn't stop there. On October 4, 1970, only two weeks later, Janis Joplin died from a heroin overdose. The sad thing was, it seemed inevitable. For months before their deaths, the vitality drained out of them as the sedative effects did their work.

Morgan could not understand the appeal of downers. "Why would anybody want to do a drug that puts you to sleep?"

Of course, for a lot of people, they wanted to escape their reality. Or it just felt good. Whatever it was, Morgan liked his reality, he loved life, and he considered drug use a mechanism to enhance life. He didn't want to go to sleep. He certainly didn't want to go to sleep forever.

As if this wasn't enough, Jim Morrison of the Doors died the following year on July 3, 1971. To many, he was a hero of rock innovation. He was a poet, and he wove the themes of his poetry into the music of the Doors to create epic acid rock manifestos. What Jimi Hendrix was to the instrumentation of rock music, Jim Morrison was to the message.

The combination of freedom from inhibitions and an insatiable desire to experiment proved to be a deadly cocktail. In the end, "If it feels good, do it" and "Try everything once" inflicted immeasurable harm on society. No one was immune, and the passing of these shining stars revealed that all was not well in Woodstock Nation.

Morgan and Cutter met in the fall of 1968 in Blacksburg. Along with others, they were the first to ignite the magical spirit of those early days. Many years later, in 1974, things had changed, and they sat brooding in a dark corner of a college bar, reminiscing about the good old days. Any remnants of beautiful people and flower power were long gone. Peace and love had been replaced by sex, drugs and rock and roll. There was no more ideology, no more lofty visions for humanity. People didn't even think of those things any more. It seemed there had been a sea change of perspective.

"Y'know Cut, just a few years ago, everybody you came in contact with was a deep thinker. Remember Bill Cosby's sister? She's the one who asked, 'Why is there air?' like she was pondering the existence of existence. We used to talk about the reasons for war, why it was wrong, what made up the human condition, what could be done to improve on that condition. All we wanted was brotherhood, and good vibes... it was enough to just groove on a good rock beat and hallucinate."

"Yeh, I know what ya mean. Where did all those people go? A whole society suddenly disappeared! Did they vanish into thin air? Was it all an illusion? And if it was... what's wrong with an illusion? It's like someone threw a cosmic switch that instantly transformed a whole generation... like an alien mother ship cruised around the world with a long vacuum hose dangling down to earth, sucking up the beautiful flower people, leaving behind nothing but dull-witted, lecherous, party 'til you puke derelicts."

Cutter went on, "Now, the only thing anyone talks about is, 'Let's get drunk, let's get stoned, hey, look at that chick!' Slobber, drool. Instead of 'Why is there air?' the deepest, most profound question anybody can come up with is, 'Hey man, got any coke?'"

Morgan laughed. It was true, the paisley, flower power ideology had morphed into sordid, self-indulgent depravity. And it would only get worse. He answered Cut,

"Where did it all go? People just got bored. Anything gets old after a while, and when they got bored, they started looking for something new and different. Now when you start looking for something new and different, you find a pink bar filled with drag queens. When you're in a pink bar filled with drag queens, a jealous painted lady accuses you of trying to pick up her boyfriend. When you say to the painted lady, 'Sorry, ma'am,' he clobbers you over the head with his purse, kicks you out the door and calls you a fundamentalist bigot."

"So..." Morgan took a drink and set it down to make his final point, "Don't be called a fundamentalist bigot. Just be glad you're bored."

Cutter shook his head. "Man, you ain't right... Here's what I think. The 'illusion' of peace and love was created out of a distorted concept of freedom. Everyone wanted to be free to express themselves with no obstacles. They wanted to enjoy all the pleasures of life, legitimate or illegitimate, without any consequences or condemnation." He went on,

"Those consequences and condemnations came from society, the way they say things 'should' be done. The hippies wanted to break all these taboos so their lives could be uninhibited. Kind of like James Dean, 'Rebel without a cause.' Rebel for the hell of it.

"Over the years, the rebels were no longer content to simply reject 'normal.' In that sense, you're right. They got bored. Now it's a contest for every generation to see how many bizarre inventions they can come up with to break the rules of the previous generation. Shaved heads, greased Mohawks, all kinds of rings and piercings and tattoos. In order to be cool, you gotta think of some new way to be different."

Morgan was enjoying Cutter's philosophy lesson. He added,

"Yeh, and when everybody is different, they all look the same. They don't know it, but all they've done is create some kind of weird, deviant uniform. Now, the only thing left that's different is to be normal, but no one wants to do that."

Cutter jumped in for the final word.

"And you know why? Because the need for acceptance is a cruel slave driver. When you crave acceptance, you wind up in bondage to your freedom."

Morgan rubbed his chin, "In bondage to freedom. Now that's an unusual concept. My knee-jerk reaction to something like that would be to get free from my freedom, if it's gonna put me in bondage." It is a prophecy that would visit him another day.

From its humble beginnings, Morgan and his friends had built up a "mountain hippie" community in the hills of Blacksburg, Virginia. The days of chain wielding, vicious rednecks were ancient history. Now, it was common to see groups of hippies chipping in together to rent country houses as they ventured further and further into the rural landscape. And it wasn't too unusual to find a longhair with a jar or two of moonshine on the shelf.

Even though all hippies shared their regard for love and peace, there was a big difference between mountain hippies and city hippies. The contrast here was just as stark as the Mendocino communal setting was to the Haight Ashbury setting. Morgan loved the country, but the spirit of action and hustle that infused the city was intriguing to him as well. He wouldn't want to live there, but it was always a novel experience to visit. This visit turned out to be a bit more novel than he had expected.

Tonight, he was hanging out with Jimmy Burnett, a friend from college who was also from his high school in Northern Virginia. Strolling along the familiar strip of Wisconsin Avenue, the sights and sounds conjured up scenes from years gone by.

"Nice night."

Jimmy threw his head sideways to let his long blonde hair blow back over his shoulders. He was a legend of the mountain hippie group, having been one of the first to grow his hair out. He was tall and lanky, with the fullest head of straight blonde hair you could imagine. The girls loved him, and he didn't have to do anything. He would just stroll and smile, and heads would turn. That's why they called him, "Smilin' Jimmy."

"Yeh, I hope we can score some hash."

Morgan was relatively short beside him, unassuming and unimpressive, almost like a side kick. He reflected,

"Last time I was here, it was all junkies. Never seen the like. Once people go to junk, you can't trust 'em. They'll rip you off in a second. It's like, once they take that step, all remnants of decency, honor and honesty go down the tubes."

"That so? I've never been around them much. Last time I was here was a couple of years ago. Seemed all right to me."

"I don't know why they do it. It's a mystery... I guess it's one last thing. I always said I would try everything once, but that's going a bit too far."

"Yeh, I know what you mean. Doesn't appeal to me either."

Morgan took stock of the scene to see if anything had changed since last year. The atmosphere had returned to a normal, night life kind of flair, but there was an obvious void of hippie vibes. Maybe the wave of junk wiped everything out, and it all went back to "normal." However, it still didn't feel normal, and he was trying to put his finger on it.

The duo continued to mosey up the sidewalk, and Morgan scrutinized a figure leaning against a lamp post. It had always been common for people to congregate around lamp posts in Georgetown, but this one had an odd look to it. Whoever it was had long, shiny, perfectly straight brown hair hanging over the shoulders, a flowery type of shirt and tight jeans. This was not your everyday hippie hair that was typically somewhat unkempt. This hair looked like it had been cream-rinsed and brushed with a lot of care. The posture was a little off, too. Instead of the typical swagger of a cool hippie, the hips were tilted to one side, and the shoulder dropped slightly like a seductive woman. Hanging down from the shoulder on a long strap was a purse. They passed on by.

"Did you see that?" Morgan asked Jimmy.

"Yeh, so what?"

"Did you think there was anything strange about that person back there?"

"You mean that girl at the lamp post? No, what's so strange about a girl leaning on a lamp post?"

"I don't think she was a girl."

"What? Whaddya mean she's not a girl?"

"Shhhh. Wait. Here comes another one."

The next lamp post had two more figures in the same general attire. Meticulously combed long hair, tight jeans, lipstick, eyeliner, and a purse adorning the shoulders. Morgan took a sharper look at their faces. If they were girls, they sure were ugly. They had to be the ugliest prostitutes he'd ever seen.

"Do you think they're hookers?" Jimmy said. About that time, one of the strange figures turned and took a long look at Jimmy, scanning him up and down. The person with the lipstick winked at him and cracked a crooked smile.

"If they are, they're not the kind you want."

"I don't want any hookers, anyway. What in the world are you talking about?"

"Jimmy, look a little harder. There's some more up ahead."

"What are they lookin' at me for?"

"All the girls like you, Jimmy... you know that."

Morgan was laughing to himself now, having too much fun. Jimmy still had a puzzled look on his face... eyebrows arched up, his forehead lined with wrinkles.

"They just like your long blonde hair. Only, these girls ain't girls. They're guys! Get it? Guys!"

"Oh crap! Are you for sure? Damn, I guess you're right. Oh no, I think I see a friend of mine from high school."

Jimmy squinted at the group, trying to make out the facial features. His mouth dropped open, no sound coming out, as he stood in utter shock.

"What's the matter, Burnett, don't you speak?"

His friend challenged him in a deep voice. Jimmy continued standing there with his mouth open, trying to get his voice back.

He shook his head, "No..., No..., I don't speak. I don't believe it. Aren't you Bobby Porter?"

"I'm Roberta now. Bobby's gone."

"But you used to get all the girls. You were the cool guy in class. Why are you doing this?"

"Like I said, I'm Roberta now. Take it or leave it, Burnett."

"Well... shoot. I'm leavin' it."

Jimmy had the same look Morgan had the first night a guy tried to pick him up years ago. Total bewilderment mixed with fear. He turned back to Morgan,

"This is insane. What is going on? Why are there so many? Why would Bobby switch to Roberta?"

They cast their gaze across the street, then looked back and forth, up and down the block. Interspersed among the pedestrians, were pockets of the same kind of people. They were hanging out, sitting on stairways with their legs crossed at the knee, their hands hanging limp at the wrist, standing around in groups of two or three.

The magnitude of the cultural shift finally dawned on Jimmy and Morgan. There were enough of these unusual beings to conclude that the next wave to wash over the hip district of Georgetown was the most unexpected. In their quest for the next high, or the next low, or the next most erotic fantasy, those who really wanted to "Try everything once" had broken the last barrier of sexual norms. First Georgetown was beat, then it was hip, then it was psychedelic, then it was junkie, now it was gay.

"Man, I gotta get outta here, this is creepy."

"I'm with you, brother. Let's split."

The car was parked all the way back on M street, a good four or five blocks away. The two mountain hippies, now totally out of their element, took off running. They bounded down the sidewalk of Wisconsin Avenue, zig-zagging around people as they navigated their obstacle course. Long hair blowing over their shoulders, jumping left, shifting right, they looked like tribal businessmen running through the airport, trying to catch a plane. All along the sidewalk, everyone they passed turned and stared. Morgan bumped into a thin, peculiar looking figurine who gasped in a high pitched falsetto,

"Oooh, you pushed me."

Morgan shoved him out of the way. "Excuse me, ma'am... er, I mean, sir." He spun around and kept on running.

Back at the car, they leaned on the hood, huffing and gasping.

"Man, that's the weirdest thing I ever saw," Jimmy said, still wheezing.

"Yeh, that threw me for a loop for sure. I've had rednecks say I looked like a girl before, but I never wanted to look like a girl, or tried to look like one."

They pulled onto M Street and headed west out of Georgetown. Cruising over Key Bridge toward Virginia. Jimmy was still shook up,

"Man, I can't get stop thinking about Bobby Porter. That just blows my mind. What do you suppose made him decide to do that? What got into all of them?"

"The only explanation I can come up with is, they've done everything else, and the only thing left is going gay. First there weren't any junkies, then everybody wanted to be a junkie. There weren't any gays now they all want to be gay."

"Yeh, you're right. I don't recall seeing anybody like that where I've been, either."

"Now that I think about it, I didn't see any drag queens at Woodstock, and I didn't see any in the Haight either. They might have been there, but you couldn't tell... it wasn't an issue. They didn't flaunt it like those people. I guess they're looking for one more thrill.

"Do you ever get to a place where you stop experimenting? Where enough's enough? Every step along the way is a choice, and I always thought I wanted to try everything once, but that's one step too far. Well, if you throw junk in there, that's two steps too far. Those are just choices I'm not gonna make."

"Me neither, brother, me neither. They can have it. I like my women just fine, thank you."

"Well, I am relieved to hear that, Jimmy. Cutter once told me I would make one ugly girl. The same goes for you."

"Gee, thanks, I think."

Bull Island

In September 1972, word went out that a rock festival would be held in southern Indiana. It was called "Bull Island," and was billed as the Woodstock of the Midwest. It was supposed to follow the same format: three days, big name bands, another gathering of the tribes. Woodstock held such a place in the heart of hippie folklore that people were constantly striving to duplicate the experience, but it was elusive. It was like chasing the wind, or grasping Jello.

Once the crowds left Woodstock, the spirit left, and it could never be recaptured. The music used to define the heart of the movement, with electric vibes in the air and love in the heart. Subsequent festivals devolved into mere concerts. Spectacles without the unity. Or if there was any unity, it was an awkwardly manufactured unity. While Monterey Pop and Woodstock had real fellowship and cultural overtones, the rest of them just became a good excuse to go wild.

As the date drew near, local courts blocked the festival from taking place, so the promoters had to move the site to a large field near Evansville, Indiana. Due to this last minute decision, there was no time to make the preparations necessary to accommodate a huge crowd. There was no water, no food, and worst of all, no toilets. The quickest way to create waste dumps was to bring in backhoes to dig long, deep trenches about four feet wide through the proposed camping areas.

With no facilities, no organization, and no law, the festival began a severe downward spiral. Many of the bands got word of the debacle and cancelled. This, of course, made the crowd mad. As the days wore on, drug abuse soared, tempers flared, waste piled up in the trenches, and the assembly turned into a depraved mob. When it was all over, those who had been there had witnessed the grotesque extent to which flower power could be twisted when the debased workings of the hippie nature were left to their own devices.

Stepping out of baggage claim in Evansville, Indiana, Morgan started looking for a ride to the festival site. A carload of longhairs pulled up on Interstate 64, and someone yelled out the window,

"Hey! You goin' to the festival? C'mon, get in."

132

Within the hour, the car pulled off the shoulder and the occupants got out. Each one grabbed his gear, and they joined the migration with high expectations. Once they reached the gate, the fence had already been broken down, and the wave flowed through the opening.

"So far, so good." Morgan's eyes were alert, checking it out.

"Looks like a rock festival to me."

The flow led into the central hub of the festival. People were setting up tents and tables to sell whatever they had. Usually it was head gear of various sorts... pipes, roach clips, hip clothing and accessories. Food trucks were preparing for business, along with some concession stands.

"Oh good. We might actually have something to eat this time. This is shaping up pretty good." Morgan saw more tables up ahead and slowed down to take a look. "Window shopping at a rock festival. Should be interesting. Let's see what they have here."

The first few tables had an assortment of baggies laid out. Morgan expected to see bracelets, beads and Indian jewelry, but as he looked carefully, he saw little green pills. The next table had sheets of paper perforated into squares with a discolored dot in the middle of each square... blotter acid. He noticed that many tables had signs on them, labelling their wares: Hash, LSD, Mescaline. The dealers hollered out their sales chants, "Step right up. Get your acid here... Weed for sale... Hashish, black Afghani hash."

At first, he was elated at the thought of a psychedelic, underground market of drugs having free reign. The police had remained outside, abdicating any responsibility for maintaining the law. So, whatever was lawless before was fair game now.

"Now we get to run our own show. This is the way we want to do it. Open drug market, free sex, and rock and roll. This is what it'll look like when Woodstock takes over."

He was feeling really good about himself until he reached some more tables along the stretch. They had signs saying "Heroin, 'Ludes, Downers." Some of the tables had syringes for sale, and in the tents behind them, he could see people shooting up.

"Oh, no. It can't be." He knew what the final outcome of that would be... death and destruction. What really shocked him was the number of people lined up to either buy the poison or shoot it up right then and there.

"Don't tell me people really want this." His fears were realized later that night as the effects of large amounts of barbiturates and heroin overcame many. They stumbled around, crashing into others, falling into campfires, weaving through the crowd, begging for free downers.

With mixed emotions, Morgan turned away from "Alice in Wonderland Avenue" to find a place to set up camp. He knew some of his friends from Virginia were supposed to be here, so he wandered aimlessly, looking for a familiar face. A couple hours later, he recognized two guys off in the distance. He waved,

"Hey, Fat Harry, it's me."

Back in Virginia, there were two Harry's, "Fat Harry" and "Weird Harry." Everyone affectionately called them "Fat" or "Weird" respectively, and didn't think anything of it.

"Look guys, it's Morgan. Hey man, c'mon and crash with us."

There were four of them, and Morgan fell in as they headed back to the camping area, far removed from the stage.

"You guys have quite a set up here. You got it made in the shade."

The tent slept six to eight people, and together they brought all the necessities: food, coolers, water jugs, and lounge chairs. Out in front, they had constructed a large fire ring of stones they gathered from the field.

"Make yourself at home, man." Morgan was impressed. What a way to do a rock festival!

"Hey Fat, I just have one question."

"Yeh, what's that?"

"Why'd ya put the tent on the edge of the trench?"

"For convenience, man. You get done with a chicken leg, you throw it over your shoulder into the trench. It's all right here at our fingertips."

"Uh, yeh, great. Have you considered the smell? Just a thought."

"Ah yes, we have already figured that in. The wind is at our back. Everything blows that way."

The promising extravaganza soon began to sour. What ensued was a total breakdown of all morals or decency. The narcotic use became rampant. Fat Harry came back to the camp one night with a stunned look on his face, mixed with sorrow.

"Man, I just passed by all these people lined up around a tent. When I got closer, there was a picnic table with a guy laying on it. This other guy walked up to him with a needle and stuck it into his arm, then rolled him off the table. As soon as he was gone, another one laid down on the table and they did it again. They were shooting them up with blue morphine and just rolling them onto the ground, using the same needle over and over. It was gross."

"Are you serious? Why do they want to pass out? I came to see the festival, not sleep through it. I didn't see any heroin at Woodstock... not all these downers, either. There's a dark cloud hanging over this place, and I don't like it."

The deterioration only got worse. Sunday morning, Morgan opened the flap of the tent and saw a straggly looking kid walk up to the edge of the trench and stare down into it.

"Hey Fat, wake up, come look at this." Fat Harry raised himself out of his sleeping bag and crawled over to the tent flap.

The kid was a total mess. His hair was not quite shoulder length, knotted and disheveled like a bad case of bed head. His shirt was torn and unbuttoned, hanging loose. His pants were halfway down his rear, sagging over his bare feet. His shoulders were stooped and rounded in a slouch... a filthy lock of hair dangling over his face as he gazed downward. Morgan thought to himself,

"Is this the picture of the typical hippie? Is this what the world thinks we are? No wonder they think we're disgusting. I think it's disgusting."

They hadn't seen anything yet. To his horror, the scraggly kid climbed down into the trench and waded into the middle of it until his legs were immersed up to his knees in three days of trash and sewage. Morgan and Fat looked on in utter dismay. It was like a surreal documentary playing out before their eyes. It could have been the ultimate scare tactic film about what will happen to you if you become a hippie.

"MOTHERS, THIS IS WHAT WILL HAPPEN TO YOUR CHILDREN IF THEY TAKE ONE PUFF OF MARIJUANA."

The sad truth was, Morgan couldn't refute any of it, because he was looking at it in real time.

As a finale to his demented performance, the kid proceeded to dip his hands into the waste, scoop it up, and pour it over his head. Soon, he was dipping it and splashing it like a five year old in a swimming pool. Fat and Morgan stared in disbelief. Without a word, they formed a defensive position between the kid and their camp. One thing's for sure, he's not coming this way. If he does, he'll end up back in the trench, bleeding.

The image of the kid playing in the sewage plagued Morgan from that time on.

"Has Woodstock Nation come to this? This isn't stardust and golden... this is space aliens in the sewage. A wasted kid, stripped of all decency, full of downers, playing in the piss? Pathetic."

The rest of the festival was a survival contest. The guys tried to make the most of it, staying together and getting high around the campfire. That night, they all went down to see the bands. The debauchery was everywhere, and the crowd had turned into a seething mob, full of anarchy. There was a wariness in the air, with everybody loaded on three days of drug abuse. Trouble could break out at any moment, from any direction. The big name bands had all bowed out, so the ones left were not famous, but they played their hearts out. The next morning, plumes of gray and black smoke billowed up from the front of the crowd. The stage was burning.

Three cops stood watch at an exit as the people filed out. Fat Harry tried to be sociable,

"Hey officer, how ya doin'?"

"Oh, I'm doin' just fine. Did you have a good time?"

He had a smile on his face, but it wasn't genuine. You could tell there was something else behind it, like he was laughing at them, not with them.

"Oh yeh, it was great. Kind of messy, though."

"Well, this guy had a great time." The cop kicked a sheet off a long form on the ground. Harry choked as he looked at the corpse with flies buzzing around, crawling in and out of its nose and mouth.

"Oh, my God." He stumbled to his knees and threw up in the grass. He slowly raised himself up and wiped his mouth with his sleeve. "I've never seen a dead person before."

"Yep. He had a great time. He was just dyin' to get here, and he got his wish. You hippies think about this the next time you want to do some drugs."

"Yes, sir."

"Let's get outta here, Morg. I've had enough of this."

Ever since his son had taken on the hippie mindset, Dad had a choice. He could shut him out as a rebellious son, or try to keep the lines of communication open. He was concerned about the sins of the lifestyle, but instead of brow beating him, he tried to get him to tell him what was on his mind. If there was an opportunity to inject some wise counsel in sideways, he would look for it.

"Y'know Dad, when I was in Woodstock and Haight Ashbury, people called me 'brother'. That really felt good. It made me feel like I was part of a universal bond."

"Is that so?" Dad shook his head and let out a sigh, as if he was disappointed. "You know, it used to be common in the Church for Christians to call each other 'brother'."

"Really? I never heard anybody say that in our church."

"Well, I guess they got out of the habit. Do you think that could be one of the reasons your movement became so popular? If the Church was showing the love you all seem to want, would that have kept you from joining them?"

Morgan thought about it,

"I don't know, Dad. Even with the brother thing and all, I know the Church would never accept smoking pot, taking acid and free love."

Dad shook his head, "Yes, thankfully you're right. I think we could agree on that. So, you're not really in it for the brotherhood, you're in it for the fun, right?"

"Well, I wouldn't want to put it that way. I guess we would like to have the brotherhood with the fun. You know, we do believe in a lot of good, moral values."

"Like what?"

"I told you about the Hog Farm at Woodstock, right? And the commune in Mendocino? They had a real heart to help each other. Also, the whole idea of "Walk a mile in my shoes" is about seeing things from the other person's perspective, trying to see life their way before you judge them. Besides that, we don't think the pursuit of status and hoarding money is important. We look down on the idea of working your whole life just to drive a Cadillac so you can show all your friends you made it."

"I see. Those are all good values. Would you like to hear my take on that?"

"Sure, give it a shot."

"You know this is not the first generation to come up with these ideals. All of those values you describe are in the Bible. About the Hog Farm. The theme I get from that is generosity, right?"

"Yeh, I guess so."

"Would it be fair to say they were putting their hard working efforts into looking out for the interests of others?"

"Right."

"That's how the early Church got started. The first Christians in Acts sold all they had and shared it with whoever had a need.

"Now, 'Walk a mile in my shoes'. Doesn't that sound a lot like, 'Do unto others as you would have others do unto you'?"

"Hmm. Yeh, the Golden Rule. Never thought of it that way."

"As far as materialism goes, you know the Bible says the love of money is the root of all evil."

"Yeh, yeh, I know. But in order to be a Christian, you have to give up everything you like. I just don't think I want to do that right now. It would be boring."

Rather than try to make Christianity sound easy, Dad held his ground.

"Just keep this in mind... the righteous values your culture espouses come from the foundation of Christ. But there is one big difference. You are trying to apply the principles of Christ, but you don't want to follow the lifestyle of Christ. You want to have your cake and eat it, too, but it doesn't work that way."

"If you're wondering why all this is crumbling around you, it's because you have left Jesus out of the equation. You want the results, but you don't want to obey the Giver of the results. Therefore, the Giver withholds His hand. Christianity will live forever because the power of Jesus works through those whose hearts are set on Him. This hippie peace and love has barely made it five years. Once the ideology goes, and the self-nature kicks in, it'll be Katie bar the door."

Bull Island, or Evansville, as some people would remember it, was the story of the Great Unraveling of Woodstock Nation. All that Morgan had witnessed since his last visit to Haight Ashbury was personified, magnified, and desecrated at this event. If the "Death of the Hippie" ceremony in the Haight was the funeral, then Evansville was the cremation.

What was surprising was how quickly the forces of indulgence and selfishness took over. In the Haight, it happened overnight. It seemed like you woke up the next morning and bars were on the windows. Most diehard hippies had trouble believing their ideals were so temporary, but it became obvious peace and love had died out by the end of the '70's. So, those who weren't sucked into the mother ship went on with life, partying into the '80's, but they never knew what happened. They just thought it was a colossal shame. Love was love, and it faded away.

Now it was every man for himself. Morgan was disappointed, but he wasn't ready to cash in his chips just yet. He had roads to travel, adventures to live, and money to make. The heart and soul of the counter-culture was still found in a green herb with the botanical name, *cannabis sativa*. As the number of hippies grew over the years, so did the demand for more pot. And that demand grew into a booming network of underground businessmen, just like the magazines said. Ounces were no longer sufficient to supply the needs of the hippie masses. They would demand pounds, and hundreds of pounds, and tons of the precious weed.

Texas

A sharp, autumn blast rushed down the valley of Blacksburg, Virginia, making this cozy hole in the wall very attractive. Only it was more than a hole in the wall, it was Middle Earth. The owners of the new restaurant were as creative as they were ambitious. It took months to gut the old building and transform it into a work of interior decorating art. The idea was to make it look like a scene from one of J.R.R. Tolkien's fantasy stories.

From the minute you walked in the door, you felt like you're in a cavern, way down, enveloped by a dark, dank cave shaft. The main room brought to mind a giant "ballroom" found on a cave tour. The floor was sunken, with four or five round tables accompanied by rounded back chairs. Along the perimeter of one wall were four cubicles that looked like dugouts in a cliff. Inside each one was a booth for four people.

Every opening was rounded, producing a secluded, comfy, underworld effect. During remodeling, the walls were sprayed with a liquid foam that dried into blobs resembling stalactites and stalagmites. The final impression was an eerie, puffy atmosphere, topped off with soft, multi-colored flood lights and Crosby, Stills, Nash and Young oozing through the built in speakers.

For Morgan, this place made the ideal secret hangout. If any of his closest friends wanted to find him, they knew where he would be. Tonight, in the fall of 1971, he was nestled in one of the cubicles, reclining in a booth with his brown suede boot up on the bench seat, grasping a cold Michelob. Savoring the ambience, he focused on a fluorescent lime stalactite hanging from the ceiling.

The door to the restaurant opened, and the sound of muddled voices filtered back from the front desk.

"Is Morgan in here?" The Brooklyn accent gave it away... Cutter.

"He's in the back. First cave on the right."

Heavy footsteps clomped on the hardwood floor until a curly headed, smiling face popped around the molded edge. "Hey, wild man, where ya been?"

"Oh, just hidin' out, as usual. Haven't seen you in a while."

"Been outta town. You want another beer?" Cutter signaled to the waiter. Two more.

"Y'know, Cut, I was just thinkin' about that. It's funny, but we used to feel so high and mighty about pot and tripping we gave up booze altogether. Remember that Andromeda concert at Ironman's when no one bought a single beer?"

"Yeh, I remember. Everybody sat cross-legged on the floor. The problem was, the bar had to sell beer to make a profit. As I recall, they never asked you back."

The waiter arrived with the beers and they both took a hard chug. Cutter plopped his bottle down.

"That didn't last long, did it? We used to make fun of the frat boys getting drunk and puking their guts out. We looked down our noses at them like they were some kind of sub-human life form."

Morgan tilted his head back, looked down his nose, and put on a British accent.

"I say, the poor fellows didn't have the 'higher consciousness' we had. They didn't know the 'proper' way to get high, like us *civilized* hippies. They were too barbaric to understand how to exercise the ethereal realms. The blaggards were simply base and ignoble, you see. To them, the psychedelic situation was bloody obfuscatory."

Morgan patted his lips with a napkin.

"My dear fellow, it would never do to pollute our minds with an alcoholic stupor. If anyone were to disparage us with such an accusation it would be a calumny of the highest order. We could never keep company with such rabble. It would be monstrous intolerable."

They rocked back and forth in the booth, hooting and snorting. Back to his Virginia mountain accent, he went on,

"So, obviously, we couldn't let anybody know we really had a hankerin' to just let go and get drunk. But, here we are, back to beer all over again. Like we never skipped a beat."

Cutter leaned over and lowered his voice.

"Hey, to change the subject, I got some news. This is top secret. Your ounce dealing days are over."

"What? OK, you got my attention. Lay it on me."

"Think back the last few years. Buy a pound, break it up into twenty or so lids, sell 'em for fifteen, make a couple hundred bucks. You know the drill."

"Yeh, so what's up? Whatcha got up your sleeve?"

"I just got back from Texas. Pulled in last night. Fuzzy put together a gig down there, and I drove one of the cars back. They offered to pay me in cash or pot, so I took my cut in pot. I ended up with eight pounds free and clear. Now I'm gonna sell it and reinvest. There's room for one more driver, so if you want to get in on it, I'll put in a word for you with the Fuzz."

"You drove a car load back from Texas?"

The imagery flooded his mind, unleashing a myriad of emotions. The thrill of a trip to an unknown land intertwined with the terror of being stopped and searched. A minute ago, he was lounging in the only world he knew, but now, an opportunity he had never imagined was staring him in the face, saying, "Take me! Take me!" A trunk load of pot? From Texas? It's a blind leap, but Cut did it. I oughta be able to do it. What if I don't do it? No, this thing's gonna get bigger, and I won't be able to stand it, watchin' the rest of 'em get rich and famous.

He raised his beer toward Cutter.

"You bet, brother. Let's do it."

On the outside, the front of the renovated building on 117 Main Street was an unassuming conglomeration of red brick and mortar.

This structure in the middle of Blacksburg, Virginia looked like nothing had changed since the turn of the century. Most of the buildings from that era had been demolished, but this one stood alone, an outdated relic, surrounded by a gravel parking lot.

The new owners put all their effort into making it look like an Old West Saloon. The support beams were made out of rustic, rough-cut wood. The dining tables were round, giving it a gambling hall atmosphere. The back of the open area was raised to form a stage for weekend bands. And of course, no self-respecting hippie bar would be complete without a great sound system.

They found the walnut bar top at an old antique shop, but it was so faded and worn out it was hard to recognize as a bar top. With lots of stripper, sandpaper, lacquer, and elbow grease, they turned it into a work of art. This masterpiece of restoration was the crowning touch of a project that would become the hub of operations for this mountain hip community. This was their Bar, owned by them, built by them, inhabited by them. Outsiders would come and go, but 117 Main Street was the center for all business and communications. As far as anyone knew, the authorities never tapped the pay phone in the hallway by the bathrooms, but they should have.

The community had taken on its own distinctive flair as it grew and blossomed. There were the usual trappings of long hair and colorful dress, but there was a rougher, wilder edge to it. Instead of hippie beads, there were chains. Their ragged hair flowed over leather vests adorned with silver studs as they smiled and flashed the peace sign.

Rockin' Rollie set his cigarette in the corner of his mouth and bent over the end of the pool table. With a folding Buck knife on his belt, silver bracelets and a natural sneer, he was the image of the Blacksburg hippie... except for the peace sign. He pumped the cue back and forth. CRACK!! The balls blasted apart in all directions, the 3 ball falling straight into the corner pocket. He grabbed the chalk and rubbed it over the tip as he glided around the table, eyeing his next move like a leopard stalking an impala. He lined up again behind the cue ball and drove the 5 ball hard into the side pocket.

The white ball bounced back with reverse English, and he was set up nicely for his next shot.

"So you need a ride South, eh?"

"Yeh, I heard you were going back to San Diego. If you have an empty seat, I sure could use a ride to Texas."

"Well, that's a long way out of our way, Dusty. But, I've got a lead in Waco I want to check out, and if it works, we won't have to go all the way to California. So, sure, if you don't mind a few detours, we'll give you a ride."

A few days later, they were deep in the scrub country west of San Marcos. The big Oldsmobile sedan bounced down the back roads of south Texas, leaving behind the assortment of oak, cedar and pecan trees commonly found in north and eastern Texas. As they travelled further west, the vegetation became sparse, with scattered mesquite trees and prickly pear cactus as far as the eye could see. A thick, reddish cloud of dust swirled up behind them on the unimproved county road. Rollie followed a crude map to the house where they needed to go. After a while, he saw a mailbox by a metal cattle gate and motioned toward it.

"I'll get the gate." Morgan jumped out, unhitched the chain, and swung the gate open wide. "I hope this is the place."

They pulled the car up to a lone modular house sitting in the middle of a wide expanse of sage brush. The door opened, and a stout figure swaggered toward the car, swinging a lever action Winchester .30-30 rifle in his right hand. His hair was pulled back into a tight, stubby pony tail underneath a Resistol cowboy hat. It was their Texas contact, Mark.

"Oh, it's y'all. Didn't recognize the car. That could have been bad, 'cause we're a little jumpy these days. C'mon in."

Morgan set his bag down inside the small living room, then found a chair at the kitchen table. Fuzzy's other driver, Fred, was already there, staring blankly at a solitaire game spread out before him. He set the deck of cards down and glanced up with a worried look. Something wasn't right.

Mark walked toward the refrigerator, still holding the .30-30 with his left hand.

"Y'all want a bar?"

"A bar?" Morgan repeated, puzzled. What kind of bar is he talking about? Does he mean a bar of soap? A candy bar?

"Yeh, a bar. Any of y'all want a bar?"

The three Virginians look at each other with an "I don't know either" look.

"What kind of bar?"

"Around har we drink Pearl. Y'all want one?"

"Oh, you mean a beer."

"That's what I said, a bar. Ya want one or not?"

"Yeh, sure, that would be just fine, don't you think that would be fine, fellas?" Everybody nodded enthusiastically.

"Yankees! I don't know what I'm gonna do with you people. Y'all ain't from around har, are ya? You're from Virgeeeenia. Well, as soon as we load y'all up, ya better get your scrawny asses back on up to Virgeeeenia. But when y'all come back, ya better be sure to find us, 'cause if y'all run into somebody else, they're liable to tie y'all up in knots and throw *all* y'all in the bull pen, just 'cause your from Virgeeeenia.

"Anyway, let's get down to business. The way we do this is, we swim the bricks across the Rio Grande to a point on the bank where we have a car parked and ready to load. On this trip, we loaded up two cars. One was y'all's, and the other was ours.

"On the way back, I was driving point, and Cowboy was driving your load. We were on the Interstate when a cop pulled Cowboy over. I gunned it and got away, and another cop tried to catch up, but I got off on the back roads and lost him. So we know this much. Your load is busted, Cowboy is in jail, one car is still on the river, and they're lookin' for this car. But, we're ready for 'em. If they come for us, we're all going to hell."

Morgan looked around at the scene in the cramped house. Two other guys were sitting in chairs by windows, each one casually resting a rifle on the sill. He saw Mark's chair by the living room window with a box of shells on the floor. The window looked directly at the gate, the direction they just came from. Now he could replay what it must have looked like to Mark when he saw their unfamiliar, unmarked car coming down the driveway toward them. He was right, it could have been bad. Real bad.

The awful gravity of the situation swelled into full blown realization.

"They intend to shoot the police if they come down that driveway! And if they shoot the police, they will shoot back, and anyone who survives will be charged with murder. Including me!"

The calmness on the faces of the Texans showed they had already settled this in their minds. They had considered the consequences, and were ready to carry it out.

Morgan tried to stay calm. This was not a pretty sight. It gave a whole new meaning to "Momma told me not to come."

"You want some speed?" Mark pulled a quart baggie half full of white powder out of a drawer and threw it on the table. "There ya go, help yourself. I think I'll do another hit while I'm at it."

"Speed? Yeh, I guess. Where'd this come from?"

"Ol' Stevie here's been making it. He's got pounds of it. We been doin' it ever since we got back here the other day."

Mark pulled out his knife and chopped up a mound of white powder, drawing it into long lines. He rolled up a bill and slid the plate across the table.

"Here ya go. Welcome to Texas."

"What happened to the other car on the river?" Morgan asked.

"As far as we know, it's still there. Nobody saw us leave, so it should be all right. We're offering $5000 to anyone who'll go down there and drive it back. You interested?"

It was an absurd question. What were the chances that the cops, or the Border Patrol, or anybody else might have seen this suspicious looking vehicle on the bank of the Rio Grande and decided to stake it out?

Morgan snorted his line and winced at the burn. He pondered the offer... Better not.

Rollie broke the silence, "Hey, Morg, we gotta split. This is not a good scene, and we have a long way to go." He and his driver walked through the dust back to their car.

"Sayonara." He waved as they spun out down the road.

Morgan turned back to Mark, "So, are we going to be able to take anything back with us?"

"Well, of course, you can buy some of Stevie's meth and take that home. Y'all might make somethin' on it to cover your expenses."

"That doesn't sound like a bad idea. I don't even know if I can sell that much speed back home, but I definitely don't want to hang around here." He looked at Freddy, "What do you say?"

"I'm with you. I've been waiting around the last two days for you to show up. We could go ahead and score the meth and head out right now, as far as I'm concerned."

Now that they had a plan, a great weight lifted off Morgan. But it was small consolation in light of what was all around them. The Texans had not moved an inch from their perches at the windows. If anything, the meth had only heightened their resolve. They had gathered more boxes of rounds at their feet, and their guns were still firmly in their grips, resting on the window sills, pointing outward.

The scenario was clear now, and everybody knew the score. If you stayed, there was no telling what would happen. The cops might come, or they might not come. There could be a shootout with everybody dead, or maybe not. Either way, sitting around racing on speed, staring out the windows with loaded .30-30 rifles was terrifying... not his idea of a good time.

"If we can just make it 'til morning," Morgan said to himself. "All we have to do is make it through the night."

The next day, driving back to Virginia, Fred and Morgan rode quietly for a long time, the magnitude of the situation they left behind weighing on their thoughts. Fred's voice was shaky as he opened up.

"That was pretty intense back there, wasn't it?"

"No kiddin'. Those guys didn't bat an eye. They were willing to die to keep from going to jail, but whoever thought it would come to that? The scary thing is, we had no idea what we were getting into. The situation was totally beyond our control. Not only that, we still don't have a load, and we're not gonna make any money." Morgan blew out some air. "I just don't know…"

Fred was silent as they cruised east on Interstate 40, staring out the window. It was an inglorious end to a maiden run, but enlightening nonetheless. Morgan tasted the bitter disappointment of suffering for other people's mistakes. And as he would find out later, it wasn't just people and situations that affected his life. It all went back to the lens. His lens on life had determined the lifestyle he had chosen, which now determined the situations he found himself in that would ultimately affect his life.

Tucson

A wadded up ball of paper sailed through the air in a lazy arc and landed on the table, next to Morgan's plate.

"Good Lord, what does he want now?"

Across from him, his friend Agent Orange dipped his steak into a blob of ketchup. They tried to find a nice, quiet place to eat breakfast, so they intentionally chose a booth at an out of the way restaurant. Unfortunately, Easy was there, too, three tables behind them, talking long and loud, as usual. Morgan was nursing some scrapes and bruises he had incurred the night before in a motorcycle wreck. He had six stitches in his arm where he had gone through a barbed wire fence. This made it all the more difficult to endure the barrage of paper wads bouncing around him.

"Hey Morg, over here!"

His neck was stiff, so he slowly turned his whole body around to confront his tormentor.

"I can't play now, Easy, I'm hurtin'. Got mixed up with a barbed wire fence last night."

Easy rocked back in his chair and bellowed, "What's the matter with you, don't you know how to ride that little bicycle? Hey, I gotta talk to you."

Oh, God, Morgan thought. He's nothing but hot air. You gotta watch people who talk too much. Loose lips sink ships and all that.

"Not now, Easy. Let me eat my steak."

"You like steak, don'tcha?"

"It's a lot better than beans and rice."

149

"What's that?

"Never mind. Just a personal joke."

"Well, I got a way for you to eat a lot of steak. A whole lot of steak."

"Yeh, I bet."

He tried to think of a way to get rid of this guy. It was no use. Easy walked over to his table and begged him for a ride into town. Agent Orange wiped his face with a napkin and bowed out of the awkward encounter, leaving them alone together.

"All right, all right. I'll give you a ride."

Cruising down Main Street, Easy launched into a wild story. He was animated, his hands waving in the air, his eyes bugged out, talking a mile a minute.

"I been lookin' all over for you, Morgan. There's a guy named Doug who used to go to school here that moved out to Tucson to get some weed. I knew him before he left, and I just saw him here, in this town, last week. It was pure accident... he was just walkin' down College Avenue. He was looking for Lord Byron, but Byron was outta town, then he bumped into me.

"He showed up here with eighty pounds just to see if we could move it, and I did it in three days. So now, he wants me to go out there, and he's gonna load us up with as much as we can handle. I need someone to go with me, and since you've been going to Texas and all, I thought you would be the perfect choice. All we have to do is get our money together, fly out to Tucson, and start making money hand over fist."

By this time, Easy was so worked up he was almost foaming at the mouth... his hands were rolling over and over, and he was just about beside himself. Morgan wondered, is this for real?

"How do I know you sold eighty pounds? I didn't see any of it."

"Just ask Moose. He moved some of it for me. After you do, give me a call. This is gonna open up a whole new door, you watch."

With a brief phone call, Moose confirmed that Easy did indeed have some pounds to sell the week before. So, even though Easy was the most unlikely of people you would expect to have a direct connection to weed from Mexico, Morgan had to admit this was a genuine lead.

Easy was an outcast, always loud and laughing, like a necessary nuisance everybody tolerated. He was uncouth and aggravating, but there was a corner of Morgan's makeup that sympathized with him. There had been times when he felt like an outcast... he knew all too well what it was like to be rejected, to be awkward and uncool.

It would be poetic justice for one of the most rejected members of the local hip community to soon become one of the richest and most notorious icons. It would be even more poetic if Morgan could get in on it. He picked up the phone. Two days later, they were sitting together on a jet, their boots stuffed with cash, flying west to Tucson, Arizona.

The wait in the living room of the suburban Tucson house was excruciating. Doug and his crew had left earlier in the afternoon to make the run from Mexico. It was similar to the Texas plan, except they carried burlap bags full of bricks over the hills by the border instead of swimming them across the Rio Grande. Before they left, they counted their money to come up with an exact figure for the number of pounds in this load. Almost as an afterthought, Doug had asked them,

"Do you guys want us to pick up any coke over there for ya? It's $30 a gram."

Easy acted like a kid about to get an ice cream cone. "All right, you bet I want some coke, how 'bout you, Morg?"

Morgan was caught in the classic peer group trap. He knew cocaine was a dangerous drug, but it was still foreign to him. He hadn't been around it, and he hadn't even tried it, but now he was going to be part of smuggling it across the border. His common sense was telling him, "no," but his fear of being thought of as a sissy told him he better do it. Fear of sissyhood won out.

"Sure. $30 a gram? I'll get 10 grams."

Easy raised his stake. "Make mine an ounce. I want to sell some when I get back."

"Fine," Doug said, "it's no problem. We just throw it in with everything else. If the weed makes it, the coke makes it."

The next day, Morgan and Easy rented a small RV camper with a cab-over bed and all the amenities. They performed a job that would become routine after a while... packing the bricks into compartments underneath the bench seats. In the ice box, they kept the commodity Morgan bought with so much trepidation, a bag of pure white cocaine powder.

Around noon, Easy backed the loaded RV out of the driveway, then moved the gear shift into drive. He turned toward Morgan with a silly grin, almost giddy with excitement.

"Well Morg, we're done here. All we gotta do is make it home."

Easy guided the camper through the suburban streets toward the freeway. The idea of making it all the way back East still seemed audacious and unreal. Yet here they were, making it happen.

A cool night settled over the northern Arizona desert as they left Phoenix behind them, cruising north to Flagstaff. Morgan reclined in the soft leather passenger seat, enjoying the sharp cut of desert air outside the windows. Easy looked over,

"Hey Morg, why don't you get out that coke and cut us up some lines?"

Dustin carefully stepped into the back as the RV bounced down the highway. The air was invigorating and the action was heady as he cut up two long lines. First, he snorted his. Then, he brought the plate up front and grabbed the steering wheel while Easy took a long whiff. The high quality cocaine immediately took effect and Morgan's heart began to race. His chest felt like it was inflating, and a rush went through his whole body. He was totally elated, and he instantly knew why this drug could be very addicting.

Morgan settled into his seat as they climbed a long rise in their ascent around Oak Creek Canyon. They crested the hill, rolling down the mountain with the stars overhead and the lights of Flagstaff in the distance. The guitar licks of "Long, Cool Woman" by the Hollies broke out over the AM radio, then the shout. Easy cranked it up. Roaring high on pot smuggling adrenaline, cocaine, and the thrill of life, they let out a long, loud whoop and pumped their fists in the air.

The saguaro cactus had given way to pine and spruce as they penetrated further and further north. The safest route home was through Colorado and the Midwest. They crossed Interstate 40, then up to the Four Corners of Arizona, Utah, New Mexico, and Colorado. After the climb over Wolf Creek Pass, they made their way to Interstate 70. This took them all the way to West Virginia and finally to their destination in the mountains of southwestern Virginia.

Safely back home, Morgan's life was instantly transformed. "One thousand, two thousand, five... ten..." His exhilaration rose as the reality sank in. "I made it. I won!"

He tucked the bills in his boot then walked across the parking lot to the Bar. As he worked his way through the crowd, two pool players lifted up their eyes and give him a nod. He paid for his beer and turned around, resting his elbows on the bar. He raised his bottle to them and smiled back, returning the respect.

"Ah, the thrill of victory. I could get used to this."

The discovery of pot connections in Texas and Tucson created a boom in Blacksburg like the days of the California Gold Rush. It soon became evident this was a big time bonanza, and many others tried to get in on the action. Before long, numerous organizations formed out of the small hip community, and marijuana began to flow in truckloads from West to East. The only thing everybody had to do was keep it all among "good people."

A penthouse apartment would usually evoke an image of a swanky luxurious suite on the top floor of a skyscraper in New York's fashion district. The interior would be appointed with elegant furnishings, brass chandeliers, lush shag carpet, and velvet window coverings.

This penthouse in Blacksburg, Virginia, however, only shared one of these attributes... it was the sole apartment on the top floor. There was no shag carpet, only old, faded hard wood floors. Where you would normally see curtains, there were sheets nailed to the window trim.

Three young hippies shared the apartment, each one pursuing his own path in life. Lurch was quiet and unassuming, not flamboyant or impressive in any way, but he was getting ready to graduate in Mechanical Engineering. Max was a biker, red headed and stocky, always smiling, his bearded face beaming out good vibes. Agent Orange also had red hair, but his face was chiseled with high cheek bones. His whiskers formed a trim line with his jaw and moustache, making him the very image of the Zig Zag man on a pack of rolling papers. Of course, he would say,

"No, I don't look like the Zig Zag man, the Zig Zag man looks like me."

Agent Orange got his name from the dreaded defoliant used in Vietnam. Nobody dared ask him, but rumor had it he had been credited with multiple kills in combat. For this reason, Morgan had his eye on him for a partner. He needed a driver, and he also wanted protection. Agent Orange had all the credentials. In this community, at least, he was respected by all... nobody messed with Agent Orange.

At night, the penthouse came alive. Somebody was always coming up with a new and unusual hobby or project. For some reason, Rollie kept his boa constrictor named Alice in a tank in the living room, even though Rollie didn't actually live there. One of the main attractions was to gather around the big terrarium and watch Alice attack, squeeze, and swallow a laboratory mouse from the Psychology department. That had to stop, though, because one day, the terrarium was empty. Alice the boa constrictor had escaped.

The real business began when the partygoers left. On this night, the closest of friends were gathered around the kitchen table for a poker marathon. It was about 2:00 in the morning, and one of them was asleep on the couch in the living room, getting some rest before rejoining them in the morning. The smell of dirty clothes permeated the small apartment.

Along the back wall of the kitchen was the sink, the dirty gas range, and the refrigerator. The wood stove was in the corner against the other wall. They got the wood table from a used furniture store, the lacquer flaking off in patches, with matching faded kitchen chairs. The only light in the room, their "chandelier," was an exposed bulb hanging on a long cord from the ceiling, dangling overhead.

"Seven card stud, Doctor Pepper," announced Agent Orange with a mischievous grin. The players let out a collective groan as he slid the deck to his right for the cut. In Dr. Pepper, 10's, 2's and 4's were wild... no purists here. The pot soon mushroomed to over $70.

"There ya go, read 'em and weep. Full house, jacks over fives."

Lucky turned over his hole cards, then used both hands to pull the pile of money toward him.

"Well, boys, that's the way it goes. First your money, then your clothes."

He got his name for an obvious reason, he was always lucky. Lucky at cards, lucky at girls, lucky at everything. He had long, dark, curly hair and a million dollar smile.

"Pretty boy smartass." Orange passed the deck to his left. Rollie hung a cigarette in the corner of his mouth and started to shuffle.

"OK, guys and dolls, dollar ante, five card draw, nothin' wild."

"That's more like it," Lucky said.

Orange barked at him, "What are you complainin' about? You just cleaned up."

"Well, I just don't like wild cards. Guess it doesn't matter, though."

"Is everybody in? Here we go." Rollie flipped cards around the table until everybody had five, face down.

Morgan picked up his hand and leaned back in his chair. Man, I love it. It just doesn't get any better than this. He fanned his cards out and saw four tens and the ace of spades. Dumbfounded, he kept leaning back until he lost his balance. The chair fell over, his head hit the edge of the cast iron wood stove and he crumbled into a heap on the floor.

"Hey Morg, you all right? What got into you? Is your hand that good?"

"Oh, not really. Just clumsy, that's all."

Lucky folded immediately.

The game flowed around the table, and he played cautiously, trying not to seem overly confident. The others watched him with suspicion. He called all bets, then turned in his ace to make it look like he needed a card. Rollie quizzed him,

"So ya got two pair, huh? Or maybe you're drawing to a flush."

Morgan tried to put on a poker face, but failed miserably.

"I'll let you know," he stammered.

On the last round, he raised once. Rollie folded. The rest of them looked at him warily and called. He laid down his four tens.

"Boy, you can't hide a good hand for nothin'." Orange shook his head. "I had you pegged the minute you fell out of your chair."

Just then, over the back of the gas range, a long, thick snake with diamond and oval markings slithered out and stopped halfway between the burners. It raised its triangular head as it observed the scene, flicking its tongue. Everyone turned around, curious to see their unexpected guest. They knew who it was.

"Alice! You're back!" Rollie jumped out of his chair and grabbed the boa. "Oh my baby, where have you been?" He hugged it and kissed it, let it crawl over his shoulders and around his neck. They all rejoiced with him over his snake that was lost, but now was found.

It was in poker games like these, and in the Bar at 117 Main Street, that meetings materialized to talk business. In the Spring of 1973, three delegations of pot dealers began to work out details to converge in Arizona. They made plans to share rides and buy in with each other, depending on who found the best deal. As the time drew near, it grew into a full blown dope dealer's convention, complete with hotel reservations and car rentals.

The Petunia Deal

With the sun high overhead, Morgan had just passed Hays, Kansas, full of expectations. It wasn't that long ago he was on this road, hitchhiking to California, only to end up in Pueblo, Colorado. But this time, he had a new, rented Ford LTD, the air conditioner was blowing cold, and he was on his way to a dealer convention in Tucson. The speed limit was 80.

He had three different contacts in Tucson, and his goal was to come out of this next run with over $100,000. With those kinds of prospects, he was feeling pretty good about things. Money was no worry, he could buy a new truck when it was all over, and he was on top of the world. "Baba O'Reilly" by The Who boomed out over the radio, and Morgan tapped out the beat on the steering wheel, singing along out loud. "Sally, take my hand..."

POW!!! BLAP, BLAP, BLAP, BLAP!!

The right rear tire blew at 90 mph, throwing the car into uncontrollable convulsions. The rear end fishtailed, and Morgan slammed on the brakes, straining to straighten it out. The car swerved to the left and plowed straight into the median, careening head on into the cars and semi-trucks coming the other way. He frantically tried to turn to the right, but the car would not waver from its deviant path.

"Maybe I can whip the rear end sideways and dig it into the grass, like they do in the movies. Hope it doesn't roll."

He spun the steering wheel left and the front of the car lurched. The rear end came around to the right... now it was broadside, skidding at 70 mph. The rear wheels dug into the grass, and suddenly it stopped. The momentum jerked his body like a rag doll, slinging Morgan into the passenger seat. He crawled back to an upright position and turned off the ignition.

"What do you know? It worked!" He rested both hands on the steering wheel, gasping for breath, and watched the cars and semis race past him. WHOOOOSH!! The big rigs blew waves of air, rocking the car as each one roared by.

He stepped out to inspect the damage. There were long gashes in the grass forming parallel lines from where he left the pavement to the final resting place. The right rear tire was buried half way into the dirt. On the other side of the car, the left rear tire was wedged against the wheel well, the force of the skid shifting the axle over at least six inches. Morgan got the tire iron out of the trunk, wedged it between the tire and the wheel well, and pried the metal fender away from the tire.

"Hope that does it. Now, maybe I can get to the airport in Hays and get another car."

He started the car, inched it backward, and it rolled. So far, so good. A long string of cars zoomed by until, finally, he had a long break in the traffic. He crept forward, ever so slowly making his way onto the shoulder, and hobbled to the exit. Every foot of progress was a good sign... one more step toward the airport.

KABLAP... KABLAP... squeak... grind. KABLAP... KABLAP... squeak... grind.

The wheel rims scraped the asphalt with a horrible metallic squeal. The bumpers were hanging loose and flapping, and the rear axle was six inches off center, making it drive at an angle. He pulled into the Avis parking spot at the airport, walked up to the counter and handed the keys to the agent.

A young, high school girl looked at him with a big smile and said, "Hello, sir. Welcome to Hays. What can I do for you?"

"They sure don't make cars like they used to."

"Yes, sir. Is there some kind of a problem? I'd be glad to help."

"I appreciate your optimism, but I don't think you'll be able to help much this time. You won't believe what I did to your car."

"Oh, I'm sure it can't be that bad. Would you like to speak to my supervisor?"

The middle-aged man shook his head and ran his hand over his bald spot, trying to figure out how to handle this one. Morgan made a feeble attempt to explain how he saved the car and himself from crashing head on into a convoy of semi-trucks. The supervisor looked at his disheveled long hair with contempt.

"I'm sorry, but we don't have any more cars to replace this one."

"But you don't understand. I have to get to Tucson. There's gotta be a way to get out of Hays, Kansas!"

"You'll have to go to Denver to get the proper authorization to get another car." He abruptly turned and walked away.

Morgan bought a ticket on the next flight to Denver and settled into a seat in the waiting area. He picked up the local section of the Hays Daily News to see what was happening. Stock auction at the sale barn. Used farm equipment. Talk about dullsville. A voice over the loudspeaker broke the silence.

"Frontier flight 496 to Denver is now boarding. All passengers please report to the boarding area."

He handed the agent his boarding pass and attempted to walk past him onto the tarmac. The agent pulled him aside.

"Sir, I am so sorry. This is just a formality, but we have to search you before we can let you board the plane. Federal regulations. We have to make sure you aren't carrying any weapons on board. Also, is there any contraband in your suitcase that we need to know about?"

So close, and yet so far away. He felt the gravity knife in his front pants pocket.

"Oh, I see. Well, I don't have any problem with that. I'm not a violent sort of person. But, actually, there is something I need to tell you about."

"Oh?" The boarding agent squinted with a frown, "What is that?"

"You see, I have a quart jar of moonshine in my suitcase."

The agent smiled, relieved. "Is that all? That's no problem. We are only looking for weapons."

Encouraged by this small victory, Morgan opened up a little bit more.

"And, before you start searching me, I guess I need to tell you that I have a marijuana cigarette in my pocket."

"I understand. Thank you for telling me. When I get to it, just nod, and I will know that's what you are talking about."

"OK, sure." So far, so good.

The agent patted him down, feeling under his arms, down his chest, outlined a long, narrow form in his front left pants pocket, and looked up at him. Morgan nodded, and he continued the search down both of his legs.

"Could you please remove your boots for me?"

Oh, no. This is gonna do it for sure. He pulled off his boots, and wads of hundred dollar bills fell out on the floor.

"That's what I really didn't want you to see."

"Oh, I'm sorry. Some people just like to carry their money with them. That's quite all right. You are free to go."

Morgan slid his boots on, stuffed the money back inside, pulled his pant legs over the tops and walked onto the plane. He settled into his seat, shaken. The plane rotated off the runway, and he stared down at the long line of Interstate 70 as Hays, Kansas faded away.

"That was close." His mind flashed back to the semis bearing down on him. "That was real close."

"Welcome to the Best Western Inn, Tucson, sir. How can I help you?"

"Yes, give me a room for two, please. Do you have anything on the ground floor, pool side?"

"Well sir, unfortunately, we have had quite a rush of people today, and pool side is all booked up. We still have one on the ground floor in the back."

"That'll be fine. I'll take it."

"All right, sir, just fill out this registration card, and I will check you in."

Morgan turned around to scan the lobby. The hotel was a beautiful display of the great Southwestern Desert. Saguaro cactus and towering royal palms hovered like a canopy over the concourse. The floor was covered with a thick, well-padded carpet displaying an intricate, Apache style design. The lobby was equipped with a couch and matching chairs upholstered with deep red leather and antique brass furniture tacks outlining the arms. The walls were painted with a mural of the desert... pastel colors of pale green sage brush, red clay hillsides and turquoise sky.

He thought he saw Daffy Donald sitting in a chair in the corner, his face buried in a local tourist guide. Daffy lifted his eyes ever so slightly to connect with Morgan. *So, this is the place. I wonder how many made it.* The front desk girl handed him his keys.

"Here you go, sir. Just go out that door and across the inner courtyard, and your room will be on the right."

As he stepped out the door, there was a large swimming pool to his right, and a smaller Jacuzzi tub off to his left. The courtyard was lush with palm trees and Southwestern plants. He took a minute to soak up the sights and sounds around him. He could hear water trickling from artificial fountains and waterfalls somewhere in the decor.

"Hey Morg, welcome to Tucson!"

The unmistakable voice snapped Morgan out of his trance. There was Easy, half submerged in the hot tub, his flabby white chest dripping wet, his arms resting on the red bricks lining the perimeter. With a bottle of Coors in one hand, and a huge, crooked grin plastered across his face, it was an image that would take years to go away.

"This is how they do it in the Mafia. Take a look around... everybody's here."

Morgan wanted to tell him to shut up, *"cause the whole world ain't supposed to know we're having a dope dealer's convention!!"* But it was no use. Easy was Easy, and it all came with the package. He surveyed the courtyard and noticed the swimming pool and lounge chairs were all filled with long haired, scraggly looking friends from Virginia. Off to the side, nestled between two royal palms was a patio table with two padded chairs. Sitting there with his back to the rest of them was the man he wanted to see... Agent Orange.

Morgan took his bags to the room, unpacked his clothes and made a call. He had a new contact to try out for this deal, but he only knew him by his last name, Gordon, so his nickname had to be Flash. Flash gave him the breakdown.

"I'm gonna have something for you by tomorrow night. Now listen up good. This one's a little different. They're selling them in bricks, not pounds, so I can't guarantee the total weight. I need to meet you somewhere tomorrow and show you a sample. We can talk some more about the specifics. If you like it, we can go on from there."

"OK, where?"

"We've rented a house just for this occasion. Meet you there at 2:00 tomorrow afternoon." Flash gave him the address.

Morgan walked back to the courtyard and sat down with Orange. He signaled for two more beers.

"Hey man, glad you made it. I sure can't pull this off by myself."

"Wouldn't miss it for the world." Orange cracked a little smile, "Got any news?"

"Yeh, I got a pretty good line on something. If everything works out, we should be done pretty quick. I've still got a rental car... Boy, you gotta hear what happened in Kansas. But, that can wait.

"Here's the deal. I'm lookin' at some samples tomorrow. If we like it, we'll do the deal tomorrow night and load you up. I'm hoping we can stay at Flash's house after that... that way, we don't have to hang out here with all these other bozos and a camper full of weed. Depending on how things go tomorrow night, I may have enough money to get some more after that. We'll cross that bridge when we get to it. When it's all said and done, you'll drive back, and I'll wait a day or so and fly back so we get there at the same time."

"Sounds like a plan. Whatever you say, chief."

When he got to the rented house, Flash was in a room piled high with Mexican bricks. There was a set of scales on a table, and three Mexicans sitting in the living room, smoking cigarettes. One was an older man who studied everything going on around him and said nothing. The two younger Mexicans were there to translate and conduct all the business.

They put one of the bricks on the scale and it read 2.3 pounds. The next brick weighed a little over 2.5 pounds. Morgan randomly picked out five more bricks from the stack, and they averaged out to 2.4 pounds. This was enough to convince him the entire load would weigh more than the customary two pounds apiece.

"Cuantas por estas?" He asked in his broken Spanish.

"Ciento cincuenta por cada." One hundred fifty each, or seventy five dollars a pound, if they averaged two pounds per brick.

He did some math. One hundred pounds, at two pounds per brick, was fifty bricks. If each brick came out to 2.4 pounds, the total weight would be one hundred twenty pounds. That meant he would get one hundred twenty pounds of pot for the price of one hundred pounds.

What an opportunity for this dealers' convention! He could offer them a price per pound or per brick. If they chose pounds, they got their pounds, but he'd get the extra. If they wanted it by the brick, they shared in the gamble. He was pretty sure he could pull this off, and if he was right, he could come out smelling pretty good.

Back at the Best Western, Morgan began to work his magic. He called the main dealers together at a remote poolside table to explain the offer. Easy was there, representing Daffy Donald, Lucky was there, representing his own group, and Lord Byron was there representing himself.

"I can fill all your orders in one deal. I'm gonna shoot straight with all of you. They are selling them in bricks. I have seen them, and they should all be over two pounds. Here's what I am willing to do. If you just want to get your weight for seventy five a pound, we will all chip in and buy the load, and I will guarantee your weight. If the bricks are light, I will make it up out of my part. But, if they are heavy, I will still give you your weight, but I keep the rest. Or, you can get them by the brick and take the chance with me."

"Aw, Morgan, are you serious?" Easy fell back in his chair. "You know how these wetbacks are... how can you trust them? All I know is Daffy wants his dope for seventy five a pound."

"So you want to buy it by the pound, is that what you're sayin'?"

"I guess so, man. Why does it have to be so complicated? I just don't want to get burned."

Lucky chimed in, "how well do you know these people?"

"They're good people. It's a different group of Mexicans, but the Americans are solid, so I am sure everything is on the up and up. Like I said, if you just want it by the pound, you got nothin' to worry about. I will guarantee it all."

"Well, it's a little too risky for me. I trust you, though. If you'll guarantee the weight, I'll get one hundred twenty five."

Morgan pulled out a pen and a napkin.

"One hundred twenty five, OK, that'll be $9375, payable up front, in cash. How 'bout you, Easy?"

"Yeh, damn. I guess we'll get the whole thing. Give me one hundred seventy five." Easy pulled out a napkin. "Let's see, at $75 a pound, that's $13,125. OK, so let's be clear, Daffy wants one hundred seventy five pounds for $13,125. Deal?"

"Deal. Byron?" Lord Byron had been observing the conversation intently, and knew how cunning Morgan could be. He knew he would never risk this much money if he didn't have something up his sleeve.

"No, Morg, I'm with you." He raised his eyebrow suspiciously, but gave him a wink. "I want bricks. Get me all you can for $15,000."

"You got it. Everybody get your money counted and bring it to my room by 6:00 tonight. We rock and roll after dark."

About an hour after sunset, Morgan and Agent Orange sat idling at a stop light on Golf Links Road. The aura of a desert city at night was all around them... Hot rods rumbling, a radio playing in a car two lanes over, the sound of Mexican music coming from behind. The street lights cast a brilliant glow on the avenues, making straight shafts of light that trailed off into the darkness. In the distance, they could see the outline of the mountains outside of town. The Tucson air was electric. The desert landscape, satisfying.

They pulled into the carport of the rented house in a middle class neighborhood. The kitchen window faced the carport, and Morgan told Orange to pull back just a little bit from the window. With the $12,000 that he had personally put in the pot, he was carrying a total of $50,000 into a house to buy marijuana from a group of Mexicans he had never dealt with before. But then, Flash would be there, so he felt confident all would be OK. Just in case, he thought up a safety measure. With a full Coors in one hand, he laid out the plan.

"You stay here while I go inside. I'm gonna leave the money here at first. If I see anything fishy, I'll throw this beer bottle through that window, and you skedaddle outta here."

"Gotcha, boss."

"If everything's cool, I'll come back and we'll go do the deal."

"What are you gonna do if they pull guns?"

"I'll run like hell. Just hang tight."

Inside, everything was like it was earlier in the day. The old Mexican was still in his chair, and the rest of them were waiting around. The pot was stacked high in the bedroom, and the scales were resting on the table, ready to go.

"Are you ready?" Flash asked, "How much do you want?"

"I want 330 bricks." Flash ran the numbers and said,

"That'll be $49,500, where is it?"

"It's out in the car. I'll go get it."

"What's the matter? Don't you trust us?"

"Nope. Be right back."

Morgan got Agent Orange and the money... and the action began. The two young Mexicans counted out the bricks and stacked them in another bedroom. Flash and Morgan counted out the money. Orange simply stood still, leaning against a wall in the living room. He discreetly caught the eye of the old man to let him know he was watching. The old man smiled back with deep dark eyes. When they were done, everybody shook hands and parted ways. Flash offered to stay with the weed, so Orange and Morgan drove off into the city lights of Tucson.

The next day, Easy, Lucky and Byron came over to weigh up their pot and load it into their vehicles. When Byron found out his 100 bricks weighed 235 pounds, he was ecstatic. However, Easy was not so pleased. He looked at Morgan's stack of bricks and shook his head,

"Man, that just ain't right. Look at all that grass you got extra. All on my dime, too!"

"Relax, Easy, some of it came from Lucky's dime. You know I gave you a choice."

Easy was still fuming, "I can't believe it turned out this way. You came out of this thing smellin' like a damned petunia! Oh well, what are you guys gonna do now?"

Morgan's adrenaline raced as he looked at his huge pile of bricks. He reflected, yeh, what *am* I gonna do now? After a deal like this, I can't stop. It's in my blood. I'm so stoked I feel like I've got a critter in my gut, roaring and hungry. Massive, hairy, sabre toothed, screaming, *"More... more!"* He laughed and turned back to Easy.

"I've got another place to stay for the next couple of days. I might try to score again."

"Well, I gotta hand it to ya. You hit the jackpot. We're headed back home. I guess we'll see ya back at the ranch."

"Yeh, Easy, be careful." Morgan gave a casual salute. "Happy trails."

Bust

Flash Gordon's house was Tucson at its finest. He had built up a good distribution network, and he was able to pay high dollar rent for a high dollar house. On the outside, the architecture was adobe stucco, with arched doorways and windows. The entryway was framed with large, rounded timbers, and matching timbers protruded from the walls at main junctions. Desert landscaping was strategically placed all around with a mature cactus garden in the front. The focal point was a giant saguaro surrounded with prickly pears, barrel cactus, and various desert flowers. A circular driveway proceeded underneath an elegant overhanging concourse. From here, flagstone rocks led to the massive, etched glass double doors.

The inside did not disappoint. One wall of the living room was devoted to the fireplace, built with solid stonework, accented with a gnarled, thick wooden mantel. The ceilings were vaulted with exposed beams that contrasted against the bone colored, plaster walls. As if this wasn't enough, frosted French doors opened to a deep blue, tile lined pool, beckoning from the back yard.

"Welcome, welcome, come on in and make yourselves at home. Meet my old lady, Diane."

"Hey, Diane, good to meet you."

Morgan and Agent Orange gazed around in wonder. "You've got quite a place here."

Flash spoke softly to Diane, "Hey baby, I've gotta talk business with these guys. Would you please mix up a couple of Margaritas for our guests?" Diane walked away into the kitchen, the guys staring after her, google-eyed. Flash invited them into the living room.

Morgan and Agent Orange settled into the overstuffed, soft leather chairs. They hadn't seen a place like this since they came to Tucson. Everyone had been climbing the ladder, so to speak, and Flash was the highest one up that they had met so far.

"You know how it is, you get what you pay for. My business has been booming since I came out here from back East, and I just thought I would enjoy it while I could. You never know what will happen tomorrow."

"Ain't that the truth? You never know what'll happen the next minute. Before we go any further, I just gotta tell ya what I went through to get here." Morgan then delivered a Hollywood rendition of the tire blow out in Kansas.

Flash laughed, "After all that, this Tucson stuff ain't nothin'!"

"Well, I wouldn't call it nothin', but I'll take this kind of excitement over that kind any day." Morgan took a long sip of his margarita. "So, back to business, I need to fill up the rest of my load and head on back."

"How much do you need?"

"I've got one more friend coming out from Virginia. With what he wants, and what I have left to get, I think we'll need about three hundred fifty pounds."

"We might be able to use the Mexicans again. I'll see if they can get some more of those big bricks."

Later that afternoon, Cutter showed up in his Chevy pickup.

"How was your trip?" Morgan handed him a Coors. "By the way, welcome to Tucson."

Cutter flashed a smile. "Remember when we were sittin' in that stall in Middle Earth, plannin' out Texas? Who knew it would lead to this? Looks like we hit the big time here."

"Yeh, Nogales is only 70 miles away. Doesn't take any time at all to get it over the border and up the highway. Can you believe we used to get all excited over ten or fifteen pounds? When I get done with this next deal, I'll be moving 300 pounds back East."

"Well Morg, there's nothin' like money. Money and drugs, ain't that what you used to say? I think you've got just about enough by now."

"Yeh, I gotta hand it to you, though. You always were the businessman. That's what the magazines say, right? We oughta be corporate executives."

"Yeh, what do they know? I'd like to see a corporate executive do what we do. Where's Flash?"

"He went to check out some bricks. We're hopin' to score tomorrow. You got any idea how much you want?"

"I've got $16,000 to work with. I was hoping to get as close to 250 pounds as I could."

"Well, you might be in luck."

The following afternoon was D-Day. The plan was simple. The Mexicans would drive the load to Flash's house in two cars. Then they would weigh it out, exchange the money, and leave everybody to package it up. The entire transaction should take no longer than two hours. Of course, those would be a very nervous two hours.

Agent Orange passed the time by playing his guitar. He loved the blues, and he slowly strummed a bouncy, rhythmical twelve bar chord progression. He bobbed his head with the beat, eyes half closed, nodding his chin up and down as he grooved along.

"Hey, Secret Agent Man, hate to break up the mood, but we gotta talk."

The red-headed veteran put the guitar back in its case and carefully closed the lid, snapping the latches shut.

"Go ahead, Dusty. I'm all ears. This things's comin' down pretty quick, ain't it?"

"Yeh, and I've been thinkin'. Just in case something goes wrong, I wanna protect you and the load from gettin' caught up in it."

"Yeh, I thought about that. What's the plan?"

Morgan pulled out his wallet. "Go do the laundry while we do this deal." He scribbled on a torn piece of paper. "Call this number to make sure everything's cool before you come back."

"And if it isn't?"

"I don't think there'll be any problem. But, worst case scenario, find a neutral place, like a mall or something, wait a few hours and make your way over to Lucky's. Do you remember how to get there?"

"Yeh, I think so. Sure hope this goes OK. I'm a little worried, working with new people and all."

"Yeh, I know what ya mean. We used 'em last time, though, and everything went all right." Dustin couldn't ignore a little knot in his gut.

Time crept by at a snail's pace while everybody waited for Flash to call. The tension in the air was heavy and thick as they anticipated the critical engagement of people, money, and large quantities of pot. Cutter and Morgan had their money counted, the numbers figured out, and they waited. Orange was at the laundromat, and Morgan could only drop down in the big leather chair and try to be patient. He drummed his fingertips on the armrest.

Cutter paced around the living room, nervously sipping his beer. He craned his neck, looking out the window to scan the clear blue sky over Tucson. It all looked normal... hot and dry. A long contrail from a commercial jet streaked across the atmosphere. Off in the distance was a little speck he assumed was a traffic helicopter.

The phone rang. Thank God! We can finally get this show on the road. On the other end was Flash,

"We're on our way. The guys had to stop and get a flat tire fixed. Be there in five minutes."

"Is there anything you need us to do?"

"Just make sure the gate on the side of the house is open so we can drive straight through to the back. Other than that, just sit tight, be calm, and don't do anything stupid."

Light 'em Up!

Dispatcher Rita Flores was busy working a car accident when a 911 call lit up the board.

"Tucson Police Department, what is your emergency?"

"This is Dave's Auto on Speedway. Some guys just brought a car in here to fix a flat, and the trunk is full of marijuana."

"Can you give me your name and address?"

"I'd rather not give you my name. If you want to catch these guys, you're gonna have to hurry, 'cause I can't stall 'em forever."

"How do you know they have marijuana in the trunk?"

"We smelled it when we put the car up on the lift. Just thought you'd like to know."

Rita passed this information on to Captain Clark in Special Investigations,

"Clark here... you say they have a loaded car at this tire shop?"

"Yes, sir. They're just about done with the job, but they'll drag it out as long as they can."

"OK Rita, put two unmarked cars on scene at once, call Air Support for the chopper, and put all the patrol units in the area on standby. We don't want him, we want to know where he's going with it."

"10-4. Units 351 and 354 be enroute to Dave's Auto on East Speedway for observation. Be advised illicit drug activity. Do not apprehend. Follow to destination and report back.

"Unit 351, 10-4."

"Unit 354, 10-4."

Rita called the Air Support Unit.

"Hey guys, this is Rita at central. We just got a call from Dave's Auto on East Speedway about a loaded car. We need Air–1 activated now. We've got two units on site, and we'll all be on this channel."

"10-4, Rita, you got it. Pretty good load?"

"Don't know the whole story yet. They said the trunk was full."

"10-4. On our way."

"Attention, all units central and east, be advised we have a bogey leaving Dave's Auto on East Speedway. Monitor this channel for progress."

Finally, Rita called DEA and brought them into the loop. Agents Reed and Sparks got the case. They checked their weapons and jumped in their Monte Carlo. Sparks looked in the mirror and checked his hair. He had to grow it over his ears and down his neck for undercover work, but he kind of liked it. He was already muscular and stout, and the long, black hair and moustache made him look really bad.

The two unmarked cars separated and discreetly parked where they could see the front of Dave's shop. They spotted the two young Mexicans milling around outside, smoking cigarettes. Soon, one of them got in an older model Chevy Impala, and the other climbed into a jacked up GTO. They pulled out going east on Speedway. Units 351 and 354 fell in at a safe distance.

"Unit 351 to central, we have two bogeys. Suspects moving east on Speedway, currently at Swan."

"10-4, Unit 351."

Air-1 was in contact with dispatch, climbing out and forming the beginning arch of a large circle that would encompass east Tucson. Depending on which direction the target went, they would be able to close in from their vantage point in short order. As the car moved farther east on Speedway, it boiled down to three marked patrol cars in that section who would join the hunt. By this time, Reed and Sparks were tuned in, on their way and ready to rumble.

Standard procedure was to surround the active site and seal off any means of escape. When the target was verified, the patrol cars would secure the front, and the unmarked cars and DEA boys would secure the back. The added bonus was the Air-1 helicopter which could track everything in a 360 degree scope from its position in the air.

"Unit 351 to central, crossing Wilmot and Speedway, moving east."

"10-4."

Air–1 continued its wide circle. Using their binoculars, they now had the cars in sight.

"Unit 351 to central, approaching Camino Seco eastbound."

"10-4."

One of the patrol cars had fallen in line behind the unmarked cars. The other two had positioned themselves at a gas station a couple of miles east, waiting for a final position report. The chopper tightened its circle, knowing they were getting close. Speedway Boulevard only went so far before it dead ended at the desert.

"Unit 351 to central, suspects turning south on Bonanza. Repeat. Turning south on Bonanza."

"10-4, Unit 351. All units respond to Speedway and Bonanza southbound."

The two parked patrol cars jumped into action... Reed and Sparks moved in to close the gap with the target car.

"There's a neighborhood on the west side of Bonanza with a big alleyway behind that row of houses. I bet that's where they are. That might be a good place to hit 'em from behind."

Sparks was energized and double checked his .357 Magnum. The Air–1 chopper banked left towards Bonanza Avenue.

The loaded cars went down Bonanza and slowly turned into a driveway. As they eased through a gate to a garage in the back of the house, Air–1 descended. The unmarked cars held back to give the target cars time to pull into their driveway and get settled. Easy now. No warning flags. Don't want them to get spooked at the last second and spit the hook.

With the baby safely tucked away, the lead car called in the strike.

"Unit 351 to central, light 'em up."

Cutter stared at the sky out the living room window. He motioned Morgan to take a look.

"Man, I don't know what to make of this, but I've been watching that helicopter go in a big circle for a while now. Maybe it's nothing', but it seems like it's getting closer."

"Keep your eye on it. I don't know what we can do about it at this point."

"Well, we might wanna think about calling it off." Cutter went back to the window. What started out as a faraway speck was now forming a smaller circle directly overhead. A cumulus cloud moved across the sun, casting a daytime shadow.

Two cars rolled into the driveway through the gate. Once they were parked in the back, the Mexicans jumped out, popped the trunks and started hauling burlap bags through the back door. The center of operations was in the dining room, which sat off to the side of the living room.

The action was frantic. Everyone moved as fast as they could, dragging burlap bags and stacking bricks. With the amount Flash bought for himself plus the three hundred fifty pounds for Morgan and Cutter, there were a good six hundred pounds of pot in the house.

Flash kept his eyes moving, going from the garage to the dining room, scoping things out. He stood next to Morgan and shared his thoughts.

"Listen, everything looks good, so far. One thing I like about this house, the garage is in the back, so no one can see us unload this stuff once we close the gate. The Mexicans have already proven themselves, the bricks are big, the pot is good... I just don't see how anything could go wrong. By the way, where's that friend of yours who stands around and looks mean?"

"I sent him on an errand. Don't want all my eggs in one basket, just in case."

Cutter hurried over to get Flash, a scared, wild look in his eyes.

"It's comin' for us. You gotta take a look. It's closing in fast!"

Flash went with Cutter to the window and stared up at the sky. Morgan still didn't believe it, and kept on working, hauling and stacking his bricks.

SLAM!! A car door shut as three cars pulled up, flashing red and blue. Uniformed men got out, running toward the house. Cutter and Flash bolted from the window, terrified.

"They're here."

"Who's here?"

"The cops, dumb ass."

Morgan panicked, pacing around in circles. What do I do? I've gotta move fast. What have we always said we would do? Surrender or run? If everybody runs, we can scatter the cops, and some of us might get away.

He looked out the back door, but his mind was filled with chaos. He focused across the pool to the back fence. It bordered an alleyway... maybe there's some hope there. The wind started blowing downward onto the tops of the palm trees. The boughs bent and flipped around wildly like they were in a hurricane.

He opened one side of the French door and ran into a wave of Tucson heat whipped up by a helicopter hovering over the parked cars, just to the side of the swimming pool. He could see the men in the chopper, one looking right at him with a bullhorn at his mouth. His heart pumping like a bass drum, he took three bounds and leapt over the pool, fell to his knees, picked himself up, jumped on the fence and pulled himself to the top.

THUMP, THUMP, THUMP, THUMP... The bullhorn blared out over the din of the pounding propellers. "Suspect running out of house, heading for alleyway. Suspect heading for alleyway."

Morgan pivoted over the six foot picket fence and dropped to the ground. The alleyway was a straight open channel before him, like a long, wide bowling lane with nowhere to hide. He took off running, the scene around him playing out in slow motion.

"Suspect running down alleyway. Suspect running down alleyway."

He looked over his shoulder and saw two men coming around the corner of the fence line, guns drawn, running full speed toward him.

"Freeze, you son of a bitch! Freeze!

THUMP, THUMP, THUMP, THUMP... The bullhorn kept up its incessant chatter, with the propellers stirring up clouds of dust. The throbbing noise reverberated in his chest. Reed and Sparks quickly gained on Morgan, his legs folding underneath him, handicapped by trying to run in cowboy boots. The fatal moment hit him when reality broke through. He could not escape, and he had to surrender to a greater force. He slowed down to a trot and raised his hands in the air.

The greater force didn't let him off easy, though. Sparks grabbed Morgan by the shirt, dragged him and slammed him against the fence. He cocked his .357 magnum and pressed it against his temple. Out of the corner of his eye, Morgan saw the hammer pulled wide open. He felt the steel barrel hard against his head. Reed pressed his gun against the other side of his head.

Two big guns. Two hammers pulled back, pressing into his temples, hands trembling with fury and adrenaline. Morgan came unglued. Everything that made up his inner being drained out... his spirit, his energy, his will to resist, everything.

"OK you jackass, you know the position... up against the wall. Spread 'em. Thought you'd get away, huh? Where's your piece?"

"My what?"

Their hands were shaking and their thumbs quivered. Please don't let them slip!

"You're piece, stupid. Why else would you run if you weren't carryin' a piece?"

Sparks patted him down with his left hand, keeping the gun hard pressed into his temple.

"I don't know. I don't have a gun. You gotta believe me."

"Oh really? We ain't gotta believe nothin' from you, asshole."

They uncocked their guns, pulled Morgan's hands behind his back and handcuffed him. With a rough push, they marched him back to the house. As they walked through the gate to the pool, he saw the rest of his friends lying face down on the patio, motionless, their hands cuffed behind their backs. They looked like a pod of beached whales that just washed up on the shore. The Mexicans were stacked up on the side of the pool, and Cutter had his face down, resting his forehead on the concrete. Morgan made eye contact with Flash, who formed his mouth into a *"Shhhhh."*

It was a dismal scene... cops milling around, writing on clipboards, joking lightheartedly and patting each other on the back. Captain Clark surveyed the site, inspecting the work of his officers.

"Good work, men. Good work. This oughta put a dent in the flow for a day or two."

Paaaaaaa... Phump. Paaaaaaa... Phump. Surrounded by middle-aged women and screaming kids, Agent Orange sat on a table mindlessly watching the clothes flop around in the big dryer. The tumbling clothes, mixed with the rumbling of the washers, filled the room with the familiar sounds of a laundromat. The air was infused with the delicate fragrance of clean cotton and laundry detergent.

He pondered his role in the pot business so far. He knew the services he provided were crucial.

"I load up hundreds of pounds of pot, drive it across the country, and act as Morgan's enforcer. It would be nice if he paid me a little better, after all, I'm not just an errand boy. But, we do go first class."

In spite of all this, Orange's military training had instilled in him a deep sense of loyalty. He would do his duty first, and worry about the money later.

With a wet load in the dryer, he folded the last of the dry T-shirts and laid them in the laundry bag. The uneasy feeling about the new contacts still gnawed at his stomach as he stepped into the phone booth. Pulling out a wrinkled piece of paper, he dropped in a dime and punched the buttons. The phone rang three times.

"Hello?" It was a male voice he didn't recognize.

"Yeh, I'm just checkin' in. Is Morgan there?"

"Hey, man, how ya doin'? Yeh Morgan's here. He can't come to the phone right now. Just come on over, anyway, we got all you need."

Orange was confused. Is this guy OK? He sounded a little too friendly, and he sure didn't sound like anyone he knew. He seemed a little awkward, like he was trying to be somebody he wasn't, or say something that wasn't exactly right.

"Uh, I don't know. Are you sure everything's all right? Who is this, anyway?"

"Yeh, man, it's all right. Just come on over, we're waitin' for ya."

"Hmmm. I don't think so. Who did you say you were, again?"

"Would you believe this is the cops, and we just busted this place with six hundred pounds?"

"Yeh, I'd believe it." SLAM! He pounded the receiver down on the hook.

"Crap! That's what I thought." Orange stepped out of the phone booth and wandered around in the parking lot, running his hands through his hair.

"This is bad, this is really bad. I hope they can't trace that call. I better get outta here quick."

He hurried back into the laundromat, yanked open the dryer door, and pulled the hot, moist clothes into the cart. He feverishly crammed all the clothes, wet and dry, folded and unfolded into a laundry sack, threw it over his shoulder, and jogged out to the truck. The middle-aged women watched him with dismay, shaking their heads, wondering why they allowed men in laundromats in the first place.

Orange drove the camper aimlessly through the streets of Tucson, eventually finding a spot in the middle of a shopping center parking lot. He pulled out a city map, gathering his thoughts.

"Now where was Lucky's house? It's been a while..."

Scanning the map for major landmarks, it came back to him, and he cautiously headed that way, looking around for suspicious cars. He knocked on the door of the old adobe style house in south Tucson. His heart was still pounding. Lucky's roommate cracked open the door and peeked out at Orange.

"Yeh, what's up?"

"Remember me? I'm Morgan's driver. Is Lucky here?"

"Yeh, come on in." Agent Orange paced the floor in the living room until Lucky emerged from the back of the house.

"Hey Orange, you still here?"

"Yeh, I'm still here, unfortunately."

Lucky sensed bad news. "We sent our load back yesterday, what's up?"

"We were tryin' to score again, but the load got busted."

Orange told Lucky the whole story from his point of view. Lucky shook his head as he absorbed the news, then suddenly looked up with a wide eyed stare.

"Is your load still in that camper? Are you sure they didn't follow you here?"

"Yes, I'm sure. I've been wandering around Tucson for two hours and I know I'm clean. I need a place to lay low 'til I know what Dusty wants me to do. He's probably gonna need some help getting bailed out, but I don't have that kind of dough. I've got 250 pounds of weed, but no money."

"Well, I can't have you stay here. We'll put you up in a hotel somewhere until this thing works itself out a little bit. Don't worry, though. We'll take care of Morgan. I'm already thinking of a lawyer I can talk to. I'll get to work on it. Here, have a beer and we'll set you up for the night."

DEA agent Sparks strutted around the bodies with his head held high, laughing and chortling like a defensive lineman who just sacked the quarterback.

"This idiot thought he could outrun me, can you believe that? Where'd he think he was gonna go? Mexico?"

He leaned down and taunted Morgan, hissing in his ear.

"Hey punk, this is what you get for trying to run away from me. You're lucky I didn't blow your brains out. They say the leader of the pack is Morgan. Is that you, big shot?"

Morgan was so deflated he didn't even think in English. He let out a soft mutter,

"*Si.*"

He turned his face down and rested his forehead on the concrete, his eyes closed. His freedom had been stripped from him in an instant. All he could do was breath. In, out. In, out. The next thing was the ride to the jailhouse. One thing was for certain. Morgan and Cut wouldn't be spending tonight in Flash Gordon's luxurious Arizona hacienda. Tonight was going to be spent on a cold metal cot.

Desperado

Sergeant Bishop waved the string of new inmates into the holding room to be processed into the Pima County Jail.

"This way, c'mon, keep it comin'. OK, two of us are going to process you people so we can get through this faster. I'll take three of ya over here on this side. You other three have the pleasure of meeting Sergeant Juanita. OK, who's first?"

Nobody jumped at the chance, so Morgan decided to get it over with. He walked into the office and sat down next to Bishop.

"Hello son, how's your day goin?"

Morgan wasn't in the mood for jokes. "I've had better."

"Now, just gimme your name, rank and serial number, and we'll get this over with. You got any relatives we need to contact?"

He shuddered to think what his parents would say. As much as he tried to get away from them, he still didn't want to bring them any grief. After all, they did come out and rescue him in Colorado. He didn't want his sister in Texas to know either, so he just said, "No."

"No? Really? Who's gonna bail you out?"

"I don't even know what my bail is."

"They'll bring a judge down here soon if they haven't already." He motioned to someone in another room. "Hey Jimmy, do they have a bail set for these guys yet?"

"I think it's $5,000."

"You hear that? Five thousand dollars. You got that kind of money?"

"Not on me."

"OK, lookin' at your report, it says you ran. That ain't good. It also says they searched you for guns but didn't find any."

"No, I don't carry a gun."

"You're in the pot business and you don't carry a gun. What if you run into somebody who does carry a gun? What are you gonna do then?"

"The people I work with are good people. They don't need –"

Bishop dropped his pen and turned to face Morgan.

"Listen son, this ain't cowboys and Indians. You say you don't need a gun now, but if you stay in this business long enough, you will. Mark my words.

"OK, we're done here. Go over to that window and get your uniform. There's a changing room around the corner. Put all your personal belongings in the gray tub, and hand it to the corrections officer. Make sure you take off all your jewelry, 'cause they like that stuff inside. Next!"

The rest of that day, Morgan got a good look at what awaited him if he got a lengthy sentence. Everybody was put together in one large open cell, teeming with inmates. The sleeping area was crammed with bunk beds arranged in parallel rows. The open area had a number of metal picnic style tables, each one encircled with men who had been there for a while. Some were reading or playing cards. Two men sat on a bench, one hunched over with a needle of some sort, inscribing a blue tattoo on the other's shoulder.

To Morgan, this was the picture of despair. "You lose your freedom because you lose control. Now..." he focused on a group of muscular, tattooed Mexicans leaning on a bunk, "it looks like they have control." He felt a tap on his shoulder and turned around.

"Hey, I'm Ricky. You wanna stay away from those guys over there. They're gonna want a payoff sooner or later, so you better find somethin'."

"Pay them off? With what? There's nothin' in here."

"I'm just tellin' ya man, you better find somethin', or else." He pounded his fist into his other palm. "I use acid. Buys me protection. Want some blotter?"

"What? Blotter? In here? Are you serious? Don't tell me you trip in this place."

"Yeh, all the time. It's great." Ricky smiled at Morgan with a crazy grin.

He looked back at the gang leaders, and the reality came into focus. His heart raced with visions of fighting and pain... "This ain't good. Somethin's gotta change."

He jumped on his bunk and went through every detail of what went wrong. There were some subtle clues he could have picked up on, but he didn't. He chided himself for being so dumb, and he could only draw one conclusion...

"You ain't as smart as you thought you was."

The next morning, the busted party was called out and herded off to a court room. Almost methodically, as if there was nothing abnormal about 600 pounds of pot, the judge reduced their bond to $1,000 each. The deputies escorted them back to the jail where they get their lunch of cheese sandwiches on stale bread, a blob of cherry Jello, and a cup of unsweetened tea on metal trays. Two hours later, a jailer hollered for Dustin Morgan.

Dreading what could happen next, he followed the jailer down a hallway. He unlocked a metal door that opened to a long, narrow visitation room. Morgan sat down on a stool in one of the little stalls, looking through a thick, plexiglass window. A few minutes later, a door opened to the room on the other side, and who was sitting opposite him but Lucky!

"Hey man, we heard what happened. What a bummer. I sure hate to see you in here like this. You look lower than a snake's belly in a wagon rut."

"You ain't kiddin'. I'm lower than that. I'm lower than whale poop, and that's at the bottom of the ocean." Morgan shook his head and laughed at his own joke.

"Well, at least you haven't lost your sense of humor. We're gonna get you outta here. I heard your bail is $1,000. Is that right?"

"Yeh, that's what they said this morning."

"Well, we're gonna spring for that. You can pay me back later. I've also contacted a lawyer we know. He should be down here this afternoon to meet you. He's one of the best attorneys in Tucson, and he's got the contacts to do a good job for you."

"How much?"

"It'll cost you a chunk, but he can do the job."

"Man, I don't know what to say. I'll make it up to you, somehow."

"That's OK. I know you're good for it. After you see the lawyer, we should be able to get you out. And, by the way, Agent Orange came by. He wants to know what to do."

"Just tell him to go home."

"That's what I thought. I'll tell him. Don't worry, Dusty. It'll all come together. We'll keep on truckin'."

The jailer led Morgan back to the cellblock. A couple of hours later, he heard the keys again. It was Sergeant Bishop with words that were music to his ears.

"Dustin Morgan, get your stuff and follow me."

Inside the well appointed lawyer's office in downtown Tucson, attorney Russell Holmes thumbed through a stack of papers. It looked pretty cut and dried. What can you do when they catch everybody red handed? Inevitably, each one of the accused had developed their own story to make it look like they had nothing to do with it. He couldn't imagine how he could paint his client as an innocent bystander when he was the only one who ran.

The only thing he had left was some technicality, some loophole, like a botched warrant, or unauthorized search and seizure. The warrant had been called in as a routine telephonic, so there wasn't much of a chance there. The authorities were good at what they did, and they knew the drill for drug busts like the back of their hands. But Holmes was a sharp defense attorney, and he wasn't ready to throw in the towel just yet.

The secretary's fuzzy voice came through the intercom. "Mr. Holmes, Attorney Weber is here to see you."

"Send him in."

"Hey Russ, another beautiful day in Tucson, eh?"

"What's so beautiful about it? You got somethin' up your sleeve?"

"Now, now, that's no way to be. Have you looked at your Morgan case lately?"

"Yeh, I got it right here on my desk. Looks pretty grim, I must say. Not much wiggle room."

"Well, you're going to have even less wiggle room now. The State has offered my Mexican driver total immunity if he'll flip."

"And what are you counselling him to do?"

"Flip, of course. They have every base covered, and there just isn't any other way out. I'm sorry, Russ."

"That means he's going to tell the whole story about my client."

"You got it. Morgan's the one they're after… they think he's the ringleader."

"What about the Mexicans? They're the ones who brought it here in the first place."

"The old man and the kid are illegals, so they're just gonna deport them. You know how that goes. They'll be back."

Holmes flipped his pen in the air, exasperated. "OK, Weber. Thanks for telling me. I sure don't like it, but you gotta do what you gotta do. I guess I need to inform my client."

After Weber walked out, he took a deep sigh, then exhaled slowly. "This isn't what I get paid for. I get paid to win, not lose gracefully."

But, any plans he may have had to get Morgan off just vanished. There was only one thing left to do… call the DA.

Morgan walked up the concrete steps, through the front door of the 117 Bar. As soon as his eyes adjusted to the dim lighting, he saw Cutter and Orange sitting together at a table off to the side. Orange waved him over.

"Hey, stranger, welcome home. They finally let you out?"

"Boy, I'm tellin' ya. We gotta stop meeting like this. When did you get back?"

Cutter leaned back in his chair, "Oh, I've been back for a couple of days. You must have made bail right after I did. You know, that was a pretty good idea for you to have Orange go do the laundry. That saved your ass."

"Yeh, it saved mine, too." Agent Orange chimed in, "That was smart thinkin'. I ain't lyin'. Sorry you had to take the fall."

"Well, I guess that's why I get the big bucks. Which reminds me, we gotta sell that load you brought back so we can get some cash. I gotta pay you, and I gotta pay my lawyer."

Cutter broke in, "Speakin' of lawyers, mine says I have a good chance of getting off."

Morgan was dumbstruck.

"What? When I bolted out the back door, you were right there in the house."

"Yeh, but I found a room with no pot in it, sat down, and just waited for them to find me. My lawyer thinks it's gonna work, since they can't prove I knew anything about it."

"If that don't beat all. I hightail it out of there, and you get off! The world ain't right."

"We're all responsible for our own actions, big boy. Besides, you need me now, and I need you. I think I have a buyer, and I got expenses."

"All right, all right, we'll take care of this tomorrow. Go ahead and call your guy. I need a buck fifty, though. We gotta dig our way out of this."

Orange motioned Morgan to an empty table and lowered his voice.

"I got expenses, too." His hand had a slight shimmy as he gave him a hard look, "That business down there was no walk in the park, and the drive back made me a nervous wreck. I appreciate you lookin' out for me and all, but I saved your whole load, and I need double for this run."

Orange looked straight at Morgan with a serious gaze bordering on threatening. Morgan was taken aback... Orange wasn't kidding.

I sure don't want to rattle up any of his old demons, Morgan thought. He peeled five one hundred dollar bills off a wad in his pocket.

"Here's a bonus for mental anguish... I'll get the rest to ya as soon as we move some of this. And yes, thanks for everything." He stood up and stretched, "I got my bonus for bein' stupid from the Pima County jail."

Morgan plopped the quarters into the slot for the long distance call. After the customary small talk with the secretary, attorney Holmes came on the line.

"This is Russell Holmes."

"Yeh, Russ, this is Dustin Morgan. I'm checkin' in from back here in Virginia."

"Yes, Dustin, I am afraid I have some bad news. You know, you have a lot of odds stacked against you."

Every time Morgan called the attorney, it was like riding a seesaw. If there was any glimmer of hope, his heart went up, giving him that uplifting, "everything's going to be OK, and you can go on living your life" feeling. If that window of hope began to close, his heart went down, and he got that "Oh my God, I'm going to go to jail, and I may not survive" feeling. That's the one he was getting right now. He stammered,

"What do you mean 'bad news', Russ?"

Holmes told him about the immunity deal the State struck with the Mexican driver, who was now going to testify against him.

"That pretty much puts the nails in the coffin, Dustin."

He saw his life spiraling out of control, back to that cell in Tucson. The anguish in his gut was so intense he doubled over. Quick thoughts raced through his mind. Should I make a run for it to Canada? Can I get rid of the witness? It just got worse and worse. He tried to keep his voice from squeaking,

"So, Russ, is there anything we can do?"

"There may be one more card we can play."

"Tell me, please. I'm all ears."

"I spoke with the district attorney, and he is willing to take a plea deal for ten years' probation. That's a long time, but it keeps you out of jail. Of course, a felony will go on your record."

After taking the plunge down to the bottom of the seesaw, Morgan was more than ready to escape the awful, sickening feeling of going to prison. He jumped at the chance.

"Take it, take it! No jail time? That's pretty good for six hundred pounds."

"Well, like they say around here, Tucson has more grass than Carter has pills. They just don't have enough room for all you guys. No weapons, no assault, no aggravating circumstances, you're outta here. Now, you'll have to come back here to finish the proceedings. I'll get a date and let you know. Call me back next week."

"You got it. You are a life saver."

Morgan set the receiver down with a sigh, and a light, lifting feeling began to seep through his chest. He quietly walked back to the table and leaned back in his chair, relishing the chill of the

Michelob. He looked at Cutter with his mop-top of curly brown hair and Orange with his Zig Zag man look and lifted his beer in a salute. What a crew! After all we've been through, we're still in pretty good shape. All I've gotta do now is sell that load.

"Are you of sound mind?"

"Yes, Your Honor."

"You are here to enter a plea of guilty to possession with intent to distribute marijuana, which is a class 2 felony in the State of Arizona. Do you understand that?"

"Yes, Your Honor."

"Do you understand that your charge carries a maximum prison term of ten years in the state penitentiary, and that upon entering this plea you will receive the sentence of ten years' probation, contingent upon the recommendation from our department of probation?"

"Yes, Your Honor."

"If, at any time, you violate the conditions of your probation, you will be returned to the Arizona penal system to serve the full term of your sentence. Do you understand?"

"Yes, Your Honor."

"So, how do you plead?"

"Guilty, Your Honor."

"Let the record so reflect. Your plea is accepted, and you are adjudicated guilty of possession with intent to distribute marijuana in excess of four pounds, which is a class 2 felony in the State of Arizona. I sentence you to ten years suspended in the Arizona Correctional System. I remand you to the custody of Adult Probation Services. Your probation officer has already been assigned. He is ready to process you immediately. That is all, this case is closed."

The gavel went down with a crack. The judge rose and walked away from the bench, and Morgan was directed to a thin, middle-aged man with a soft, friendly grin. He held out his hand and shook with a firm, but caring grip.

"Mr. Morgan, my name is Jeremy Rombach, and I have been assigned as your probation officer. I want to do everything I can to help you with your probationary sentence. Please come into my office and we can complete all the details. We should be able to process you quickly and get you on your way."

Morgan was taken aback by the sudden display of niceness. Where did all this come from? He followed Rombach through the courthouse to his office. Once inside, the probation officer settled in his chair and pulled out some forms.

"OK, first of all, we need to establish your conditions. Then we will work out what you need to fulfill those conditions."

"Uh oh, here it comes," Morgan thought, "they're going to rake me over the coals now, for sure."

"Now, as the judge said, if you get arrested again for any crime, your probation will be revoked. Do you know what that means?"

"He said I would have to serve my whole sentence. I am guessing that means all ten years?"

"Yes, that's right. All ten years in the state penitentiary. So I suggest you think carefully about your lifestyle and the choices you make. It could be something as simple as a DWI. Boom! Off you go."

"OK. Yeh, that's something to think about. Is there any chance of getting off probation any sooner?"

"Yes, if you keep your nose clean and make all your required reports, we can recommend an early termination in three to five years. Of course, that is based on you keeping the stipulations of your probation, which brings me to the next point. During the term of probation, you must remain employed, or enroll in an accredited form of education. This includes trade schools, community colleges, anything that will help you to pursue a career. Do you have a job at this time?"

"I have a band in Virginia. Does that count?"

"Well, that may do for now, but eventually you are going to have to find a full time job. Now, we need to define the parameters and responsibilities that you will have. You are under the supervision of the State of Arizona, but you live in Virginia, is that correct?"

"Yeh, that's my permanent residence."

"Now that I'm thinking about it, fill out all your contact information here, please." He slid the paper and a pen over to Morgan.

"We do have one more issue we need to resolve. In order to place you on probation, we need the name of one contact in case of an emergency. We also use this person as a reference. So, who can I put down?"

Morgan winced. What a mess! Sis is gonna have to be the one, but I sure hate to do it to her. But, they're not gonna let me out of this part again. He leaned forward,

"I guess I'll have to use my sister in Texas. They're good, solid people."

"Ah, very good. Do you mind if we call her now?"

"Now?"

"Yes, we can't process the application until we have contacted a reference."

"Well, I guess I don't have a choice. Yeh, go ahead." How do I get myself in these situations? First, they're gonna let me die on the operating table if my parents don't answer the phone, now, they're gonna cart me off to a jail full of father rapers and mother stabbers if my sister doesn't answer the phone.

Rombach returned with a smile.

"Well, Dustin, you can stop worrying now, we were able to contact your sister. She did vouch for you, so there should be no more problems getting you processed."

"Really? You got a hold of her? What did she say?"

"She said, 'please don't put him in jail.'"

"Is that all?"

"She also said that they would be willing to have you stay with them to get away from your bad influences if that would help. I told her that would be up to you.

"So now, moving on, we can either transfer your supervision to Virginia, or you can report to us by mail once a month. Which would work out best for you?"

"I'll just report once a month if that's OK."

"Splendid. Next we come to travel privileges. Do you need to travel as part of your job?"

Morgan still thought of his pot distribution business as is his job, so he said,

"Yes, I would say that my job requires me to travel."

"Fine, fine," Rombach typed 'unlimited travel'. "Now, due to the nature of your offence, we will have to restrict international travel. Will that be a problem?"

He couldn't believe his ears. Unlimited travel with no local supervision, and they're asking if it's OK if they keep him from going to Mexico? The only reason he went there was to browse the markets for trinkets and tequila with a worm in the bottle.

"No, no problem at all. I don't need to go out of the country anyway."

"Good, good. Well, that pretty well wraps things up. You will be getting a package from this department that will have all your reporting forms and conditions in writing. Before you go, please sign here indicating that you understand and agree to everything we have discussed."

Morgan signed on the line, and Rombach extended his hand.

"Thank you, Mr. Morgan, you are free to go."

The lights of the airline cabin were dim, most of the passengers sleeping. The flight attendant occasionally walked the aisle, checking to make sure everybody had everything they needed. Morgan rested his head against the wall, peering out the oval window of the Boeing 707 into the darkness of rural America.

It had been almost two years since he left the probation office in Tucson, and he still couldn't believe his luck. By getting off so easy for such a big bust, he felt like he had beaten the rap, and had a license to let it all hang out. Even now, Agent Orange was out there somewhere, driving a truck full of weed back across the country, while he was nursing a Tanqueray and tonic at 30,000 feet.

The bust had changed him. He had met the enemy face to face, making him more hardened, more wary, more calculating. But it had also triggered a wild abandon, as if he had to get all he could before disaster struck. He was addicted to the lifestyle, and the constant barrage of partying began to warp his character, stripping away all sense of drive. It drained out his work ethic, so that it was all he could do to perform a simple task like changing the oil in his truck.

The probation office started to raise a fuss about a job, so he answered an ad for a construction crew laborer. The work wasn't that bad after he got out in the fresh air, but getting up at 5:30 AM every day of the week was pure torture. He made the 7:00 AM start time most days, but one morning he had no choice but to show the foreman his bloodshot eyes and ask for the day off.

It didn't take long for him to start daydreaming about the money and the freedom he had running dope. He knew all he had to do was get back in that truck and head out West, and everything would be better. Better than working, anyway. So, here he was in the air, flying back to Virginia, trying to keep the show going.

But the thrill was gone. Unless you could call being scared witless that you were going to get pulled over for a routine traffic violation, and the cop was going to find your load of weed, and you were going back to Arizona for ten years, thrilling. So, the thrill was still there, but the glamour and the lustre were gone. Instead of the vibrant, strong, happy ball of energy Morgan used to be, he was slipping downward like a whirlpool in the Mississippi River.

Back at the 117 Bar in Virginia, Agent Orange's load was safely stashed away, and the psilocybin mushrooms performed their magic on Morgan's mind. Sitting at one of the round tables in a remote corner, he was once again sipping the same old Michelob, tasting the same old metallic twangs, listening to the same old music, and watching the same old surroundings.

He hadn't allowed himself to get attached to any one girl, preferring to keep his freedom to play around. Tonight he realized the tradeoff for all this freedom... he was alone. For all his friends and acquaintances, he didn't have anyone to trip with, no one to hang with. He was tired of the old stuff and didn't have plans for any new stuff. He was on probation, spending too much money on cocaine, and he didn't want a career of carrying lumber for a construction crew.

Maybe it was the mushrooms in his brain, or maybe it was a still small voice, but the impression grew bigger and bigger that he needed a change. He needed to get out of here. His mind flashed back to his childhood bedroom at Mom and Dad's where he concocted the scheme to abruptly leave and hitchhike out West.

He was overwhelmed with the rush of doing something he hadn't done in a long time... just get up and go! Go! Get out of here! Go into the wilderness, into the night, into the unknown. By yourself? Yes, by yourself! You've always got the one companion who never leaves you, is always there, patiently waiting. She doesn't care if you're drunk, or tripping, or early or late... as long as she is with you. She doesn't complain, doesn't criticize, doesn't whine. Yes, she's been sitting out in the truck for hours now, just waiting for you to come back. That's what I need to do. I need to get up right now and go out West. I need to go to Colorado.

Morgan sloshed his beer and dribbled it down both sides of his mouth. He wiped his face with his sleeve and stumbled out the door to his truck. He was tripping hard now, and too drunk to be driving, but he had to get out of town and ramble on. He opened the door and dragged himself into the driver's seat. Sitting faithfully in the passenger's seat, overjoyed at his return, was his female companion... his blonde German Shepherd, Ralph.

"Ralphie, girl, guess what? We're goin' to Colorado! What do you think about that?"

Pound, pound, pound.

Her tail beat against the seat cushion as she licked his hand and whimpered with glee.

"You know you're just a dog. You're not a human, and you can't talk. You're never gonna talk, even though you think you can talk. Now just get all that out of your head."

Pound, pound, pound.

Morgan pulled out of the parking lot and carefully maneuvered through town. Once he was out on the open road, he lit up a joint, put in a Led Zeppelin tape, and moved the selection to "Ramble On."

He pounded out the beat on the steering wheel, trying to work up the burn he used to get when he was doing something adventurous. It didn't come. It collapsed like an air mattress with a hole in it.

"Why? What's it all for? More money? More kicks? More glory?"

He had already been there and done that. He spent all his chips on adventures gone by, on thrills already experienced. Nothing was new. The brotherhood and the vibes hadn't been around since Woodstock Nation fizzled. Pot dealing had its rewards, but even that was biting him in the rear.

In his drug and alcohol fogged mind, a strange desolation began to creep in. The bottom was dropping out, and Morgan sensed a deepening twang of helplessness. His mood changed, and the high powered, wild man music just didn't cut it.

He ejected Led Zeppelin and slid an Eagles' tape into the eight track. When it got to "Desperado," the opening strains struck a chord in his soul. He sang with it out loud. He didn't just sing it out, he shouted it out, into the night, with all his heart.

"Desperado, why don't you come to your senses...?"

The message of the ballad articulated every struggle, every dilemma, and every philosophy he had lived out, and was now living out. Tears rolled down his cheeks as he rolled through the darkness, playing it over and over and over again.

PART TWO

The Invitation

The rays of the morning sun pierced through the truck window, striking Morgan on his eyelids.

"Oh God, what happened?" He raised himself up in the seat, shielding his eyes, and saw he was in a rest area.

"C'mon, Ralph, let's find out where we are." They got out of the truck and stretched hard. Ralph sniffed the cool morning air and looked up at Dustin, wagging her tail. They walked over to the map of Kentucky. The "you are here" pin put them 25 miles east of Lexington.

"Ah, it's good to be back on the open road..."

The sensation came back of release from whatever was holding him down. His thoughts returned to the hitchhiking days, and it was an amusing irony. After all these years, he still didn't know where he was going, but he knew he was on the right track by simply getting away.

"Sometimes you just have to extract yourself from your situation and see where life takes you," he said to himself. He looked up at the white, cotton ball clouds, then gazed around, mostly to the west. At least this time, he had a truck. And a dog named Ralph.

They spent the next two weeks in Colorado, moving from one campsite to another. Morgan ran into surprisingly few people, so he spent the evenings around his fire, musing about life in general. There was something magical about the air in the Colorado high country. The pines and spruce added a fragrance that went beyond the sense of smell into a lofty feeling of being in the mountains. Maybe this was the point John Denver was trying to make in his song, "Rocky Mountain High." He didn't get any earth shattering revelations or mystical experiences, he just cooked his rainbow trout over the fire and stared up at the stars. Ralph was in dog heaven.

One day, he heard a radio announcement that the Eagles were going to be at the Red Rocks outdoor amphitheater west of Denver.

"What's it all about, Ralphie?" Morgan sang in a mock falsetto voice, trying to imitate Dionne Warwick. Lying down, with her head resting on her two front paws, Ralph raised her eyebrows as if to say, "What now?"

"Can you believe it? If anything can make sense out of life, an Eagles' concert can. C'mon, let's pack 'em up and move 'em out."

About eighty miles from the concert, he stopped at a store to get a chilled bottle of Blue Nun wine and popped a little green pill. From then on, he sipped the wine, listened to his Eagles' tape, and enjoyed the beginning rushes of LSD.

Outside of Red Rocks, the traffic jammed up, waiting in line to enter the parking area. The attendant waved his arm and pointed to the row he wanted him to use. He said goodbye to Ralph and cracked a window to give her some air. Then he locked the truck and started the climb up to the amphitheater.

Half way up the trail, he found a place to take a break. He was trying to achieve the perfect blend between the wine and the acid, thinking it would make the music sound better. He chugged the Blue Nun, determined to finish off the bottle. At this point, it was warm and didn't even taste good, but he forced himself to gulp it down out of principle, or duty, or just plain cussedness.

The concert goer's streamed past him as he sat down again, huffing and puffing from the steady incline. Suddenly, he lurched over and heaved a gush of vomit. He moved away from the crowd and heaved again and again. The onslaught finally subsided, and he was on his hands and knees, in the red dirt, slobber dripping from his mouth.

"Boy, this is glamorous."

"Way to go, buddy," someone yelled out. "Drink much? The party hasn't even started yet." He endured more laughter and scorn. Right now, he was too sick to care.

Within a short time, the stomach spasms went away. His breathing got back to normal, and with a little care, he climbed back up on his feet. He blinked his eyes and took a look around. The awesome display of rock formations, sheer red cliffs and sculpted facades astounded him. The concert area was set in a bowl, surrounded by walls carved by nature with lines of red horizontal strata in a myriad of colors.

As if Red Rocks wasn't magnificent enough, LSD would make all that wiggle and vibrate with kaleidoscopic effects. By now, Morgan's brain should have been generating all manner of patterns, but it wasn't. Fully expecting the usual colors, he squinted his eyes trying to force them into being. He waved his hand back and forth... no trails. Then came the dreadful, shocking conclusion. When he threw up, he threw up everything in his system. He was stone cold sober... he was straight!

The concert was mediocre at best, as if listening to a band without the benefit of psychedelic mental stimulation was an endurance contest. Disgusted that he wasted all that time and money trying to get a buzz, Morgan scuffled down the mountain to his truck and his dog.

"Oh Ralph, this is ridiculous. Talk about worthless... I can't even get high right!" She assured him that *she* loved him by vigorously wagging her tail.

"Yeh, yeh, I know." He stepped into the driver's seat.

"I guess we've worn out our welcome here in Colorado. Time to go back home. To what, I don't know. Do you? C'mon, give me a clue."

Ralph raised her nose for a pet and licked his hand. Morgan rubbed her head and ears and tried to think of something other than just driving straight back to Virginia. The plan was not hard to come by, in fact, he probably knew it all along somewhere deep inside.

There was someone who really did care for him, who would really like to see him. He avoided going there before, because they were from another world, but he knew he would be welcome if he came. It was sort of on the way back, and a few more miles, so now would be a good time to step out of his comfort zone and see what was on the other side.

"OK Ralph, you talked me into it. It's a really good idea, by the way. Good thing I got you with me to keep me straight. We're gonna be like Davy Crockett. 'Y'all can go to hell, we're goin' to Texas.'"

"Do you want another cup of coffee, Dustin?"

Sis leaned against the kitchen counter in her ranch style house in Reno, Texas. To Morgan, it seemed really big and western, with a stone fireplace in the living room and four bedrooms. What was so different was the atmosphere... so straight and devoid of the revelry he was used to. But, one thing about the straightness, it was also peaceful, absent any air of danger, or intimidation, or uncertainty. It was a very comfortable place to have a heart to heart talk with his older sister.

"Sure, that second cup is always a kicker. By the way, you really helped me out with the probation deal in Tucson. You're the reason they didn't send me up the river.

"That was a shock. And, yes, I could not imagine you in jail, so I told them we would do whatever it took to keep them from putting you there. But, Dusty, do you really have to keep on living like this? You know how much I worry about you."

"I know, I know. I don't want you to worry about me either. It's just that I love the adventure of running pot. It gets in your blood. Of course, when they chase you down the alleyway and stick loaded guns into your head, the glitter begins to wear off a little bit."

"I would think so. Do you want to tell me about it?"

"Tell you about it? Are you sure?"

"Yes, I want to know everything. You know we don't get to see each other but once in a blue moon. C'mon, spill it. Girls, drugs, life, long hair, music. Just tell me what's on your heart."

"Have you got any more coffee?"

They did this for the next two days. Got up early in the morning, sent the boys off to school, and cleaned up breakfast. Then, they reloaded the coffee pot and talked and talked. For Morgan, it was like opening a pressure valve in his mind. It was such a relief to just vent.

He explained all his philosophies of life, the hippie ideals, and Woodstock. But he didn't do all the talking. Sis was playing this very wisely, knowing there might be an itty-bitty crack in his facade in which she may be able to plant a seed.

"Dusty, have I ever told you the story about how your brother-in-law and I got saved?"

"No, I've never heard all the gory details."

She rolled her eyes, "They are not gory, I assure you. One day we heard a knock at the door. I opened it up, and a man was standing there who we had never met before, and he said, 'Hello, my name is Eric, and I have good news!'

"We said, 'Welcome stranger. We sure could use some good news right now.' This man we had never met sat down in our living room and said to us,

'God so loved the world that He sent His Son down to earth, Who became a baby, grew up among us, and then went to the cross to die. Now, God's law says the penalty for sin is death, and we have all sinned. So, either we have to die, or someone else has to die in our place. That is called a sacrifice. When God's Son died on that cross, He sacrificed himself for our sins. He died in our place so we could go to heaven. All you have to do is believe Jesus died for your sins and receive Him as your Savior, and you will be able to live with God forever. And besides that, He will put His Holy Spirit in you, Who will give you power to live a godly life, and He will make your life more abundant and full of blessings. Now isn't that Good News?'"

Sis went on, "We looked at each other and knew instantly that was what we wanted, so we asked Eric what we needed to do, and he led us in a prayer to repent, believe in Christ, and ask Him into our hearts, and Boom! We were saved! We've never been the same since."

"Well, I can vouch for that. You guys have definitely been different since you first told me about it."

"So how does that affect you? What do you think about what he said? By the way, that man turned out to be Pastor Eric from the First Presbyterian Church. That's where we go now, obviously. You would really like him."

Morgan juggled many thoughts as if this was a mathematical equation, or a riddle to be solved. He had grown numb to God in recent years, some of his friends proclaiming the Bible was just a book of fairy tales, made up through the ages in an attempt to explain away the mysteries of life. The story of Jesus was fantastic and other worldly, to say the least. He had grown up with it, so it was nothing new, but he had never really believed it like they were now. The other part, that gave him the most trouble, was the part about living a holy life.

"Oh, I don't know, Sis. The way I see it, if I believe in Jesus, I'll have to give up all my fun, pour out my booze, throw away my pot, and say 'aw shucks, and gosh darn it," I'll be honest... I'm not ready to do that right now."

"It's not a matter of you giving it up... God will give you a desire to give it up, and then He will take it away from you when you ask Him."

"Well, that's even worse. I don't want God messing with my mind to get me to stop wanting to do things I want to do right now. If I ask Jesus into my heart, I'm opening myself up to a mental overhaul I never signed up for. No, like I said, I'm happy for you guys, but I'm enjoying life too much now to change things."

"You didn't seem to enjoy the part about going to jail for ten years."

"Touche, you got me. No, that part I don't like, for sure."

"So what are your plans? What do you want to do with your life?"

"Honestly, I don't know. I talked to Dad once about flying. Do you remember when we flew from Albuquerque to New York? I was five years old then, and they let me sit up in the cockpit with the pilots. I never forgot that, and that's the only thing I can say I ever wanted to do. Fly airplanes. Maybe there's something there."

"Yeh, maybe so. Where do you think you'll go from here?"

"Guess I'll go back to Virginia and try to sort things out. I'm pretty much stuck in my routine right now."

"Well Dustin, you don't have to be stuck in anything. I'll offer you the same deal I told the probation officer. If you want a place to stay to make a change, you can come here. But I have to tell you, you've got to come here on our terms. We have your two little nephews to take care of, and we don't want them learning any of your bad habits. So that means no smoking, no drinking, no dealing, and no shenanigans. You have to come to church with us on Sundays at least, and you have to get a job. If you get to the point where you are willing to do that, you are more than welcome. I know the Lord has better plans for your life, little brother."

You Get Tired of Steak

The headlights bounced on the Interstate as the truck sailed through the gentle hills of Tennessee. Ralph was curled up in her usual spot on the passenger's seat, glad to be out on the road. Morgan pondered his direction from here. What about what Sis said? Is there even the smallest inkling to take her up on her offer? She definitely painted a different picture of what life could be like. A viable alternative, so to speak... what about the pot business? What about the glory of being a folk hero in a unique time in history? What about the friends, the parties, the adventure? A week ago, you thought that stuff was futile.

What about Christianity? Is it real? He harkened back to a pot luck supper Sis took him to a couple of nights ago. He felt like a fish out of water, but the church people were really nice, and they seemed genuinely interested in his well-being.

"This is my little brother, Dustin." Sis introduced him with a beaming smile, so happy for him to see what good Christian fellowship was really like.

"Well, hello Dustin, I'm glad to meet ya." A tall, middle-aged Texan grabbed his hand and shook it with a crunching grip. "It's good to have you in the house of the Lord."

"It's good to be here," Dustin replied, shaking the tingles out of his fingers.

No wimpy Christians here, that's for sure. He could throw that excuse out the window. In his short time in Paris, he got a different picture of what the day to day life of a Christian was really like. These Christians were strong and hardworking, tough but gentle, on top of the world. They radiated self-confidence and were absolutely unashamed to be known as believers in Jesus. On the contrary, they were proud of it. It was a portal into another culture... one foreign to him, but not as far away as he thought. Morgan had a good feeling inside that they would be the ones you would want on your side in the middle of a fight. Of course, they were Texans.

Maybe they're not all hypocrites. Maybe it's not a sham. But, the gulf between where he was and where they were was deep and wide. He remembered how he felt, mingling with the gray haired ladies and the straight laced young men, his long hair hanging down over his shoulders. Everybody went out of their way to make him feel welcome, like they never noticed he looked like a cave man. He knew there was a catch somewhere, though. Nobody had to tell him if he became a Christian, all that would have to change. He fully expected to have to cut his hair and change his attire if and when he became one of them.

"I mean, that's just part of the deal," he mumbled to himself.

Up ahead, he saw a large white form on the side of the highway. The closer he got, he made out what seemed to be a big group of people. He slowed down to see men and women and children, hitching a ride. A lot of people helped him when he needed a ride, so it was time to pay it back. From what he could see, this was a strange group, though.

He got out to analyze the situation. There were about fifteen people, all dressed in white robes, the men with long, stringy hair and beards, the women and children looking like the commune types.

"Hey brother, thanks for stopping. God be praised."

A murmur went up from the group, "Yes, praise God, bless the Lord."

"What are you people doing out here? It's the middle of the night!"

"We are Children of God." At the mention of God's Name, they all looked up to the sky and said,

"Bless God, bless God, thank you Father."

"Okay, great. Where are you going?"

"We have a colony up the road a ways. If you can give us a ride, I am sure the Lord will bless you."

"Well, let's see. We can squeeze as many as possible in this camper. Three of you can sit in the front with me. Try not to step on my dog."

"Oh, bless you, brother." They conversed among themselves to work out a plan, and the women and children stepped into the back of the camper. Once they were loaded up, Morgan pulled out onto the Interstate.

Children of God, eh? If the Lord is trying to get my attention, He sure has a strange way of going about it. In the last forty eight hours, I've seen two polar opposites of what Christians should look like. One group wears suits and ties and short hair, the other group looks like Moses. One group is totally straight, content to drink coffee and tea, but I don't know about these guys. He looked over with a mischievous grin.

"You wanna smoke a joint?"

He didn't care so much about getting high as he wanted to see if the holy hippies had really forsaken the world. Surprisingly, they declined. That's interesting... they have some standards, after all. I mean, what's the point of turning religious if you don't have standards?

This brought him back to the church group in Texas. Which one of these groups truly represented what it meant to be a Christian? His answer lay in the effect each group had on him when he met them. When he met the Texas Christians, he knew he was in a company of people who represented something completely different from where he was.

When he met the hippie Christians, he couldn't tell if they were any different until he offered them a joint. He could only imagine what the Texas Christians would have done to him if he offered *them* a joint. Some people might criticize them for having Cadillacs, but be honest, who doesn't want to be rich? That whole "rich is evil" thing is bogus. Wasn't that why he was dealing pot... to get rich? And what about the straight appearance? At least you could tell they were Christians by looking at them.

He couldn't say the same for the Children of God. When he first saw them, he had no idea they were Christians. They looked like refugees from a commune somewhere, like the one he stayed at in Mendocino. It wasn't until they started chanting, "Bless God, praise God," that he knew they were Christians, and then he wasn't so sure. If Christ is supposed to change you, they didn't look changed at all.

"So, what about outward appearance? Is it really meaningless? Aren't you supposed to look like what you are? After all, I'm doing all I can to "say" I'm a lover of adventure, acid and the Revolution through my looks. My long hair and Levi jacket say I'm wild and free. It's not a fashion choice, it's a fashion *statement* to the world, telling them I reject all the norms of the *Establishment*. When you put it that way, it's no wonder people judge outward appearance.

"Now, looking at this group of Christians dressed up as hippies, the only conclusion I get is if I adopt their ideals, I'll look like them. But wait a minute, I already look like them! So what's to change? If I adopt the ideals of the Christians back in Texas, I'll look like them, and they're offering a clear choice of a different life. At least they're portraying an accurate description of the product they're selling. No deceptive advertising, so to speak. No, I think I want my Christians to be Christians, and my hippies, hippies, thank you. That way, I don't get confused."

Two hours later, Morgan pulled off at an exit to get some gas and let out his passengers. He parked on the far side of a large convenience store parking lot and went to the back to open the door. The overcrowded group dressed in white robes climbed out one by one and walked by Morgan with far off smiles on their faces.

"Thank you, brother, bless you." The leader walked past him with his head tilted back, staring up at the stars and mumbling.

"What did you say?" Morgan asked.

"Bless God."

"Yes, Bless God," they all repeated in unison as they walked across the parking lot toward the store. Morgan watched them from behind and shook his head.

Ripley's Believe It or Not says truth is stranger than fiction, but some things are just stranger than truth. After gassing up, he climbed back into his truck, glad to get rid of his unconventional troupe. They were nice people and all, but weirdness was just not comfortable to be around. Ralph was already back in her spot, curled up in the passenger's seat, gazing up at him with a look of contempt, like she didn't know why she had to give up her seat in the first place.

"OK, Ralphie, what did you think of that?" Ralph raised one eyebrow and gives two wags.

"Yeh, me too." Dustin chuckled, "Pretty strange. I think it's time to go home. Maybe we can get back to normal for a while. Whatever normal is."

That next weekend, Morgan was back in the Bar on Main Street, sitting at the same table he was at three weeks ago when he stumbled out the door to go to Colorado. It was no use. He couldn't make sense out of anything he discovered on his pilgrimage. Deep down in his heart, he knew his sister was right, but the thought of turning straight was repugnant to him... he just couldn't swallow it at all.

When he visualized himself with his hair trimmed around his ears, wearing collared plaid shirts and wing tips, he physically shuddered. His brother-in-law had explained to him very clearly that he didn't need to do these things to become a Christian, but as a Christian he would want to change. He understood all that, but he looked at the final product... it didn't matter how it happened, it just happened.

Not changing, if he became a Christian, wasn't an option either. It made no sense to give up sex, drugs and rock and roll while still looking like you were doing sex, drugs and rock and roll. He believed in truth and honesty, and that to him would be a great farce, not to mention a huge contradiction of being someone on the inside you didn't look like on the outside.

Morgan quickly slipped back into a continuous stupor of running around, doing nothing all day, and drinking the night away. It wasn't long before he got bored and disillusioned. Is this all there is to it? Is this what life is all about... the end game? Getting to the point where you don't have to work so you can eat in nice restaurants, drink champagne, get high, and have steak and eggs for breakfast?

When he left Woodstock, he had an obsession to escape the beans and rice syndrome of handouts and communal living. So, after a successful run, he would have a Victory Dinner to celebrate everything about his lifestyle... the risks, the daring, the rewards and the glory. But after a while, he got an unexpected revelation.

"No matter how good something is, if I do it enough, it becomes monotonous. No more electricity, no more wild fever, just old, out of control routine." The inevitable conclusion hit him.

"You get tired of steak."

The words of "Desperado" visited his mind many times. He knew the things that were pleasing him could hurt him somehow. He was not accomplishing anything... just spinning his wheels. A nagging feeling told him he wasn't staying even, either. Danger was lurking out there, somewhere, inevitable, ready to strike the moment he least expected it. He was actually losing ground, going backwards instead of forwards, and he'd better do something about it.

He filled out the probation form and took a walk to the post office box across the street. After dropping in the report that secured his freedom for one more month, he slid into the pay phone booth.

"Mr. Rombach, this is Dustin Morgan calling from Virginia."

"Well hello, Dustin, how are things up your way?"

"OK, I guess. Just checking in."

"Have you got a job yet?"

"No, not a full time one. It's hard to find a job around here."

"Well, you better find something soon, Dustin. I can't let you go unemployed forever, and I would hate to have to bring you back here."

"Yeh, I would too. Listen, what would happen if I moved out to Texas with my sister? Is that all right with you?"

"I think that would be an excellent idea. I don't think the environment you're in is doing you any good. We could postpone the work requirement for a couple of months for you to get settled, but you would still have to enroll in school or get a job eventually."

"Yeh, I know, but you said you could put off the job thing for a little while?"

"A little while, Dustin. But only for a little while."

"That's all I need to know."

Dustin walked back into the air conditioned Bar and ordered another Michelob. He had one more reprieve from work, but his time was running out. The afternoon wore on, he shot a little pool and played some pinball, whiling away the day with meaningless diversions. By dinner time, he was already lit.

117 Main Street was packed, and the band was cranked up so loud you couldn't hear the person next to you. A cloud of smoke hung in the air with heads bobbing to the beat and billiard balls breaking in the back. Morgan milled around, talking to friends and scanning the crowd. It used to give him a great sense of satisfaction that this place had become the hub of a thriving hip community here in his own town. But his lack of purpose nagged him, weighing hard...

He couldn't escape the significance of what the probation officer said, that it was only a matter of time before he would have to face reality and get a job. His future was staring him in the face, and he had to make some decisions. If he made the wrong ones, things could get mighty ugly. The chapter was coming to a close when he could eternally squander his days, floating along in that big inner tube on the endless river.

Virginia had always seemed better to him than Texas, but now a sense of dread filled him with the certainty that if he stayed in Virginia, he would either die or go to jail. This tilted the odds dramatically to the point where Texas actually seemed like the better choice. Indeed, if he took his intuitions to heart, it was the only choice.

He walked over to the bartender and changed out a five dollar bill. He plunked his quarters into the pay phone around the corner, by the bathrooms. The one the cops should have tapped.

The phone in the kitchen of the ranch style house in Paris, Texas, rang two times. Sis picked it up and said, "Hello." Out of the receiver came a loud, horrendous noise that she deciphered to be rock music and people shouting. Again, she said,

"Hello? Who is this?"

His voice was muffled, barely audible. "Hey Sis, it's me, Dustin, can you hear me?"

"Dustin, is that you? What are you doing? Is anything wrong? Where are you?"

"No, nothing's wrong. I'm in the Bar. I'm just calling to see if your offer is still good for me to come out there."

"You want to come out here? Now?" She almost choked. "And you're calling me from a bar? It doesn't sound like you're quite ready to come out here."

"Oh, I'm ready all right. I'm more than ready. Don't worry, I'll be good."

"When do you think you'll get here?"

"I'll be leavin' in the morning. It'll take two days. I should be good and dried out by then."

"I hope so, Dusty. You know the rules."

"Yeh, I know the rules. So it's OK?"

"Yes, little brother, it's OK. Be careful."

Sis hung up from the phone call she had been praying for since the probation officer called three years ago. She turned to her husband and said,

"Honey, guess what? Dustin is going to take us up on our offer. He's coming to live with us. What do you think about that?"

Morgan's brother-in-law dropped his paper and raised his eyes to meet hers.

"All I gotta say is, if he gets out of line, or if he messes with our family, I'll break every bone in his body."

Salvation

Pastor Eric followed through with a powerful drive off the first tee. Since Dustin had played the game in high school, the Pastor saw this as a good way to break the ice. Eric was a strong, stout Scotsman with a quick wit and a zeal for excellence that included his golf game... he had a handicap of three.

"So, Dusty lad, I hear you're goin' to give Jesus a try, eh?"

"Well, I don't know about that. I guess that's part of the bargain for coming out here. Maybe if I sit through enough of your sermons, some of it will rub off on me."

"Believe me, boy, if God wants to rub off on you, He's gonna rub off. You can count on that. Y'know, I was a pretty unlikely candidate for Jesus, just like you."

"Oh really? You look pretty straight and narrow to me."

"Oh no, laddie. I grew up in the back alleys of New York. I was a fighter and a brawler, you might say. My family wasn't Christian, either. We all had to grow up in the streets... it was hard."

"What kind of fighting? Gang fights?"

"Well, that was part of it, but I did some boxin', too. Golden Gloves and all that."

"So you're a street fightin' pastor."

Morgan grinned... he was starting to like this guy.

"Well now, Dusty, I said that's what I used to be. I had a lot of bitterness bottled up inside that I had to get rid of, you see. I'm not out to beat up the world anymore. One thing I can tell ya, if you have any bitterness, you better get rid of it. Give it to Jesus, or it will rot you from the inside out."

"That's not really a problem with me... I'm a pretty upbeat guy. I try to get along with everybody. My problem is, I don't want to give up anything. I'm having too much fun to want to change."

"So yours is revelry and carousing, eh? Well, everybody's got their own burden to bear, so to speak... their own inner struggles, and no two people are the same. But, we all need Jesus. One night I came home from a revival meeting and said, 'Dad, guess what? I just got saved... I'm going to follow Jesus.' He said to me, 'Well, son, if you're going to do it, make sure you do it with all your heart.' I never forgot that, and I don't regret a minute of it."

"You know, the problem is, I always used to think Christians were weak and wimpy. Every one of them talks with such a soft, sing-songy voice I can hardly stand it. They're trying to be so nice and all. Sometimes I just want to punch 'em in the mouth."

Pastor Eric, the street fighter, cocked his head back and roared.

"Oh laddie, you better watch out for those Christians, now. You're liable to get more than you bargained for."

He had that look of total self-confidence Morgan had seen in so many of these Texas Christians... not an ounce of fear, in complete command of the situation. Morgan wished he had that much courage and boldness. He could imagine what Pastor Eric would have done with that crowd of rednecks in Hardee's. He wouldn't have had to swing a punch. One look from him, and they would have backed off, and before you knew it, he'd be preaching Jesus to the whole drunken bunch.

Two more golfers teamed up with them to make a foursome for the rest of the course. As they played from hole to hole, the other two carried on a salty conversation, laced with profanity and racy talk. Morgan knew better than to cuss around a pastor, but Eric didn't let on about his vocation. His golf game spoke for itself, and the foul-mouthed partners were impressed by his skill. On the eleventh tee, Eric sent a beautiful drive down the par four fairway. The ball rose slightly and hooked faintly to the left, rolling to a stop over 250 yards away.

"Damn. That's a hell of a drive, Eric," the tallest golfer exclaimed. "By the way, what did you say you do?"

Pastor Eric slid his driver into his bag, turned to them with a wide grin and a twinkle in his eye and said,

"I thought you'd never ask."

The next Sunday, Morgan's brother-in-law introduced him to one of the elders in the church.

"Dustin, you need to go down to the admissions office at the community college and sign up for my class. I teach a Continuing Ed course on Building Construction that will help you get a job. If you stay with it for the whole semester, I can take you from basic framing all the way through finishing out a house."

Morgan hesitated, mainly because the end game was one more construction job, but he knew he had to do something. He put it off as long as he could, then dragged himself into the Junior College admissions office.

"I'm sorry, sir, but that class is filled. You won't be able to take it again until next spring."

"It's full? Well, ain't that a shame."

At first, he was overjoyed that he cheated work one more time. But then, driving around town, he had a pep talk with himself,

"What am I thinking? I have to do this. If I'm going to do anything, I need to get some training, and I'll actually come out of this class with some skills. I won't have to haul lumber anymore, I'll be the one doing the building. But just when I'm ready to bite the bullet and sign up for the class, it's full. There's gotta be a way."

He thought back to Sunday's sermon. "Pastor Eric has been talking a lot about prayer lately. I wonder if this would be a good time to try Jesus and see if He's really there."

Still driving around, Dustin spoke out loud into the air,

"Jesus, here I am, talking to You. If You're really there, I need something. I ask You to make a way for me to get in this Building Construction class. If You do, I'll believe You did it, and I'll switch over to Your side." Now let's see what happens.

After running some errands, Morgan pulled up to Sis's house and walked in the back door.

"Hey, Dusty, I just got a call for you from the College."

"What? What do they want?"

"It was the girl from the admissions office. She said one of the students cancelled that class, and if you still wanted it, she had an opening."

Morgan couldn't believe it. Was this just a coincidence? Should he tell Sis about his prayer? No way... if he did, he would never hear the end of it. What about his deal with God? Was it time to pay up? No, it couldn't be. Better keep this quiet.

The whole family talked to Jesus and about Jesus all the time, as if He was a real person, living in the air all around them. This was a different attitude towards God than what he grew up with. He had always gone to church on Sunday with his parents, but during the rest of the week, Jesus was not in the picture. Mom and Dad were moral, ethical, hardworking people, but they didn't talk to God on a regular basis. They didn't act like there was someone else in the room, so Morgan had no reason to think there was such a thing as a living Jesus watching over them.

Now, this new reality was being forced upon him. Not harshly, or menacingly, but by default. This was how his sister and brother-in-law saw it, this was how everybody in the church saw it... "On Christ the Solid Rock I Stand." He was even getting used to the old hymns. He didn't mind, everybody was extremely nice, and he was making friends in another world from those he had back in Virginia. It's just that everything was so, well... so straight.

The effects of drying out began to make themselves known. The construction crew started work at 7:00 AM, and that meant 5:30 AM wake up. This time, it was hard, but it wasn't torture. The more he did it, the more he got used to it. On the job, he carried lumber, cut rafters, walked plate lines, and generally got back into shape. These were tough, country Texans and they teased him mercilessly. Even the hippie on the crew was someone you didn't want to mess with.

One day, Sis brought up the big question again,

"Dusty, what do you want to do with your life? I would really hate to see you waste what God has given you. Just let yourself go and dream about something you never thought was possible."

Morgan visualized a jet airliner. "All I can think of is flying."

"Is that what you really want to do?"

"Let's put it this way. If somebody gave me the chance, I would jump on it in a heartbeat."

"Dustin, with God everything is possible. If the Lord wants you to fly airplanes, by golly, you're gonna fly airplanes! Just imagine, in a few short years, you could be sitting in the cockpit of a 727!"

The reality of the image filled him with a rush of joy, painting a broad smile on his face. "I've never allowed myself to think that far. That's incredible. Do you really think God would do that for me?"

"Of course, Dustin. He'll do it if you let Him. He'll walk by your side, if you walk by His side. So, let's get on with it! We know someone at church who used to be in the Air Force. He can point you in the right direction."

Dustin was suddenly overwhelmed by the possibility of such goodness. "It seems your church is full of good contacts."

"The Lord makes a way, brother, the Lord makes a way."

He was starting to believe her.

Now that he was firing on all cylinders, he quickly completed the Private Pilot ground school course with a home study program. Dad helped him buy a used Cessna 150 two-seater plane for the price of a used truck. He parked it at a small grass strip outside of town, and learned how to maneuver in every conceivable takeoff or landing situation. Crosswinds, soft field procedures, short field procedures, short and soft field procedures.

There was an old hay shed near the approach end of the strip, so whenever the wind came from that direction, it would swirl around the barn and cause waves of turbulence and wind shifts right at touchdown. He mastered them all, and by the time he passed his Private Pilot flight test, he could take off and land anywhere. The next step would be professional flight school.

A Process of Faith

Matthew, Mark, Luke and John. Morgan finally forced himself to read the Bible, starting in the New Testament. He became intrigued with how Jesus could read people's minds. Numerous times, the text would say, "knowing their thoughts, Jesus said such and so." How could He know their thoughts? You can rig outside things like sickness, or happenings, but thoughts? They're invisible. No ordinary man can reach inside and play with your thoughts.

The more he read, the more he wanted to know if what he was reading was actual history or a collection of made up stories. When he got to the book of John, the claims about the divinity of Jesus seemed preposterous. He was there at the creation... all things were made through Him... He came down from heaven as the Son of God and could give eternal life. Either all this was true, or He was the greatest con-artist who ever lived.

Coincidentally, the next Sunday, Pastor Eric preached on it in church. He uttered Morgan's thoughts straight from the pulpit,

"Either He is who He says He is, or this is the greatest hoax in history!" He went on to prove from the Bible that it was all true.

Later that week, Morgan kept reading in John when the idea dropped in him about the Roman Empire. He always had a fascination with the ancient Greeks and Romans. He was awed by their power and the level of civilization they had achieved in the ancient world. He loved the Roman movies that came out when he was young. Most of them were about Jesus, but he was enthralled by the Romans legions. Now, a strange chain of logic began to link together.

"How come no one ever questions whether the Roman Empire ever existed? You never hear anyone say, 'Oh, the Roman Empire is just a myth, it never existed, it was just a fairy tale people made up to explain away history'. That would be ridiculous. But why are people certain it did exist? Well, there's pottery, and inscriptions, and ruins. That may explain the civilization, but what about individuals? What about Julius Caesar? Does anybody have his hairbrush, or his toga? I guess there's a sculpture of him somewhere, but the reason people believe Julius Caesar existed is because someone who lived when he did wrote about him in a document that was passed down from century to century, saying he existed.

"Here I am, reading a copy of the Bible that is a document passed down from that same era, written by people saying Jesus existed. How many copies of the Bible are there? Don't they say it's the world's best seller? Add up all the Bibles that have been printed since the time of Christ, and you have the most documented Man in history! Based on sheer evidence alone, if I believe Julius Caesar walked the earth, I've gotta believe Jesus walked the earth."

This was a major turning point. He was now convinced the historical Jesus was a real person, and the accounts of Him in the Bible were accurate. That left one part unresolved. Did He really rise from the dead? He had been listening to enough sermons to know this was the turning point of the whole argument. It was a surreal fantasy to believe that Jesus came back to life after having been killed all the way.

All the way was important, because doubters claimed He really was not dead. But if He was all the way dead, like everybody else who dies, and then woke up and started walking around again... Whew! That's crazy! Who believes that? Do all those prim and proper Christians believe that? That's like something they ought to tie you up for and call in the men in white suits.

As much as he marveled at the far-fetched notion that Jesus really came back to life and rose up into heaven, he knew a spark was smoldering inside his heart. Once he had it settled that Jesus lived on this earth, the next step of believing He was sent by God began to take hold. More sermons from Pastor Eric, and more mingling with the salt of the earth Christians began to pound it in bit by bit. He went with some church people to a week-long seminar on Basic Life Principles, and during one of the breaks, a young man his age walked up to him out of ten thousand people.

"Do you know Jesus as your personal Lord and Savior?"

"Uh, I don't think so."

"The Lord told me to come over and tell you something. He wants you to know Romans 10, nine and ten. It says, *'if you confess with your mouth the Lord Jesus and believe in your heart that God has raised Him from the dead, you will be saved. For with the heart one believes unto righteousness, and with the mouth confession is made unto salvation.'* I'll be praying for you."

He turned and disappeared into the crowd.

A few more weeks went by, and the struggle intensified. Morgan was not without other voices, whispering in his ear. All day long, the carpentry crew listened to outlaw country on WBAP, 820 AM. The fun-loving music of Waylon & Willie, Hank Jr. and David Allen Coe had replaced the far out strains of acid rock. The uncontrolled wails of Jimi Hendrix had been exchanged for the beautiful twangs of a pedal steel guitar. The country western sound was rowdy and down to earth, fanning the flames of having a "good time."

The conflict was becoming intense, and Sis plainly saw the fight as a spiritual battle. She knew the Holy Spirit was wooing him one way, and the devil was tempting him the other way, even though Dustin refused to believe he was being man-handled by spirits.

One glorious evening, though, God broke through. The family was sitting around having evening prayers, and Sis asked Dustin if he would like to confess Christ for his life. Finally, he knew he had no reason not to. He believed in Jesus, he was pretty sure that He was who He said He was, and that He did indeed rise from the dead. Knowing all this, it would be dishonest to say, "Yes, I believe Jesus rose from the dead, but I'm not going to say it out loud." If he knew it inside, but refused to say it outside, wouldn't that make him a liar, a hypocrite... the very thing he used to accuse Christians of being? He couldn't live with that, so he said,

"Fine, let's do it."

"Oh Dustin, Praise the Lord. Here, let's all gather around. Now, is there any particular Scripture you would like to use?"

"Well, that verse the guy from the Seminar gave me would be a good one. He said God gave it to him to give to me."

"What one was that, again?"

"Romans 10:9 and 10."

"That's right. That is going to be *your* verse. OK, I'm going to lead you in a prayer, and all you have to do is repeat after me. Is that all right?"

"Sure, Sis, go ahead."

Sis, his brother-in-law, and his two nephews knelt around Dustin, and she began to pray,

"Dear Father, we lift up to You, Your precious child, Dustin. Lord, You know the struggles he's been having and his need for a Savior, Your Son, Jesus Christ. Now Lord, we ask that you fulfill Your Word in Dustin and give Him Your eternal life as he confesses Jesus before You.

"Now Dustin, repeat after me... Father, I repent of my sins."

"Father, I repent of my sins."

"I ask You to forgive me."

"I ask You to forgive me."

"I confess with my mouth the Lord Jesus."

"I confess with my mouth the Lord Jesus."

"And I believe in my heart that You raised Him from the dead."

"And I believe in my heart that You raised Him from the dead."

"Father, please save me."

"Father, please save me."

"I ask You to come into my heart."

"I ask You to come into my heart."

"Thank You, Jesus."

"Thank You, Jesus."

Sis lifted her head and looked Dustin in the eyes... tears streaming down her face as she broke into a wide smile. She threw both arms around his neck, sobbing and laughing at the same time. The rest of the family closed in, hugging him and patting him on the back.

"Oh Dusty, you did it, you did it." She stood back, and took another look. Her eyes opened wide with a jolt of astonishment as she saw the Holy Spirit descending on him. She turned and embraced her husband and two sons.

"Oh, dear Lord, it happened, it happened!! We have to call Mom and Dad. Oh dear Jesus, Praise You, Lord."

Morgan was still sitting there, wondering what to make of it all. His sister was ecstatic, so full of joy she was almost incoherent. His natural inclination was to expect some kind of high, or rush, or something physical. He did feel elevated, however, maybe even a little light-hearted... but no matter how hard he tried, he was just not as excited about getting saved as everybody else was.

He didn't want to let anybody down though, least of all his sister and brother-in-law who had put up with so much to get him to this point. So, he went along with the formalities of telling Mom and Dad he got saved, and answering everybody's questions at church. He said the prayer because he believed it, and it was an inescapable truth he needed to acknowledge, but in spite of all this, he hated to admit it... he was almost glad to get it over with.

From that point on, everybody expected the change to come over Dustin he had been trying to avoid. The sad truth was, he still didn't want to change. He did feel a new camaraderie with the people at church, though, because yes, they really did believe that Jesus was God's Son, and that He died all the way and rose again from the dead. Now he believed that too, and that made him part of a new fraternity. He was one of them, by a shared faith, even though he wasn't ready to drop everything and live like them. He had moved a great distance from where he used to be, but now he was stuck in the middle.

The day after his Private Pilot check ride, Ralph climbed up in the passenger's seat of the old Cessna 150. Morgan threw his backpack in the rear compartment, and they took off from Paris, Texas. Eight hours later, he flared over the runway in his old stompin' grounds, Blacksburg, Virginia. He had plans to go to flight school in Florida, but he felt the need to see his old friends one last time. He had to know if anything had changed.

"Ohhhhhh, rockin' down the highway..." The fast, driving beat of the Doobie Brothers' tune gave him a charge of electricity, making his heart pound violently. The bass guitar kept coming back to the same note, pounding the song in him like a hammer. The sensations were amplified considerably by the marijuana in his brain. This was

the first joint he had smoked in nine months, and it felt like a brand new high.

But it wasn't the same. Before he got back, word had gone out that Morgan found religion, and people were now asking him about it everywhere he went. In the Bar, at parties, sitting around in circles smoking dope. He tried to blend in, but he was totally out of place... it was obvious to everybody he was a different person.

Just the other day, he was in the Bar getting a sandwich, looking around at the familiar surroundings. This was his home, his hideout. It was here that he felt the camaraderie, the victory, the honor of being one of the elite. He felt as much of a bond with the Bar as the people in it. How could nine months away make him feel like such a stranger? And if he didn't belong here anymore, where did he belong?

An old acquaintance sauntered up, beer in hand, and scrutinized him with scoffing eyeballs. Tom was a philosopher, one of the "intelligencia" who knew the real truth. They used to share the same views, but this time, he laughed at Morgan with dripping sarcasm,

"So... tell me about Jesus."

The ridicule was a stunning blow. He was being mocked in his own Bar! In a vain attempt to salvage his dignity, he denied it vehemently.

"Rumors! Rumors! Where do people get all these rumors? I am not a Jesus Freak!"

Now, riding in the back of a car full of well-meaning friends, who had just sent him out to space with a joint of Jamaican buds, his heart was racing with the high speed rock, his mind rolling along a mile a minute. A voice cut through clear as a bell.

"So you're going to deny Me? You know you just denied Christ in front of your friends."

The voice was inescapable, he knew Who it was. He knew from reading his Bible that if anyone denied Christ before men, He would deny them before the Father. But he didn't want to tell them about Jesus. He didn't want to be an ambassador of Christ sent from Texas. He just wanted to go back to where he was and have fun without a guilty conscience.

"Yeh, yeh, I know, I know," he muttered to himself. He tried to block the voice out of his mind. He shook his head, trying to throw off the pesky Spirit.

"Hey Morg, what's the matter? You OK? You got a funny look on your face. Who are you talkin' to?"

"Huh? Nobody. Yeh, I'm fine. The Doobie Brothers sure sound good. You've got a great system."

"Yeh, I just put it in. It really rocks, don't it?"

Morgan rested his head on the seat back and closed his eyes. He knew he was trapped.

"Oh boy, what have you done to yourself now?"

If it was answers he wanted from his short trip to Blacksburg, he got them. Not the ones he wanted, but it was pretty obvious he could not stay in the past. Sitting in the confined cockpit of his Cessna 150, he yelled, "Clear!" and fired up the engine. He ran his hand over the instrument panel and set his altimeter. A great comfort filled him, now realizing that his vertical speed indicator and directional gyro were his new best friends.

He sat back and grabbed the yoke, feeling the vibration of the engine...

"This is home now. This is where I belong."

Jamaica

The one-bedroom efficiency was advertised as a "bachelor's delight." It had three rooms... a living room, a kitchen, and a bathroom. It was the end of August, and the small apartment in tropical Florida had no air conditioning. Morgan didn't mind, though. He was on his own once again. This time was different, however... he was there for one purpose only, to get all the advanced certificates and ratings he needed to start a career in aviation.

For once in his life, he had no one to answer to as far as peer pressure went. In this town, His life was an empty canvas, and he could paint it however he wanted it to be. He cut his hair for flight school, and he looked about as normal as you could get, so now he had a choice. Would he be Mr. Straight Guy or Mr. Party Guy?

In Blacksburg, he left behind a character embellished with years of notoriety. But here, everyone related to him according to his new persona... a flight student nerd with the social appeal of a possum. Even though he met a group of locals who took him in, he seemed invisible to pretty girls. Dustin accepted his lowly position as a byproduct of starting all over in a new area, but he wondered, "Will I ever get it back? *Should* I ever get it back?"

After getting the keys to his apartment, he walked three blocks to the nearby 7 – Eleven. He came back and unpacked the supplies from his maiden shopping run. The issue was settled with the first thing he put in his small refrigerator... a six pack of Budweiser beer.

A year later, Dustin passed his Instrument Flight Instructor exam, which would certify him for his first flying job. When he autographed Dustin's logbook, the Federal Examiner said,

"You fly a good airplane, Mr. Morgan. You seem to have the natural intuition it takes to make a good Instrument Instructor."

Encouraged by this vote of confidence, Dustin launched his career, taking on students and charters to the Bahamas. However, he had also set a course that would dismantle everything he gained in Texas. He wanted so badly to have things like they used to be, he thought he could bludgeon his spiritual resistance into submission by cramming beer and pot into his system. He was determined to desensitize himself against the checks and balances the Holy Spirit was putting up, but every step he took was like a pick axe to a stone wall, letting the world leak in. Then came his first real test.

Joe Rossi strolled into the office of the fixed base operator at the local airport. He was a little high strung, wearing a polo shirt, Top-Sider boat shoes, and a silver ring with a skull and crossbones. Although he looked like your average, tropical businessman, his charming smile belied the sinister nature of his mission.

After being discharged from the Marines, he set up an operation in Jamaica, specifically designed to smuggle marijuana to the United States. His decision to enter the business was based on a simple matter of economics. He compared the selling price against the cost and overhead, and knew that no other enterprise could give him that kind of profit margin.

Like so many others who came to this conclusion, the fear of getting caught was not an issue. It was a caution, to be sure, but he felt like he was immune from capture. It just added to the game of "catch me if you can." After all, he was a Marine, trained in tactical combat. He gloried in the planning, the reconnaissance, the deception, and he was absolutely sure he would win. So far, he was right.

Joe had spent years building his flourishing smuggling business. He bought land in Jamaica and converted it to a pig farm as a front for his trade. From the vantage point of a local farmer, he could secure all the contacts he would need. He knew who grew it, who handled it, and who could deliver it to a secluded loading point.

Until now, Joe's mode of operation was to use a sailboat. As he got more successful, he acquired a residence in Grand Cayman, where he spent most of his time. He paid his local foreman, Carl, to oversee the pig farm while he was gone, and to supervise the ground crew when they were moving a load.

During normal life, Joe kept his boat docked in Grand Cayman or in one of the marinas in Montego Bay. When it was time to fill it up with bales, he would coordinate a rendezvous off the north coast of Jamaica, and Carl's crew would quickly load them from shore. From that point on, it was Joe's job to navigate the high seas, through wind and rain and peril of night, and bring the load safely into one of the many inlets that dotted the Florida coast.

But after a couple of close calls, Joe got tired of the boat smuggling routine. He was weary of the long, monotonous voyage and worn out battling the stormy Atlantic. The obvious solution was to use an airplane, but how would he do that? It took a lot more to turn himself into a pilot than to become an amateur sea captain. He had to meet someone he could persuade to fly a load, and the only way to do that was to take some flying lessons.

He signed up with various flight instructors at airports in South Florida, but they all seemed too straight-laced. He had to be careful who he approached and how he approached them. He was getting discouraged that he would never meet anyone who would want to risk their flying career to bring back a load of funny freight. That is, until he walked into this little charter and flight instruction outfit in Vero Beach.

"Yes sir, how can I help you?" The perky brunette dispatcher greeted Joe.

He looked around the office of the small fixed based operator, or FBO. The dispatcher's desk, pilot supplies counter, and pilot lounge were all positioned in one big room. On one side, the lounge consisted of a couch and two love seats, arrayed in a horseshoe shape around a small TV set. A coffee table sat in the middle, with neatly arranged aviation magazines stacked on the shelf underneath. On the other side, a long, rectangular glass case held Ray-Ban sunglasses, aviation maps, log books, and a couple of ties with airplanes on them. Overhead was a wooden propeller with a clock in the middle. You could hear the crackle of tower and ground control coming over the radio by the back wall. Joe answered,

"I saw your ad for the solo special. What's that all about?"

"That is our current promotion for people like yourself who have always wanted to fly, but have never given it a try. It is $495, and for that you get ten hours of dual flight instruction that should result in your first solo flight. The instructor will then endorse your log book, and you will be on your way to your Private Pilot Certificate! By the way, the log book is included."

"Sounds good to me, sign me up." Joe pulled out five one hundred dollar bills and handed them to the girl behind the counter.

"Very well, sir. Let me get your change and a receipt." She handed him a five dollar bill and a logbook. "When would you like to start?"

"As soon as possible."

"All right. Our instructor is flying right now, but he should be back in an hour or so. Let me check the calendar. It looks like tomorrow morning will be your first flight. You can meet him this afternoon if you like, and you can get some of the preliminaries out of the way."

"OK, tomorrow morning will be fine. I'll wait for him."

"Good, good. I am sure you will like him... His name is Dustin Morgan."

A collage of aeronautical charts covered the entire wall of the briefing room. By connecting the maps of smaller sectors together, the company had created a huge aviation map showing the entire southeastern United States, the Bahama chain, Cuba, Haiti and Jamaica. This created a big picture which greatly enhanced flight planning for long distances to the islands.

Dustin used this room for pre and post flight briefings. The company had already moved him up to charter work, getting the occasional flight to one of the Bahama destinations, such as Freeport,

Bimini or Nassau. After he got his multi-engine rating, the opportunities increased, with charters and corporate customers to every imaginable island and cay in the chain. It was not long before he became an expert on the Bahamas, which would come in very handy, very soon.

After eight flying lessons, Joe and Morgan were beginning to open up to each other. They went out for drinks a time or two, and even though Joe hadn't said anything about being a boat smuggler from Jamaica, Morgan had spilled the beans about Tucson.

Joe couldn't believe his luck. Once he learned Dustin was a veteran dope runner trying to be good, he knew he had his man. He slipped in a reference to Jamaica here and there, until he felt like the time was right.

"So, have you ever thought about flying any dope?"

"To tell you the truth, I actually vowed not to use my flying to fly drugs." Joe's heart dropped. "But I have to admit, the thought is tempting." Joe's heart came back up again.

Back in the planning room, Joe walked up to the map board and scanned his hand over the middle of Jamaica, intently looking for landmarks. He pointed to a valley.

"I've been trying to put together a run out of Jamaica. I have access to two strips. One is here, and the other is," he moved his hand over a few inches to another valley, "right here."

He turned toward Morgan, trying to gauge his response, then made his pitch. "I'll pay you ten thousand dollars to fly it back with me."

Dustin shot back, "You'll have to pay me a lot more than ten grand to get me to do it."

Joe knew he'd been had. He lowballed Morgan to see how green he was. Well, that didn't work. "OK, what's your idea?"

"I think we should split the load, since we both have the same chance of dyin'."

A cheapskate at heart, Joe winced. However, now he knew Morgan's true colors. He'd just shown he'd done this before, and that could come in handy.

"Well, after hearing your stories, I know you can handle it. I can work with you on the price. It's just a matter of whether you want to go for it or not. Do you think a Cherokee Six will hold three hundred pounds?"

Dustin had absentmindedly slipped back into dealing mode. "Oh yeh, easy."

Voices from all directions immediately invaded his mind.

"Wait a minute! What are you doing? Planning out a load from Jamaica in an airplane when you said you would never do that? Stay the course! Stay the course!"

"How much did he say? Three hundred pounds? You would get one hundred and fifty pounds at $250 a pound... That would instantly put you back on top. Shoot, most pilots wouldn't even know what to do with that much pot, but you don't have that problem. One call to Virginia and, BAM! Done.

"And another thing... all the girls think of you as a goofy flight instructor. And all flight instructors look like used car salesmen. Cocky, full of themselves, straight goons. You know that's what you look like. No wonder you can't get any chicks. You know this, too. If you come back as a doper pilot with $30,000, you'll be an outlaw, and you won't have that problem anymore. Remember, ladies love outlaws."

What he couldn't see was that he was a player in a timeless spiritual battle. His will was leashed to two long reins going up into the heavens. On one rein, Legion pulled with promises of pleasure and glory. On the other, the Holy Spirit pulled with exhortations to be loyal to Jesus.

Right now, the bad side was winning. One last voice pleaded in the background, fading away, "No, Dustin, No! Don't do it!"

He gazed at the spot in Jamaica where Joe had his finger.

"I don't know, Joe, I'll have to think about that one. I'm sure we'll talk about it some more."

The tug of adventure played on his strings, and he knew he wasn't putting up much of a fight. He did his best to hold out, but he was collapsing like a house of cards.

The Way Love Goes

"Morgan, you gotta get over here, haw, haw, haw!!"

Chuck was in his usual form, half blasted in the middle of the afternoon. Morgan was at the airport office, finishing up paperwork.

"OK Chuck, calm down. What are you talking about?"

Morgan went along with Chuck like a necessary evil. He was one of the friendliest people he'd ever met, and Dustin didn't have many friends in Vero Beach. But Chuck was not one of his kind. He was in his forties, not a hippie in any sense of the word, and he had one very obvious problem. He was a full blown alcoholic.

"There's hot chicks running around here everywhere!"

"Is that so?" Morgan was skeptical. "So what do you want me to do?"

"I said, 'get your ass over here.' I got you lined up with a hot date. You gotta see her."

"All right, all right, I'm comin'."

Morgan pulled up to the beachside duplex, and Chuck opened the door, a big grin plastered on his face.

"C'mon in here. You're gonna like this. I met Mom last night, and she has a beautiful daughter. Now, just sit down here on this couch, and I'll be right back."

A few minutes later, he walked a cute, young, brown-haired girl out to meet him. He tried to put her at ease.

"Now don't be nervous. This is my friend, Morgan. You're gonna like him, I promise. After all, he is a pilot."

She stood before him with obvious contempt.

"Here she is, Morg, haw, haw. What'd I tell ya? Ain't she gorgeous? This is Lisa."

Neither one of them knew just how to act. Morgan's eyes bugged out as he looked her over, and she was disgusted that she was now on display. But they both knew they had been put in an awkward position, so they said, "Hi," and agreed to go along with Chuck's plan.

The rest of that afternoon, Chuck cajoled Morgan into stopping at every bar they passed to get a drink. He talked non-stop, like he had to entertain everybody all the time. Hunched over his fourth martini, Chuck raised his head and turned toward Dustin.

"Hey Morg, ya know what I'd rather have?" His eyes were glazed over with a mischievous twinkle.

"No Chuck, tell me, what would you rather have?"

"I'd rather have a bottle in front of me than a frontal lobotomy, haw, haw, haw!"

Lisa rolled her eyes. They went to a steakhouse for dinner and drank some more. By this time, Dustin was totally sloshed and put on a terrible show. He was wearing a Levi jacket over a white T-shirt. Lisa tried to humor him by making a bow tie out of a napkin and pinning it to his undershirt with a toothpick. She was appalled at his behavior, and his only saving grace was that he was a pilot. That meant he had accomplished something to get there and wanted to go higher. Compared to the guys she'd known so far, that said a lot.

After dinner, they went to Morgan's house. His roommates, Steve and Roger, were on the back porch with a cozy fire burning inside a small ring. The house bordered a small man-made pond, and the veranda was surrounded by tall palm trees. The sound of Steve's harmonica floated over the gathering.

"C'mon Morgan, get your guitar. Let's play some Waylon and Willie."

One new thing Dustin had put on his canvas was the outlaw country he picked up in Texas. It fit like a glove in small town Florida and helped stem the tide of disco. Acid rock had lost its moxie. Who knows, if Waylon Jennings, Willie Nelson and Hank Williams Jr. hadn't come on the scene, the world may have been taken over by the Bee Gees and Donna Summer. Where would we all be then? Better to not think about it.

Morgan got his Guild D50, affectionately named "Maxine," and went through "Good Hearted Woman" and "Luckenbach, Texas." Steve followed along, moaning away on his harmonica. Everybody around the fire joined in, singing along like they were in summer camp. Then, he picked out the opening guitar strain of a song from the album, To Lefty from Willie by Willie Nelson. He started to croon,

I've been throwin' horseshoes,
Over my left shoulder.
I've spent most all my life,
Searching for that four leaf clover.
Yet you run with me,
Chasing my rainbows.
Honey, I love you too,
That's the way love goes.
That's the way love goes Babe,
That's the music God made
For the whole wide world to sing
It never gets old, It only grows.
Losing makes me sorry,
You say, "don't you worry."
Honey, I love you too,
And that's the way love goes.

"That's the Way Love Goes"

Written by Lefty Frizzell
Recorded by Willie Nelson

Morgan sensed Lisa standing behind him. He had given up long ago on trying to impress her. He knew he hadn't been the best gentleman in the world, and he figured he had blown it completely. He turned and looked, not knowing what to expect. Much to his surprise, she was smiling. The down to earth, Western swing love song had touched a soft spot in her some way, in spite of himself. Thanks, Willie.

The next time they went out, Morgan took Lisa fishing at an irrigation canal in a local orange grove. Ralph was uneasy, sniffing back and forth between Dustin and Lisa. Lisa put on her doggie voice, talking for Ralph.

"Hey, what's going on? I tawt I was de only girl around here."

Ralph looked up at Lisa, then back at Dustin, nervously wagging. Lisa mimicked, "Dad! Dad! Dere's something wrong here! Dere's a girl in da fishin' hole! You better do something!"

Dustin petted Ralph and gave Lisa a wink, "Oh, don't worry, Ralph... don't you worry."

He tied a cinch knot and threaded a purple Mr. Twister on Lisa's hook. After pinching on a split shot about six inches up the line, he handed her the rod. In order to show her how to cast, he had to stand behind her and wrap his arms around her. He also had to hold her hands in his and go through the motions of operating a spinning reel. Once she got the hang of it, he went over to his pole to rig it up.

"Got one! Yahoo! What do I do with it?" The two pound largemouth surfaced with a splash.

"Holy Smokes! I got it, I got it. Just reel in and drag it to me. Here, I haven't even got my rod ready yet, and you caught a fish. That ain't fair... Actually, let me finish putting this worm on... OK, take my rod while I put your fish on the stringer."

Morgan handed Lisa his rod and grabbed her rod. He removed the hook and threaded the stringer through the fish's gills. Lisa cast again and glanced at Dustin as the plastic worm slowly sank.

"So tell me about yourself. What are your plans?"

"Well, in the long run, I'd like to make the airlines. That seems so far off, it's not even real. Right now, I'm hopin' to make enough money to go out West."

"Why out West? Are you going by yourself?"

"It's something I've always wanted to do. Don't know why, but I've seen the Rockies, and that's where I'm goin'."

Lisa looked back out to the water and said to herself, "Not without me." Her rod jerked, and she squealed with delight,

"Whoopee, I got another one!"

"Doggone it! Stop that! I can't even get around to fishin', I'm so busy taking yours off the hook!" So the girl can fish. Put a check mark by that one. On the way back, Morgan breached a topic that was top secret.

"If I told you something that was classified information, could you keep it to yourself?"

She cocked her head, "Sure."

"Would you be upset if I suddenly made $10,000?"

"Shoot no, are you kidding?"

"What about $20,000?"

"Heck no. What are you up to, anyway?"

"I've got a chance to do a pot run from Jamaica. It could be dangerous, but if it works, we'll be able to go to Wyoming and get away from it all."

Lisa was shocked. Did he say, "We?" Then she considered the run.

"Dangerous, you say? No kidding it's dangerous! Aren't you afraid something could go wrong, or you could die in a plane crash?"

"You can get killed walking across the street. That's how I look at it. People spend their whole lives trying to keep bad stuff from happening. They starve themselves and jog five miles a day, trying to stay 'healthy,' then fall down dead from a heart attack. They turn down opportunities to see the world because they're afraid of flying, then get run over by a Mack truck in front of their house. Maybe I'm crazy, but I refuse to let fear keep me from experiencing all that life has to offer."

She confessed to him, "You don't know how bad I want to get out of my town. It is a dead end street... day in, day out, the same old thing. Nobody has any plans except to work their menial jobs, then huddle up in the local bar. I want to do something with my life, and you are the only man I've ever met who wants to do something with his. I feel the same way. I might be scared to death, but I'm not gonna let that stop me from doing what I need to do."

Morgan was impressed. "A lot of people are too afraid to think that way. But if we pull this off, you'll know what standing on top of the world feels like."

"You sound like you've been there before."

"Oh yeh... It's all or nothin', but the *all* is well worth it."

"That kind of dream has never crossed my mind. I never thought it was possible."

"So you don't mind if I fly a load of marijuana from Jamaica and make a lot of money."

"If you think you can do it... Go for it!"

Oh, for a woman's appreciation and admiration. Men will crawl through broken glass for it. That was all he needed to make up his mind. But if he was going to do it, he knew he'd have to do it all the way. He was no longer a flight instructor. Dustin immediately shifted into smuggling mode... the world of planning and logistics for a clandestine operation.

Legion laughed with glee, and turned to his hordes,

"My boys, that was easy, did you see that? Like a sheep to the slaughter. We got him again."

After giving Joe the go ahead, he made a phone call to the one he had always counted on when the chips were down.

"Hello, Agent Orange? This is Morgan. Get yourself a ticket to Florida, we've got work to do."

Voices and echoes bounced around the Orlando airport as Morgan craned his neck to find his friend. It had been a couple of years since they ran their last load out of Tucson. The long hair was gone, and the sloppy dress was gone. He had on a gray suit, and Lisa was wearing a full length red dress. Morgan wanted to impress Orange with a new look... he wanted to make a statement something like this,

"We're in a whole new ballgame. This is Florida... I now have specialized training, and this time, we're going international."

A familiar voice shouted out from behind.

"Hello, Chief." Orange looked up and down at Morgan's outfit.

"You sure look spiffied up. Who's this?"

"This is Lisa. Lisa, meet Agent Orange. You're going to get to know each other pretty well the next few days."

Lisa looked at Orange and smiled, "You look just like Jimmy Buffett."

Morgan chuckled as Orange shot back. "No, my dear, Jimmy Buffett looks like me."

After pulling his suitcase off the conveyor, Morgan and Lisa took Agent Orange on a long drive to a private airstrip with a dining club. On the way out, he described the highway system and the directions back to the house. Morgan turned to Orange,

"It sure is good to see you again."

Orange's eyes were sparkling with excitement. "Yeh, it is. I didn't expect this. Thought you were out of the business for good. My life just went flat after Tucson. No thrills, no chills... it was bad. I guess I needed something to keep my mind occupied since 'Nam."

"Well, this should tickle your gizzard." Morgan laughed as he got an idea. "Now I have a purpose in life. My contribution to society is to keep you from goin' wacko. Hey, I got some Piper baseball caps for the crew. Try this one on."

"Thanks, man. Do you think it's red enough?"

"Yeh. I told everybody we're gonna call ourselves the Red Cap gang."

"The Red Cap gang, huh?" The Vietnam vet pulled his visor down, slanted his eyes, and looked sideways, "Sounds pretty dangerous."

The guard at the resort barely looked up as they passed through the gate. They parked the car and took a stroll around the airstrip. Morgan pointed out to Orange how the planes were parked, and where they would most likely pull up.

"Now, you realize, the only reason you are here is for Plan B. The last resort. If we end up here, that means something went wrong at the first drop zone. I don't know what could go wrong, but I never like to put all my marbles in one bag."

"Kind of like the laundromat?"

"That's right. Like the laundromat. On the night we come in, just come out here and eat a nice steak at the club. After it gets dark, make your way over to your car and wait. Hopefully, you won't have to do anything, and you can come home after 10:00."

"And what if you do come in?"

"Well then, we'll have bales of weed coming out of our ears."

The Longest Run

Joe and Morgan used the giant spread of aeronautical charts in the briefing room to plot out their run. The first leg would go from Vero Beach, Florida to Kingston, Jamaica. Joe would go down ahead of them to make all the arrangements for transporting the pot to the airstrip. Morgan would fly down with Joe's wife, Margie and meet him that night at a predetermined bar for a rendezvous. On D-day, Morgan would file a flight plan west, from Kingston to Grand Cayman, but he would divert to the landing strip where Carl would load him up.

At this point, Margie would get out of the plane, and Joe would get in. They would then reverse course and head east for the group of islands known as the Turks and Caicos. There, they would land on a small island with a caretaker named Timmy and unload the bales before going on to clear customs at Grand Turk. The next day, they would leave Grand Turk, pick up the bales at Timmy's strip, and fly back to Florida. Finally, they would land at an uncontrolled airport in Florida where Joe's handpicked ground crew would be waiting to unload the plane. No problem.

Morgan and Margie cruised through the densely populated slums of Kingston. These weren't quite as bad as the ones he saw in Haiti, but they were no prize, either. Most of the structures were put together with corrugated tin, and you could only imagine what would happen to this place if it were hit by a hurricane. After miles of shacks and emaciated natives, they weaved through the middle class areas of Spanish Town, just west of Kingston. Margie knew the way to the rendezvous point, and handled the communications with the driver. They soon settled into a booth in a quaint Caribbean bar.

Morgan was in pirate heaven. The Jamaican rum had a particularly deep, thick, syrupy twang that captured the tonic of the tropics. Sing-songy West Indian accents filled the air, and the irregular beat of reggae music bounced merrily... people bobbing and swaying to a Bob Marley tune. He relished the ambiance of a dope run out of a banana republic.

After an hour or so, Joe showed up with his crew chief, Carl. He introduced Carl to Morgan. By this time, Morgan had a good buzz going. He gripped a bottleneck of Jamaican rum, squinted his eyes, turned slowly and growled,

"I am the Captain of my ship. From now on, you will address me as Captain Morgan."

Carl held out his hand.

"Ay, ay, Cap'n. Glad to meet you, mon. Welcome to Jamaica."

Joe sneered, "Captain Morgan my ass. You get us back and I'll promote you to General."

He unfolded a map, pointing to a landing strip west of Kingston.

"OK, this is Number One. We will be there in the bushes, waiting for you. If for anything goes wrong, go on to Grand Cayman... we have a place to stay there. If that happens, I will call tomorrow night, and we can move the pickup to Number Two which is over here."

He pointed to another strip in a different part of the island. Morgan's heart sank, knowing it would be extremely difficult to find this strip. They had never flown over it, and it was just a makeshift dirt runway in the densely forested valley. After a few more rum and Cokes, Joe left with hearty handshakes all around and a hug for Margie. Carl patted Morgan on the back with a gentle squeeze.

"Soon come, mon. Soon come."

Morning broke. Morgan filed his flight plan for Grand Cayman, took off out of Kingston, and headed west. Number One had a long asphalt runway, used for local air traffic and maneuvers by the Jamaican Defense Force. He was on edge as they peered out the windshield, looking for a long, straight line in the distance to come into view. First there was a clearing, and then it appeared... a paved strip. At one end of the runway was a speck. The closer they got, the clearer the details... it was a twin-engine airplane, poised for takeoff.

"Margie, look! That's an airplane down there! We can't land with an airplane on the runway."

"I wonder if it's JDF. I hope Joe didn't get busted."

They flew around the strip, and Morgan dipped his wing to get a better look. The plane was definitely brown, and what was worse, it was now moving. Margie strained to get a better look.

"Yep. That's JDF!"

Morgan pushed the throttle to the stops, dialed the navigation radio to 115.6, and set a course for Grand Cayman VOR.

"What's he doin', Margie, is he following us?"

"He's climbing out and making a left turn... still turning left... Yep, he's following us!"

Fear seized his body, draining his energy. All his dreams of a flying career, of anything positive about his future were in jeopardy now, fragile, about to pop. If he got caught, he'd end up spending years in a Jamaican jail. That's worse than an American jail! He craned his neck over his shoulder to see if the tenacious pursuer was still there, like a cop chase in the air. He's there. The coast line appeared ahead.

The radio crackled,

"Piper 84 Foxtrot, state your position."

"84 Foxtrot is 95 miles west of Kingston, 8500 feet, enroute to Grand Cayman."

"84 Foxtrot, roger."

The pursuit plane followed behind until they were 20 miles west of the Jamaican coast, then disappeared. They didn't hear another word for the rest of the trip. After a long hour and a half over the water, Grand Cayman came into view. Tower cleared them to land, and Morgan set the Cherokee Six down on the runway. With a tentative sense of relief, he called ground control to taxi to Customs. Both of them were certain they would be dragged away in handcuffs by the Grand Cayman authorities, eager to question them about their peculiar behavior. They anxiously searched the tarmac, looking for signs of law enforcement, but no one was there to greet them.

Relieved, they parked the plane, cleared Customs, and took a taxi to an area of the island called West Bay. Morgan's nerves were shot, and the only elixir was large quantities of rum. The bad part was, he had to do it all over tomorrow. Fly back into Jamaican airspace, find the strip, load the pot and get out of town. And there was no turning back. What was he going to do? Say, "That's all, folks!" and fly back to Florida? He didn't even have enough money for gas.

That night, Joe was on the phone. Margie handed it to Morgan.

"Morgan, listen to me. Can you hear me?"

"Yeh, I can hear you." Morgan's voice wobbled.

"What's the matter with you? Are you drunk already?"

"Yup, pretty much. Better hurry before it gets any worse."

"OK, here it is. Number One at one. You got that? Number One at one."

"You gotta be kiddin'. Back to Number One?"

"Trust me, Morgan. I'll tell ya about it later. Just be there. Number One at one, got it?"

"Yeh, I got it." He handed the phone back to Margie.

Shaking his head, he strained to focus on the aeronautical chart and make the calculations to arrive back at the same strip the next day at one o'clock.

"He wouldn't tell you to come back if he didn't have a reason." Margie tried to assure him as they lined up on the final leg for a landing at Number One. As Morgan rolled out, he passed armed military men strolling alongside the strip. He came to a stop at the end and Carl opened the side cargo door. A truck backed up to the plane. Margie jumped out, and Joe got in.

"Ahoy, Captain. Top o' the mornin' to ya'," he laughed. Carl stuck his head in the door and raised his hand toward Morgan.

"Be calm, mon. Be calm. Every ting is goin' to be OK."

Three Jamaicans rapidly threw bales in the back of the plane and filled it up in less than a minute. Carl latched the door and gave it two pats. Morgan revved up the engine to taxi to the takeoff end of the runway, rolling past soldier after soldier with machine guns hanging on their shoulders. The plane was loaded to the gills.

Joe turned to Morgan. "I got into a poker game with the commanding officer last night, and we worked out an arrangement." He smiled. "It's much easier this way, don't you think?"

"I guess. As long as they don't shoot us before we take off."

The rest of the trip was uneventful. The drop-off at Timmy's went smoothly, as planned, and they landed at Grand Turk. Morgan had filed a flight plan from Grand Cayman to Montego Bay, but he figured the Jamaicans would be too incompetent to keep track of him, so he could land in the Turks and Caicos as if he had come from anywhere.

They strutted into the customs office, and the agent greeted them like old friends.

"Very well, so glad to see you. We were wondering where you were. Did you get lost? Montego Bay is looking for you."

Oh great, Morgan thought, I've heard that sarcastic tone before. They both looked at each other, not knowing what the other was going to say. Joe went first.

"You see –"

"No, no..." The thin agent held up his hand. "That's OK. I am afraid we will have to keep you here until we straighten this out."

The jail had three cells, and they were full. Joe somehow talked Customs into letting them stay at the local hotel, as long as they came back first thing in the morning. On an island in the middle of the ocean, where could you go? Walking away, Joe whispered,

"Well, it could be worse."

Sitting around a small, circular table on the veranda of the hotel, the two marveled at their good fortune. Jail cells don't get any better than this... hanging out at beachside, languishing in the lazy atmosphere of a distant out island. A soft breeze whished through the palm trees, while waiters strolled around the tables, bringing drinks and appetizers.

"Good evening, I am Cedric, your waiter. What can I get for you to drink? Our specialty today is conch chowder and shrimp salad."

Joe answered first, "Rum and coke for me."

Cedric turned to Morgan, "I'll have some conch chowder and a Beck's"

"I will be back shortly with your order." He bowed and walked away.

While they waited, Joe launched into a story about his days as a boat smuggler. Morgan was fascinated by these tales, and they had vaulted Joe to the status of genuine, Caribbean dope runner. But his standing in Morgan's eyes was constantly being challenged by his rude and noxious behavior. Joe was an egomaniac, and right now, he was in his glory.

"Morgan, you seem to be a thoughtful guy..." he rubbed his chin, "Now tell me, what does it *mean*, Morgan? What does it all *mean?*"

Morgan knew what Joe was getting at. He was mocking Dustin's weak attempts at morals and relishing his role of spoiler. Right now, Joe was the face of the bad side, and Morgan was in no position to refute it.

"It's just a game, don't you see?" Joe raised his eyebrows and laughed hideously, "just a game!"

They sat for a while, drinking and gazing at the turquoise water. Suddenly, Joe pounded the table.

"Morgan, I got it, I got it!" He grabbed Morgan by the collar and pulled his face up to his, "You know what we're gonna tell those guys? We're gonna tell 'em you been sleepin' with my wife!" Dustin pulled away and wiped off his face.

"With Margie?"

"Yes, with Margie! You been flyin' all over the Caribbean with her the last few days, how do I know you haven't been?"

"No, no, Joe. That hasn't been goin' on. She's too faithful."

"Listen, these cops know we're hidin' somethin', and all we gotta do is give 'em somethin' to believe. Tell 'em you been flying around Jamaica with my wife while I've been on business. Then tell 'em you flew me all the way here from Grand Cayman and bypassed Montego Bay because she was there and you didn't want me to find out. Make sure you throw in some juicy details, and they'll love it!"

Morgan was breaking so many rules, he didn't know where to begin. Unlike Joe, he put a lot of stock in being honest. But the truth was nothing to Joe. He'd lie at the drop of a hat, and now Morgan had to go along with it. It may have sounded strange, but he felt worse about lying to Customs officers than he did about flying pot.

The next morning, the agents suspiciously went for the sordid fairy tale, laughing among themselves. They really didn't care where the goofy duo came from, and they really didn't want to mess with them anymore, so they were soon on their way to Timmy's strip.

Morgan rolled the plane off the grass runway next to a clump of scrub palms. Joe jumped out and painstakingly dragged the bales into the plane two at a time. The minutes seemed like hours, and it felt like they were in slow motion, swimming in mud. Any time now, Morgan expected to see a plane overhead. This would be followed by a landing of armed agents and immediate arrest. Joe slammed the cargo door and jumped in the passenger's seat. He had that crazy smile and wild look in his eyes.

"OK, Captain, it's your turn now, show me what you got."

He turned the plane around and taxied back to the far end of the grass runway. The big question was if it was long enough for him to take off at maximum gross weight. The engine idled while they gazed at the grass strip before them. Short, scrubby trees lined the runway on both sides with those at the end forming a formidable wall. Morgan's heart raced as he fondled the handle of the throttle. He pressed his feet hard on the brakes, drew in a deep breath, and gradually pushed the power all the way to the stops.

The engine roared with the tachometer showing 2700 RPM. Mixture was full, prop full, two notches of flaps. He released the brakes. The plane rolled very slowly, using up precious runway trying to pick up speed. The temptation on a short field take off was to rotate too quickly, but Morgan kept the nose down. The trees at the end moved closer and closer, larger and larger.

The airspeed indicator moved past the stall speed, and he tried to pull it off the ground. No dice. The plane was glued to the runway, the high angle of attack keeping it from accelerating. If something didn't change, they would crash full speed into the trees. Joe had both hands braced on the dashboard, his knuckles white, his mouth frozen in a horrible grimace.

Morgan had no choice. He crammed the yoke forward, against all rational sense, and lowered the nose. The speed picked up, and the wall of trees filled the windshield. He pulled back one more time. The airplane separated itself from the clutches of the earth, the trees passing so close underneath he swore he could hear them scrape the belly. He immediately lowered the nose to fly at treetop level until he got to best rate of climb speed. Then, as he started to climb, he gradually raised the flap bar one notch. The plane responded by climbing faster. Finally, he raised the flaps completely, and they were on their way.

Joe exhaled violently,

"Damn, Morgan..." He wiped his brow with his hand, breathing heavily. "You had me there for a minute."

"Oh, really? Shoot, that was nothin'. Just your everyday take off. You look a little squeamish."

"No more wise cracks. Let's go home."

Darkness descended over the Florida coast as Morgan flew a normal route toward the landing zone. Joe looked out of the side window. "Man, these clouds are thick. Can you see the strip?"

They stared intently, trying to find a break in the overcast.

Morgan replied, "No, it's socked in. I should have known this was comin', but they really didn't forecast it like this. The weather said, 'partly cloudy'. That usually means you can see through the clouds."

"It's not your fault. But if we can't get in, we'll have to use Glenn and Lisa, and I really don't want to roll bales out of the plane in front of the Customs office."

"That's all right, I got it covered." Morgan looked at Joe out of the corner of his eye, with a sly grin.

"What do you mean, 'you got it covered?' I'm the one who put this thing together."

"Yeh, but you didn't think of a plan B, now did you? And believe me, Glenn and Lisa waiting at the Customs building is not a Plan B."

"Shut up, this is no time for jokes. We gotta think of somethin'."

"We don't have to think of nothin'. Like I said, I got it. I've been in this business for a long time, and I never do anything without a Plan B."

"O, so you got a Plan B? C'mon whiz kid, out with it."

"Remember that resort strip we went to for lunch the other week... the one where you did some takeoff and landings? I have a driver waiting there."

"You have a driver there? Now?"

"Right now. And what's more, they have landing lights. It's a public strip, but chances are, nobody will be there. Of course, there's the guard shack. But look, we can't keep flying around in circles. If we don't make up our minds, we're gonna run out of fuel."

"So, is this guy gonna run off with our weed? How well do you know him? What's his name?"

"He's my driver from the Tucson days. We've done plenty of runs together. He'll be there, and he'll get it back to us. That's his job. His name is Agent Orange."

"I like him already. I guess we don't have much of a choice... OK, let's go. If he's really there when we get there, I think I'll give him a big kiss."

"I wouldn't do that if I were you."

Morgan called Unicom and announced their arrival at the small uncontrolled airport. He entered the downwind leg, doing all he could to look like a normal plane coming in for a landing. He touched down on the lighted asphalt strip and rolled out. As they taxied back to the parking area off to the side, a human form appeared in the distance, walking toward them. Joe leapt out of his seat to intercept whoever it was before they could see the plane. He walked up to the unknown visitor and shouted over the noise of the idling propeller,

"Are you Agent Orange?"

Getting a "yes," he hurried back to Morgan, dragging his finger across his throat. Morgan pulled the mixture control back to the stops, the engine died, and the propeller came to a halt. Orange pulled his rented Ford up to the side of the plane, and they frantically pulled out the bales and stacked them in the car. The trunk was soon full, and they crammed the rest into the back seat and passenger's seat.

"Do you think we got enough?" Morgan asked Orange.

"Looks like it. Comin' out of our ears. Just like the old days, right?"

"Just like the old days. I hope you know you're a life saver. Is anybody in the guard shack?"

"Yeh, but he's half asleep. We do have a problem, though. I sure hate to drive back to town with these things uncovered like this."

"Well, let's see. Everybody take off your shirts and lay them over the tops of those bales in the back seat. Joe, give me your coat."

Morgan wrapped Joe's coat around the bale in the front seat, buttoning it up the front. Orange saw what he was doing and took off his red baseball cap. Morgan then flipped up the collar of the coat, and wedged the hat inside. He got a pair of sunglasses from the glove box and slid them under the visor of the cap.

"There, meet Mr. Cool!"

The situation was so bizarre, they didn't know whether to laugh or be worried. Morgan stood back and shrugged, "We did all we can do." They shook hands and pledged to meet again in a couple of hours.

"*Hasta la vista.*" Orange waved at Morgan.

"Yeh. *Adios.* Back at the ranch."

The night was calm at the Ft. Pierce airport. In the parking lot by Customs, Lisa and Glenn waited in a 1972 Chrysler Imperial. Their primary purpose was simply to be there when Morgan and Joe arrived. That was innocent enough. However, they were also the last line of defense in case something went wrong with the drop. Plan Z. This meant they might be called upon to load up the pot in front of God and everybody.

Like all the other players in this scene, Lisa didn't think she'd have to do that, or that she would get caught if she did, but she was not as numb to it as everybody else. Sitting in the car for hours at the airport, she had plenty of time to let it all play out in her mind.

Glenn interrupted her thoughts. "Hey partner, are you ready for this? You're with me all the way, right?"

"Yeh, sure."

She really wasn't ready, but she only had to consider the alternative. "I've been out on my own since I was sixteen, working and sleeping and dealing with small town people. Catty women at work. Abusive men. I've been lied to, cheated on, betrayed." Morgan's tales of snowcapped mountains and awesome beauty had sparked a longing to go far away, to places unknown, to leave it all behind.

"Dusty wants to go out West. Oh, my heart burns whenever I think about it. Driving way out there, with him... what a chance to get free! He wants someone to run with him, as the song says, and that one is going to be me."

None of this had been lost on Morgan. When he offered to take her for a ride in his tiny Cessna 150, it was a test. He was impressed when she didn't flinch, but acted giddy about how exciting it would be. He found later, she was lying. Now, with her volunteering to be in the pickup car, he could see she was a woman of deep loyalty and courage. He had never given any thought to marriage, but she was proving to be a breed apart from the others.

One thing was different this time, though. He had never admired a girl for her character before... things like courage, diligence, and loyalty were never a part of the picture. Now, in Lisa, they were. The big question was, "Is admiration the same thing as love?" His previous ideas of love had been grossly distorted by his past. So, like everything else good and proper, Morgan was going to have to have it beaten into him slowly and painfully.

Now it was beginning to get late, and she felt a twang of worry. What if they crashed? What if they got busted?

"Glenn, don't you think it's been a long time? Shouldn't they have been here by now?"

"Yeh, but you never know about these things... all kinds of stuff can happen. I wouldn't start worrying just yet. I tell you what, I'm gonna put on my lucky red baseball cap."

Just then, Glenn saw a man walking toward them. Lisa figured it was someone from the airport, or a security guard. Glenn thought he know who it was. He got out to confront the stranger.

"Can I help you?"

"Hey there, do we have any members of the Red Cap gang here?"

"You got it, bubba."

Lisa was momentarily confused, then suddenly realized who it was. She ran toward him, relief and joy flooding her heart. She wrapped both arms around him and squeezed harder than she had squeezed anybody in her life. Tears streamed down her cheeks.

"I didn't know it was you. Oh, thank God it's over. Now we get to go to Wyoming!"

The Guajira Run

Morgan still couldn't believe what happened with the Jamaican load. After all they went through, the bales were moldy, and he barely made enough to go out West with Lisa. By the time they got to Portland, Oregon, he had to take a job driving a freight truck to stay alive. The Northwest was cold, wet and miserable, and he couldn't get a flying job. Not only that, he was three thousand miles away from where his last flying job was! Last but not least, his drinking drove Lisa away, and he had to rent a house with two ugly guys. He always knew failure in a dope run meant death or jail, but he never imagined it could mean exile to a foreign existence.

He came back to Florida alone, knowing he had treated Lisa badly. He didn't like to think of himself as a jerk, but he had to admit that's what he was. It was either that or settle down, and he just wasn't ready.

His old boss gave him his job back, flying freight, even though one day he pulled him aside and said,

"I heard you were flyin' pot in 84 Foxtrot."

To which Morgan said, "Who told you that?" He suspected the Customs agent had smelled it in the airplane.

"I... don't remember who told me, but you better watch it."

Was he giving him a tip or a warning? Locking eyes, Morgan nodded, "Thanks."

Sipping a hot cup of coffee and nursing a hangover, Dustin sat back on his couch, watching the next episode of Wile E. Coyote

(Carnivorous Vulgaris) and Road Runner *(Acceleratii Incredibus)*. Wile E. Coyote sailed over the cliff for the third time, with a *"poof"* at the bottom of the canyon. Morgan laughed again, wondering if he'd ever get tired of watching his favorite cartoon.

With the Miami Herald spread open on a coffee table he kicked his feet up and browsed through the paper. On the second page was a headline, "Coast Guard Seizes Fifteen Tons of Pot at Sea." The article described a ship with a foreign registry, full of undocumented workers, loaded with pot. Stories like this had become so frequent, they had long since left the front page, being relegated to the inner realms of the paper. Invariably, some vessel, whether it was a boat or a plane, had been nabbed by law enforcement with an enormous amount of weed on board. There were the usual pictures of Latin American men in handcuffs, sitting in a group, armed agents hovering over them, and stacks of marijuana bales on the deck.

The audacity of the smugglers seemed to know no bounds. One group was caught in a sting known as the "Canary" operation. The plan was to use a Boeing 727, fill it up with pot and land it on a strip where they would unload tons upon tons without being seen.

As he read these stories, over and over, day after day, they worked on a soft spot that had never been scratched. The botched Jamaica run left a bad taste in his mouth... it didn't satisfy him, because it wasn't a full pay out. He was supposed to be rich. He was supposed to be on top of the world, and he had done his part, but it still eluded him. If he was going to put his life on the line, by golly, he was going to reap the rewards... someday.

One balmy, Florida night, Morgan sat back in his recliner, watching a news host interviewing a veteran drug pilot. The guy was a grizzled old salt of at least sixty years old who looked like a weather beaten, retired airline pilot. Maybe he was. He talked about flying a DC-6 down to Colombia and landing on a strip with a dog leg he had to negotiate on landing and takeoff. As a popular air cargo plane, the DC-6 had four Pratt & Whitney 2400 horsepower engines, and a payload of fourteen tons.

Morgan marveled, "a DC-6? Now, that's a big plane! Where in the world would you land something like that?"

However, not everybody was so skilled at bringing in big airplanes full of dope. While working as an instructor in Miami, a DC-6 went missing from an airplane refurbishing business next door to his flight school. Everyone knew what it had been stolen for, and nobody thought they would ever see it again. The other pilots sat around laughing and joking about what kind of guts it took to fire up a DC-6, taxi it out on the ramp, take off and fly to Colombia. They calculated how much money a load that size would bring, and how much the pilots would probably make.

Morgan had to admit this level of caper was way out of his league. He couldn't see himself doing anything like that... the chances of getting caught were just too high, and the penalties would be outrageous. People in some places got five years for distributing a hundred pounds. What would you get if you got caught with twenty thousand pounds? They would have to pump air to you under the jail! He had guts, but not that many guts.

That night, the same plane showed up back on the ramp at the same airport, surrounded by flashing red and blue lights with eight tons of pot on board. The crew had somehow neglected to check the weather before attempting their audacious stunt, and the winds had shifted around to come from the north at thirty miles per hour. Flying up from the south, it lowered the ground speed, which reduced the range, which caused them to run out of gas before they could make it to their landing site. The plane was so big, they had to put it down at Miami International!

While everyone else blathered on about the incompetence of these poor souls, Morgan silently contemplated the dark side of the spectacle.

"These pilots are men just like me. They were free yesterday, but now they are in handcuffs, going down to the jailhouse. They might have families. They certainly have mothers and fathers and people who know them. If you're a Colombian national, you get deported, but if you're an American drug pilot, you're not so lucky."

Scenes like this made Morgan content to bide his time flying charters to the Islands. He needed to build multi-engine time, and he'd never get tired of conch chowder and Beck's in a clear bottle.

He even made a feeble attempt at telling himself he wouldn't fly any more dope. He really didn't have to worry about it, though... He didn't have the contacts.

"Morgan, we've got a flight for you with Mr. Tucker to Orlando to pick up his plane. Be here at 7:00 AM sharp." Chief pilot John Culligan barked out the assignment like an Army drill sergeant. "Can you fly a Piper Apache?"

"I can learn real quick. Can't be too hard."

"OK, I'm comin' along to ferry our plane back. You and Tucker will come back in his plane. He needs a pilot, 'cause he's not comfortable flying it himself. He doesn't have enough hours."

"Sure, no problem."

Culligan shouted back over his shoulder, "And no diversions!"

In Orlando, Tucker paid for the repairs on the Apache, and the pilots got in their respective planes. Culligan took off first, leaving Morgan and Tucker to fly back together. As they rolled down the taxiway, they passed by a long string of service ramps, full of parked airplanes.

"You see that Aztec over there?" Tucker pointed out a light twin nestled among other small planes. "That's a doper. So is that Cessna 421 next to it."

"What? Really?"

How does he know this? His intriguing passenger mentioned some more facts and figures, gauging Morgan's response. As they flew back to the home base, he got the feeling this plane had been used for this purpose before. He did wonder why there were no seats in the back. Tucker talked around in circles, never saying it directly, but sending the message in every other way, *"I am a pot smuggler with planes and an entire operation ready to go. Would you like to fly for me?"*

Morgan wasn't ready to jump in head first yet... he was still a long way from it. The venture of flying all the way to Colombia in a twin-engine airplane was a daunting task, and he still figured the risk outweighed the reward. However, the constant barrage of media coverage was having an impact as it continuously massaged his passion for adventure and intrigue.

One investigative editorial in a South Florida newspaper exposed some very fascinating information about the pot flying industry. It gave a detailed description of a desolate piece of land that jutted out into the Caribbean from the north coast of Colombia called the Guajira Peninsula. This barren wasteland was scarred everywhere with dirt landing strips created by drug running groups with bulldozers. From the air, it looked like a massive, oblong expanse of sandy beach where someone had taken a big stick and scratched lines all over it, in every direction. In time, this otherwise useless piece of real estate became the primary jumping off point for marijuana coming out of Colombia. The reporter said it was estimated that over three hundred pilots in South Florida had made *"the Guajira Run."*

As Morgan read this story, it ate away at his core. He didn't want to admit it, but his craving for excitement was burning once again. Flying a load was the only daring enterprise left in this day and age. It was the modern equivalent of being a rum runner on the high seas or a pioneer with an irrepressible urge to go West, wondering what's on the other side of that horizon.

The spell gnawed at his gut. He knew it was dangerous, but he also knew the danger was his door to a new world. It was his horizon. If he could face it and get through it, he would escape his role as a droll flight instructor and don the mantle of notorious pot pilot. And now, it was more than an ethical question. It was a dare. The newspaper article had unwittingly slapped him across the face with a challenge.

He looked in the bathroom mirror of his one bedroom apartment and peered into the hazel eyes staring back at him. As if looking deep into his own soul, he asked the guy in the mirror,

"Can you make the Guajira Run?"

"OK Ralph, let's go see Mr. Big." She jumped into her front seat and Morgan drove out to the ranch style hacienda on the outskirts of Ft. Pierce, Florida. He knocked twice. Tucker opened the door, and Morgan told Ralph to wait outside. Sitting on her haunches, she pricked up her ears, and began her shift as guard dog.

"Well, Dustin, you finally decided to call. I'm glad you did. So you think you're ready to go for the big time, eh?"

Dustin looked around at the rustic beauty of the Florida ranch. "Yeh, looks that way."

"Let's go back to my office, and I'll show you how we do this. You want a drink?"

Tucker grabbed a beer and led him to an office that had been converted into a very specialized flight planning room. The room had maps covering one wall, like the collage in his briefing room when he was a flight instructor. A small red stick pin was nestled in the middle of a large peninsula on the northern tip of Colombia. The entire route was marked out with thumbtacks and string, from the Guajira on the bottom to the drop zone at the top.

"These are the landing strips we use down there." He pointed out some markings on the Peninsula. "It is an eight hour flight one way in a Piper Navajo, so we leave at 7:00 AM in order to make the pickup and drop it back here around midnight or so. You'll have aux fuel tanks, and we'll go over all that. They can light the runway down there with 55 gallon oil drums, and we have radios for talking to the ground crews. Do you have any Navajo time?"

Morgan's head was reeling. He had never seen anything like it. *This really is the big time... These guys know what they're doing!*

"No, not really. I helped ferry one once, but I only got to handle it a little bit. I did get to land it, though."

"Well, we've got some work to do before you're ready. I'll meet you at the airport tomorrow, and you can get some practice in. You also need to fly with Toby and Scooter so they can show you the drop zone and how it works when they're kicking the bales out. It's not easy. Toby is ground crew chief, and Scooter is going to be your chunker. You need to work closely with both of them. Your lives may depend on it.

"Oh, one more thing. You're probably wondering how much you'll get paid. The first run is $25,000. After that, it's $30,000, and if you do five runs for us, we give you a bonus of $30,000. We believe in rewarding our pilots for a job well done. Just to show you I mean business, come here and take a look."

Tucker opened a briefcase with hand-tooled leather on the outside. Inside, it was full of stacks of one hundred dollar bills.

"This is fifty thousand dollars, and there's a lot more where that came from. You don't have to worry about getting your money. We've got lots of money. If you stay with us, you'll have lots of money, too."

Morgan had to admit Tucker had made his case. Talk about employee satisfaction! Now what was he going to do about it? If he had been waiting for the right connection to make a run to Colombia, this was it. If he never goes, it won't be because he didn't have the opportunity. And what had he been telling himself? If you don't do it, you'll never know what's on the other side. The alternative is a life doomed to sameness... a life of not knowing what you could have done. It's just not acceptable... it's not an option. The hook was set deep down in his heart as a wide grin spread across his face. He looked Tucker in the eye and put out his hand.

"Whatever you say, Boss."

On the way home, he pulled into a 7-11, and Led Zeppelin's "Whole Lotta Love" pounded out of the radio... a flashback from a bygone era. Morgan turned it up loud. The rumbling energy of the wild rock made his blood boil, transporting him back to the notoriety of the old days. He thought it was gone forever, but now it was waiting for him on the other side of that horizon. He cracked a little smile.

Go For the Gold

An early morning mist wrapped the tropical vegetation with a moist dew. This was a new day in many ways. The Navajo Chieftain was still new to him... he only had about five hours in it from the drop zone training. He barely knew it well enough to start the engines and take off, and it was a lot more airplane than he ever had in his hands before. That made it daunting, but Morgan was thrilled. All pilots like more power, and this baby had power.

It was also his first trip to Guajira. After all he went through on the Jamaican run, this was a different story. He had a real airplane, he was flying with a real organization, and he was going to the real Colombia. No more rinky dink games... the run he pep-talked himself about in the mirror had come to life. Right now, it was all an unknown barrier, but sometime after midnight, he would be on the other side, looking back.

He walked up the steps and stooped through the door into the hollowed out cabin. No seats, two 55 gallon drums lying horizontal behind the cockpit, and an empty void that made it all seem very out of whack. A little check hit him, reminding him he would be coming back with it full of illegal bales. He really didn't have a choice, but now would be the last time to call it off. Sliding into the pilot's seat, he shuffled his body to get comfortable and fastened his seat belt. He turned to Scooter who was buckled in next to him, sitting quietly.

"Well, I guess it's time to go for the gold."

"Yeh, buddy, let's do it."

Mixtures forward, props forward, throttle cracked, battery switches on, magnetos on, boost pumps on. Morgan pushed the rocker start switch and the left engine came to life. He checked oil pressure and adjusted the throttle to 1000 RPM. He repeated the procedure for the right engine. The powerful Lycoming turbocharged 310 horsepower engines put a beast in Morgan's hands as he manipulated the throttles for taxi.

On takeoff, the tremendous amount of unleashed muscle urged the plane forward like a coiled spring eager to break loose. He advanced the throttles, and the spring came to life, pressing them back in their seats as they accelerated, rotated, and climbed out. Morgan raised the landing gear and flaps, and they cruised through 8,000 feet with the Florida beach disappearing behind them. The early morning sun cast its bright orange rays over the horizon of the wide Atlantic Ocean. It was a beautiful Caribbean day for an eight hour flight "down South."

Emilio Garcia was sitting in the Toyota Land Cruiser he used to maneuver through the scrub land of Guajira. Emilio was younger than most leaders of a smuggling team, but he was educated and highly intelligent. He didn't intend to stay in the business, but at this point in time, it was paying the bills and helping him pursue a bigger dream. So for now, he waited calmly, with his hand-held radio laying on the seat next to him. It came alive.

"*Bandito, bandito*, do you read me?"

In the cockpit, Scooter was trying to reach the Colombian ground crew. The outline of the Guajira Peninsula had just come into view, and he had a chart spread out over his lap. He looked down at the pencil markings, then up at the land mass in front of them. Both crewmates intensely scanned the area, comparing the features before them to the depiction on the map. They knew they were close, and there were many strips to choose from, but it was really important to get the right one. He pressed the button on the mike again,

"*Bandito, bandito*, this is Americano, over." Crackle, scratch, static.

Emilio picked up the radio, "*Americano, si. Necesitas la luz?*"

"What'd he say?" Scooter looked at Morgan.

"I think he wants to know if we want lights. Tell him, yes."

"Yes, yes, we want lights."

"*La luz, si?*"

"*Si, si.*"

Emilio gave a sign to two of his men, one on each side of the runway. They put a torch to the first oil drum, then ran down the strip, lighting each drum as they passed it.

From the air, suddenly, right in front of the plane, a string of lights appeared, igniting in sequence down a line. They formed the perfect outline of a runway. Morgan performed a standard left hand traffic pattern and lined up with the lights. He gripped the throttles hard to steady his hand.

"This is it. Don't come in high or hot. You gotta stick it the first time."

Flaps down. Landing gear down. The grass strip rose up to meet them. Floating just above the runway, he was too fast, using up too much ground. In desperation, he pulled the throttles off. The Navajo sank.

WHAM!! The impact was so hard he looked out to both wings to make sure the landing gear wasn't poking up through them. He rolled out and taxied back. Waiting at the beginning of the runway were two vehicles and a group of Colombians.

"Gotta trust the Boss on this one. He's done it before... I hope they don't kidnap us and hold us for ransom."

"*Bienvenidos a Colombia*. I am Emilio. Did you have a good trip?"

"Yeh, thanks, it was all right. It's the trip back that counts."

There were at least ten Colombians milling around, two on either wing, pumping avgas into the Navajo. Four more were hard at work passing bale after bale through the side door and stacking them inside. The rest walked around, scanning everything like secret service agents. Two of them had fully automatic rifles, the rest of them had pistols stuffed into their belts.

Emilio was very businesslike, sitting on a bale, marking down the weight of every package. Morgan tried to start a conversation.

"You got a pretty good thing goin' here, Emilio."

"Yes, but I tell you, my friend, I am only doing this to raise money for law school."

"Law school? I didn't think smugglers went to law school."

"Oh yes, amigo. It is my path to be legal."

"Hmm, interesting. So what do you plan to do with a law degree?"

"Of course, I am going to have my own law firm to defend the smugglers."

"Oh, yes, of course."

Morgan gazed down the runway and absorbed the scene. Dusk was settling, with the roaring flames of the oil drums lighting up the strip. Oh, the price you have to pay to be a part of romantic folklore! The silhouette of the airplane getting loaded with pot, sitting at the edge of the runway, surrounded by armed Colombian natives... what a sight! This was the image that used to plague his imagination.

"This is why I do this. The glory, the romance, scratching the itch." He let out a sigh, "It feels good, real good."

"Hey, we're ready, let's go."

Scooter tapped him on the shoulder, snapping him out of his spell. They belly crawled across the top of the bales toward the front of the plane and dropped into their seats. The moist bouquet of a plane full of weed overwhelmed him, stoking the passions. A short Colombian tapped on the side window of the cockpit, waving. Morgan opened it.

"Por su jefe."

He handed him a small, square package, and Morgan gave it to Scooter, who quickly tore open a corner to discover a brick of dark red Colombian buds. The cream of the crop for the Boss. Morgan nodded back as he shut the window.

"Gracias."

Morgan fired up the engines and lined up for takeoff. A Colombian with a machine gun slung over his shoulder stood on the side of the runway, waving him on. He moved the throttles to full, gathering speed as scrub brush rushed past their wings. They rotated off the ground, and Morgan raised the flaps, then lifted the knob to raise the landing gear. The three green landing gear indicator lights went out, showing they had retracted. They continued the climb to an altitude of 10,500 feet and set their course just west of north for the trip back home.

The climb was laborious, however, and the fuel flow was more than it should have been. Scooter didn't know anything about airplane performance, but it didn't sound right to him.

"Something's wrong, man," he said to Morgan.

"Yeh, maybe. We'll see what it looks like when we level out. I know I retracted the gear... all the indicator lights are out."

After an hour in level flight, the gauges were still reading a little high, so Morgan re-calculated the amount of gas they would consume by the time they got there. The answer was not good. Over an eight hour period of time, the tiny deviation in fuel flow would cause them to run out before they got there. He tried to explain this to Scooter.

"Man, I don't know about all that, but I do know that this plane is not acting right."

"The only thing that could have gone wrong is if the landing gear didn't go up all the way, but I've never had that happen before. I guess we can recycle it."

"You better do somethin', or we're not gonna make it."

Morgan slowed the airplane down to landing gear extended speed and firmly pushed the gear handle down. *Thump, thump, thump.* All three green indicator lights glowed green. After he was sure they were all the way down, he grabbed the gear handle again and pulled up hard, making double sure it went all the way up and locked in place. The quiet thumps of gear retracting into their housings told them they hit home. Once they got back to cruise, their speed was better, the fuel flow was where it should have been, and everything seemed fine.

"See, I told ya." Scooter said, somewhat perturbed that Morgan didn't listen to him in the first place.

The Navajo was now flying normally, but the fuel they burned had put them in a dangerous predicament. Even with optimal performance, they would arrive at the drop zone with under ten gallons total. That would be the same as running on fumes.

Morgan devised a plan to drain every drop out of each tank on the airplane, leaving gas in only one tank to feed both engines. He would leave a very small reserve in another tank in case he needed it for a last minute switch. First, he would burn all the fuel out of the auxiliary 55 gallon drums.

The Navajo had two fuel selector switches in the cockpit. One for the left tank and one for the right. Both switches had three positions, outboard, off, and inboard. A crossfeed switch enabled both engines to run off of a tank on either side. Morgan set the left fuel selector to "inboard," the crossfeed to "left to right," and opened the line to the drums. When the aux tanks were exhausted, he resumed his plan by running the fuel out of the right side tanks first.

"OK, here we go." He set the crossfeed switch to "right to left." The airplane was now running off the right outboard tank. He let the fuel get close to empty and braced himself. The engines sputtered, and the plane sank slightly. He lifted the lock pin up and slid the selector switch to right "inboard."

Scooter was nervous. "My God, Morgan, what are you doin'?"

The engines picked up the fuel from the inboard tank and came back to life.

"I have to do this, Scoot. It's the only way we'll have enough fuel to make the drop."

When the fuel in the right inboard tank was exhausted, it sputtered again. Flying at night, over open ocean with no land in sight, the plane died and sank. He moved the crossfeed from "right to left" to "left to right." After an eerie two second silence, it caught again.

"Oh dear Lord, you're gonna give me a heart attack."

"Listen man, this ain't any easier on me than it is on you. If it's any consolation, it looks like it's working. Let's just cross our fingers and hope we have enough to get us there."

Now, pulling from the left inboard tank, he ran it almost all the way down, leaving a tiny bit for a final reserve. Then he switched to the left outboard tank. This was it, the last one left, and the lights of the Florida coast were coming into view.

Toby and his ground crew nervously awaited the call over the walkie-talkie. Pilots had been known to do some crazy things on their maiden voyage. He had done all he could to prepare him, showing him landmarks and flying dry runs.

"Morgan's first run. It's all up to him, now. He does seem a little wet behind the ears, and he looks like a high school kid. I sure hope the Boss was right."

"Big Boy, Big Boy, this is Starbuck, over."

All right, here we go. "10-4, Starbuck."

"We're twenty miles out, thirty three passengers."

"10-4. Thirty three." Toby turned to the ground crew eager to get started.

"OK, boys, the game is on. We're lookin' for thirty three bales. Lights, camera, action!"

Two ground crew guys jumped in their trucks and switched on their headlights. Two more, at the end of the drop, did the same. Any minute now, they could expect an airplane with its side door hanging open to come floating over them at treetop level.

On a clear night, you could see the shadows of the palms forming outlines against the sky, the full moon and the stars overhead.

Overlaid with a Navajo gliding along, spitting out rectangular packages one by one, Toby always wanted to capture this image in a framed picture. With a scant glow of early dawn in the background, he would title it, "Sunrise over Florida."

Scooter was in the back, and the door was down. Morgan saw two white lights straight ahead, right where they should be. He had the plane configured for slow flight. Altitude was good... airspeed was good. The airplane was performing perfectly, except for one thing. All the fuel gauges had been on empty for too long.

Light on – light off! Scooter started chunking the bales out the door. Morgan concentrated on power, altitude, and airspeed. He was very close to the ground, the palmetto vegetation passing under his wings. His left hand was on the yoke. His right hand holding the fuel selector switch.

WHOOSH! Both engines died at once! The plane sank, silently, and night shadows of trees rose up to meet him. Out of fuel... So close to the ground. He imagined the pain he was going to feel as they smashed into the palm trees. A strange calm came over him.

"No fear. No fear. Just do what you can do."

He pulled the lock pin and moved the fuel selector from the "outboard" hole to the "inboard" hole. The left engine caught, swinging the airplane to the right. The bales fell from their stacks, rolling on the floor. The right engine caught, countering the force of the left. Morgan struggled to maintain control of the plane as it bucked and swerved like a wild bronco.

Meanwhile, Scooter bounced around in the back... bales dislodging all around him, ricocheting off his body. There was nothing for him to hold onto.

"What are you doing?" he screamed, his voice full of terror.

A tumbling bale knocked his legs out the door. He grabbed at the carpet, leaving tracks with his fingers. The 100 MPH wind pulled hard, trying to rip him from the plane. He flailed his feet until his left foot found the bottom step, then, pushing with all his might, he lifted his body over the threshold. Wiggling and squirming, he belly crawled the rest of the way into the plane.

Up in the heavenly Control Room, Jesus watched all this, shaking His head. He called two of His angels, Clarence and Fred, and explained their assignment.

"Do you see Dustin down there, getting ready to crash into those trees? He's really been a hard nut to crack. I saved him back in Texas, but he's making it awfully hard on himself. Now, I've got a plan for his life, and he can't kill himself before he accomplishes it, so I'm going to send you two down there to help him out. Clarence, you've done this kind of work before, but you're going to need Fred here for backup."

"OK, Lord, what do you want us to do? Should I wear the nightgown I died in like I did last time?"

"We don't have time for that. Just take along Old Fred here and help him earn his wings. The biggest priority right now is to keep him from flying into those trees at the end of the drop zone."

"But Lord, he's breaking the law! He's flying a load of pot into the country!"

"I can see that, but believe Me, the benefits of saving him are going to be well worth it. You and Fred fly on down there. Get underneath those wings and lift him over those trees so he can live to see another day. Clarence, you have left wing... Fred, you're on the right. Don't worry, I'll take care of him later."

Morgan couldn't answer Scooter, he was too engrossed in regaining control of the airplane. Inexplicably, both engines regained smooth operation, and he climbed out, gaining precious altitude. Rather than trying to shout to the back over the engine noise, he flashed the interior lights to signal Scooter to close the door. Scooter pulled it up and locked it, then climbed over the jumbled pile of bales. He slid into the right seat, shaken and furious.

"What in blazes is going on? I almost went out the door back there."

"We ran out of gas. I got us on the very last of the last. It's probably just a few drops. There's no way we can go around again. We're gonna have to find a place to land."

He looked out to the east and saw a rotating beacon.

"That must be Ft. Pierce. We gotta go in there. Do you think we can pull it into Red's?"

"Naw, he wouldn't like that. Not full. We have strict orders not to bring anything into that hangar that ain't legal. We're gonna have to dump it on the side of the runway."

Scooter decided to take charge. From this point on, the operation was more in his realm of expertise than Morgan's. He coached him,

"Just take it easy, now. The one thing we gotta do is look normal, so let's do everything by the book. Got your lights on?"

"Yeh, here they come."

Morgan flipped the switches for navigation lights and strobe. The lighted runway loomed into view.

"OK, now think landing. Just go through what you normally do to get ready for a landing."

Morgan flashed into checklist mode. He didn't have time to pull it out and read it, but the basics were the same for most planes. Mixtures – full, props – full. Landing lights – on. Flaps – first position. Landing gear – down. Check for all three green lights – two main gear – nose gear. Flaps – full. Approach speed – 100 knots. Double check landing gear.

They floated over the runway as he dropped with a slight thud on the two main gear. He powered back, raised the flaps, and braked hard. The main runway on this airport went alongside the principle establishments: Customs, the FBO, the lighted parking lot. The secondary runway, the one they're on, was shorter. It dead ended in a desolate, unlighted area surrounded by scrub palms and bushes. At the very end, a dirt and gravel opening led to two private hangars.

"Pull over here." Scooter jumped out of his seat to the rear cabin door. "I'll throw them out, and you take the plane up to Red's. You can wait there, or whatever you want to do. I've gotta drag all these into those bushes and get 'em off the runway."

Morgan carefully guided the big twin off the runway, powered back to idle and waited. Scooter dropped the door and rapidly pushed the bundles out, forming a scattered pile of bales in the grass. He stepped down and shut the door, giving Morgan a thumbs up.

He taxied down the gravel pathway to Red's hangar, and shut the plane down. Breathing a big sigh of relief, he had two choices.

"I know I can let Scoot take care of that weed by himself, but I only get paid if the load goes through. The longer that stuff stays out in the open, the better the chances of somebody seeing it. So, if I want everything we just went through to count for something, I gotta get out there and finish the job."

Scooter couldn't believe his eyes when he saw the pilot walking toward him through the grass. Like everybody else in the organization, he figured he was just a flight instructor nerd who looked like a used car salesman. It wouldn't have surprised him one bit if he had taken off down the road, ass and elbows, like he was running all the way to Miami.

"Hey, you need some help?" Morgan grabbed a bale and dragged it toward the brush.

"Yeh, man, I thought for sure you'd be too scared to come back."

"Naw, I ain't skeert. Done it before."

Tucker handed Dustin a paper bag with $25,000. "Son, that was one fancy bit of flyin' you did last night. You only had two gallons left in the bottom of those tanks."

Dustin took the bag and looked inside, full of hundreds and twenty's. Praise from the Boss was great, but money in the hand was better. "Yeh, it got pretty hairy there at the end. Glad we made it."

"Well, like I said, the next bag will have $30,000 in it if you're up for it. You'll have to commit to four more runs, though. You need to think about it, 'cause once you're in, you're in."

He was back in black, on the other side of the horizon. Everything he expected to happen, happened. Instant status... he was a star, a legend, Commander Starbuck. The hunger in his blood came alive, and he recognized it... the critter! Only this time it was different. Before, it just wanted to be fed. Now, it was sinister, with an agenda, and it had a name. Its name was Legion.

The first thing he bought with his new fortune was a bright orange, one dollar T-shirt that said "UNEMPLOYED." The next thing was a big bag of cocaine.

The last time he saw Scooter, he looked a lot worse for the wear. His eyes were black, his face black and blue with highlights of red, and his mouth was ringed with cuts and scabs. He had more than a couple of teeth missing. He had been on another run down to Colombia, but this time, the pilot did worse than anything Morgan had done.

"Man, you don't look so good. What happened?"

"We crashed at the end of the runway, loaded down. We both went face first into the instrument panel. They had to drag us out of the wreckage and take us to a hospital. We didn't have any passports, so we jumped on another doper coming back."

"Man, that's crazy!"

Scooter was defiant, "You win some, you lose some. Hazards of the trade. As soon as I'm all healed up, I'm goin' again."

It was a matter of pride. He had to get back on that horse. Morgan understood all that, but a strange air of desperation crept over him as he considered Scooter's mangled face. He had finished his five run commitment, but the risks were very dire, and he couldn't control them all. Am I in too deep? Can I even get out? Maybe I can retire after a couple more runs. At least I deserve a break.

In the summer of 1981, he called his old drummer, Gregg, and they put together a fishing trip to Grand Lake, Colorado for an annual pilgrimage they had crowned, "Mackinaw Madness." A few years back, on his trip out West with Lisa, they had stumbled on a run of lake trout and hooked into some fifteen pounders. The conditions were just right that year, but they never lined up like that again. Nevertheless, the possibility of landing one more huge trout kept Gregg and Morgan coming back year after year.

With visions of snowcapped mountains in his mind, Dustin threw his clothes into a suitcase, dropped in a vial of coke and counted out a wad of one hundred dollar bills. While he was out there, he intended to look into some land.

"Who knows, maybe someday I can back to Colorado for good."

Maryland

"Bomb, Bomb, Bomb... Bomb, Bomb Iran,
"Bomb, Bomb, Bomb... Bomb, Oh, bomb Iran..."

Moose's wife pointed to the rectangular bumper sticker on the back of his new F150. It had a white background with "Bomb Bomb Bomb" in red and "IRAN" underneath it in black. She explained to Morgan,

"That's the sentiment around here. Everybody's mad as a hornet about those hostages."

From November 4, 1979, to January 20, 1981, Iranian militants took sixty-six American diplomats and citizens hostage for 444 days. What became known as "The Iran hostage crisis" enraged Americans everywhere, even the hippies. Almost instantly, calls were going out to bomb Iran, nuke Iran, or whatever had to be done to get our hostages back. Among the first to jump on the bandwagon were Morgan's friends in Blacksburg.

"So much for being anti-war," he quipped, "I guess when they mess with us, all bets are off."

"Well, they better not come around here, that's all I gotta say."

He was back for New Year's Eve to make arrangements to ship some Colombian up to his old friends. By now, he had completely regressed to the state he was in before he left to go to Texas. His persistent efforts to shake off the guilty twangs of the Holy Spirit had pretty much succeeded, and he had managed to reconstruct his old life and build on it. He now had more money, better connections, and a new existence in the tropical paradise of Florida.

When he left Texas, he had started up a path towards a flying career that would lead to a legal income, a job with great skill and responsibility, and a future with unlimited promise. He loved flying, and he wanted that to happen, but he didn't want to leave out the fun or the adventure. His plan was to keep his old lifestyle, make enough money to build a nice nest egg, and then continue with his flying career, like nothing happened.

Unfortunately, every step was based on the assumption that nothing would go wrong. However, he failed to consider Murphy's Law, which went something like this,

"If anything can go wrong, it will.

If there is a possibility of several things going wrong, the one that will cause the most damage will be the one to go wrong.

If a bolt is dropped while working on the engine of a car, it will fall to the ground and roll underneath to the exact center of said car."

Plenty of unforeseen problems had already plagued Morgan in his dealing career, but so far, he had been able to overcome them or work around them. Maybe it was luck, or maybe it was his lot in life. Whatever it was, his lot was about to change.

"I sure would like you to fly for me, Dustin."

The smuggler was a local businessman named Dave. Dave had a local charter service, but Morgan was not impressed. Compared to the Boss, Dave was a greenhorn, a wannabe drug smuggler, and Morgan wanted nothing to do with him. He turned him down, but Dave continued to pester him. Apparently, he had a load backed up in the islands, and he didn't have a pilot, so he was getting desperate.

The week after the first offer, Christy, the company dispatcher, assigned Morgan a charter flight to Maryland. It seemed normal enough, so he plotted the course and filed a flight plan. Before he left for the airport, he got a call. It was Christy.

"Meet me at the McDonald's parking lot before you get here."

"Sure, what's up?"

"I need to tell you something."

He pulled into the parking lot, and she walked over to his window.

"I just thought you'd like to know, Dave went to the Bahamas yesterday morning and came back last night. I don't know what he's up to, but I figured I should tell you."

"I'm guessing you don't know for sure what he brought back?"

"No, but I do know what kind of business he's been doin' lately, so beware."

"OK, thanks. I don't know, I'm just getting tired of foolin' with him. Maybe it's a regular charter. I already accepted it... if I turn it down now, he'll probably fire me."

"Well, it's your call."

Morgan was pre-flighting the airplane when Dave walked up with his partner. They set their suitcases in the back of the plane, but Morgan was suspicious of one in particular. It appeared Dave was trying to pass off his coke as an inconspicuous carry-on bag. That way, he wouldn't have to pay Morgan thousands of dollars as if he was a partner in the run. Morgan just wanted to get it over with, so he put it out of his mind, hoping it would turn out to be a regular flight. He could always plead ignorance if Dave got caught.

Once in Maryland, they settled into a friend's house in town. Morgan grabbed a beer out of the fridge and dropped on the couch to unwind. His worst fears were confirmed as he watched Dave unpack. The suspicious briefcase was full of uncut Colombian cocaine, and he was meeting a buyer for it that evening. Dave tossed a quart Ziploc bag to Morgan and said,

"Here ya go, Dustin. Have an ounce for bringing us up here."

He wasn't going to refuse an ounce of pure cocaine, but it was far from what his normal fee would have been if he had agreed to the flight in the first place. Nevertheless, he stayed up all night doing the coke while waiting for Dave to show up. Around dawn, he finally nodded off in his hotel room.

"KNOCK, KNOCK, KNOCK!!"

"Uh, what?" Morgan pushed himself up and shook his head. It was 8:00 AM. "Who could that be? Probably housekeeping."

He cracked the door, and three men pushed themselves through, forcing their way into the room. A long-haired man moved toward him with the muzzle of a pistol pointed straight between his eyes. In his other hand, he held up a badge.

"Maryland State Police. Trooper White. Are you Dustin Morgan?"

"Yeh, what's this all about?"

"Up against the wall." Trooper White handcuffed him immediately. "You're under arrest for conspiracy to transport cocaine into the state of Maryland. You have the right to remain silent. Anything you say can and will be used against you in a court of law. Do we have your permission to search the room?"

"Sure, go right ahead." Morgan didn't have any kilos, and that's what they were looking for. *Dave must have gotten busted. If I had only listened to Christy. All I can do now is act like a charter pilot. Surely they can't charge the pilot for something a passenger did.*

The detectives turned everything upside down. One of them came out of the bathroom.

"Hey, looky here." He held up an empty glass vial. "Pulled this out of his suitcase."

Trooper White looked indignantly into Morgan's eyes.

"This is enough to charge you with conspiracy." He turned to another detective. "Take him down to the station and book him."

Across the table from Morgan, a judge sat next to an armed detective. She questioned him,

"It appears that you have been arrested in Arizona before. Is there anything you want to tell us about that?"

Somehow, his arrest in Arizona was still on his record even though it was supposed to have been expunged. Not knowing how much they knew, he decided to be truthful.

"Yes, I was arrested for possession with intent to distribute in Arizona."

The detective sneered and said, "How many tons was that?"

"It wasn't a ton, it was only six hundred pounds."

"Six hundred pounds? I was just kidding. Oh boy, we got us a live one here."

The judge looked at him with a stern, disapproving attitude.

"You're bail is set at $250,000."

He winced, and the detective laughed mockingly, "I'm telling you, son, you fly with the crows, you get shot with the crows."

Morgan replied sheepishly, "Why so much?"

"Because I thought it was necessary."

"Hey, we got a newcomer."

The bearded, scraggly-haired inmate sized Morgan up as he stepped into a small crowded cell. The guard slammed the door behind him with a heavy metallic "CLANG." The cell was no bigger than a large living room, with two bunks along one wall, one against each of the other two walls, and a toilet out in the open, only a few feet from the metal table where they ate. The one-man shower stall was next to the toilet. There was one empty bed left on a top bunk, so he threw his leather flight jacket on it. It would be his pillow for the next month.

The conditions seemed unfit for human habitation, the putrid smell from the toilet permeating the air. But after a few days, amid all the turmoil in his brain, he started to get used to it. The first night inside, they passed around some weed in a makeshift pipe, and the cook sold them fried oysters for $1.00 a plate. Later that week, his lawyer came up from Florida and bought him a small black and white TV for the cell. For the next few weeks, Bonanza and Happy Days were his only links to sanity.

Two weeks later, it got worse. The lab results for the empty vial came back positive for trace amounts of cocaine, and they added a possession charge to his indictment. The days and weeks rolled on, with no relief in sight.

One day, he heard the rustle of jailhouse keys, and a deputy opened the thick metal door.

"Dustin Morgan, get your stuff and follow me."

He brought him out of the cell and walked him to a conference room. Waiting inside was his Florida lawyer, Gus Patterson.

"We're gonna get you out of here, Dustin. I got some paperwork on your lot in Florida and put it up for collateral for your bail. With your reputation as a smuggler, I was able to convince them it was worth well over $250,000. They don't think you'll show up for trial, so they figure it'll be easy money."

Morgan couldn't believe his ears. He had bought a quarter acre lot to build on in Florida, and his house was about half way done, but he had no idea Gus could leverage it to bail him out. Four hours later, they were on a plane to Orlando.

Patterson took a sip of his Jack and ginger and set it on the drop down tray.

"I don't know about this conspiracy charge. We should be able to get around that. The possession charge is only a trace, so we should be able to get probation for that. All in all, I think we can get through this whole thing with nary a scratch. Just be patient."

Morgan was still reeling from the squalor he had left behind.

"I hope you're right."

He told Patterson about Dave and what an amateur he was, but it didn't really help. The authorities in Maryland were absolutely sure they had cracked a well-organized cocaine smuggling ring, and they intended to put them away for a long time.

Jesus told his angel, Clarence, he was going to deal with Morgan in His own time, and that time had come. Now, the lever on the Big Panel was switched to "On," the motors came to life with a roar, the gears rotated, the screws turned, and the press began to close.

"Dustin?" Her voice was cracking.

"Mom? What is it? Is something wrong?"

"Your father just died."

He was speechless. There was no one in the world he loved more than his Dad. The sense of loss overwhelmed him, and he went through the night like everybody else who had suddenly and unexpectedly lost someone dear to them. He went over and over their relationship from years gone by. He relived the highs, the lows, the difficulties. He lamented the ways he had disappointed him. He wore himself out going through the "what ifs" and "if only's."

A few months later, Ralph developed a strange cough. Morgan took her to the vet, hoping all she needed was a treatment of antibiotics. He called back in two days, and the vet said she had pneumonia, but he could pick her up. He stepped in the door of the vet's office, and she came bounding up to him, wagging her tail, so glad as always, and started coughing up blood.

"Hey, what gives? You all had her here for two days, and now she's coughing up blood?"

They told Morgan to wait in the lounge while they took her to the back. Fifteen minutes later, a very distraught high school helper came out and said,

"We put her up on the table to see why she was bleeding, and she just died."

"She died? What do you mean, 'She died?' Ralph is dead?"

"Yes sir, she just started hemorrhaging internally, and died on the table. The doctor would like to do an autopsy if it is OK with you."

"Yeh, I guess, what does it matter now?"

After the autopsy, they carried a large black plastic bag out the back door of the clinic and helped Morgan put her in the truck. He struggled to fathom that his closest companion for the last ten years was now a lifeless form in a trash bag. All he could do was bury her on his lot. Walking around in circles, beside himself with grief, he flailed his arms and pulled his hair, not even knowing what to do with his hands. How could he go through life without Ralph? The answer wasn't what he thought he needed, but it was pretty obvious he didn't know what he needed, and he never would if left to his own devices.

In order to conquer himself and reach his full potential, he'd have to go against all he wanted or felt. It takes pressure to crack someone from their misplaced resolve, and some need more pressure than others. For Dustin, that pressure had to come from an outside Source, because he would never do it to himself. But, you have to break an egg to make an omelet. You have to chip away the rough edges in order to craft a diamond.

The Kleenex

"Kaboom! Pow! Boom! Boom!" The rocks exploded one after the other as Morgan skillfully manipulated the controls of the firing spaceship. He held the left button down to rotate the ship, tapped the thrust button, and simultaneously pounded the fire button to spray a moving circle of bullets at the enclosing rocks. He anxiously awaited the inevitable flying saucer to appear from the side, spitting out its deadly return fire.

"Weedlweedlweedlweedlweedlweedl, Blam!" He's hit. Game over.

At 3:00 in the afternoon, the Bootlegger lounge was dark and cool while the Florida sun blazed outside. The jukebox bounced out "Tennessee River" by Alabama. Morgan dug in his pocket for another quarter, content to while away the afternoon immersed in a screen full of incoming asteroids. He felt a tap on his shoulder,

"Hey, Dusty, how are you doin'?" It was Lisa.

"Lisa!" His heart lifted at least three notches. In times when so much bad had been going on, she was a breath of fresh air.

"How did you get here? When did you get back?"

"My job sent me back to Cocoa Beach on business, so I came down here to find you."

"Really? To find me, after the way I treated you on that trip?"

"Yes Dustin, you didn't expect me to come all this way and not look you up, did you?"

"Let's go over there and talk." He pointed to a table in the corner. "Hey, Rick, two Mich's over here."

Rick snapped to attention with a salute, "Yes sir! Commander, sir! Two Mich's comin' right up, sir!"

Lisa looked at Dustin with a curious glance, "Commander?"

"It's a long story... here, have a seat." He pulled out her chair.

Morgan poured his heart out, glad to have someone who would listen and who would care. He told her about the bust and the third-world jail in Maryland... about his Dad dying, about Ralph dying, about Colombia and his money going down the drain into the hands of his lawyers. Lisa took it all in, nodding her head, thinking to herself,

"He's just about to break. It won't be long now. I can tell he loves me, he just doesn't know it yet. I hate it for him, but this might be what it's going to take for him to come to his senses."

Reality closed in more as they got back together and Lisa got pregnant. He was scared now, more scared than he'd ever been on a dope run. His freedom was in real jeopardy, and the very thought of being married was death to life as he knew it... It was like biting the dust.

One day Dustin went to Lisa's apartment to talk. He followed her with his eyes as she walked from the kitchen to the sofa. She was six months pregnant and radiantly healthy. She set her tea cup on a table and began brushing her hair. It was sun-bleached bronze, long and glistening, and he was stirred by her beauty. It wasn't a lustful stirring, but a warm admiration of who she had become... a mature and determined mother to be.

"Y'know, I've been thinkin'. I mean, I know this means a lot to you, but well, I just don't know..." Dustin fumbled with his hands. Tears rolled down Lisa's face.

"Dusty, what is the matter with you?" Her voice was loud and shaking. "Can't you see I love you? Don't you love me? You need me. I need you. We need each other! You can't go on like this, getting busted, going to jail. Your whole world is crumbling around you and I'm right here! What's it going to take?"

She broke down, sobbing. "Just go home until you figure it out."

From that time on, he fought, he squirmed, he agonized, and Scott the Great entered the world. Gradually, he began to soften, and found himself feeling a little bit proud of having a baby boy.

"Why don't you bring your girlfriend and your son over to our house so we can meet them?"

The Boss had found some common ground with Morgan other than flying pot. He married a sweet young wife named Cindy, and she was pregnant with twins. His offer to come out to the ranch was almost too weird... who ever heard of an invitation to a formal, social dinner with a dope smuggler? So the girls could talk about their babies?

When they got there, Cindy had the house in immaculate condition. She had an unlimited budget to equip her kitchen and interior with anything she wanted. She replaced all the curtains and furnishings and bought brand new matching place settings. The dining room table was a picture of elegance, with ornate candlesticks, linen napkins, and genuine silverware.

After dinner, Lisa and Cindy hit it off, having a great time talking all about baby clothes, and how cute they were, and what fun it was going to be. Cindy was especially happy to see that Morgan was taking more of an interest in Scott.

"You know, if a little boy doesn't have a man in the house while he's growing up, he's gonna squat to pee."

She should have been a child psychologist.

"Man, you only paid me $35,000 for that last trip, and I set up the whole deal."

Grady presented his case to the Boss in a small, out of the way lounge. They had just completed a run from Jamaica with new contacts Grady arranged. Not only did his people provide the weed, they made all the connections for a protected loading at an airport, along with a secure takeoff. Grady even flew as chunker with Morgan, so he wanted to be compensated for that on top of everything else.

"What are you talking about, Grady? We're sellin' that pot for $250 a pound. You should have all of $45,000 for that run. I don't think that's too bad for a trip to Jamaica."

"Well, that stuff wasn't any good, and all I could get was $150. That just ain't enough for all I did."

It was obvious Tucker wasn't going to budge, and Grady started to boil inside. He knew his connections would mean big money for the Boss in the future, and he felt he should be included more as a partner than a hired hand. He was the enforcer for the organization, and his duty down there was to rough people up for slipping low quality grass in the deal. It was an uncomfortable situation, but Grady didn't fool around. When they left the island, more than one

Jamaican had bruises on his face. Apparently, the Boss didn't think Grady would try anything with him. This was a mistake.

The black sedan pulled up quietly in the horseshoe driveway in front of the Boss's home. Two figures emerged from the vehicle and moved toward the house. One remained with the car, ready to drive away at a moment's notice. Grady and Rocco paused by the door in the garage, their loaded pistols tucked into their belts. They nodded at each other.

"SMASH!" Rocco kicked the door in... Grady followed. Cindy came running down the hallway, towards them, her only concern to protect her unborn twins. The Boss had been in a deep sleep, but he slowly shook off his fog and realized someone was in the house. Grady brushed Cindy aside and headed for the bedroom. He caught the Boss rising out of bed, coming down with a bone crushing blow to his left eye, pulverizing the soft tissue.

Out in the kitchen, Cindy screamed at Rocco,

"What are you doing? I'm going to call the police!"

"Now, now, Mrs. Tucker, nobody's gonna call anyone. You just settle yourself down."

Rocco spoke in a soft, overly calm tone as he clipped the phone wires with his cutters. He'd done this kind of work before.

"You behave yourself, and you won't get hurt. We came here to teach the Boss a lesson."

Tucker reeled back from Grady's punch and fell on his pillow. He reached underneath and pulled out a 9mm pistol. In a flash, the gun was pointing at Grady, and he had him beat to the draw. Squinting his damaged eye, fighting the pain, he could still see him through his good eye.

"Don't go for it, Grady, I'll drill ya for sure. Now back on outta here and get out of my house!"

He followed Grady out of the room and saw Rocco in the kitchen, with Cindy in between them.

"Get out of the way! Get down! Rocco, put your hands up. I'll shoot whoever goes for their gun first. Now get out before we have a real problem."

Rocco and Grady slowly backed out the door and retreated to their car. The Boss followed them through the garage with his gun raised. They eased themselves into the car seats, then without warning, Rocco and Grady fired toward Tucker. He ducked behind the water heater, using it as a shield and returned fire. Bullets pinged into the water heater like hail on a metal roof. The tires squealed on the pavement as the terrified driver tried to escape. The car lurched out of the driveway while Tucker emptied his clip into the back of it. The last thing he saw was the glass falling out of the back window.

The next day, Morgan and Lisa were cruising around and drove by the Boss's house. The driveway was full of people, some with large video equipment, others circled around Tucker, who was standing outside the front door. A police car was parked in the grass, but it didn't look like the Boss was getting arrested. In fact, he was smiling.

"What do you think is going on there?" Morgan asked Lisa, "looks like a press conference or something." He kept on moving, not wanting any part of it. They ate lunch and went back by the house. The crowd was gone.

Tucker came to the door, his left eye a horrible color of purple and red, almost swollen shut.

"What happened to you? Did you make Cindy mad?"

"Y'know that last load we did with Grady? Well, he didn't think he got paid enough, so we had a little disagreement. Come here, let me show you somethin'"

Tucker took them to the garage and pointed out the bullet holes in his water heater. He recounted all the details of the botched raid, laughing like he was telling a fish story.

"So what did you do? Is that why all those people were out here earlier?"

"I called the cops and pressed charges for attempted murder, that's what I did. The press picked up on it and came out here to get a story. I told them Grady had a chip on his shoulder and this was what happened. Then I told them they had enough fun with me for now, and I sent 'em home."

"So what happened to Grady? Did they arrest him?"

"Oh yeh. You can't go around shooting at people and not get arrested. I think they set his bond at a hundred grand, or something. I heard he spilled his guts."

"What do you mean, 'he spilled his guts?' Doesn't that mean we're all in trouble?"

"I don't think so. The cops just look at this as a family quarrel. They'd just as soon we killed each other off. Besides, who's gonna believe a drug smuggling, New Jersey thug?"

Lisa was not amused by any of this. In fact, she was petrified at the reality of what just happened. What if they had been here with Scotty? What must it have been like to be in Cindy's shoes?

She suddenly realized the danger of the business Morgan had been in since she was out West. It was like an episode of *The Untouchables* or *Dragnet* had suddenly come to life. One look at the bullet holes in the water heater and she had enough. She just hoped he got enough before he got killed. She was a homebody at heart, and all she ever wanted was to settle down and have a house full of kids. She knew that would scare Morgan off if she mentioned it, but there was a speck of light at the end of the tunnel.

Sis had been sending Morgan a monthly issue of a Christian ministry called "Changed Lives." It was a little pamphlet with messages about getting saved and testimonies of people who had left bad lives behind. He usually threw them out without reading them, but only after they had graced the living room coffee table for a couple of weeks. Just seeing the cover, and knowing that Sis was still reaching out to him from the other side, had an effect. Now that everything else was falling apart, maybe it was time to try church again. He wondered what Lisa would think about it.

"I have to admit, she's passed every test I've thrown her way. She went flying in my little rattle trap, she waited in the backup car, ready to drive a load of weed… she's already gone above and beyond the call of duty. I've got one more for her, though, and this may be the real hurdle.

"Lots of people do daring things, but the very thought of a church service scares them to death. That takes courage in a different realm, where you step off the cliff and let God have control over your life. That's the real unknown, where eternal pioneers tread, and not too many people have the guts to go there. I wonder if she'll be up for that."

Lisa jumped for joy and wrapped her arms around his neck.

"Really? Oh, Dustin I've been wanting to go to church since I was a little girl, only nobody would take me, and if they did, they could never explain it to me. Where are we going? When are we going? This is so exciting! Dusty, this is the best thing you could ever do for me. I can't wait." She planted a big kiss on his cheek.

Morgan wanted to slap himself.

"What have I done? I should have known... she's fearless. She's not scared of anything. I'm the one who's scared of changing my life. Oh well, I can't back out now, I've already put my foot in my mouth."

The next Sunday, they went to a Nazarene Church the next door neighbor lady had been inviting him to for the last year. The visiting preacher droned on and on about things Dustin didn't understand or care about, but then he struck a nerve. He pointed to the back of the church where the nursery was, where they left Scotty, and started howling about the kids,

"What about the children, your babies back in that room? What kind of life will they lead? Will they grow up knowing the goodness of the Lord, or will they have to experience the heartbreak of living in a world of sin? What kind of life are you going to give them? How are you going to raise them? It's all up to you... their future is in your hands. Are you going to train up your babies in the nurture and the admonition of the Lord, or are you going to leave them to the howling pack of wolves?"

He went on and on, pounding his fist on the pulpit as he pounded his point home. The words hit Morgan like a brick. He felt like the preacher had singled him out and was talking directly to him.

"How could he know what's going on in my life, what I am thinking?"

He started shaking and trembling. He knew he had been living a lie... he knew what he should have been doing. The Holy Spirit took this opportunity to strike. Then came the altar call. Morgan was helpless, incapable of resisting the pull. He took hold of Lisa's hand and dragged her out of the pew. She was totally bewildered, thinking he wanted to leave early and was heading toward the door. But when he turned the other way, towards the front, she was mystified.

At the altar, he exploded with uncontrollable sobs and cries as she knelt beside him. She still didn't know what he was crying about. The pastor knelt down on the other side, put his arm around Dustin's shoulder and started to pray. One thing she noticed, that she could do something about, was that Dustin's nose was running like a geyser, and his face was a slobbery mess. This was her moment to shine. She reached into her purse and produced the one earthly thing Dustin desperately needed at this moment. A Kleenex.

It's Not Working

"Hey Morg, so what are ya gonna do now?"

His roommate was prodding and teasing him, knowing he had some tough decisions to make. Doug Buck was one of the friendliest people Morgan had ever met. A local Floridian, he had a deep southern drawl and a grin that could charm a rock. When he smiled, his eyes sparkled with good vibes. He was also six feet tall, with thick, hairy arms and the stride of a biker. When that smile went away, it was a whole new ballgame.

"You got a baby boy, and you got a girl who will follow you anywhere. You know she is devoted to you... you'll never have to worry about her goin' out on you. That means a lot."

Morgan shifted uncomfortably in his chair. "Yeh, I know. That does mean a lot. That may mean more than all the other things combined."

"Of course, that means you'll have to settle down to one woman." Buck's grin lit up his face... he was enjoying his little game.

"I hate to say it, but you're right. I've been realizing a lot of things lately. Scotty is my responsibility, and as much as I try to avoid it, it's starting to grow on me. Lisa is the most faithful girl I've ever met, and I know that's the key ingredient to a lifelong partnership. You can have the hottest girl on the planet, but if she's not faithful, your life will be miserable. I've already been down that road.

"Back in Virginia, a long time ago when I was in college, I used to come down from my trips by walking in the woods behind the campus. When the fog settled into the trees at night, the dark, tangled forest looked like a scene out of an Edgar Allen Poe story. One night I was sitting on a log, strung out on mescaline, and I was thinking through all the things I wanted in a girlfriend, or a wife. I was actually pondering the concept of whether I ever wanted a full time wife.

"It was like I could see ahead in the future, and I imagined myself being in my forties, still trying to play the field. It seemed kind of asinine that I would keep on running around like a kid, cruising the bars, chasing skirts... everyone I knew would be married with families, and then Boom! It hit me. In spite of all my friends, and associates, and my community of hippies, I could end up living by myself. The likelihood that this scenario could actually come to pass scared the hell out of me. It still does. It bothered me so much I shouted out loud into that, gloomy, misty darkness,

'I DON'T WANT TO TURN FORTY ALONE!!'

"Well, it looks like this is my chance. I can see a door opening from another world, and I think I need to walk through it. I've been considering some things I thought I would never consider before."

Buck's grin disappeared. "You can't be serious. Are you thinking what I think you're thinking?"

"Yeh, Buck, I am serious... I think the time has come for me to do something crazy."

The decision whether to go with Lisa followed him everywhere. It was the first thing on his mind when he got up, when he rode around with his friends, or when he was sitting quietly in a bar, nursing a beer. It was a tricky situation. Morgan, like any other red-blooded American man, would rather fly a plane load of dope into the country any day than deal with sensitive, emotional issues that required him to show his feelings. As a pilot, the only way to get through something like this was to go through the checklist.

"She is faithful. Check.

"She is honest. Check.

"She is pretty. Check.

"She has a brain. Check.

"She can fish. Check.

"Do I respect her? Yes.

"Do I admire her? Yes.

"Am I attracted to her? Yes.

"Do I love her? This is the sticking point. It all hinges on this. C'mon, is it there? Is it there? .... YES!"

A rush of euphoria whished through him, and a smile broke out on his face. "Now, what are you gonna do about it, Commander? Are you man enough? Do you have the guts?"

The moment had come... It was time to bow the knee.

Since he didn't have a ring, he decided to get a token that would certify his intentions to replace it with a real one when he could. He sneaked into Lisa's apartment and rummaged around until he found a jewelry box. He pulled out a nice looking ring, and thought he was real clever to get one that already fit her hand.

It was the moment of truth. He steeled himself like a soldier going to battle. If he was Catholic, he would have crossed himself. He made reservations for that night at one of the nicer restaurants in Vero Beach. The plan was simple. He would start driving to the restaurant like normal, but on the way there, he would pull over on the side of the road and ask her to marry him. Then, with her all happy and excited, they would celebrate in a romantic setting, with a great meal and all the trimmings.

"What are you doing? Why are we pulling over? Is there something wrong?"

"No, there's nothing wrong. There's something I want to tell you."

Dustin fumbled around in his pocket, trying to find the ring he pulled out of her jewelry box. The irony hit him that he had made tens of thousands of dollars running pot, and still couldn't afford to buy Lisa an engagement ring. That sense of failure dealt him a heavy blow.

"What are you going to tell me?"

The next blow was the reality that the words that needed to come out of his mouth right now were, "I love you." He tried to articulate them.

"I...." he paused.

"What, Dustin?"

The revelation hit him that by saying, "I love you," he was breaking down all the walls that he had put up between them in the past. He was humbling himself before Lisa and surrendering to her. The wall in his heart began to crumble. The dam broke. He exploded with anguished moans and cries... his sinuses let go, and his nose and mouth exploded as well, running like a river. In between heaves, he forced out the words.

"I...don't know what to say... I ... have to get this out... I... love... you ... and... I.... want... to... marry you.... Will... you... marry me?"

He bawled and cried so hard the tears ran down his face and dripped off his chin. Lisa dug in her purse for the ever-present Kleenex. What a tormented soul Dustin must be! She looked at this sobbing, heaving, broken man with sympathy and compassion. She did like what she was hearing, though.

Suddenly, flashing red lights appeared in the rear window. The trooper walked up to the car and shined his flashlight onto Morgan's face.

"Is everything all right here?" he asked. Dustin was still gasping for breath, so Lisa came to the rescue.

"Yes, officer. Everything's OK. I think he's trying to propose to me."

"Well, buddy, I can't help you there. You're on your own. Just thought I'd take a look. By the way, you look terrible. You take care of him, ma'am."

"Yes sir. I will." She meant it.

After the trooper pulled away, she patted Dustin on the leg and looked him in the eye. With a straight face and a calm voice she picked up the conversation where it left off.

"Do you have a ring?"

Dustin was glad he was prepared for this,

"Yep. Got it right here. Let me put it on you."

He took hold of her hand and slid the ring on her finger. It was about a full size too large. He was confused... why is this not fitting her perfectly?

"Where did you get this?" The look on her face changed.

"Oh, I just picked it up somewhere."

"This is my sister's ring! It was in my jewelry box. How did you get it?"

"Uhhh... does this mean 'no'?"

"Bom, bom, ba bom. Bom, bom, ba bom."

The church organ filled the air with the triumphant opening strains of the Wedding March. Everyone rose to their feet. The display of honor for the bride sent a jolt through Morgan, and a lump rose in his throat.

"Here she comes, Morg. Ain't she gorgeous?" Buck whispered in his ear as Lisa slowly strolled down the aisle, her hand locked in her Daddy's arm.

Buck was resplendent with his huge frame, his fu man chu moustache, and his formal tuxedo. He performed his best man duties with an exquisite flair... encouraging and uplifting, making sure Morgan didn't pass out. A blanket of comfort descended... a strange sense of calm and inner relaxation, assuring Dustin he was doing the right thing. He realized later it was the unique gift reserved for those who bend to His will... The peace of God.

The reception at Marvin Gardens was a gala of friends and family and champagne. It was the last big party of the old crowd he was going to see. He didn't know it at the time, being absorbed in all the festivities, eating, drinking, and dancing. However, it became blatantly clear when it was time for them to depart. His friends had masterfully transformed his pickup truck. Along with the bras tied to the radio antennae, and the cans tied to the bumper, they had used white shoe polish to declare in big block letters along the side,

"COMMANDER STARBUCK BITES THE DUST!"

"Dustin, here's a letter from the district attorney's office in Maryland. What do you suppose that could be about?"

Dustin closed his eyes. Damn! Here it comes again.

"Do you remember the bust last year, and how I had to spend a month in that dungeon?"

"You mean the deal with Dave? I thought that was all over with. Didn't he pass a polygraph?"

"Yeh, they dropped the conspiracy. The problem is, they found an empty vial in my suitcase that tested positive for coke. They added a possession charge, but I never heard anything about it until now."

"How did an empty vial of coke get into your suitcase?"

"My guess is, it was left over from one of my trips to Colorado. I didn't even know it was there."

Dustin tore open the envelope and scanned the official looking document.

"Well, honey, it looks like I have to go to Maryland. They've set a trial date in December, and I have to be there. I guess I better let work know I'm gonna need a couple of days off."

A large board hung on the wall of the Director of Operations' office at Devoe Airlines, a small commuter based at Opa Locka airport in Miami. On it was a schedule showing the availability status of every pilot. Sue, the assistant director, assigned the notations... "A" was for active, meaning they were currently flying the line. "S" was for standby or on call. "V" was for vacation.

One of the pilots spent his off days flying a charter down to Haiti. For some reason, the authorities would not let him go, so now he was in a Haitian jail cell, waiting for someone to get him out. Sue put a "J" in the box by his name, indicating jail. Four days had gone by so far, so he had a line of "J's" stretching along the chart.

Morgan had been flying the last ten months as captain on the Navajo for this small commuter, and everybody regarded him as your everyday, normal pilot. No one bothered to ask him where he got his Navajo time, and he wasn't about to tell them. Now, however, that would change as he tried to explain to Sue why he needed time off to go to Maryland.

"So you have to go on trial for possession of cocaine?" she asked.

Morgan knew that sounded really bad, so he tried to spin it the best he could.

"It's like this. I didn't know it was there, it was a long time ago, and it was empty –"

She held up her hand and looked straight at him. "And how did an empty vial of cocaine end up in your suitcase?"

"You see, there was this guy that wanted to fly some coke up there, but I didn't want to be a part of it. He wound up getting busted, but believe me, I had nothing –"

"Right, right. I'm gonna call Bob in here."

Bob was the Director of Operations. Morgan had known Bob since his first flying job in Miami. He didn't know how much he knew, but at this point, he figured the only way to keep his job was to be honest.

"All right, Morgan, I understand you're a coke pilot and you got caught, and now you gotta go to Maryland."

"No, no, I swear, I did not willingly take that load of coke up to Maryland. The guy tricked me, but I still got caught with an empty vial of my own stash."

"Oh, I see. Y'know, I've been wondering for some time now, how did you say you got your Navajo time? When I knew you back at the old job, all you could fly were small twins."

Morgan sat back and let out a big sigh. This was one of those situations where you had to throw all caution to the wind and just blab it out.

"OK, here goes. I flew some weed in a Navajo, and that's where I built my time. I think I flew almost two hundred hours in it before I got on with you guys."

"So you're a doper, and we're supposed to act shocked. Let me tell you, nothing shocks me around here anymore. I got one captain in jail in Haiti, and another one who's been flying dope from Colombia. I take it you don't do that anymore?"

"No, sir, I don't. I'm trying to make a career out of my flying now. I want to move on."

"Well, officially, we should terminate you. Unofficially, we need you to fill Conner's spot in the rotation. So, for now, we'll put you on probation, pending the outcome of the trial."

"I really don't think anything is going to happen up there. It's just a trace amount, and I should be able to work it out somehow."

"I hope you're right, I don't want to have to fill up your row with "J's." We're gonna end up with more 'J's' than 'A's'. I've gotta find enough pilots who aren't in jail to fly the airline!"

"All rise."

The judge walked in and took his seat at the bench. Morgan sat at the defendant table while his attorney, Dean the preacher, and the prosecutor huddled at the front. Dean was not really a preacher, but he looked the part... tall and thin in a dark black suit with long hair combed straight back, like a Pentecostal Bible thumper from the sawdust trail.

The proceedings were not going well. There was an air of animosity toward him in the chamber, and he could tell they did not consider him to be an upstanding member of society. They were not impressed that he was a Captain on a commuter airline. The judge was somber, the bailiff looked repulsed by him, and the prosecutor acted like an attack dog. Finally, they adjourned, and Dean motioned for him and Lisa to step out of the courtroom.

"This is the scoop, guys. They have the lab results and all the evidence they need to convict you of possession of cocaine. Since you gave them permission to search the motel room, there is nothing I can do as far as the warrant goes, so my hands are tied. They still think you had a part in the conspiracy, even though Dave passed his polygraph. I know it's not supposed to influence your other charge, but this is small town Maryland, and it does.

"So, it's come down to this. They want to give you four years for this charge, and they're not budging. The only other thing we can do is take it to trial, but I don't have much hope for that, either. As a matter of fact, if we did that, it could be worse."

"Four years! Are you serious?"

"That's what they said. Believe me, I fussed and fumed, but that's their final offer."

"So what happens now?"

"Well, if it was less than a year, you could serve it in the county jail, which would be much nicer. However, that's not the case. They'll take you straight from here and put you in a holding cell. Tomorrow, you will go on a bus to the state pen. I'll give you both a few minutes to talk."

Dustin's head was spinning and tears rolled down Lisa's cheeks as he looked into her eyes. Last week he was flying passengers, and tomorrow he was going to the penitentiary. He started to swoon, and they embraced, breaking down on each other's shoulders. He took off his watch, gave her his wallet and pulled his wedding ring off his finger. Morgan tried to stay in charge by giving her instructions.

"Just go home, take care of Scotty... I don't know what else to say."

Trying to lighten the moment, he tried a joke, "I guess they'll have to fill in a row of "J's" on my chart."

Lisa got an idea, "Do you think we should pray?"

"Pray? Has it come to that?" Dustin sighed, "I guess we can give it a try."

They bowed their heads together and asked God to do something to help them.

Dean the preacher saw them grieving and praying together and thought of one last plan.

"Wait here, guys, I'll be right back."

A few minutes later, he walked out of the courtroom, a very slight smile in the corner of his mouth.

"I don't know what changed, but they have agreed to suspend three and a half years of the sentence, leaving you with six months to serve in the county jail. I also got them to agree to give you some time to get your affairs in order and report after the New Year. So, they're not going to haul you off in leg irons today."

Thank the Lord, he dodged the state prison bullet. There would be more bullets to come, however. Morgan would still have a cocaine conviction on his record, which would then lead to a one year suspension of his pilot's license. His only hope was to keep his nose clean so he could have it re-instated when the suspension period was over. At this point, that was still a tall order.

"Sis, I know you tried hard, you did your best, and it's all my fault, but some bad things have happened, and some wrong decisions were made. Well, to make a long story short, I am going to have to go to jail for six months."

There was a gasp at the other end of the line. She immediately came up with a plan.

"What about Lisa and Scotty? Where are they going to go?"

"We haven't figured that out, yet."

"I wish you had told me about this sooner so we could have been praying. You need to trust us to go through these things with you. Please bring them out here to stay while you do your time."

Back in Miami, Dustin and Lisa started planning for situations they never dreamed of.

"Your sister is the religious one, right? The one you stayed with in Texas before I met you?"

"Yes. I gotta warn you, they'll try to get you saved. Are you ready for that? Actually, they can't force you to be saved, but they will take you and Scotty to church with them."

"I don't even know what it means to get saved. Nobody ever explained it to me. Even after we went to that Nazarene church, you never told me what it was all about down at the altar."

"Well, I guess I better tell you now. You see, I got saved in Texas, but I've been fighting it ever since. When I went down to the altar, God was speaking to me about my responsibility to raise Scotty up as a Christian. I knew it was the right thing to do, but I didn't want to live like a Christian, so how could I bring him up to be a Christian? I was all torn up inside... that's why I was such a mess."

"So you've been saved all this time, and you never told me?"

"Yep, that's about the size of it."

"Why not?"

"Because I knew if you got saved, you would go runnin' off with Jesus and hound me to death about all my bad habits. I figured, if you didn't know any better, I could have some peace and quiet.

"Of course, when you get saved, you're supposed to become humble and submissive, so maybe it wouldn't have happened quite like that, but the cat's out of the bag now. Yes, I am saved, and if you go to Texas, you'll probably get saved, too."

"I think I would like that. Getting saved in Texas. It has a nice ring to it. We sure need a change from the way it's been."

"Yeh, we haven't been getting along too well, lately. I'm not sure what the answer is."

"Well, I know one thing. If you think I'm gonna go out there and turn into some kind of humble and submissive wife, you got another thing comin'."

"Yeh, Yeh, I know, I know."

Dustin just smiled to himself. If the Holy Spirit could turn *him* around, like it seemed He was doing, Lisa didn't have a chance.

"Mr. Morgan, welcome to our humble resort. The county built this new facility for us last year, and you are one of the first ones to try it out. I know you had the pleasure of serving in our old lock-up, so I am sure you will find this one more to your liking."

"Charmed, I'm sure."

Mom had just dropped him off at the brand new county jail in Maryland to serve his sentence. The warden knew him from his time in the old jail, and was treating him like an honored guest. Dustin tried to use his acquaintance to his advantage.

"Is there anything I can do to make my time go easier?"

"You mean work wise? Oh, yes. If you want to work, we can put you in the kitchen, and you will get to stay in the trustee cell. That is our privileged class, if you will. In the regular cell blocks, each cell is barred and locked, and they can only come out for meals and rec time. In the trustee cell, you can roam around freely in the open areas."

"Well, that's for me. I know if I work, the time will go by faster."

"Sure thing, Mr. Morgan. We'll set you right up. Just get changed over there in that dressing room, and I'll show you the way."

His new uniform was a bright orange prisoner suit. They took away all of his personal belongings, with the exception of a toothbrush and a comb. He was allowed to keep a gift that his sister and brother-in-law had given him. A new Bible, personally engraved with his name in gold print. The jailer walked him down a long corridor to his cell.

"CLANG!" The barred, metal door closed behind him... again. In front of him was the open area of the cell block where the TV and eating tables were. Pay telephones lined the opposite wall. In the back was a passageway with four individual cells on the left and four on the right. There was one upgrade from the old jail that was a significant blessing. It had private showers and toilets. He slowly walked between the cells, glancing inside to get a look at his new roommates. He found a room at the end with no one in it, stark and barren.

"I guess this one's mine. Welcome to my new home," he groaned.

He dropped his roll of bedding on the metal bunk and looked around at the cinder block walls. The analogy was painfully obvious... his physical surroundings perfectly depicted the state of his life.

"Stripped. I am now stripped of everything. No house, no family," he looked down at his orange suit..."no clothes. It's gone, and who did it? Was it the cops? The system? Dave and his idiotic mistakes? No, it was me. If I don't take the blame, there's no way I can fix it."

He took in a deep breath and exhaled slowly, his mind projecting a video of all that got him here. He saw the empty vial of coke in his suitcase and rewound it backwards. It took him to a trip to Colorado. He saw joints around a campfire, lines on a mirror, friends passing a bottle of brandy. More scenes brought back fond memories. Hendrix at Woodstock, partying at Marvin's, the pirate bar in Jamaica, the fire lit strip in Colombia. His heart burned with the fervor of doing a run, shaking hands all around, counting the money. He sensed the warmth of the brotherhood, and then it all came together.

"Ah, but that is the culprit. My love for the hippie life... flower power, peace and love. I've been living my life through a psychedelic lens, and it has been steering every decision I've made. Drop acid, go to San Francisco, drive to Tucson, fly to Colombia. Not to mention my 'missionary zeal' for the Cause... the Revolution. Yeh, I'm tryin' to go straight, be a pilot, but the force that's still calling the shots is that old lens. Those kaleidoscope eyes. And in the end, all those eyes have done is lead me right here."

He stared at the blank, pale yellow walls of his prison cubicle and took a deep, hard look at his plan... keep his old lifestyle, build a nice nest egg, and keep on flying.

"As long as I stick to that plan, the vulnerability will never go away... like stripes on a tiger. I got busted with 600 pounds of pot and walked, but a microscopic trace of cocaine got me four years. And no amount of precautions will guarantee it won't happen again. I can't impose enough checks and balances on myself to prevent a forgotten roach in the ashtray, an open container in the car, or an empty vial in the suitcase. And next time, it'll lead to the state penitentiary."

With a slab of sheet metal for a bed, and four cinder block walls for a room, he could only come to one conclusion.

"It's not working."

Deliverance

The preacher greeted his flock as they filed through the door in the small Texas church. He was a big man with a daunting presence and a beaming smile. A young lady with a troubled look walked by and held out her hand. He gently smothered it with two huge palms and looked into her eyes.

"Hello sister. My name is Pastor Sandy, do you know Jesus?"

Lisa had never had that question put to her before. What does he mean "know Jesus?" How can you know someone who's invisible?

"I... know about Him," she answered.

In Pastor Sandy's sermon, he explained what it meant to know Jesus, and she was sure he was preaching to her. He said Jesus knew her name, and He loved her.

"He loves me?" The words warmed her deep inside. "How can He love me after all I've done? Am I even worthy of love?"

Sandy described the cross, and God's forgiveness through His Son. Lisa was in awe, drinking it in, overflowing with joy. Then he explained how to receive Jesus and know Him as her Savior. Lisa figured it required the normal effort to study, gain experience, and do good works. But that was not the case at all. All she had to do was believe.

As the Pastor prepared his congregation to receive communion, he took special care to emphasize everyone's need to give their heart to Jesus before they participated. He went on to say,

"All of you who take the bread and the cup are acknowledging your faith in Christ and your desire to live for Him."

The elders passed the communion trays around. Lisa jumped at the first opportunity to confess Christ, taking the bread and cup as they passed. Sis was sitting next to her and saw the smile on her face.

She didn't need any coaxing, because she had no love lost for her old life. She had been miserable, knowing nothing but heartache, so she laid her sins at His feet and ran to Jesus with open arms. As she walked out of the church, shaking Pastor Sandy's hand, tears streamed down her cheeks. He smiled with a deep inner satisfaction... he knew another one had come home.

Dustin dialed the pay phone in the open area of the cell block. He stood with his back against the wall, looking down at his orange jump suit, and waited for Lisa to pick up. During their weekly phone calls, she went on and on about all she had been learning, growing by leaps and bounds.

"Do you remember B.J. Thomas?"

"Yeh, he sang pop songs, like 'Raindrops Keep Fallin' On My Head.'"

"Well, guess what? He's a Christian now, and he's putting out Christian music. He sings 'What a Friend We Have in Jesus' with Barbara Mandrell, and it's great! You should hear it. I thought that since he was from the old days, you would like it."

Dustin was not surprised. Lisa never was a hippie, and she didn't understand the movement. To her, all the music was the same, she never listened to it for the message. But to him, Top 40 artists were sellouts to the big producers. They were commercial, not genuine believers like the *real* rock bands. Now, she wanted him to get all excited about Barbara Mandrell and B.J. Thomas? "Little Green Apples" was a long way from "Street Fightin' Man!"

"I knew it. I knew she was gonna get saved right off the bat. Now here it comes. She wants me to dive in with her to this new Christian music. I'm tryin' to do this God thing, but if she thinks I'm gonna give up the Rolling Stones for B.J. Thomas, well... I just don't know if I can do it!"

The change came at a good time, though. The cold reality of the jail cell had forced him to re-consider many things. After the dramatic revelation that his old plan was not working, Dustin abandoned it to devise a new plan. He started in Genesis and read his Bible from cover to cover. He made a formal vow to raise his family up in the Lord. He didn't know what that entailed, but assumed it included going to church. He knew he still might not want to go to church personally, but he took the bold step of promising God he would take Lisa and Scotty every Sunday, whether he wanted to go or not.

Four and a half months later, he walked out to the curb in front of the jailhouse and got in the car with Lisa and Mom. The top priority after his release was to get away from his old life. He knew how susceptible he was to the pull of his friends, so going back to Florida was not an option. Nowhere on the East Coast was going to be an option, either. The only solution he could think of, that actually let them pursue a new life together, was Colorado.

In *How the West Was Won,* Linus Rawlins said the Rocky Mountains were so high, he ran into a man with wings, playing a harp. Dustin and Lisa had come to Grand Lake, Colorado, almost 9,000 feet above sea level. Just a few more steps up one of those mountains, and who knew Who they would run into.

Dustin carefully backed the pop-up camper into the campground site, looking at Lisa in his side view mirror.

"A little to the left. More, more. Now straight back. Perfect." She held up both hands.

The Forest Service Ranger had made them campground hosts with a permanent site at the water's edge. Now their front yard was a perfect view of snowcapped peaks framing a high mountain lake.

"Dustin, do you think we could go to that charismatic church in town? I'd like to see what they do down there."

"Sure, why not? If we're gonna go with Jesus, we might as well go all the way."

Dustin had attended four different churches in his life. He grew up in a Presbyterian church with his parents, but nothing from Sunday School stuck. In Texas, he really liked Pastor Eric and his church, and he gave a lot of credit to them for his transformation.

The Nazarene church in Florida had a sweet, older congregation, and the Baptist church they had been trying out in Grand Lake also had a lot of nice, well-meaning folks.

The one thing they all had in common was the atmosphere. Prayers, announcements, three hymns and a sermon. The doctrine was supposedly different, but he couldn't tell. They all preached about God and Jesus, and they all sang out of a hymnbook.

While she was in Texas, Lisa received the Baptism of the Holy Spirit, and could now speak in tongues. He knew *that* was different, but, what are you gonna do?

"I thought Jesus rising from the dead was bizarre, so what's so crazy about this? She acts like she's talking to Jesus, personally. That's a different realm than I am used to. In church, people talk *about* Jesus, not *to* Jesus."

Living Word Christian Fellowship was a different story. The minute they walked through the doors, the music was lively, with a rumbling bass drawing them in. Immediately, he noticed he was surrounded by people his own age. Most churches he had been in were full of old people with a few young ones here and there. This one was just the opposite, and it encouraged him. Then there was the music. The songs were not familiar, but they were lighthearted and energetic. Up on the stage was a praise band, with guitars, electric bass, a piano and a drummer. These were accompanied by two or three singers who looked like they're having the time of their lives.

"You mean you can have fun being a Christian?" he mused.

The music had a beat, and it was lively, but it felt nothing like a rock concert. Instead of projecting wild mayhem, the air was full of worship. Instead of showmanship and out of control ego on display, the players had their eyes closed, raising their hands to the Lord. The effect generated a positive sense of praise that permeated the congregation. All around, people were waving their arms in the air, tilting their heads back, singing along and uttering praises under their breath.

Then unexpectedly, something happened that Dustin had never heard in his life. The music gradually died out, but the guitar and the bass quietly lingered on one chord. Everyone swayed in silent prayer. Then, spontaneously, beginning with one or two people in the congregation, they hung on a musical note, singing in unintelligible sounds. More joined in, adding their own unique resonances... the praise group singers came in at musical intervals that built into multi-level harmony until the whole room was singing in tongues with an ethereal blend. It sounded like a chorus of angels in heaven.

"Well, what do you think?" Lisa asked when they got back to their camper.

"I gotta admit, that's not like any church I've ever been to. I think I like it."

"Can we go back?"

Legion was losing his grip on Dustin's soul, and he was not happy. It was so much easier when religious things were repulsive to him, but now that he had found out what it was like to feel God's presence, things were getting tough. Of course, it didn't help that God lit a fire under Dustin's back side in that Maryland jail and burned out a lot of his taste for the old life.

Now, instead of detesting straightness and yearning for pleasure, he was actually beginning to embrace the qualities of responsibility and self-control. It wasn't that he wanted to deliberately exercise restraint, it's just that, by physically moving his family to Colorado, he had put himself in a place where there was a lack of worldly influence, and an abundance of spiritual influence. In spite of all this, Legion knew he was still up for grabs. All he needed were the right tools.

The Attack

Five miles back on a gravel road, the walls of Morgan's cabin gradually took shape.

A worker shouted "This one's cut, lift her up."

Morgan operated the controls on a crane and lifted the long, three-sided log from the cutting table. The cables swung the log to two men straddling the unfinished wall. The first one to reach it pulled it toward him while Morgan gently lowered the other end to the carpenter in the back. They adjusted the big timber to lay down on the mark, then used sledge hammers to drive spikes through it into the log below.

One Saturday morning, his lead carpenter, Steve, offered him a joint.

"Hey, you wanna burn one?"

The pot quickly took over their brains as Dustin pulled out some garage door instructions. It became readily apparent they were too complicated for their state of mind. There were multiple plastic bags of nuts and bolts and springs, and the diagrams might as well have been blueprints for a skyscraper. He handed the sheet to Steve, thinking he would know what to do, since he was the lead carpenter, but he was sadly disappointed. Steve took a couple of seconds to look it over, browsed through the box full of parts, looked up at Morgan with red eyes and shook his head.

"Ain't no way, boss."

"But I thought you knew how to put in garage doors."

"Normally, I do, but not today. Can't make heads or tails out of it. Guess we'll have to go home."

So much for pot not affecting your abilities. Morgan got in his truck and headed back to the campground. He popped a Coors and put in a Marshall Tucker tape. The free flowing Southern rock soothed his soul. Cruising through the evergreens, he warbled "Heard It In A Love Song" out loud, tapping his fingers on the steering wheel. Back at their site, Dustin eased the truck into the small parking space and got out.

"Honey, I'm back."

He stretched, taking in the magnificent view, then turned to go to the camper and stumbled on a rock.

"Nice one, Dusty." Lisa poked her head out the door. "Did you remember we have a pot luck supper at the church tonight?"

"What? Oh, no. I forgot. I just smoked a joint and drank three beers."

"Well, we signed up to go, so we have to go. I've already made a green bean casserole. Why do you let yourself get like this anyway? I thought you wanted to straighten out."

"I do, I really do. It's just so doggone relaxing, and it makes me feel so good... the blue spruce whooshing by my window... Marshall Tucker taking me home."

"Well, you might want to chew a mint and comb your hair. We gotta get down there."

The fellowship hall was full of their new found Christian friends. Everyone was open and talkative, acting like there was nothing wrong with Dustin. His eyes were so bloodshot they were burning, and he knew that some of them could tell he was high. One disadvantage of being in a church full of people your age, a lot of them probably went through the same things you did, so you're really not fooling anybody. Some churches would shun him for such behavior, but much to his surprise, nobody said anything about it. They hugged him and talked to him as if he was sober as a judge.

He was starting to like these pot luck suppers more and more. The love was definitely in the air. He hadn't felt any sense of fellowship and community since the Woodstock spirit burned out. Now, here it was again, surfacing in, of all places, a church! Could Dad have been right? Had he just discovered a secret cache of Christians who called each other "brother"?

A much bigger issue was at play, however. Once again, when he arrived in Colorado, he had a Holy Spirit Wall surrounding him to ward off the temptations of Legion. But, just like in Florida, every time he smoked a joint or drank a beer, he allowed a crack to form that let the enemy reach in and take more control. This time, because his commitment was stronger to follow the Lord, Legion had to pull harder on his leash.

"Dustin, shouldn't you be getting home to your wife?"

It was late, almost closing time at the Lariat Saloon. The bartender lady was a friend of his, so he felt he could confide in her somewhat. He told her about getting married, having a son, spilling irrelevant dribble the more he drank. He even told her he was going to church. Like most down to earth people who just want to have a good time, she thought it was great that he wanted to go to church, just don't expect her to go.

This was the first time Dustin could distinctly feel a force pulling on him. The fact that he had no business in a saloon, talking to a female bartender from the old days was pretty obvious. He went there because it gave him fond memories of good times in the past. He just wanted to have a beer or two, maybe find an old friend, and then go on back to the camper. That was at six o'clock.

Around nine o'clock, he knew Lisa had made supper, had already fed Scotty and put him down, and was probably wondering where he was. Now the battle became more pronounced. He needed to turn around, slide down off the barstool and walk out the door. He needed to restrain himself from staying there, but he didn't. He couldn't.

Walking away from the bar and toward responsibility was hard. The soothing comfort of beer was easy, and the atmosphere of the bar was relaxing. So he held onto his mug, clinging to his freedom, moving his hand to signal for another beer. The later it got, the more intense the struggle became, until, sloppy drunk, he said to himself,

"What in the world is making me stay here? I better get on home."

He made it back to the campground, staggered out of the truck and tried to find the first step of the camper. As he lifted himself up, a foot came out of the door and kicked him in the chest, pushing him backwards. He sprawled on the ground and rolled into the fire pit, laughing.

"When you sober up, you can come in. I'm not gonna let Scotty see you like this."

"Yes, dear."

He tried to get in the hammock and fell out the other side. Finally, he crawled back into his truck and passed out.

In the heavenly Control Room, all of this was playing out on a wide screen monitor, a really wide screen. It was 53,000 light years wide by 30,000 light years high. The terminology for this giant monitor was the Life Illuminating Grand Housetop Transcript, which formed the acronym LIGHT. On it, everything done in secret, along with every thought and intent of each person's heart was projected, producing the same effect as if they were shouted from a housetop. A multitude of heavenly angels were watching the action.

When Lisa's foot came out the door and shoved Morgan into the campfire pit, a cheer went up,

"Way to go, Lisa! Atta girl!"

Jesus looked on and reproved them,

"Now don't you think that shows a little lack of respect for her husband?"

"Yes, Lord, but he didn't deserve any respect. You are right, as always, but Lisa has been trying to serve You, and we're just naturally on her side."

"Well, trust Me, this show isn't over yet, and Dustin is one of Mine, so let's do all we can to make him succeed. In times of temptation, he needs our help, just like everybody else."

Jesus turned to Legion,

"Are you enjoying yourself with My servant, Dustin?"

"Oh yes, he is so easy. He's like a puppet on a string. Pull him this way, he goes this way. Pull him that way, he goes that way. If You open up a bigger hole in Your Wall, I can make him do much more. Remember his cocaine addiction? And his lust? I've got demons assigned to him specifically for those cravings. I can make him do horrible things."

"Unfortunately, it looks like he needs more pressure to crack all the way. Go ahead and have your way with him, just don't let him kill himself. When he comes out of this, he will be a mighty soldier for the Cross."

"Morgan? A mighty soldier for the Cross? Ha! There's no way."

"Have I ever been wrong?"

In the fall, the aspen leaves turned a bright yellow color, spreading a patchwork of gold throughout the high country mountain ranges. Every hillside and valley became a brilliant display of evergreen interspersed with gold. Meandering through this extravaganza of Colorado color was the county road that led to Dustin and Lisa's cabin. Every day, Dustin drove this stretch to and from the building site, and every day he was stunned by its beauty.

On the way in to work, his mind was preoccupied with the tasks associated with the construction of the cabin. On the way out, Legion's demons launched their attack. In spite of the colorful imagery all around him, he began to see mental images drawn from old memories of drug induced euphoria. Driving down the road, he was flooded with visions from those episodes... pornographic images flashing up like they were on a screen, cocaine rushes going through his body as if they were real. Legion replayed them over and over again until he had to pull off the road. The visuals were so intense he couldn't see to drive.

"My God, what's happening to me?"

Dustin held onto the steering wheel and rattled his head, trying to shake the thoughts out of his mind. He looked around to concentrate on the view outside the truck. In a few minutes, the images subsided enough for him to make it back to Lisa. He acted like nothing happened.

He was locked in a spiritual battle on a galactic scale, but he refused to acknowledge it. He thought it was all in his mind and that he had control over it. He didn't know where the images came from, but he figured they were left over from his old days, and he just had to deal with them. The very idea that he could be possessed by demons was an insult to his manhood. It was a threat to his autonomy, to his sense of freedom. Of course, he had no idea how the spiritual realm worked, and he wondered if there really was one, but,

"It just makes sense that I should have the final say over what goes on in my own mind."

Pastor J. R. knew about spiritual things. As the man of God who built Living Word from the beginning, he had founded the church on preaching a personal Jesus. This was why the members talked *to* Him instead of *about* Him. J. R. made the Bible come alive, regarding it as an instruction manual for life. When he read out of the Gospels, Jesus seemed to jump out of the pages.

When Jesus was healing the sick in the Bible, He was right here to heal our sickness today. When He was casting out demons in the Bible, He was right here to cast them out today. At the end of every service, people went forward to receive healing and deliverance. The place was full of joy every Sunday as people shared their stories about what Jesus did for them during the week.

This environment caused the spiritual attraction in Dustin's heart to grow, but the temptations of the flesh continued to multiply as well. There was a giant tug of war going on in the heavens, with Legion and his army of demons pulling on their leash, while Jesus and the angels pulled on theirs. The lustful visions tormented him almost daily, constantly increasing with one final goal... to make him buckle and turn the visions into action.

"Honey, I found a used refrigerator and stove in the Denver want ads, so I think I'll go on down there tomorrow and get them for the cabin."

"Are you going to be back for dinner?"

"Maybe. I might look up a buddy of mine from Virginia while I'm there. He moved out here a couple of years ago."

Lisa turned away with a slump as she peeled a potato.

"Why would he be looking up an old friend from Virginia? I know we haven't been getting along very well lately... he's got something up his sleeve."

She knew she hadn't been able to keep herself from nagging him about his habits, and she regretted it.

"But, doggone it! Why can't he just leave it all alone and give his heart to Jesus like I did? That would make it so much easier. Now, he's going to look up an old friend, whoever he is. I hope I didn't drive him off. I guess my own struggle is criticism. I shouldn't be surprised... his sister warned me the enemy would try to get to me like this."

Legion had finally broken through. After an exhausting onslaught, Dustin conceded he might as well give in and get it over with. With this decision, Jesus withdrew His hand, allowing Legion to have total access.

Early in the morning, Dustin headed over the mountain pass to buy the fridge and the stove. The used appliances were in a bad, inner section of the city, and he spent half the day finding them and loading them in the truck. He could already feel the pull on the inside, urging him to get the coke. As he headed in the direction of his friend's house, he knew something was going on.

"Why am I driving this direction, knowing I'm going to buy cocaine? I know it's wrong. Lisa is sitting there, back in the mountains... I'm sure Jesus doesn't approve, either. But, it's kind of like it was back in the Saloon. I just have to do this."

Legion laughed as he deftly manipulated the strings on Dustin's heart, "C'mon, boy, go that way, now come on over this way. That's right. You're mine, now."

Dustin turned one way, then another, steadily heading for the destination where he could fulfill his craving. Once he got to the house, he handed some money over to his friend who returned an hour later with two grams of white powder.

"I shouldn't be doing this. I know I shouldn't. I have no resistance left. It feels like I'm being pulled around with a rope tied to a ring in my nose."

Finally, Legion hauled Dustin into the parking lot of a hotel, and walked him inside.

"OK guys," Legion said to his horde of demons, "he's all yours. Let 'im have it. Drag him so far down he'll never want to go back. He'll give up his pathetic trial with Jesus. Shame him... Humiliate him. His dirty little secrets will be with us, and we'll have him forever."

The new day dawned. Dustin rolled out of bed after a few futile hours of trying to sleep. He could hear the sound of maids knocking on doors down the hall and panicked, realizing he had to destroy all the evidence. His head started to clear as he got dressed and scurried out to his truck. On the way through the parking lot, he dropped a paper sack into the trash dumpster.

The Victory

"Holy crap! How am I gonna face Lisa? I was supposed to be home last night."

It took all his concentration to navigate the fast moving Denver traffic, and as he climbed the grade going out of town, a blanket of remorse enveloped him.

"How could I do that? I can't believe I went through all I did to carry that out. Somethin's not right. Something or somebody had control of me. What am I saying? I don't believe in a spirit world that can get inside your brain and make you do stuff, do I? Can it be?"

Dustin pondered the significance of being controlled by something else. The idea was disturbing and unsettling.

"I'm not free. This isn't freedom. This is junk, trash, garbage. I need real freedom. I don't just *need* it, I've *got* to have it. It's a matter of life and death."

His heart was pounding. Breathing heavily, he lifted his eyes upward,

"This calls for desperate measures. Here goes... Lord, is that what went on yesterday? If it is, I want out. I can't go on like this. I need You. Yes, that's right, I really do need You."

He was almost embarrassed, as if there were people around who could see his weakness. The sweet taste of sin the night before had turned bitter in his mouth, and he knew his only hope was to go begging for help. His repentance began as he realized his need for a Deliverer and lifted his eyes toward heaven.

"Oh God, please help me."

The Father, Son and Holy Spirit had been watching the whole show on the LIGHT screen. This was the spark they'd been waiting for. He had just come to his senses and realized his sorry state.

A shout went out, and a round of applause rose up among the angels. It swelled and spread until it crescendoed into a mighty thundering roar of cheers and joy.

The Father turned to the Son and the Holy Spirit and said,

"Looks like he's ready. Let's go down to Colorado. Let's go get My son."

Dustin got a little twang of that peace he felt a couple of times before.

"Is that a 'yes'? If it is, I gotta know. If that was the devil pulling me around like a rag doll, well... I can't have *that!*"

"Well then, what are you going to do about it?"

"What? Did You say something? I recognize that voice. Lord, I felt like I had no control over myself yesterday, like I was being dragged around by the nose."

"You were."

"Well, that's no good. I've spent all my life trying to be free from others ordering me around, and now I've got demons ordering me around? That's no good! How do I get rid of them? What do I need to do?"

"Confess."

"Confess? To who?"

"To Lisa."

"Oh no, Lord, not that. Anything but that. Do I have to tell her everything?"

"Yes, everything."

"Why? Do I have to tell Pastor J.R. too? Can't we come to some kind of agreement?"

"No. No agreements. I need you one hundred percent. Lisa is part of you, and if you keep it a secret from her, you will create a wall that will stop the flow of My Spirit. Pastor J.R. is your spiritual authority, and he is responsible for your spiritual welfare. By confessing to him, and to Lisa, you will strip Satan of his blackmail, and you will open the gates to all My power."

"That's what I need, Lord. All Your power. I can't do this myself. If there's some other-worldly force dragging me around in chains, then it's way more than I can handle. I need You to take away those visions. So, You're telling me the only way to release Your power and conquer the enemy is to confess?"

"Yes, Dustin. *'He who covers his sins will not prosper, but whoever confesses and forsakes them will have mercy.'*"

"So if I don't confess to Lisa, and I try to cover it up, the visions will come back, and I'll be stuck in the same rut I was in before?"

"That's right. It takes total surrender to be free."

In a flash, all the memories of Dustin's Woodstock past appeared. He was standing at the top of the bowl, tripping, looking down at the magic multitude. The bonds, the adventure, the brotherhood. It was time to put it all on the altar, but the decision was no longer a debate... it was a dire emergency. He shouted out loud as he cruised past Idaho Springs,

"Satan, you've had it! You done messed up this time. I'm callin' in the Big Guns. I'm callin' in Jesus! I'm a FREE MAN! Do you hear me? I AM A FREE MAN! I'm gonna confess everything to Lisa that you made me do. You're NOT gonna tie me in chains. You're NOT gonna keep me in bondage. I will not allow myself to be your slave for the rest of my life."

An ugly little demon turned to Legion and asked, "Do you think he'll do it?"

"I don't know. I hope not."

The rest of the way home, Morgan talked to God, getting more psyched up as he went. He knew he was on the verge of something great, but he didn't know how it would happen. No matter how he put it, Lisa was going to be hurt.

He pulled up in the driveway. Confrontations were always awkward, and this one was going to be the most awkward yet, but he was so disgusted at how he performed yesterday, and so determined to get free today, he felt his very life depended on going through with it. He took Lisa to a quiet room where they could have their privacy, held her hands in his, and told her the whole story.

"The Lord told me I had to confess to you to be free. I don't want to hurt your feelings, but this is something we have to go through."

"How do you know the Lord spoke to you?"

"I've been talking to Him for the last two hours, all the way over the mountain from Denver. He told me everything I need to do."

Lisa broke down in sobs. She could tell Dustin had been with Jesus.

"Do you think you need to be delivered?"

"Absolutely. It's very clear to me I have been taken over by demons. That's the only explanation that makes any sense. When I realized I was being herded around Denver, it really woke me up. I believe it now. I'm going to see J.R. after this, and I'm gonna have him pray for me."

On the way to the church, Morgan prepared himself for whatever the pastor might do.

"Lord, how am I going to know if I'm delivered? Let's see, it was the visions and the images that compelled me to commit the acts. So, that would mean, if I don't have the visions anymore, I won't have anything to compel me. So, how does this sound? I would like to make a request. I will know that You have delivered me if the visions go away. Deal?"

Morgan knew this was a big request. "How strange is it that there is a force powerful enough to invade my mind and flood it with unholy thoughts? And how much stranger would it be for another force to come in and blow away the first force? And yet, that is exactly what needs to happen. And if it happens, I'll know it, and I will know Who did it.

"OK, Dustin, so what is your problem?"

Pastor J.R. and his associate pastor, Terry were in the office at the church. They didn't really know Dustin that well, other than to notice he didn't seem as sincere in his relationship with the Lord as most of the other members. They had him sit down in a chair, facing them, and he went through the whole story, starting at the top.

Dustin told them about the visions, the compulsion, the trip to Denver, all the sordid details. It was a long and tortuous narrative. He suffered unspeakable humiliation as he revealed his secrets to these two godly men. They were stoic and unflinching as they absorbed his account. Finally, he was done, and he sat in the chair with his head bowed down, his arms resting on his knees, totally deflated.

"And what do you want us to do?" J.R. asked him.

"I want you to pray for me. I want to be delivered."

"That's why I asked you. It's important for you to voice your request out loud. I definitely think we can help. OK, stand up."

Morgan was a little confused. He expected them to stay seated, bow their heads and mutter a prayer like he had always seen people do. He stood up with his head still bowed, thinking he was going to pray. Pastor Terry prayed in tongues under his breath as Pastor J.R. approached him.

"Lift up your head and look me in the eye."

A change came over Pastor J.R. Instead of the nice, soft spoken church pastor, his eyes came alive, and his whole persona flushed with boldness... he was on the attack. A look of fire lit up his face, and he strode toward Dustin like a lion. Morgan's eyes made contact with J.R.'s. He started to shake. J.R. pointed his finger right at his face and spoke directly to the spirits. He snarled,

"You demons of lust and drugs and drunkenness, I command you to come out of this man now, in the Name of Jesus Christ!!"

In the heavenly realms, the screams of Legion and his demons resounded like tormented echoes going down a well as they spiraled into the pit of hell. The angels watching the LIGHT screen saw the hordes tumbling down to Hades as Jesus cast them all out of Dustin Morgan. They erupted in a deafening sea of applause and shouts and praises. Thousands and thousands of angels sang, "Worthy is the Lamb!!" and "The Lord, my God, my Strength, my Song, has now become my Victory!!!"

Morgan just stood there. J.R. looked over at Pastor Terry and said, "Well, what do you think?"

"Oh, I definitely felt a release. I feel very good about it."

"Is that all?" Morgan was still a little bewildered.

"That's it. It doesn't take much when you have God on your side. You did the right thing, Dustin."

Morgan shuffled down the front steps of the church and walked to his truck. Along the way, he talked out loud to himself.

"Some very strange things have been going on today. First, my Pastor casts demons out of me, then, I don't feel anything. Oh well, I'll know soon enough whether those visions come back or not."

Driving down the highway, he started to feel lighter and lighter, like he was floating six inches above his driver's seat. A Presence hovered right in front of him, slightly above and to the left.

"Who is that? Jesus, is that You?"

All the way back, Jesus was right there, all around him, so close he could touch Him. Dustin reached out and grabbed the air, over and over, laughing out loud with a gusher of release that erupted out of his belly. As the reality of what just happened sank in, he exploded with joy. No visions now, no visions the next day, no visions for the next year, no visions for the next twenty years.

He was in awe of God. Physical miracles were one thing, but when God entered the battlefield of his mind, conquered his oppressors, and threw the bums out, he was certain there was another realm, and He was the King. Morgan knew it. He was sure of it. Jesus had rescued him from the clutches of Legion and his demons, and he owed Him his life.

Lisa paced around, anxiously awaiting his return. She busied herself with normal duties... taking care of Scotty, doing chores. All the while she prayed,

"Please God, please God, *please* God. Show Your power. Save Dustin with Your mighty, outstretched arm. Deliver him, Jesus."

The truck door slammed. Dustin bounded up the stairs and ran into the house. He wrapped his arms around Lisa, squeezing her so hard she lost her breath.

"I'm Free! I'm Free! I can feel Jesus! He's right here. Can you feel Him?"

Tears rolled down her cheeks. "Yes, Dustin. I can. I can feel Jesus. He's right here. Oh hallelujah, praise You, Jesus."

It was a really good day. What a wonderful gift. It just happened to be Morgan's thirty-third birthday.

Grenada

Every small town in Colorado had a unique flair, and whenever you strolled down the sidewalks, they seemed to share the same atmosphere. They all started out as little old towns with a history of mining, or trapping, or fishing. Some of them had streams running through the village. They were quaint, built out of clapboard, with stone and brick facades on the storefronts. Metal benches adorned the sidewalks on the outside, and rugged pine tables graced the inside. And in every mountain town you had that fragrance... the aroma of high country air and evergreens.

Mark and Dustin had just picked up some building supplies from a hardware store in this cozy town in the foothills. Morgan loved Idaho Springs because it was the first small town you hit as you left the urban sprawl of Denver and began the ascent into the glorious Rockies.

"Whaddya say? Let's make a little detour for a hot cup of coffee and a donut."

Mark was a new friend from Living Word who offered to do the wiring on Dustin's cabin, just to gain the experience. The two cabin builders had just stocked up on building supplies from a hardware store and were trying to find an excuse to linger in this tranquil mountain village. Finding a small cafe, they ordered some coffee and cinnamon rolls. Dustin settled in a wooden booth, sipping his cup, and looked out across the street. There, beckoning him from a small saloon, was a glowing neon Michelob sign. It was a blast from the past, intruding into his new life from the other side of the road. It was saying,

"Dustin, I'm here. Come on in. Remember all the good times we had? You used to have a ritual, remember? Every time you went up the mountain, you would stop in a bar in the foothills and have a couple of beers to celebrate. Well, you're getting ready to go up the mountain, and here I am. Come on, Dustin, just have one beer. One beer won't matter."

Dustin was amused that a neon sign could say so much. It was true, almost a decade of expeditions had gone by where he followed this ritual. He couldn't deny that a part of him was drawn to carry on the tradition. The contrast was stark, and the choice was clear. The church side of him was here, in a coffee shop, with his church friend, representing his deliverance. And the saloon side of him was over there, with the tinkling glasses, the smell of liquor, the crack of billiard balls in the back.

One thing was different this time... he was fresh out of combat with the devil, and now had a new respect for what could happen if he went back. He was petrified of losing his wall of protection and being dragged off in chains. So, for once, he could look objectively at the Michelob sign and have a talk with God.

"Lord, do You see that Michelob sign? It's calling me in there to have one beer. Just one for the road. Now, I know You have delivered me from a whole night of partying with six, or eight, or ten beers, but what about the "innocent" side of drinking? The harmless, little, 'one' beer? Have I also been delivered from 'one' beer?"

The voice came back immediately,

"Yes, Dustin. You are delivered from one beer. Let Me tell you what will happen. Just like that door to the saloon opens up into another world, with another set of experiences, one beer will open a door to the complete array of temptations you just left. One beer will unplug a hole in your wall that will let all the bondages of drugs, lust, and drunkenness flood back into your life. It'll be like pulling your finger out of the hole in the dike."

The image of one beer opening the floodgates of hell jolted him. He imagined a scene out of *Dante's Inferno*, with deep, fiery red canyons, and ledges with devils standing on them.

"OK, Lord, great. I'll take it. I'm delivered from one beer."

On the morning of October 25, 1983, Americans woke up to an announcement by President Reagan.

"Early this morning, forces from six Caribbean democracies and the United States began a landing, or landings, on the island of Grenada in the eastern Caribbean...

"Let me repeat: The United States objectives are clear - to protect our own citizens, to facilitate the evacuation of those who want to leave and to help in the restoration of democratic institutions in Grenada."

The following summer of 1984, an affiliate pastor of Living Word was the guest speaker for the Sunday service. This pastor was from the island of Trinidad, located just off the northern coast of Venezuela and due south of the island of Grenada. Because of her contacts, she had made arrangements with a ruling judge in Grenada to establish a mission training center on the island, using a donated property. Her message this morning was focused on describing the details of the property, laying out the goal of the mission, and recruiting church members to form a mission team to do the work.

She delivered her message with a strong voice in the West Indies dialect.

"We have a property down there that has been donated to use as a teaching center for the people of Grenada. After the invasion, they are very open to hear the message of the gospel, so we have a great opportunity. My friend, Judge Patterson, will open his house to us, and during this time of unrest, he is one of the ruling authorities on the island. The property is an abandoned mansion that we will restore into working condition. So, we will need plumbers, electricians and carpenters, as well as anyone else who feels God is calling them to go. At the heart of the teaching ministry will be a satellite dish that we will erect to broadcast Christian services to the people. We will hold crusades, and we will go door to door, talking to people individually, whatever the Lord leads us to do."

Morgan's heart burned as she spoke. He turned to Lisa,

"I don't know why, but I feel like the Lord wants us to go to Grenada."

"I think you're right... it would be a great trip to take together. Of course, we have to find someone to take care of Scotty."

"I wonder if Sis would help. We could drop him off in Texas on our way to Florida, catch a plane out of Miami, and go to Grenada. That would be great!"

The open concourse of Miami International Airport felt like home again. Morgan and Lisa strolled briskly down to the far end where the commuter airlines and charter operations were located. He had spent a lot of time in this section of the airport, flying for his first twin-engine job, and then for Devoe airlines as a commuter captain. He hadn't been back since he left for Colorado, and he was hoping to find some of the old crew members hanging around.

The counter was deserted, and stripped bare. No computers, no papers, no nothin'. It was a ghost town. He got the attention of an agent at the next counter and asked her where everybody was.

"Didn't you hear what happened?"

"No, I've been a little out of touch."

"Get a newspaper from the bookstore over there, and you'll see. You're in for a surprise."

Just then, the announcement for their flight came over the PA system,

"Eastern Airlines flight 483, non-stop service to Bridgetown, Barbados, is now boarding at gate D7. All passengers please report to gate D7 for boarding on Eastern flight 483."

They walked fast toward concourse D and found a bookstore on the way. Dustin hurriedly got a Miami Herald and tucked it under his arm. A news ticker on a TV monitor said something about Devoe Airlines, and he saw images of people walking in handcuffs. They arrived at the gate just in time to board. The gate agent checked their tickets and motioned them down the ramp. Working their way down the center aisle of the plane, they settled into their seats and waited for takeoff.

"Now, I wonder what that lady was talking about. Let's see, OK, here it is."

Dustin's eyes opened wide as he read the headline on page 2,

"Devoe Airlines Busted in Cocaine Smuggling Sting."

Dustin read on in disbelief as the article labeled the owner, Jack Devoe, as the alleged head of the organization, with many of the staff also indicted as co-conspirators. One of the accused runners was a line pilot who was a friend of his. A strange shudder went down his spine.

"There, but for the grace of God, go I."

"What did you say? What's going on with them?"

The Boeing 727 accelerated down the runway and rotated. The metaphor was too surreal as Morgan watched Miami recede beneath the wings, the big jet carrying them away. He turned to Lisa,

"Do you remember when I told you one of the guys at Devoe offered me a trip to South America right after I got out of Maryland?"

"Yeh, you said something was going on."

"Well, I turned him down, because I was fresh out of jail, and I wasn't ready to go through all that again. He said, 'It's your choice. You could do one run, get a new truck, and go on out to Colorado.' He flashed all ten fingers five times to indicate they would pay me $50,000."

"One thing that kept me from doing it was a vow I made not to fly cocaine. I never heard of anyone dying from smoking pot, but I *have* heard about people dying from cocaine. I knew, that if I brought in hundreds of pounds of coke, somebody, somewhere, would die because of it.

"I didn't want that on my head, so it wasn't that hard for me to reject the offer. But if I had done it, I would be in this article with the rest of 'em. And with my probation in Maryland, I would go straight to the big house up there after they got done with me down here... I'd be locked up for the rest of my life! It really could have happened!"

Lisa patted him on the arm, "Well, Dusty, it didn't happen. And here you are, leaving all that behind and going on a mission trip for Jesus down to Grenada."

Morgan almost hyperventilated from the stark reminder of what he had been delivered from... not just drugs and addiction, but a life in prison, with no chance to see Scotty grow up, or to raise a normal family. No way to fulfill any dreams, enjoy the world, none of that. He began to tear up with an overwhelming rush of gratitude. He reached over and took hold of Lisa's hand.

"This is so amazing. God is using this article to show me what my life would have been like if He hadn't delivered me. Now we're flying in this plane, literally leaving that all behind, climbing through the clouds like we're going up to heaven. And when we get to our destination, we're going to tell people what God has done for us, and what He can do for them.

"It's just too much. I can't believe I'm holding a newspaper in my hand with the evidence of my former bondage, while being carried away to serve Him in a new country."

He squeezed her hand a little harder and marveled as he stared at the clouds passing below.

The small turbo prop glided low over the waves and lined up on the runway at Pearls Airport on the east coast of Grenada. On final approach, Dustin and Lisa saw a disabled Russian AN-2R biplane and a tank off to the side. A blown up transport truck lay upside down like litter on the beach. All of them were painted in a drab, military olive color. The tail of the plane bore the logo of the USSR... the dreaded hammer and sickle.

"My gosh, this is spooky!" Dustin looked over at Lisa. "Russian military equipment right out the window? I guess they really did have a war."

Grenada was a purging, cleansing experience. Dustin and Lisa felt like the mission trip was doing more for them than they were doing for the people. Every evening, members of their team gathered on a street corner, played their guitars, and sang praises. Morgan's heart warmed him as he basked in the confidence that he was right where he needed to be.

While they were singing, many locals gathered around to listen or join in, clapping along in their rhythmical, island beat. Suddenly, Pastor Terry stepped out in the open air and proclaimed a message about the saving power of Jesus. They were having a revival right here in the middle of the street! A couple of local islanders raised their hand to get saved and walked up to the Pastor. He laid his hands on their heads and they bowed in prayer. Dustin whispered in Lisa's ear,

"I tell you what, we never would have seen anything like this in the old days. This is like being a part of history. I bet people felt the same Spirit when George Whitefield preached in the colonies, or when Paul was on Mars Hill in Athens. I had no idea being a Christian was anything like this."

During the day, they took picks and shovels and walked a mile or so from the judge's house to the abandoned mansion on the mission property. The building had been so abused by squatters it was almost beyond repair. At the very least, it would need a lot more remodeling than this crew could do in just a week. But they tried, and it gave them an opportunity to get to know the people.

The group of four workers was hot, sweaty and tired. Walking back from a hard day at the center, they spotted a quaint little hole in the wall on the side of the street.

"Hey man, all that work gave me a powerful thirst. What do you say we stop in that little place up ahead and get some cokes?"

Dustin tried to share some advice,

"You know, down here, just because it has a "Coca Cola" sign in the front doesn't mean it's a corner drugstore with a soda fountain."

"What? What are you tryin' to say?"

"That place is a bar. As a matter of fact, every place down here is a bar, and the only place you can get a coke around here is in a bar."

"And how do you know so much about island bars?"

"Well, let's just say I've spent some time in these parts."

They set their shovels in a corner and went in. Just as Morgan settled on a stool at the counter, a young Grenadian man ambled over from the pool table to strike up a conversation.

"Hey, mon, where are you from?"

Over the years, Dustin had made it a habit to analyze people who were trying to get to know him. He profiled their hair, their age, their clothing, and most importantly, the look coming out of their eyes. This particular native came on as if he was friendly, and genuinely interested in learning about Dustin, but there was an underlying slyness, or a hardness. He had his reasons for being a little suspicious.

Like all internal conflicts, the political situation in Grenada was complicated. Underground groups, aligned with communist ideals, overturned the country's constitution and set themselves up as their own government. It was called the People's Revolutionary Government, and their army was the People's Revolutionary Army (PRA). Along with the PRA was a militia composed of volunteers from the Grenadian people. They had close ties with Russia, and began receiving large amounts of assistance from Cuba to build an airport. From this airport, they could accommodate large shipments of whatever might come from Russia. This buildup turned into something very ominous that the United Stated could not tolerate in its own backyard, so President Reagan decided to drive them out. When it was all over, the revolutionaries simply dissolved back into the population.

Now, Morgan was sitting next to a local young man in his 30's with a cool, confident attitude, drinking a beer and asking him where he's from. Could be innocent, or he could've been talking to a ruthless, underground guerilla fighter who used to be part of overthrowing the government.

"I'm from the states, actually from Colorado."

"Oh, dat's nice, mon. Welcome to Grenada." He was studying Morgan, looking into his eyes like he knew something.

"Yeh, thanks. It's beautiful down here."

The Grenadian's incessant stare made Dustin uncomfortable.

"What are you doing here, mon? You're a long way from home. Ya know, da pipple are very glad to see you, ya?"

His words bounced along with the familiar Caribbean sing-song. Dustin settled into his seat and started to relax, reminiscing about the days he spent in Jamaica and the Bahamas.

"We got this property up the road, with a big mansion on it, and we're trying to fix it up, but it's in really bad shape."

"Oh, dat building up der. Ya, dat's de one de soldiers stay in. Dey mess it up pretty bad, right?"

"Yeh, they did, they sure did. It's gonna take a long time to fix it up."

"Oh no, mon. Soon come. Soon come."

"Yeh, yeh, soon come. Not soon enough."

"So what is dis mansion for, my friend?"

"We want to have a center to teach people about Jesus Christ."

He knew if he threw down the "Jesus" word the guy would either want to know more or run away.

The Grenadian kept looking at him, right into his eyes. Dustin fidgeted and sipped his coke.

"You been in de Caribbean before."

Dustin choked, spraying the drink out of his mouth.

"What did you say?"

"I said, 'You been in de Islands before.' I am right, ya?"

Dustin was stunned. Why did he say that? What does he know about me that I don't know? Immediately, his mind flashed through the natives he had crossed paths with to remember if he had ever seen this guy before. Of course, that would be a huge coincidence. He had never been this far south, except for Colombia. "Did he see me in Columbia? No. Can't be. How about Jamaica? Is he friend or foe? Is he a cop or a smuggler? Can he pin anything on me?"

"Yeh, I've been in the Islands before, what makes you say that?"

"Because you understand us. I usually have to repeat every ting I say, but you don't even notice it. You talk to me like it is second nature to you."

Morgan laughed, "Well, you got me there."

The two examined each other, trying to read what was really behind the outward facade. Both of them knew the other had a much bigger story to tell than the one you could see.

"Yeh, buddy. I guess I showed all my cards, and I didn't even know it. I've been down in the Caribbean quite a lot. But, that's all you're gettin' out of me. This time, I am here for the Lord, and I am trying to do what I can to lead people on this island to Jesus."

"Well, I hope you accomplish your mission, my friend." He held out his hand. They shook hard, exchanging a heartfelt bond.

"Thank you, brother, thank you."

Back in Colorado, Dustin and Lisa settled into their new Christian life. They finished the cabin and moved in just in time for spring to fill the aspens with a luminescent green glow. At their housewarming party, the atmosphere hummed with the warm fellowship of their Living Word friends, many of them veterans of the Grenada trip. He looked around at the house full of happy people, his happy wife, the cabin symbolizing a new path in life. A girl from the youth group walked up to him, holding a cup of hot cider.

"Mr. Morgan, you have a really nice house here. You did a great job on it."

"Well thank you, Eileen. The Lord has been so good to Lisa and me since we came up here. I feel like you and everybody from this church have become our new family."

"That's what I wanted to say. You know, when you first walked through the door of our church, I was afraid of you."

"Afraid of me? Why?"

"You had a look about you. Your eyes were constantly moving, like you were checkin' everybody out. Sometimes they were so red, I just sensed a spirit of wickedness. But now, you don't have that anymore. You're the same person, but..." she hesitated, trying to find the words, "you're not the same person. Does that make any sense?"

Dustin laughed, knowing exactly what she meant.

"Yes, Eileen, that makes perfect sense. And thanks for telling me, that makes my day."

The sounds of a guitar arose from a corner of the living room, playing one of the songs they sang on the street corners of that far away island. It was a song the locals taught them that went something like this:

I got a new life,
I got a new life!
If anybody asks you,
"What's the matter with you, my friend?"
Tell 'em that you are saved, sanctified,
Holy Ghost filled, water baptized, Jesus is mine
I got a new life.

Everybody joined in with all their might, clapping the island beat, and a big grin spread across Morgan's face.

"I finally made it! I really did. I made it to the other side. I used to think people on that side were mannequins from an outdated era, but here I am. I'm back from breaking on through to the "other" other side."

He looked at his friends again, "What really happened is, I came over to God's side. Whatever side He's on, that's the one I want to be on. And I don't feel bored... on the contrary, this is probably the best I have felt in a long, long time."

His year was up, and Morgan applied to get his suspended pilot's license back. To prove he was of good moral character, he explained his conversion to Christianity and his deliverance. The FAA got these stories all the time, so they were not impressed. Dustin and Lisa prayed hard, however, and as always, God came through.

But this was only the beginning. During this "honeymoon with the Lord," Dustin received so many answers to prayer he had to keep a journal. He talked to God constantly while driving around, asking for help on mundane tasks.

"Lord, I need a cord of firewood for our wood stove. This guy is selling it for $100 a cord split, but Lord, I'm gonna ask You to get it for me for $50 a cord uncut."

Dustin walked into the man's house... he said $100 a cord. Dustin said, "I need to get it for $50 in uncut lengths."

The man said, "Let me think about it," walked into another room, and came back out.

"I don't know why, but you can go ahead and load your truck up with eight foot lengths, and I'll take $50 for it."

To get all his certifications for a flying job, Dustin had to pass a flight test for Airline Transport Pilot, Multi-Engine Flight Instructor, and Instrument Flight Instructor. There was only one problem... he needed an airplane. Not just any old airplane... he needed an instrument equipped, complex twin-engine airplane.

This one needed some extra pumping up. Asking the Lord for a $50 cord of firewood was one thing... but a twin-engine airplane? He took a deep breath and blurted it out into the air.

"Lord, I know this sounds ridiculous, but I need a twin-engine airplane that I can fly for the cost of gas. Will you show me how to get one?"

In Granby, Colorado, this was no easy task. There was only one twin engine airplane on the ramp at the airport. The good news was, it belonged to the same equipment contractor he rented a crane from for his cabin. Soon, he was driving around town, talking to God again.

"Lord, I'm going to this man's house who owns this airplane. When I talk to him, would you please do whatever You have to do so that he will rent his plane to me for the cost of gas?"

His wife answered the door.

"Yes, ma'am, I heard your husband has a twin-engine airplane down at the airport, and I would like to talk to him about renting it."

"Oh, OK. I don't think he rents it, but come on in, I'll get him."

Morgan sat down in front of Harold Williams, dirty from working, hair messed up, wearing a flannel shirt and work boots, about as far from looking like a pilot as you can get. Fortunately, Harold looked the same.

"So you need an airplane, eh?"

"Yes sir. I'll be honest with you. I lost my license for cocaine possession, but since we moved up here, I became a Christian and Jesus delivered me from everything. Now, I need a twin to get my ATP back, and I need to do some hood work to get my CFII."

"Well, son, I appreciate your honesty. None of us are perfect. Did you know I was a Christian before you told me that?"

"No, I made a vow to the Lord that I would tell anybody about my deliverance that needed to know."

"Well, then, that proves it to me. Can you teach multi-engine?"

"Are you kidding me? I ran a multi-engine rating school in Miami for almost a year."

"Then you can give me a refresher course in my airplane and get me up to speed on emergency procedures?"

"Absolutely. I can put you under the hood, and we can pull engines all day long."

"Well then, you got yourself a deal. I've been looking for a multi-engine flight instructor up here for a long time. You can help me, and I can help you. I provide the plane, you provide the gas, how's that sound?"

"Sounds like a plan."

One day, Lisa handed Dustin the phone with an expectant smile on her face. "It's for you."

This was the call he thought was way too much to ask for. The job he applied for would put him in a Swearingen Metroliner with powerful turboprop engines, bigger than anything Dustin had flown before. It had breathtaking thrust on takeoff, it climbed out like a jet, and it cruised at flight levels up to 30,000 feet with pressurization. All of these advanced features made this plane a natural launch into the major airlines.

Dustin knew this job would take him to the final step, and he could almost taste it, it was so close. He was on the verge of hitting the big time and realizing his dream, in spite of the myriad debaucheries of his past. He took the phone from Lisa,

"Hello."

The chief pilot from a regional airline in Denver was on the other end.

"Hello, Mr. Morgan? We've gone over all your information and we would like to offer you a job as first officer. Are you still interested in flying for us?"

After accepting the job, while trying not to stumble all over himself, he took a moment to meditate on all that had brought him to this place. His hippie days were gone, his drug dealing days were gone, his habits were behind him, and now, the Lord had given him a second, third and fourth chance.

The real miracle, he knew, was not the outward answers of firewood and airplanes, but the inward freedom he had over his life. He now had the discipline and sharpness to master a jet airplane, the inner release to pour his attention into his family, and the complete confidence to attack any situation.

With a sigh of relief, he hung up the phone and turned his eyes toward Lisa.

"Honey, we're back in the flying business. Let's pack it up and move to Denver!"

She put her arms around his neck and gave him a kiss, looking at him with adoring brown eyes, like the night he sang Willie to her.

"I am so proud of you, Dustin. But you know you have another new job."

"What's that?"

She laid her head on his shoulder and hugged him hard. A tear of joy rolled down her cheek.

"You're going to be a Dad again. Congratulations!"

His knees buckled and she held him up. He was going to need another Kleenex.

Captain Porter and First Officer Morgan had just completed an overnight stay in Williston, North Dakota. Early in the morning, they began their route home, making short hops along the way. The last leg went from Rapid City, South Dakota to Denver. After pulling up to the gate at Stapleton International, they gave their salutations to the passengers as they disembarked... "Goodbye... thanks for flying with us." From there, they taxied to the remote operations center for the commuter airline.

Morgan pulled out his logbook to enter his times, then the captain nudged his arm,

"Hey, Morgan, look at all those people standing around outside our building."

"Yeh, I wonder what that's all about."

Lisa was in the kitchen, warming up a bottle for their seven month old daughter, Jennifer. Scotty was still asleep in a back room.

Bump. The sound came from the garage. The hairs on the back of her neck stood up, and she ran to get Jennifer.

"What was that? I could swear I heard something in there."

She didn't have long to wait. The doorbell rang, and her heart sank with dread. "Why am I feeling this way? We haven't done anything wrong." She cradled Jenny tighter and cracked the front door. At first she didn't see anyone, then she noticed a man in a gray suit standing off to the side. The agent had his hand on his gun, leaning sideways to the door, and peered around the jam toward Lisa. With his other hand, he held up his badge and identified himself,

"Agent Hopkins, Colorado Bureau of Investigation, is Dustin Morgan here?"

"No," she looked quizzically at the plain clothed investigator, "he's at work. Is there a problem?"

"We just need to talk to him. Are you sure he's not here?"

"I think you have the wrong person. It must be some other Dustin Morgan."

The agent in the garage came out and stood beside the one at the door. Lisa was shocked,

"What are you doing in my garage?"

"Just routine surveillance, ma'am. It's standard procedure for an investigation. Who does he work for?"

"He works for Pioneer Airlines. He said he would be home this afternoon. Is there anything you want me to tell him?"

"No, that's fine. That'll be all. Have a nice day."

Lisa was befuddled. Yes, this could have happened a long time ago, when Dustin was on the other side of the law, but he had been legal for four years. She had grown so accustomed to their Christian lifestyle, it seemed like they had always lived like this.

"What could they want with him now? We go to church, we read our Bibles together as a family... we've even been on a mission trip." Ninety percent of her was certain this was some kind of mistake, something that could be taken care of with a little straightening out. Ten percent made her skin crawl.

"Will you look at that? Two cop cars on the ramp right where we are supposed to park. They must want a passenger off our plane… but wait, we don't have any passengers. We dropped them off at the terminal. So, that only leaves you and me."

Porter looked over at Morgan, "so what did you do?"

Morgan shrugged, "I didn't do nothin', I don't think." He started to tremble.

They went through the shutdown checklist, and the captain double checked Morgan.

"Did you get the bleeds?"

"The bleeds are off."

His arm was numb as he reached to turn off switches overhead. He peered outside at a line of people in front of the operations building… every employee from the company, staring at their plane. Dustin could recognize the faces, and they had very dour looks on them. Two of the crew scheduling girls were wiping their eyes.

He could not fathom they were there for him. He still couldn't imagine what he could have done. Then a faint memory popped into his head… the gunfight at the Boss's house. What was it he said about Grady… that he spilled his guts? But that was over four years ago. What's the statute of limitations? Five years? The odds began to swing the other way.

It was the co-pilot's job to go through the cabin after each flight to pick up the trash and crisscross the seat belts. The captain turned everything off, and Morgan headed to the back of the plane. The front stair step door dropped. The captain exited and a police officer stepped into the plane. Dustin's heart pounded like a drum, his hands clammy. He slowly raised himself up, turned around, and looked the officer in the eyes. Out of his mouth came words Dustin never wanted to hear again.

"Are you Dustin Morgan?"

CREDITS

www.ingramcontent.com/pod-product-compliance
Lightning Source LLC
Chambersburg PA
CBHW032240010726
47494CB00002B/571